The
HEART
of the
GARDEN

VICTORIA
CONNELLY

LAKE UNION
PUBLISHING

Text copyright © 2018 by Victoria Connelly
All rights reserved.

Published by Lake Union Publishing, Seattle

www.apub.com

Amazon, the Amazon logo, and Lake Union Publishing are trademarks of Amazon.com, Inc., or its affiliates.

ISBN-13: 9781612187044
ISBN-10: 1612187048

Cover design by @blacksheep-uk.com

Printed in the United States of America

To my dear friend, Brent, with love.

'The past is not dead, it is living in us, and will be alive in the future which we are now helping to make.'

—William Morris

Prologue

She liked to walk around the maze alone – once the housekeeper and the gardener had left for the day. That was when Morton Hall became hers again and she would walk through the panelled corridors, her feet soft and silent on the patterned rugs, passing the rich tapestries depicting Arthurian legends and doomed lovers, and the enormous paintings in jewel-bright colours.

It was her great-great-grandfather who had built Morton Hall in the 1860s with proceeds made from the Industrial Revolution. She'd never thought of it as a particularly attractive house; she'd never been a fan of the Victorian Gothic style. Its interiors were too dark for her liking and, many a time, she'd joked that she was going to whitewash the whole place with a nice cheap emulsion. She wouldn't, of course, because she knew that she was living in a little piece of history and that it wasn't hers to change. She was merely a custodian who was passing through, so she endured the dark corners and the oppressively patterned curtains and wallpaper.

But what would become of the house and garden after she died? This problem weighed heavily upon her as her health was deteriorating, but she also realised that she could do pretty much whatever she wanted, couldn't she? She could hand the whole place over to the local cat rescue if she wished. Just imagine the fun those darling animals would have scratching their claws on the priceless tapestries. Or maybe she could bequeath it to one of those heritage trusts, although she had to admit that the idea didn't really appeal to her. The house would simply be one of many open to the public. It wouldn't change anybody's life or make any real difference, would it? It would simply be yet another national treasure.

She'd had many approaches over the years from people wanting to buy the house or its collection. A Russian had once offered her an eye-wateringly large seven-figure sum and was affronted when it had been turned down. When she'd asked him what he'd do with the collection, he'd said most of the pieces would be kept in a vault. All that beauty and colour shut away where nobody could gaze upon it. She could never agree to such a thing.

Art dealers galore had forged a way to her door too, begging to rehome her Rossettis and Holman Hunts. Each one of them had been sent away empty-handed. She wasn't selling, it was as simple as that.

She'd had one idea about what to do with the place. She'd been in the maze when she'd had it; she had all her best ideas in the maze. At first, she'd shrugged it off. It would be too complicated, too idealistic. It wouldn't work. It *couldn't* work.

Or could it?

She took a settling breath, putting all thoughts of wills and other worries to the back of her mind as she walked down the wide staircase with its deep-crimson carpet and ornate balustrades carved from oak. She crossed the hallway towards the enormous front door and let herself out into the garden. It was in the garden she could breathe properly, come alive again, be herself. She never tired of it. In all the long years she'd lived at Morton Hall, she had never been bored by the garden. Or, at least, one small corner of it.

Crossing the herringbone path, her slippered feet sunk into the cool grass and she took a deep breath of evening air. It was late September, and she could smell woodsmoke from the cottages in the village. The nights were drawing in, the year was winding down and everything had that melancholic feel about it. One could no longer pretend it was summer. The warm days were over and there was a chill to the air now that meant long sleeves were necessary.

She entered the maze at the west side. There were two entrances and this was the one she favoured. She could navigate her way through the maze blindfolded if she wanted to. She knew each curve, each false path and how long it would take to get to the centre.

It hadn't always been that way. As a young girl, she'd been frightened of the long leafy walls, thinking them monstrous. The dead ends had confused her. But, as she'd grown, the maze had become a great refuge. She would often steal into the kitchen and pinch a few biscuits from the tin, sneak a cushion out of the east drawing room, which she knew wouldn't be missed, and choose a book. Then she would pick one of the sequestered dead ends of the maze in which to hide herself. She would sit there for hours, wondering blithely how she'd ever managed to be scared of the maze for it was her very best friend now.

Hiding there infuriated her family, who would shout her name from every corner of the garden.

'She's in that maze again!' she'd hear them call.

'Well, I'm not going in after her!'

She'd smile then, knowing she was safe and that she'd be left undisturbed to read her book.

She didn't read in the maze any longer. She simply walked in there. It was the only place she felt any love for. It was her green sanctuary, her place to think or to empty her mind.

It was also the place she'd been going to meet her lover all those years ago. Only, he'd never shown.

Chapter 1

There were five bedrooms, a dining room, a sitting room and a study at Garrard House, but Anne Marie didn't feel comfortable in any of them. The house – modern faux Georgian with large, symmetrical windows and high-ceilinged rooms – was owned by her husband, Grant Keely, and, no matter how hard she tried, she knew it would never feel like home.

There was just one place she'd managed to carve out for herself in their four years of marriage: the tiny bedroom at the far end of the landing. It was the room nobody else wanted and was used for all the bits and bobs of family life like unused exercise equipment, an empty fish tank, a broken record player from the 1980s and bin bags full of old clothes that nobody hated enough to part with. But, in this room, Anne Marie had set up a little workstation – somewhere she could edit in peace and quiet.

She was just about to finish making notes on a chapter from a novel by a favourite client of hers when the alarm on her mobile sounded and her fingers instantly stopped typing even though she'd been mid-sentence. She would continue tomorrow because she mustn't be late now.

She saved her document, closing it with a sigh. Then she pushed her chair back and stood up, stretching her arms and circling her shoulders. She felt stiff, but that was normal.

Walking along the magnolia-coloured landing and on down the stairs to the white-painted kitchen, she filled the kettle with fresh water and reached into the cupboard for a very particular mug. A few moments later, she took the cup of tea into the living room and looked at the clock on the mantelpiece, waiting for the second hand to reach five. When it did, she gave a little nod and walked towards the study on the ground floor. The door was closed; it was always closed. She raised a hand and knocked gently. He didn't like it if she knocked too loudly.

'Enter.'

She opened the door and came face-to-face with the familiar view of her husband's back as he hunched over his desk. His computer was on, but he was handwriting something on an A4 pad, using a disposable blue ink pen. He got through dozens of them, filling bins around the house. Anne Marie hated the waste, even having nightmares about whole landfill sites dedicated to her husband's used pens. She'd once bought him a beautiful silver fountain pen, hoping that he would convert to a more sustainable way of writing. He had kissed her sweetly and the pen had been placed in a drawer, never to be seen again.

Now, she placed his mug of tea on the coaster. It was his five o'clock mug. She'd once brought in his three o'clock mug and he'd looked at her as if she'd lost her mind.

'Is it five o'clock already?' he asked now.

'It is. The clock chimed,' she told him in case he thought her careless with her timekeeping.

He leaned back in his chair and removed his glasses, pinching the bridge of his nose and rubbing his eyes. At fifty-two, his once dark hair was now streaked with silver. Anne Marie liked that. It gave him the distinguished English-gentleman look – the look she'd fallen for when she'd gone back to university as a mature student at the age of twenty-five. Grant had been her lecturer, and how dashing she'd thought him with his steel-rimmed glasses, his slate-grey eyes and his ability to quote reams of poetry. How in awe of him she'd been, and how bowled over when he'd started paying her attention. They'd married shortly after she'd graduated.

'Are you making any progress?' she asked him, daring to reach out and touch the papers on his desk.

'Don't!' he cried. 'Please.'

She withdrew her hand as if she'd been bitten. 'Sorry.'

'I need to keep these in order.'

'Of course.' She waited a moment before continuing. 'Is there anything I can do to help?'

'No,' he said. 'Thank you.' He looked up at her briefly. 'Have you had a good day?'

'Yes,' she said. She had learned to say no more than this because he never really heard her if she elaborated, and she knew that her own job must seem so dull and unimportant to him.

She looked at the piles of books on the desk. He was working on a book about an obscure nineteenth-century poet, but Anne Marie had doubts that anyone would really be interested in him. When she'd dared to mention this, Grant had snapped at her, saying that it was the very obscurity of this poet that made him fascinating, that he was going to uncover the mystery of this writer and reveal his story to the world for the first time. Anne Marie had backed down, acknowledging that her husband obviously knew best. And who knew? He might well have an award-winning book on his hands, though she secretly doubted it. Academic publications tended to have small print runs; at best, it might receive a handful of reviews that nobody would read before being shelved alongside so many other dusty tomes in universities across the country and periodically taken out to torture students with.

Meanwhile, the angst of research and writing, of impressing his peers and adding to his credentials in the hope of promotion was taking its toll, and she could see that his shoulders were hunched so much that they almost touched his ears, and his brow was furrowed, no doubt harbouring a headache. Anne Marie at once took pity on him.

'Have you thought about what you'd like for dinner?' she asked softly. 'I could make lasagne. The girls like that.'

'Lasagne it is then.'

She waited a moment longer in case he wanted to add anything, but he picked his glasses up and put them on again and his head bent down towards his notepad, and she no longer existed.

She looked around the room for a moment, noting his framed certificates: the degree, the MA, the doctorate. There were photos of him receiving each of them, a funny little statue he'd been awarded for one of his books, and shelf after shelf of the books themselves. A lifetime's work.

She swallowed hard. What had she achieved? She'd always been part of somebody else's life, and hadn't really been very present in her own. She was nothing more than a bit player – a support actor. When she'd made the decision to go back to university to study literature, she'd been filled with excitement at the possibilities that might lie ahead. Perhaps she'd write a book of her own one day, she'd thought. Well, she'd got as far as editing other writers' books at Oxford University Press, and had then gone freelance to enable her to work from home so she could take care of Grant and his daughters but, somewhere inside her, that dream still lived on.

It was as she remembered this that her eye caught sight of the photo of Lucinda, Grant's first wife, which still had pride of place on one of the bookshelves. It was a picture of her in the garden at Garrard House, standing under one of the laburnum trees, her two young daughters beside her. Lucinda had been so beautiful, with her willowy frame and long blonde hair, and Anne Marie was quite sure that Grant still felt her loss. How could he not? She had been the perfect wife, and Anne Marie was just a poor substitute. A second-best second wife. It was a role she seemed destined to play, she thought as she left her husband's study, closing the door quietly behind her so as not to disturb him. He hated it when she closed the door too loudly.

It was now ten past five. Everything was by the clock at Garrard House and all the important things were usually on the hour. Just as Grant's cup of tea was at five o'clock, so dinner was at seven. Six was too early and eight was too late, she'd been told when they'd married. She remembered making him dinner one evening shortly after the wedding. She'd been so excited to cook in his kitchen – *their* kitchen – and had called him through when the meal was ready.

'What is it?' he'd said, looking completely baffled as he'd entered the kitchen.

'I've made you dinner.'

He'd stretched his arm out to look at his watch. 'It's only quarter past six.' And he'd left the room, returning to his study where he'd very firmly closed the door.

She'd chased after him that time. That one time.

'Grant? Aren't you going to have your dinner?' she'd asked after charging into the room without knocking.

'I'll have it at seven,' he'd told her. 'Close the door on the way out.'

She'd done her best to keep his dinner warm, but it had spoiled and he'd pulled an agonised face as he'd worked his way through it.

'Things are so much easier if you work to a timetable,' he'd told her.

So, between five and six, she tidied the house, did the ironing, folded clothes away, picked other clothes up, vacuumed in the rooms where she wouldn't disturb Grant, and dusted in those closer to his study. At six o'clock, she stopped and began pottering around in the kitchen, gathering ingredients for dinner. They ate at the kitchen table during the week and in the dining room at weekends or if there were guests.

At five to seven, Anne Marie set the table with the white plates she'd heated up in the oven. She'd once tried to persuade Grant to use something with a little colour, but he'd merely shaken his head.

'White is classic,' he'd told her.

So the beautiful blue-and-terracotta dinner set she'd brought with her into the marriage remained at the back of a cupboard. Occasionally, if Grant was away on a training day, she'd serve dinner on her own plates. His daughters would look at her in alarm, but they allowed her that little rebellion without making a fuss.

There were many changes she'd tried to make that had been squashed, although she had had success with the bed linen and the bedroom curtains, but only because they'd been so horribly faded. Grant really had expected his new wife to sleep in the same bed linen as Lucinda.

Tossing the salad in a big white bowl, Anne Marie glanced at the clock. Two minutes to seven. Close enough. Grant surely wouldn't bellow at her for that. She left the kitchen in search of everyone and ran straight into Irma in the hallway. She was putting her coat on.

'Irma? Dinner's ready.'

'I'm going out,' Irma told her as she wrapped a scarf around her neck.

'Where are you going?'

'None of your business. You're not my mother.'

If Anne Marie had been given a pound for the number of times that comment had been flung her way, she could have afforded to send her two ungrateful step-daughters to boarding school where they might learn some manners. At least the words no longer hurt her, she thought. They had at first and she hadn't worn the wounds well. Now, they merely left her numb.

'Does your father know?' she asked instead.

Irma sighed. 'Yes!'

'And when will you be back?'

'Ask Dad.'

'I will,' Anne Marie promised and watched as the fifteen-year-old walked right out of the door without a backwards glance.

One daughter down, one to go, Anne Marie thought to herself.

'Rebecca – dinner's ready!' she called up the stairs, unsurprised when there was no answer. 'Rebecca?'

Anne Marie sighed. She could hear music playing from the girls' bedrooms and knew that she couldn't avoid a confrontation of some sort. Rebecca (never Becky – Anne Marie had once tried to call her that and had been frozen out for a whole week) was thirteen and was just as tall as her older sister, but still had a lot of emotional growing up to do. She made the most of her position as the baby of the family and had her father wrapped around her little finger, and Grant always took her side over Anne Marie's.

Reaching Rebecca's bedroom, Anne Marie paused before knocking on the door, lightly at first and then with more force.

'Rebecca?' She opened the door and the scowling face of Rebecca greeted her.

'What?' she snarled.

'Dinner's ready.'

'I'm not hungry.'

'It's lasagne. You like lasagne.'

For a brief second, Anne Marie believed she saw Rebecca's resolve waver, and she thought about approaching her, sitting on the bed next to her to see if she could make some sort of connection. It might be easier without Irma around. Anne Marie had often observed how Rebecca was always quick to follow her older sister's lead, but Irma wasn't here now, was she?

'Rebecca – listen—'

'I said, I'm not hungry.'

Anne Marie stood there for a moment. As an adult, she could insist that her step-daughter turn off her music and come downstairs and eat, but what would be the point of that? It would just mean more unnecessary fighting and she really didn't have the heart for it.

'If you change your mind—'

'I won't,' the girl said.

11

Anne Marie looked at her, wondering how a human being could live in the same house for four years and be treated with nothing but love and respect and yet show absolutely no reciprocal emotions whatsoever. When she'd first taken on the role of step-mother, the girls had seemed docile enough, but she'd mistaken their innate shock at her presence for acceptance. They'd simply been sizing her up and biding their time before they'd rebelled. Well, Anne Marie was sick and tired of their games now. She just wasn't going to play them anymore.

She went downstairs, returning to her husband's study, knocking on the door gently.

'Enter.'

'Dinner's ready, darling,' she told the side of his head.

'Oh, Annie, I haven't time to eat,' he said, briefly looking up from his papers. 'I've got to crack on with this.'

She opened her mouth, but then shut it, leaving the study and returning to the kitchen. She walked towards the oven, put on the oven gloves and took out the dish of lasagne. Grabbing a serving spoon from the worktop, she walked over to the pedal bin and opened it, giving the cheesy-topped dish a little nudge with the spoon, and watching it slide into the dark depths.

She then walked through to the hallway where she grabbed her coat from a hook by the door and swapped her slippers for a pair of ankle boots. It would still be light for a little while yet which would give her time.

Garrard House was on the outskirts of Parvington in the south of Oxfordshire, a pretty village which sat in the heart of the Chiltern Hills. It was a paradise of open fields, secluded woods and the beautiful chalky Ridgeway footpath. She would often take herself off on summer evenings or crisp winter mornings and just walk, inhaling the clear air and observing the small changes that each season brought. But there was one place that drew her more than any other – more than the lush fields and the verdant woods – and it was to this place she went now.

Nobody knew that she came here because she hadn't told them. Who would care? Grant wouldn't be interested and his daughters would be even less so. The place was her wonderful secret.

She passed the large houses and the sweet brick-and-flint cottages lining the main street of Parvington and then she turned right into the churchyard of St Peter's. It was a modest church with a squat tower upon which perched a golden cock weathervane that glinted in the last rays of the sun. But Anne Marie wasn't visiting the church. She was going somewhere quite different.

Passing the lichen-covered eighteenth-century graves whose angels and skulls were still perceptible and seemed to watch her every move, she walked towards a dark hedge, stopping at a little wrought-iron gate which was partially hidden by a cascade of ivy. She wasn't sure what had made her walk towards it on that summer's evening, two years ago, but she was so glad she had when she discovered what was at the end of the narrow path on the other side: a garden – a beautiful, neglected garden. At first, she'd been mesmerised and had walked with very little thought as to where the overgrown path might lead her. She'd been so caught up by the romance and the adventure of it.

When she'd come upon the large Victorian red-bricked house with its tower, its battlements and arched windows, she'd been truly terrified that she'd be caught. Though there was nobody around, it was clear that the house was lived in: several windows were open and neat curtains fluttered in the breeze. Anne Marie had hastily retreated, but the pull of the garden proved too much for her and she made frequent visits because it was clear that nobody ventured into the greater part of it and that was such a shame.

After some research online, she'd discovered that the place was called Morton Hall. It had been built and owned, she'd read, by the Morton family with Emilia Morton, spinster, still in residence, but there was very little information about her. She'd asked Grant about it one evening.

'The old Morton place? Ghastly piece of Victorian Gothic,' he'd said, which seemed rather harsh, Anne Marie thought, even though the architecture had inspired a certain amount of fear in her. 'Why do you want to know about it?'

'Just curious,' she'd told him.

'Not a lot to know really. Owner keeps herself to herself. Doesn't have anything to do with the village, but I hear she has quite the collection.'

'Oh?'

'Artworks, furniture – mostly from the Arts and Crafts period. I've heard it's rather spectacular.'

Now, as her light footsteps took her along the path once again, she thought of the house with its single occupant, wondering what she was like and if she was happy to live alone even if she was surrounded by great beauty. And why hadn't Anne Marie ever seen her in the garden? She could understand why she didn't frequent the overgrown part, but there was a section of the garden that was beautifully maintained.

As far as Anne Marie was aware, there was only one gardener who worked at Morton Hall. She'd seen him from afar. He was tall with broad shoulders. He looked no more than thirty-five and had fair hair which was normally hidden under a peaked cap. She usually managed to avoid him because he always seemed to be working around the maze and the topiary hedges.

Why didn't he garden anywhere else? She wanted to shout out to him – *Hey! Over here. Are you going to do nothing about this walled garden?* But, of course, she never did.

It was puzzling how it was only part of the garden that was maintained. But it meant that she had a whole world to escape into – a place that seemed to truly welcome her – and she would spend hours walking along the overgrown paths, spying the statues of forgotten gods and broken mythical creatures, fountains that no longer sang with water and a long lean-to greenhouse that no longer groaned with produce. It was beautiful and melancholy all at once, possessing the wild beauty of something unloved and untouched.

Anne Marie walked around it now, her legs brushing through the long grasses. She liked this special time at dusk when the shadows were lengthening and the last robin of the day was singing in a tree.

She found an old stone bench to sit on. It was in a secluded corner of the walled garden and her frequent presence there had flattened the grasses around it so that it looked almost habitable now.

As she made herself comfortable, her stomach gave a rebellious rumble, making her regret the decision to bin the lasagne, but she'd been so mad. How much of her time was spent looking after Grant and his daughters? And yet she was made to feel invisible. Her role was simply to serve them. Other than the hours she spent at her computer, she didn't feel like she had any sort of life and that was rather sad, wasn't it? To live in a house that didn't feel like your home.

The garden at Morton Hall was a place she could come to try to forget about her life but, tonight, she couldn't help dwelling on it. She wasn't happy and, if she was totally honest with herself, she hadn't been happy for quite some time now. She was very good at denying her feelings, burying herself deep in her work, but that could only go on for so long. The real Anne Marie had to surface every now and then and the tidal wave of pain would hit her anew.

You're not leading the life you want, a voice would whisper. *You've got to get out.*

But to do what and go where?

Anything. Anywhere.

She closed her eyes, listening to the robin's sweet song, aware that the air was cooling and the sky was darkening. Taking a deep breath at last, she got up, wending her way through the long grasses and thistles towards the path back to the churchyard. Just once, she glanced behind her at the Gothic exterior of Morton Hall. She wasn't ever likely to see inside it and yet she couldn't help wondering what it was like. She'd very much like to glimpse the collection that was hidden away there.

It was as she was thinking about the works of art that might be inside that a woman suddenly appeared at one of the upstairs windows. Anne Marie gasped and, for one dreadful moment, was paralysed where she stood, knowing she'd been seen and anxious as to what might happen next. But nothing happened. The woman at the window simply stared down at her. Anne Marie was the one to break the spell, turning away and fleeing down the path and on through the ivy-hidden gate into the churchyard.

When she reached home, Irma was still out, Rebecca was still in her room and Grant was still in his study. Anne Marie hadn't been missed. She never was.

Chapter 2

Cape Colman had been working in the grounds of Morton Hall for five years, but had never met the owner. He'd never even seen the elusive Emilia Morton. Well, he'd caught little glimpses of her at an upstairs window in the west turret, but not enough to know what she really looked like.

Every order he was given came through the housekeeper. Mrs Beatty was a stern woman in her sixties with a big bosom and eyebrows which hovered menacingly over her black-rimmed spectacles. She also handed him his wages at the end of each month. His job was simple: to keep the maze, hedges, topiary, and the borders around them, the house and the driveway, in tip-top form. No other part of the garden was to be touched. The old Victorian kitchen garden, with its long greenhouse and glorious old espaliered fruit trees, the rose garden full of fabulous old varieties, the fountain and the statues: all were left to rot, crumble and run riot. Never visited, never loved. It was a crying shame, but who was Cape to argue? He might have longed to take his shears and scythe and get to work clearing the area, restoring it back to its full Victorian splendour, but his orders were very specific.

He'd once made the mistake of clearing the ivy and brambles away from one of the statues. He'd seen its face peeping out of the undergrowth and he couldn't resist setting it free, revealing its beauty to the world. The next time he'd arrived at Morton Hall, he'd been reprimanded by Mrs Beatty. Just what did he think he was doing? Cape had tried to explain, but he'd been told that it wasn't his job to think for himself. He'd hated being spoken to like that and he'd very nearly walked away, but the garden meant too much to him to do that.

His father had been a gardener, although he'd never had the training that he'd made sure Cape had received. He was more of an odd-job sort of gardener. He'd plant, shape and cut a lawn, he'd happily hack his way through any overgrown borders, but he'd be less happy designing one from scratch. He had aspirations to learn more about the history of gardening and was passionate about visiting the great gardens of England. Cape remembered some of their trips together with great affection. They'd spent many a happy day at Blenheim Palace, which wasn't too far away, but they'd journeyed further afield too, taking in the incredible landscape gardens of Stowe, Chatsworth, Petworth and Woburn. It had instilled in Cape a great appreciation for wide open spaces and a desire to spend as much time as possible outdoors, which was why he valued his post at Morton Hall so much.

His partner, Renee, didn't share his enthusiasm and she'd made it quite plain that she hated him working at Morton Hall.

'I don't know why you go there,' she told him. 'You could be doing more proper work – work you get good wages for.'

She was referring to his design work.

'But I do that as well,' he told her. 'And I like the garden at Morton Hall. It's special.'

'Anybody could cut the hedges.'

'Not as well as me,' he asserted. 'Besides, I get a kick out of being there. It inspires me.'

No matter how many times he told Renee that, she never seemed to understand. He'd taken her there once, on a perfect September day when the golden light had fallen upon the garden like a blessing, but she hadn't been able to see the beauty in the place. All she'd seen were the nettles and the briars and the rather austere house in the middle of it all. It had upset him, but it didn't surprise him. For a beautician, Renee was quite remarkable in her inability to see the beauty in the natural world. But what upset Cape even more was that Renee strongly objected whenever he took their ten-year-old daughter with him. Poppy adored the maze and it thrilled him to see her running around the leafy playground. Mrs Beatty had given him permission to bring his daughter with him once a month, but the girl was to be kept under strict supervision and must not make any noise. Miss Morton didn't like noise, he was told.

Cape told his daughter not to venture further than the garden that was in his care, not only because those were the rules, but because he'd seen the danger and desolation that lay elsewhere: the broken shards of greenhouse glass, crumbling walls and thistles, and the nettles and briars that would sting and lacerate the young girl's legs if she dared to stray from the path. Luckily, she hadn't shown any interest in the rest of the garden. The maze was adventure enough for her, as were the topiary birds and beasts that her father tended to. She was fascinated by them, giving them all names as if they were her personal playthings, and asking after them in between her visits. There was a peacock she'd named Percy and a bear called Freddy. The horse was called Starlight and the dodo was Arabella. Cape smiled as he remembered.

'Why Arabella?' he'd asked at the time.

'She looks like an Arabella, don't you think?'

Cape often wondered if Poppy was going to become a gardener too one day. How his father would have adored her. It was the great sadness of Cape's life that he'd been taken away so soon. Poppy had been a baby when he'd died from complications arising from a rare form of dementia. Had he recognised his only granddaughter? It had been hard to tell. Cape's mother had died when he was just seven years old and the loss of his father was a devastating blow. He'd thrown himself into his work, dedicating more time to it than was healthy, but he thought he had the balance right now.

And, oh, how he loved his days at Morton Hall. Yes, his job there was pretty unexciting as jobs went – there wasn't much scope to flex his own creativity when he was simply keeping things in order with a pair of shears and a hoe, but he got so much pleasure from that. He felt more like a zookeeper than a gardener when it came to looking after the topiary animals. No wonder Poppy had named all the hedges – they really were characters in their own right and, officially, they were alive, weren't they? He might not talk to them the way Poppy did, but he cared for them greatly.

Then there were the abstract shapes – the hedge that looked like a great fat wedding cake, the spirals and the pyramids, and others that were indescribably odd.

'They're every shape at once,' Poppy had said when she'd first seen them.

But each had a distinct personality, there was no denying that.

It seemed such a shame that they were only enjoyed by one person. Well, he assumed the owner enjoyed them. Miss Morton never came out into the garden when he was there, although he came across occasional traces of her presence. He'd once found a book on a bench by the topiary hedge shaped like a wedding cake; another time he discovered a whisper-thin scarf in the maze. He'd hoped to return the scarf to Miss Morton in person and had dared to enter the main house via the servants' stairs. The ground-floor rooms in that quarter were open to him so that he could make himself a cup of tea in the most basic of kitchens and use the toilet. It was one of those toilets with the cistern up on the wall. Poppy had never seen anything like it and had refused to go near it when she'd first encountered it, fearing it was going to fall off the wall and squash her. It had taken all of Cape's powers of persuasion to get her to use it.

After Cape had found the scarf, he'd ventured up the servants' stairs. He'd never dared to do that before: he'd not been invited to or told where they went and he'd never asked but, for some reason, he'd felt compelled to try to find Miss Morton that day.

The stairs were bare of any carpet and the walls, which were white, were cool and rather austere-looking. A door soon greeted him, but it had been locked and so he'd gone up another flight, finding a door that opened onto a dark landing lined with tapestries. His eyes were just adjusting when the buxom figure of Mrs Beatty appeared, silhouetted at a doorway.

'*Mr* Colman!' she'd bellowed. '*What* are you doing in here?'

He'd held out the scarf as if in explanation. 'I found it in the maze. I wanted to return it to Miss Morton.'

'*I'll* take that!' she'd said, charging forward and snatching it from him.

'I'd really like to return it myself,' he'd said.

'Miss Morton does not see visitors.'

'But I'm not a visitor – I'm her employee.'

'Yes, and your place is in the garden. Kindly return there.'

They'd stood, staring each other down in a battle of wills. Cape had given in first with a weary sigh. The woman was impossible. All he'd wanted to do was say hello to his employer. Was that really asking too much?

'Can you tell Miss Morton that I—'

'Out now, please.'

He hadn't dared to climb the servants' stairs since.

He often wondered if, one day, he'd look up from his clipping to see Miss Morton standing there. She'd introduce herself, apologise for not having done so before and they'd become great friends. Cape would like that. He longed to ask her about the history of the garden, for there was only a little information about it online and in the local library and that wasn't the same as getting to know the garden through the owner, was it? That's what he wanted – the private, *personal* history of the garden. What a treat it would be to wander through the maze with her and to ask her about her family's use of it. It seemed such a shame that he never saw her enjoying it.

But there was somebody he knew who loved the garden as much as he did. Well, he didn't *know* her exactly, but he'd seen her countless times although she wasn't aware of that.

She had long red hair, which caught in the slightest of breezes, and an anxious look about her as if she knew she was trespassing and feared getting caught. He longed to put her at ease, but instinctively knew that, if he made an approach, he would scare her off for good. So he left her alone, pretending not to see her, pretending that he didn't hear her footsteps along the path. Who she was and what solace she found in the garden, he didn't know. Much as she intrigued him, he left her to herself because he knew that gardens were sacred places and that people came into them to be still and to think private thoughts.

Plus, he liked knowing that there was someone in the garden other than himself. It made him feel less alone and made the place seem alive, which was so vital for a garden.

And so the days went by with Cape trimming and tidying, and the red-haired woman coming and going. It sometimes seemed that his days would always be the same, and there was absolutely nothing wrong with that, he acknowledged.

It was a cold day in January when Mrs Beatty made a rare appearance in the garden. He caught sight of her crossing the path and went to meet her, his heavy boots leaving their great imprints on the frosty lawn.

'Everything all right?' he asked as they met. There was something different about her, something less rigid in her manner. Her face was paler than usual and she was twisting her hands around themselves. 'Mrs Beatty?'

'Miss Morton died last night,' Mrs Beatty said at last.

'Oh, God! I'm so sorry.'

She nodded. 'She'd been unwell. For a while. It wasn't totally unexpected, but . . .' She swallowed hard, the rest of the sentence forgotten.

'Still, it's a shock, I'm sure.'

She nodded.

'Did you want me to go?' Cape asked, suddenly realising that his presence might no longer be required.

Mrs Beatty shook her head. 'No, stay today. And in the future. Your job will continue.'

'Okay,' he said, breathing a silent sigh of relief.

'And there's something else,' she said. 'She left you something.'

Cape frowned. 'Miss Morton? Really?'

Mrs Beatty nodded.

Cape felt stunned. He couldn't think what it might be. The pair of shears he'd become so attached to perhaps? Or one of the smaller topiary plants in a pot?

'You'll hear more in due course. That's all I can say.'

He watched as Mrs Beatty turned around and disappeared into the house. He stood there for a while, his breath fogging the air as his frown deepened, and a great weight of sadness fell upon him at the loss of the woman he had never met.

Chapter 3

Cape usually tried to avoid Henley-on-Thames if he could. Not only was the traffic always bad, but the shops were neither to his taste nor to his budget. But he'd received a letter from Mander and Murray Solicitors and it had seemed important. It was something to do with the estate of Emilia Morton. He'd tried to question Mrs Beatty about it as she'd left the house one day, but she'd simply shaken her head.

'It's not for me to talk about,' she'd told him.

The whole business was totally baffling.

He parked his car over the river and walked across the bridge, marvelling at the beauty of the Thames, which was an astonishing blue on this January day, flanked by impressive boathouses and the distinctive tower of St Mary's church dominating the skyline.

It was as he reached the other side of the bridge that he noticed the woman in a winter coat and black boots. She'd been looking out across the river and had just turned to continue on her way as he'd approached, but he was pretty sure that it was the red-haired woman who came to the garden.

All of a sudden, he became self-conscious as it was obvious they were going in the same direction and he appeared to be following her. He slowed his pace as she turned right over the bridge. He turned right too. It was definitely her, he thought. Although he hadn't seen her face clearly, she had the same way of walking as the woman who frequented the garden, and her long red hair was unmistakable.

Her pace had picked up now. A moment later, she turned right again. Surely she wasn't going into the solicitors' as well – was she? Cape could see it up ahead.

The office of Mander and Murray was situated in an impressive three-storey Georgian town house that overlooked the river and it seemed that the red-haired woman was, indeed, going there too. He paused a moment, not wanting to reach the door at the same time, allowing her space to go in first before he slowly followed.

The reception was a plush affair with a big shiny desk behind which sat a woman who greeted him with a smile. He told her his name and she asked him to take a seat.

Cape crossed the room and cleared his throat as he dared to sit down next to the red haired woman. She looked up from her magazine, her brown eyes not seeing him at first, but then her gaze caught his and her lips parted as if in recognition.

Cape gave a tentative smile.

'Are you here to see Mr Mander?' he asked.

'I – erm – yes,' she said. 'Are you?'

He nodded. 'Yes.'

There was an awkward pause when he wondered whether he should introduce himself, but then the door opened and a man walked in, closely followed by a woman. The man looked to be in his late thirties and the woman in her forties.

'Here to see Mr Mander,' the man said as he walked up to the desk. 'Mr Everard.'

The red-haired woman, who'd returned her attention to her magazine, looked up after the man had announced his name and gave a little nod to Mr Everard as he sat down. Cape wondered how they knew each other. Not well, judging by the fact that they didn't exchange even the most basic of pleasantries.

The woman, who was also there to see Mr Mander, announced herself as Miss Cardy and took a seat next to Mr Everard. Neither spoke to the other.

Mr Mander was a very popular man, Cape thought as three more people entered the solicitors', each one of them there to see the very same man. The red-haired woman put her magazine down and Cape noticed a puzzled look on her face before she turned to face him.

'Are you okay?' he asked her, leaning forward slightly to see if he could assist her in any way.

'They're all from my village,' she whispered.

'Really?' he said, and she nodded. 'And they're all here to see Mr Mander.'

She chewed her bottom lip. 'I wonder what's going on.'

'You think they're here about Miss Morton?' he asked.

'Are you?' she asked, her tone surprised.

'Yes.'

'So am I. I got a letter,' she began, picking up her handbag from the floor, opening it and taking out a neatly folded letter. 'I don't understand why it was sent to me. I never knew Miss Morton.' She handed the letter to him.

'It's the same as mine,' he told her.

'Excuse me?' a woman's voice said.

Cape looked up. The young woman who'd just taken a seat was watching him and the red-haired woman now. She looked to be in her early twenties and had short blonde hair and was wearing a long black coat and biker boots.

'Can I see your letter?' she asked.

The red-haired woman passed the letter to her and she took a moment to read it.

'It's the same as mine,' she announced, her forehead wrinkling in consternation.

'And mine,' Cape said.

'We're *all* here to see Mr Mander?' the red-haired woman asked, her voice louder now, causing the others in the reception to look up.

Mr Everard sat forward on his seat. 'You all get one of these letters about Emilia Morton?'

The woman he'd walked in with nodded, as did the older man and woman who'd arrived afterwards.

Mr Everard shook his head as if in annoyance. 'What's this all about?' he demanded, standing up and walking towards the reception desk. 'Why are we all here?'

'Mr Everard,' the receptionist began, 'please take a seat. Mr Mander will be with you shortly and he'll explain everything then.'

Looking somewhat appeased, Mr Everard returned to his seat.

'This is getting stranger by the minute,' Cape said to the red-haired woman.

'I wonder what's going on,' she replied.

At that, a man in a dark-navy suit entered the reception.

'I think we're about to find out,' Cape said.

'Good morning, everyone. Sorry to keep you waiting. I'm Gabriel Mander. If you'd like to follow me.'

The seven of them were ushered down a corridor lined with framed certificates and then into a meeting room with a large pale table sur-rounded by a dozen chairs. There was a huge sash window which looked out over the Thames, but it wasn't the river Cape was interested in as he sat down next to the red-haired woman; he was anxious to hear what Mr Mander had to say.

Tea and coffee were passed around and Mr Mander sat himself down at the head of the table, a neat folder in front of him.

'Okay, we'll get straight down to it. This is a rather unusual piece of business,' he began, his hands flat on the table before him. 'I'm sorry I couldn't go into any detail in the letter sent out to you all, but this really needed to be explained and discussed in person.'

'Please proceed,' Mr Everard said unnecessarily.

'Indeed,' he said. 'My client – my former client – Emilia Morton of Morton Hall, Parvington, has instructed me to let you know that her house and garden have been left to the village of Parvington. This is to include all contents of the house and monies. The entire Morton estate.' He paused as if waiting for some kind of reaction. Cape, for one, felt breathless at this piece of news.

'But that's crazy.' Mr Everard was the first to speak. 'None of us knew her. Did we?' He looked around the table.

'I never even saw her,' the young blonde-haired woman said. 'She was some kind of recluse, wasn't she?'

'Why would she leave the house to us? It doesn't make any sense,' Mr Everard continued.

'Well, I've just been instructed to tell you her wishes,' Mr Mander explained. 'I don't have the reasons behind them, I'm afraid.'

'What's it all worth?' Mr Everard asked.

'Again, I don't have that information. You would have to get an estate agent to value the property and grounds. The contents are a different matter entirely. I believe there is a sizeable art collection. Nothing, however, is to be sold. As I mentioned, everything is to be left to the community as a whole.'

'But what do we do with it all?' the red-haired woman asked.

'That, again, is to be determined by yourselves. Miss Morton, I believe, chose you all very specifically, believing that your different backgrounds and skills would help you make the right decisions going forward.'

Cape looked at his companions around the table. This was the most bizarre situation he'd ever found himself in. Did Mrs Beatty know about this? Did she know who had been chosen for this odd task and, indeed, had she played a part in choosing them? And what was her role to be, he wondered? And was his own role merely to continue cutting the hedges? There were so many questions circling his brain that he couldn't even begin to guess the answers.

'So the house is to be owned by the community in perpetuity?' a mature woman whom Cape hadn't really noticed asked now.

'Yes,' Mr Mander said. 'Initially, your role will be to restore the house and garden.'

'The whole of the garden?' Cape asked, thinking of the jungle beyond the part he tended.

'Yes.'

'That's quite a job,' Cape said.

'And there will be a small salary for each person for the time they spend at the garden. Miss Morton was adamant that nobody should be out of pocket, and there is a fund set up to pay for any equipment needed,' Mr Mander said. 'The terms of the will state that the house and garden will belong to the community once a full calendar year has passed from today's date. During that time, each volunteer must contribute at least five hours a week to the project. Once the year is over, a trust fund will be in place to cover annual costs of the hall and garden.'

'And when does that run out?' Mr Everard asked.

'It won't run out in your lifetime,' Mr Mander said. 'The Morton fortune is pretty sizeable, but there is a limit to how much money is to be released each year. The idea is that, in the long term, the community will work together to make the hall pay for itself.'

'To run it as a business?' the mature woman asked.

'That, I think, was Miss Morton's idea.'

'She expects us to give up our jobs?'

'That decision would be yours,' Mr Mander said.

Silence fell for a moment as everyone weighed up the information they'd been given.

Mr Everard groaned. 'I really haven't got time for this. It's just the sick mind games of a lonely old woman.'

Cape frowned at the angry words. 'I think she meant to be totally sincere with this gift.'

'Look,' Mr Mander interrupted, 'this is a lot to take in and you don't have to make any decisions today, although it's suggested that you form a committee to organise things.'

'Great,' Mr Everard said. 'I just *love* committees.'

'That way, you'll all know what you're doing. Miss Morton has provided you a list of all your contact details which you have in the envelopes being passed around now.'

'How did she get our details?' Mr Everard asked.

'Does it matter?' Cape asked.

'I'd like to know,' Mr Everard said. 'She didn't know me. I never had anything to do with her or her family and all of a sudden I'm involved in this crazy scheme!'

'Well, I think it's an amazing opportunity we've been given here,' the red-haired woman said. 'I've seen the garden and it has enormous potential for our community.'

Cape nodded. 'I've been working in the garden for several years now, and I agree. We've got to try to make this work.'

Everybody seemed to be considering this when Mr Mander spoke again.

'Now, it's not my position to advise you, but I'd take this information away with you and just think about it for a while. Visit the garden, look at the house. Mrs Beatty's details are written down for you here. She's the housekeeper and will show you around if you make an appointment. She's suggested that you meet there early next week.'

Mr Everard muttered something under his breath.

'Was there something you wanted to say?' Mr Mander asked him.

'I feel like a pawn in a really warped game,' he confessed. 'There's something distinctly off about all this, don't you think?'

'*Off*, how?'

'I don't know – weird. Like something Miss Havisham from *Great Expectations* might dream up. Hey! We're not being filmed, are we?' he asked, suddenly looking around the room. A few other heads turned in alarm too.

'No, you're not being filmed,' Mr Mander assured him.

'Because I won't be messed around with.' He got up from the table and was about to leave when Mr Mander stopped him.

'Take this, please.' He handed him a manila envelope. 'Read it and get in touch if you have any questions.'

'Questions you can't answer, you mean. Like why the hell this old biddy left her fortune to a bunch of strangers?'

'I'll do my best to help,' Mr Mander assured him, and Cape watched as Mr Everard left the room.

'I have a question,' the young blonde woman piped up, looking unsure of herself.

'Miss Hartley, isn't it?'

She nodded, and Cape saw her swallow hard before she spoke. 'Was she alone? I mean, was Miss Morton alone when she died?'

Everyone at the table turned to face the young woman, their eyes filled with concentration and a sudden compassion, as if they'd not yet thought of Miss Morton as a real person until now.

'I – erm – I believe her housekeeper was with her,' Mr Mander said.

'Good,' the young woman said. 'It would be awful if she was alone, wouldn't it?'

The mature woman looked a little uneasy and shifted in her chair and, when Cape glanced at the red-haired woman, he swore he could see tears swimming in her brown eyes.

Mr Mander cleared his throat. 'Any other questions before we wind things up?'

Everyone looked too dumbstruck by what had passed to think of anything to say and they began to get up, taking their manila envelopes and picking up their bags and coats before leaving the building.

'Hey,' Cape said as he held the door open for the red-haired woman. 'You want to grab a drink somewhere?'

She looked at him, obviously surprised by his question. 'Well, I—'

'I'm Cape,' he said. 'I'm the gardener at Morton Hall and, well, I don't know about you, but I'm a bit dazzled by all this. I'd really appreciate talking to someone right now.'

She nodded hesitantly. 'I'm Anne Marie.'

They shook hands and then moved onto the pavement as somebody tried to get out of the door behind them.

'Okay,' she said in a little voice. 'Let's get a drink.'

'There's a cafe just up ahead,' he told her and she nodded.

The two of them walked in silence up the road, mingling with the shoppers as a cold wind did its best to pummel them.

The cafe was busy, but they spotted a table towards the back and sat down as the waitress cleared it, shedding their coats and scarves before ordering: Cape a coffee and Anne Marie a chamomile tea.

'To calm my nerves,' she said with a hollow laugh.

'This is a very unusual situation, don't you think?' Cape asked after they'd been served their drinks.

She nodded. 'Did you know her?'

'I worked for her, but I never met her.'

'Isn't that a bit odd?'

Cape gave a little smile. 'I always thought so, but I didn't have much choice in the matter. I tried to meet her once – not long before she died – but the housekeeper turfed me out. My place was the garden and I never saw Miss Morton there, although I hoped that I would one day.'

'I wonder what she was like,' Anne Marie said, taking a sip of her tea. 'Nobody seems to know.'

'She wasn't very old,' Cape said. 'Just fifty-four, the papers said. I thought she was much older. Mrs Beatty always said she was fragile and was very protective of her. I think the two of them had been together for years. But I was imagining this really ancient lady confined to her house.'

'You say you never saw her in the garden?' Anne Marie asked.

'That's right, but I know she went out into it. I found a scarf of hers in the maze one day.' Cape ran a hand through his hair. 'I wish I'd had the chance to speak to her. Especially now, after what she's done for us.'

'Why do you suppose she's done this?'

'Well, she didn't have any family, did she?' Cape said.

'But to leave the place to a group of strangers. Isn't that odd?'

'What else could she have done with the place?'

'Given it to the National Trust or something?' Anne Marie suggested.

Cape took a sip of his coffee, which was good and strong and just what he needed, and noticed a slim gold wedding ring on Anne Marie's left hand, nestled next to an engagement ring. So she was married, he thought, realising that this strange set of people Miss Morton had thrown together knew absolutely nothing about each other.

'What do you know about the others?' he asked.

'Not much,' Anne Marie confessed. She pushed her hair out of her face and frowned, as if trying to recall the group that had sat around the table in the solicitors'. 'There's Kathleen Cardy.'

'Which one was she?'

'The woman with the neat dark hair and the bright red lipstick,' Anne Marie said.

Cape nodded as he remembered.

'She lives in one of the thatched cottages in the village. The one that caught fire last year. Half her house burnt down. It was so sad. I think she lost a lot of stuff.'

'God, that's awful.'

'It takes some getting over,' Anne Marie said. 'And she was running a small bed and breakfast from there too. I'm not sure how she coped while it was all being repaired. There's still workmen in today. I see their vans when I go by.'

'Is she on her own?'

'I think so.'

'That's a lot to cope with.'

'Yes, it must be,' Anne Marie said, shaking her head.

'What is it?'

'I was just thinking how awful it is of me for never asking how she's doing. I mean, she's practically a neighbour and yet I've never spoken to her. I just read about her in the paper and never thought to reach out to her. Oh, God, I feel terrible now.'

'Don't beat yourself up,' Cape told her. 'We all lock ourselves away in our own worlds. Maybe you'll get a chance to talk to her now.'

'I hope so,' Anne Marie said.

'So what do you know about Mr Everard other than that he's very vocal?'

Anne Marie gave a tiny smile. 'His name's Patrick and rumour has it that his wife left him. Just upped and went one night. He woke up and she was gone. There was a note, I hear, saying something like "Don't try to find me". He's got two young sons he's bringing up on his own.'

'No wonder he said he hadn't got time for any of this. Is he in Parvington too?'

'Yes. Aren't you?'

'No. Bixley Common.'

'It's nice out there.'

'Yes. Good and remote. I like the countryside and the footpaths. But I think I might be the only one not from the village,' he said.

'But you were Miss Morton's gardener. She must have thought highly of you. An honorary villager, perhaps.'

'Yes, perhaps.'

Anne Marie suddenly smiled. 'I didn't quite catch your name. Caleb, was it?'

'Erm, no. It's Cape.'

'*Cape?*'

He smirked. He was used to this sort of interrogation when people first met him.

'C. A. P. E. Cape.'

'Cape.' Anne Marie said the name again. 'That's – well – unusual.'

He shifted his boots under the table and scratched the back of his neck. 'Yep,' he agreed. 'You could say that.'

'Is it short for something?'

There was no point hiding the truth from her so he cleared his throat.

'My dad was a Lancelot "Capability" Brown nut. We used to spend almost every weekend visiting gardens designed by him. I loved it, but I wish he'd been half-sensible and called me Lancelot. I would've got Lance for short then. That's not a bad name, is it? But saddling me with Capability. I was ribbed mercilessly at school. It was a nightmare!'

'I can imagine.'

'And you're Anne Marie . . .'

'That's right.'

'It's a pretty name,' he said, noticing the way she cast her eyes down and started circling the rim of her teacup with her finger. 'You don't think so?'

'It's okay,' she said.

He watched her for a moment, biding his time.

'You visit the garden, don't you?'

'What?' She looked up, her brown eyes wide.

'I've seen you there.'

Her lips parted as if she were about to deny it, but then she nodded. 'I'm sorry. I didn't mean to trespass.'

'Don't apologise.'

'I didn't know anyone knew. I never meant to disturb you.'

'You didn't disturb me.'

'I only ever went to the part of the garden that wasn't used.'

'I know,' he said quickly. 'It's fine.'

'Really?' She looked anxious and Cape was desperate to put her at ease.

'I'm glad you came. There's only one thing that bugged me.'

'What's that?'

'Why didn't you ever say hello?'

'To you?'

'Absolutely to me!' He gave a laugh.

'But I didn't know you'd seen me. Why didn't you say something?'

'Because I got the feeling you wanted to be alone.'

She didn't deny it. 'I'm sorry.'

'Really, you don't need to apologise.'

'I had no right to be there.'

'I think it's nice that you visited the garden. Gardens are meant to be enjoyed and it always struck me that the grounds at Morton Hall were completely wasted.'

'Yes,' she agreed. 'I couldn't believe somebody would own such a place and let the garden get so overgrown. I once brought a pair of secateurs with me to snip around my favourite bench.'

'I noticed.'

'You did?'

'I often sit there myself.'

'Why is that part of the garden never touched?'

'That's a question I've asked a hundred times,' Cape said.

'It's such a shame. It could be so productive. The greenhouse, the walled garden—'

'And it will be,' he said. 'If we can drum up some enthusiasm amongst this group we're a part of now, just think what we might be able to achieve.'

Anne Marie's eyes seemed to light up. 'We could grow our own fruit and vegetables.'

'And plant some new trees,' Cape added. 'Old varieties like the ones the garden would have once had in abundance.'

'And can we grow squashes and gourds and huge pumpkins?'

'If you're willing to do the work, you can grow whatever you want!'

She was smiling now. He liked her smile. It lit up the whole of her face, banishing the melancholic look he'd seen there before.

'I'm ready to pull out my wellies right now,' she said.

Cape grinned. 'Look – here's an idea. I'm at the garden tomorrow. Why don't you come by and I'll show you the maze and the topiary garden ahead of everyone else arriving?'

'Really? I'd love that,' she told him.

'Great. What's a good time for you?'

'I could probably get there for ten. Is that okay?'

'Meet me at the cedar tree. You know it?'

She nodded and the two of them stood up to leave the cafe.

'I wonder why she chose us,' Anne Marie said as they walked out onto the street.

'Perhaps Mrs Beatty will know.'

'Will she be there tomorrow?'

'She's there every day. Even since Miss Morton died.'

'Do you think she'll be working with us?'

Cape took a deep breath. 'It's likely she'll be overseeing things. I can't remember what Mr Mander said now. Maybe there's something about it in the paperwork he gave us. Anyway, I'm sure we'll find out soon enough.'

They were walking across the bridge now. The wind had picked up and little waves danced on the Thames.

'I wish I'd met her,' Anne Marie said.

'Mrs Beatty?' Cape asked in surprise.

'No! Miss Morton.'

He nodded. 'Me too,' he said with a wistful sigh. 'I think she must have been quite a lady.'

Chapter 4

Emilia Morton always knew that there was something not quite right about her brother, Tobias. Ever since he was a young boy, he'd been unpredictable, petulant and prone to mood swings, but Emilia had never given it much thought until the summer she finished university and came back home to Morton Hall. It was 1983, but it might as well have been 1883 at the old Victorian house. Her record player and beloved LPs were hidden away in an oak cabinet and there were no posters of her favourite pop stars in her bedroom – the William Morris wallpaper simply wouldn't allow it.

'You have to respect this house,' her father had once told her. 'Just imagine you're living in a museum. Try not to touch anything you don't need to.'

Emilia had been a nervous wreck as a child, and her bedroom, as beautiful as it was, had always felt like somebody else's with its heavy oak furniture, intimidatingly large paintings and the ornate silver mirror she was too scared to look into. There was no room for her to be herself in there. She had a few paperback novels which she kept on a little shelf, but her mother always tutted whenever she saw them.

'Can't you put those away, darling?' she'd ask. 'They don't really go with the room, do they?'

It was the same with her toys. Her childhood dolls, her scrapbooks, her games and her colouring books: everything had to be hidden away from view in a large oak chest under the window. Emilia hated that chest. It reminded her of a coffin and she imagined her dolls were being laid to rest each time she put them away. It was the same for Tobias. The few personal possessions he had were to be packed away at the end of each day, and heaven help him if he dared to leave any of his toy soldiers out on parade. He'd once left a little army of them on the south terrace and their father had flown into a fit of rage when he'd seen them.

When she visited friends' houses, she marvelled at the freedom they had. Their rooms were pastel-coloured paradises full of light and life. They had posters on the walls torn out of magazines and stuck with Blu Tack and sometimes even Sellotape. *Sellotape!* Just imagine if she put Sellotape onto her 1874 wallpaper, Emilia thought.

There were toys too, in great fat heaps on the bed, on the floor, *everywhere.*

'Doesn't your mum ever tell you off?' she'd asked one of her friends, Lucy.

'What for?' Lucy had said, clearly baffled.

Emilia had had a small taste of freedom at the girls' boarding school she'd been sent to when she was ten years old. She'd shared a room with three other girls and they'd been allowed to put a few posters up on the wall behind their beds. Emilia had chosen one of a chestnut horse, one of a giant panda and another of a male singer with hair longer than hers.

Being sent to a boarding school at such a young age might have scared most girls but, for Emilia, it had been a wonderful release from the oppressive atmosphere at Morton Hall. Charles and Joanna Morton were far more focussed on their respective careers than they were on their children. Charles was a banker, though the Morton fortune was sizeable enough that his salary was barely needed to keep Morton Hall going. Still, he took pride in his job and insisted on working.

Joanna was a designer, taking her inspiration from the Arts and Crafts interior of her marital home. She was good at what she did and had an enviable portfolio of clients, but she spent money as soon as she earned it, buying period pieces of furniture for the house until it was so crammed that Charles was forced to put a stop to it.

Emilia still remembered that fight because it had frightened her so much. It had been during her first Christmas holiday since she'd gone away to school, and her parents' voices had risen up through the house. She and Tobias had come out of their rooms and stood at the top of the stairs, listening.

'What's going on?' the ten-year-old Emilia had asked.

Tobias, who was fifteen, shook his head in disgust.

'Dad's not happy with Mum,' he'd told her.

'Why not?'

'He's asked her to stop working.'

'But Mum loves her job.'

'Yes, but Dad thinks she should be at home.'

'What would she do at home? Wouldn't she be bored?'

Tobias had shrugged. 'Women are meant to be at home, aren't they?'

Emilia had wrinkled her nose. 'Why?'

'Because it's their place. If Mum was at home, we wouldn't be at boarding school.'

'But I like boarding school.'

'She should be a proper mum and stay at home.'

Emilia had looked at her brother as if trying to work out if he was joking, but he looked deadly serious.

'I think Mum should do what she wants,' she said at last.

Tobias had crossed the landing towards her, placing a finger under her chin, examining her with those penetrating eyes of his.

'What do you know about these things?' he'd said. 'You're just a girl.'

Emilia had watched as her brother had stormed off to his room.

'You're just a girl.'

It was a refrain she'd grown up with because Tobias was very good at putting her in her place.

'You're just a girl.'

Was that what her father was telling her mother?

That's when Emilia had first understood that Morton Hall was a house run by men. Women were just passing through and were expected to do what they were told.

She'd been dreading finishing university and coming home, and even more so since her parents had died. That tragedy had happened the summer Emilia had turned eighteen. Her parents were meant to be on their way back from a trip to Italy where they'd been viewing a rare Rossetti painting in a private collection. They'd promised Emilia a party to celebrate her big day. Only they'd never returned. On the last day of their trip, Joanna Morton had gone swimming. A passer-by had said that she'd swum out into the sea and lost control very quickly. Charles had gone in after her and neither had returned. The sea had claimed them: their bodies were never found.

The painting that they'd bought hung in the long gallery now. It was very beautiful, but it wasn't worth the price of two lives.

At twenty-three, Tobias had taken over the running of the house, employing Mrs Beatty to help. He'd given up his job at his father's bank, stating to Emilia that he didn't need to work – and he told her the same thing when she graduated three years later. When she replied that she wanted a job, he'd laughed.

'Why would you want to work when you don't have to?'

'Because I don't want to be stuck in this house all day,' she'd said. 'And I have a degree. I should use it. I've studied hard and I'm good at languages, all my lecturers said so, and I think I could do really well if I—'

'You should manage the house,' he'd interrupted.

'What, like an old-fashioned chatelaine?' she'd joked.

'Exactly,' he'd said in all seriousness, giving her that controlling look of his she'd grown up with. 'It's your role now, Emilia. It's your duty. There's Mrs Beatty, the gardener and the two cleaners to manage. That should be enough for anybody.'

His tone of voice had told her that he would brook no opposition.

And, that summer she'd graduated, she found herself falling into the role surprisingly easily if a little reluctantly. She had thought about just leaving one day, of circling a job in a newspaper and waving good-bye to her brother and her family home, but Tobias had filled her with so much self-doubt that she was too scared to do it.

'You wouldn't know how to survive outside Morton Hall,' he'd told her and she'd believed him. How foolish she had been, but when you've been told something so many times, it's hard to think anything else.

So she took up her new role – the role he had handed to her. She was the woman of the house now and, she suspected, would be until Tobias found himself a wife. It was hard to imagine her brother married; he'd never even mentioned having a girlfriend. But marrying was what the men of these houses did and he'd want Morton Hall to himself once he had found the right woman, wouldn't he? Emilia would have to move on. These houses weren't made for daughters or sisters. They were men's houses. She'd been allowed to study for a degree because the money was there. It was all about show. But she wasn't actually meant to use it. That wasn't part of the plan. She was to fall in line with what the man of the house wanted, that was all.

But, oh, how trapped she felt in that place. It hadn't taken long for the claustrophobia to set in. Morton Hall had been built by Arthur Augustus Morton at the height of his powers in the Industrial Revolution. He'd built the house and amassed the wealth that their family still enjoyed today from the textiles industry, and there was no denying that it was a house filled with beautiful things, but beautiful things weren't enough to make Emilia happy, she soon discovered. She knew that some of her university friends would envy her for not having to work and for having a magnificent home handed to her. Take her bedroom, for example. It was known as the Acanthus Room, named after the William Morris wallpaper that covered its walls with huge green leaves. It was a lovely room with its stained-glass window by Edward Burne-Jones, featuring his characteristic willowy figures, and the hand-knotted carpet which was only to be vacuumed through a gauze. Rumour had it that John Ruskin had visited the house and pronounced the room 'one of the loveliest in England' and Emilia had no doubt that it was, but it just wasn't *her* and every hour she spent in there felt draining and depleting.

The garden, at least, provided an escape for her. It always had. It had been the only place where she and Tobias had been able to run around as children without fearing they might damage something. Even though Tobias always had a dreadful fear of the maze and never ventured in there, they still enjoyed the garden together. They could be proper kids there, wild and free, and she still felt that wonderful spirit of freedom when she was in the garden even now she was a grown-up.

She was just returning from a walk around the garden one sunny morning when Tobias grabbed her by the arm. He'd sprung out of the shadows in the hallway, catching her unawares.

'Tobias!' she cried in alarm. 'You scared me.'

'Come with me,' he said, practically dragging her up the stairs.

'What's the hurry?'

'Wait till you see what I've found,' he said, his voice unable to suppress his excitement.

'What is it? *Tobias!*' The pressure of his hand on her wrist was beginning to burn. Luckily, they'd reached the top of the stairs and he relinquished his hold, ushering her into the bedroom at the end of the corridor. It was the room that had belonged to Clarissa Morton – the first lady of Morton Hall, wife of Arthur Morton.

It was a long time since Emilia had been in this room. The house had so many rooms but so few of them were used now and so they were wrapped up in dust sheets. Tobias had obviously been uncovering the furniture in this room because there was a heap of ghostly sheets in the centre of the carpet.

'What have you been doing in here?' Emilia asked him.

'Just looking at what's mine,' he said. He'd always been blunt.

Emilia walked towards the bed. The bed itself was quite plain with a simple sprigged bedspread over it, but it was the fact that it was a folding bed with great oak-panelled doors around it that made it a real show-stopper; each of the panels had been painted, depicting a beautiful dreamy Pre-Raphaelite woman with pale skin and cascading hair. The piece had been commissioned by Arthur Morton especially for his wife and it was stunning, although Emilia couldn't imagine sleeping in it, surrounded by so many faces. It might be a work of art, but it was also the stuff of nightmares.

'Stop staring at the bed and come and see this,' Tobias said. He was standing by the large wardrobe at the far end of the room and had opened the double doors. Emilia walked across the thick rug and gasped as she saw the contents.

'Are these all original?' she asked as she stared at the row of dresses.

'All Victorian. You know our family never threw anything out.'

'But they must be worth a fortune!' Emilia said.

'They're not for sale. They belong to our family.'

Emilia nodded. It was a knowledge she'd grown up with. Everything the Mortons had amassed stayed at Morton Hall. Nothing was ever sold, lent or given away.

Instinctively, Emilia's hand reached into the wardrobe. Each gown was wrapped in a protective sheet in an attempt to keep the moths at bay and she dared to bring one out, laying it on the bed.

'It's so long and heavy,' she whispered as she unwrapped it.

'The fashion of the time,' Tobias explained.

Emilia had seen the many family portraits of her ancestors and had frequently marvelled at their clothing with the high lacy necklines, the long skirts in sumptuous materials with pleating and ruches. They were a world away from the jeans and jumpers of the 1980s.

'These should be in a museum. The V and A!' she exclaimed.

'Just let them try to get their hands on these,' Tobias said. 'Try one on, Emmy.'

'What?' She looked at him, trying to gauge if he was being serious.

'I think you're about the same size as Clarissa.'

'I couldn't,' she said with a gasp.

'Of course you could,' her brother told her. 'What good are they just hanging in the wardrobe? I think they should be worn.'

'They're too delicate.'

'There's years of wear in them.'

'I don't think I should—'

Tobias took a step forward and was suddenly very close to her. She looked up at him. His eyes were dark and she saw him swallow hard.

'Try the dress on, Emilia.'

Their gazes locked. She was the first to blink and look away, her hands hovering over the dress on the bed.

It took a few moments to release it from its wrappings and her mouth parted in wonder as she took in the ebony-green dress with the delicate buttons and the exquisite lace.

'Put it on,' Tobias whispered.

Emilia's hands were shaking, but she had an undeniable urge to indulge in this most outrageous of dress-ups.

'Turn round.'

Tobias nodded and Emilia began to shed her twentieth-century clothes, realising how cool the room was once she was standing in her underwear.

It took a great leap of courage for her to pick up the dress from the bed and she took a moment to hold it against her, the fabric cool and silky against her skin. How beautiful it was, she thought. Too beautiful for her to wear, and yet her brother was insisting that it wasn't and so she slowly stepped into it.

'Shouldn't I be wearing a corset or petticoats first?' she asked, unsure of the clothing etiquette of Victorian times.

'Doesn't matter,' Tobias assured her. 'It's the dress that's the important thing.'

'It might not look the right shape on me,' she said, dipping her arms into the long, lacy sleeves.

'It'll look just fine.'

A moment later, Emilia had done as much as she could on her own.

'I need help,' she said, and Tobias turned around, assisting her with the hooks and eyes at the back.

Finally, she turned to face him. He took a few steps back, his eyes gleaming with a strange light.

'You look incredible,' he told her. 'Every inch the Victorian angel.' His hand reached out as he moved forward again and stroked her red hair. It was a habit that he'd had as a young boy and she hadn't minded. It was affectionate, protective even, but now it seemed strange and it was all Emilia could do not to flinch.

'Here – help me take it off,' she said, suddenly not wanting to be in the dress.

He shook his head. 'Keep it on.'

'What?'

'Just for today.'

'Tobias – no – it's not right.' Suddenly, she felt scared by his request.

'Why isn't it right? This dress is mine and I want you to wear it.'

'But it's too valuable. It'll get spoiled.'

'Not if you wear it carefully like a Victorian lady.'

'But I'm not a Victorian lady. I'm a twentieth-century one and I'm a clumsy one at that.'

'Not in this dress,' he told her, his hands on her shoulders.

'Come on, Tobes, help me take it off. I can't undo the hooks on my own.'

He shook his head. 'You're wearing the dress, Emmy.'

She watched as he started to turn to leave the room, but then he stopped.

'I've got a friend coming to stay,' he told her. 'Jay Alexander.'

She didn't respond. She felt furious with him and didn't trust herself to speak.

'Now – go and look at yourself in the mirror,' he said. 'You'll love what you see.'

Emilia felt anger and frustration boiling inside her as her brother left the room and she had half a mind to find the nearest pair of scissors and cut her way out of the dress, but she knew she could never do that. It was far too beautiful and precious. For a few moments, she stood help-lessly in the middle of the room. She had to admit that the dress was a perfect fit, which she found a little unnerving. She took a deep breath and walked across to the full-length mirror that Tobias had uncovered.

'Oh!' she cried as she looked at her reflection. With her long red hair and pale skin, she truly did look as if she'd stepped out of one of the family paintings. She hadn't realised until that moment how much she looked like her ancestors.

She walked across the room, the dress swishing about her. She liked the noise it made, but she couldn't imagine wearing it around the house.

'Emmy? Come downstairs,' her brother called.

She left the room, realising as she did that she was barefoot under the long dress, which didn't feel at all right. She'd have to find a suitable pair of shoes. At that thought, she shook her head, suddenly annoyed at herself. She wasn't going to give in to Tobias. Wearing a dress like this all day was a ludicrous idea.

When she reached the top of the stairs, Tobias was waiting for her in the hall below and he looked up at her with the kind of smile that made her anxious.

'You look beautiful,' he said.

'I need to take it off,' she told him.

He shook his head. 'You'll wear the dress for the rest of the day.'

'Don't be silly.' She tried to laugh, but found she couldn't.

'You know I'm *never* silly,' Tobias said.

She swallowed hard at the tone of his voice. 'But it isn't right,' she protested.

'Says who?' He made a point of turning around and gesturing at the empty house. 'It's just you and me here, Emilia. We make our own rules. And I say *this* is what's right.' He held her gaze and she was just about to interrupt him when he continued.

'You'll wear the dress. And, tomorrow, you'll wear another one.'

Chapter 5

While Cape's partner Renee had never been interested in his career, their daughter Poppy was always fascinated by the plans he drew up for the gardens he was working on and would gaze at them with eyes full of wonder. She was standing there now in his study, her hands on her hips as she surveyed his latest piece.

'What's that bit?' she asked, pointing to a group of three circles.

'They're hydrangeas,' he said. 'You remember what a hydrangea is, don't you?'

'Of course. They're the big flowers with big leaves.'

'That's right.'

'Why have you painted them purple?'

'Because that's the colour the client has chosen.'

Poppy wrinkled her nose. 'I like pink ones.'

'I know you do.'

'You should give her pink ones.'

Cape smiled. 'Ah, but you have to listen to what your client wants. You can't plant what you want in somebody else's garden. You can advise them if you think they're making the wrong decision, but the choice is theirs.'

Poppy seemed to consider this for a moment. 'I think she's making the wrong decision,' she declared. 'Would you like me to tell her for you?'

Cape laughed. 'I'll pass on your message and see what she says, okay?'

'Okay!'

He watched as she skipped out of the room and then he took a deep breath. It was the day after the meeting at the solicitors' and he hadn't yet told Renee about what had happened. He hadn't shown her the letter when it had arrived either. Something told him not to, but he'd have to let her know what was happening sooner or later, he supposed, getting up from his desk and stretching.

He walked through to the living room. The curtains were drawn and the lamps were on and Renee had lit the wood burner. He had to admit that there was something wonderfully cosy about winter evenings even though he missed the long summer nights when he could be planting out and digging until the last streaks of light had left the sky with a fierce passion. If he wasn't out working, he would be walking along the footpaths that threaded their way through the valley. There was one in particular he liked to frequent. In the summer, the dust from the track would coat his boots and the swallows would screech in the sky, darting in and out of the farm buildings he passed as he slowly climbed uphill towards the woods. Then he would turn around and survey the countryside beneath him. It was a gentle landscape of hills, dotted with farms and small cottages, and he loved it.

He knew he was easily pleased. He was happy with his lot in life, but he knew that Renee wasn't and her anxiety weighed him down. He'd done his best to ignore it, but it sat there like a malicious devil between them, ready to tear their life apart.

He watched Renee now. She was sitting on the sofa, flicking through a magazine about hair. There was a stack of similar ones on the coffee table in front of her. There was also a pile underneath the coffee table and in the basket by the fire. He wasn't sure if she meant those ones to be used as kindling or not and thought he'd better ask before ripping them up.

'Poppy upstairs?' he asked her.

'She's deciding what to wear to a party next week,' Renee told him, not looking up from her magazine.

'Well, if she's anything like you, that should occupy the rest of the evening.'

'Very funny!' Renee said, pulling a face at him.

He sat down on the sofa next to her.

'You finished work for the evening?' she asked.

'I think so. I've got a bit of a headache.'

'You need glasses.'

'I don't need glasses.'

'You should have an eye test,' she told him.

'I'm fine.'

'You spend half your life squinting at little maps and plans. It isn't good for you.'

He appreciated her concern, but he was quite sure it was unwarranted.

They sat in silence for a while, Cape closing his eyes and enjoying the toasty heat from the wood burner as he listened to the gentle flip of Renee's magazine pages being turned.

'I spoke to Martina again,' she suddenly announced.

Cape knew what was coming next, dreading it and hoping against hope that he was wrong.

'Is she well?' he said, not daring to open his eyes. If he kept them shut, the problem might just go away.

'Yes. *Very* well. She doesn't have to put up with these long cold winters in California, does she?'

'But winter can be fun. We've got our fire and there's nothing prettier than our valley when it's snowing, is there?' He opened his eyes. 'Remember the first time Poppy sledged down the hill? She said she was an angel flying over the vall—'

'She's even got film work,' Renee interrupted.

51

'Who?'

'Marti!' she said in exasperation. 'Can you imagine? If *I* worked with her, I could be doing make-up for the stars!'

Cape frowned. He hated it when she talked like that.

'But you live here,' he pointed out, 'so that's not likely to happen, is it?'

'We could move,' she said, and he could both see and hear that she was gritting her teeth. The idea of moving to join her sister was something she'd been impressing upon him for a few weeks now. He'd been ignoring her, hoping it was just a phase, a pipe dream that would fade away into the background as the realities of life took over and buried it, but that wasn't happening. If anything, it was getting worse and he was finding it impossible to ignore now.

He took a deep breath. 'My work is here,' he told her, thinking that would silence her on the subject.

'But you could easily work there,' she said. 'And just imagine the money you could make designing gardens in Beverly Hills!'

Cape grimaced. He could think of nothing worse. His joy lay in the green and verdant gardens of England, but he could see that she was serious about this.

'Poppy's school is here. She's settled, she has friends.'

'She'll make new friends,' Renee insisted. 'Kids adapt and this experience will be so good for her. Just think, we could probably afford a place with our own swimming pool over there or live somewhere near the sea.'

Cape frowned, wondering what on earth made Renee think that. California sounded expensive to him.

'I think you're getting carried away,' he said.

'I'm not getting carried away. I want to do this, Cape,' she said, 'and, if you don't want to do it too, I'll have to do it on my own.'

'You'd go out there on your own?' he asked.

'Well, Poppy would come with me.'

Cape's stomach felt as if it had dropped about a yard. 'You're kidding, right?'

'I'm not kidding.'

Their eyes locked together for an agonising moment while Cape tried to still his racing mind. And then he remembered that he hadn't told her yet.

'The garden,' he blurted.

'What garden?'

'Morton Hall.'

'That ugly old pile? You want to stay here because of that horrible old—'

'You don't understand – listen to me for a moment,' he told her with some urgency now. 'I've been given an opportunity. Miss Morton died and she's left the house and garden to her village and I've been chosen as one of the people to organise everything.'

'What are you talking about?'

'I need to be here. I can't just up and leave. This is a unique opportunity for me to create something really special. You know I love that garden and I've been wanting to get my hands on the derelict part since I started work there. Well, that time's come.'

'So you'd turn down a chance to live in one of the most beautiful parts of the world so you can cut down a few nettles and thistles? Is that what you're saying?'

'Listen, this could be big for us,' he said.

'Big – how? You said the place has been left to the whole community – not to you.'

'But my input – my guidance – I think I could really make a mark there.' He reached out to her and took her hand in his. 'Listen, if you still feel this way next year, we can talk about it then. Just give me some time with this garden, okay?'

Renee stood up, throwing the magazine she'd been reading onto the coffee table.

'It's always about you, Cape, and it's just not fair.'

'Renee – don't be like that. Please, darling!'

He watched as she left the living room, her feet heavy on the stairs a moment later, and he didn't have the energy to follow her.

Grant left Garrard House at the same time as his daughters on the morning Anne Marie was to meet Cape at Morton Hall. She hadn't told her husband about her appointment, nor had she told him about the strange bequest of Emilia Morton. She had the feeling that he'd somehow dampen the excitement she was feeling. Why had she been one of the *chosen ones*, he'd be likely to ask her. She could just imagine Grant putting himself forward and spoiling everything, and she didn't want that. This was her little adventure and she was going to keep it to herself for as long as possible.

The January air nipped at her fingers and nose as she left the house swaddled in her thick winter coat and hat. She walked through the village, entering the churchyard and wending her way through the frosty grasses towards the little gate. It was a journey she'd made so many times and yet this one was different because she'd been invited to Morton Hall. She had a role to play now at this magical place.

Cape had told her to meet him at the cedar tree and she knew where that was. It was impossible to miss the wonderful old tree with its great girth and enormous limbs that stretched out across the lawn. Anne Marie had often wondered how old it was. Older than the hall, she believed. Perhaps it had stood in the grounds of an older property on the same site. She'd have to look into that. It would be interesting to learn more about the history of the property.

Looking up at the dark red-brick Gothic house, she couldn't help feeling sad that it had lost the last member of its family. Could houses feel such things, she wondered? Grant would tell her not to be so stupid, but she was suddenly feeling melancholy about the whole business of Morton Hall and found that her imagination was taking her in all sorts of strange directions. She had only seen Emilia Morton – if indeed it had been her – for that one brief moment at one of the windows, the arched one to the right on the first floor, she thought, and yet she couldn't help but feel the loss that came with her passing.

'Hello!' Cape's cheery voice suddenly broke through her thoughts.

'Hi,' she replied.

He frowned and nodded to the path behind her. 'You came in through the church?'

'Yes.'

'You should've walked up the driveway. I think you've got permission to do that now.'

'I didn't think. I mean, I'm used to coming in this way,' she confessed.

'Come by the main entrance next time,' he told her.

'I'll try, but I can't promise.' She was aware that he was studying her, as if trying to make her out, so she pointed towards the topiary to distract him.

'Ah, yes – you've not seen this part of the garden at all, have you?' he said.

'No.'

'You sure you never sneaked in when I wasn't around?'

Her mouth dropped open. 'No! It's much too close to the house. I'd never—'

He laughed. 'I'm teasing.'

She gave him a guarded smile, noticing that he was wearing a thick woollen jumper that was unravelling at the back and which had a big hole where his right elbow jutted out. He was also wearing large conker-coloured boots and Anne Marie began to worry that the little ankle boots she'd chosen to wear wouldn't be suitable, but she wasn't expected to do any actual gardening today, was she?

'Let me show you the beasts first,' Cape said, leading her along a path lined with a low box hedge. Everything was so neat and tidy and Anne Marie marvelled at the frosted spider webs that glistened everywhere. January could be a bleak month, but it could also make one gasp at its beauty.

But the cobwebs weren't the only things in the garden to take her breath away. As they turned a corner, the great fat topiary display greeted her.

'Heavens!' she exclaimed. 'How did I never know this was here?'

'Not many people do,' Cape said.

'It's incredible!' She took in the gigantic peacock, which looked so regal and haughty, the cuddly-looking dodo and the magnificent horse.

'Do you like them?'

'Like them? I *love* them,' she enthused.

Cape's smile stretched across the whole of his face. 'I secretly think of them as mine. Mine and Poppy's.'

'Poppy?'

'My daughter,' he said. 'She's ten. I'm allowed to bring her here once a month. She loves the animals and the maze.'

'I bet she does.'

'You have children?'

'Step-children.'

'Bring them here – I'm sure they'd love it.'

She shook her head. 'I don't think so.'

He looked surprised. 'No?'

'They're – erm – not those kind of girls.' She could see the confusion on Cape's face.

'Not the kind of girls who like gardens?'

'Yes. Or doing anything with me,' she said and then bit her lip. What had made her say such a thing to a virtual stranger? She cleared her throat. 'They wouldn't enjoy it.'

'Okay,' Cape said. 'No worries. Well, we'll enjoy it instead, right?'

'Right.'

He gave her a warm smile that helped to banish the dark mood she was bound to fall into if she spent too much time thinking about her family.

'So, tell me about the topiary,' she said, turning her attention to the beautiful garden.

'Well, it was created for the original owners, Arthur Augustus Morton and his wife Clarissa. I believe they started with a design for the maze and then created these box hedges to give this part of the garden a sense of structure. The topiary beasts and shapes came slightly later. It was something that was popular in Victorian times although not everybody liked it. The *Gardeners' Chronicle* called topiary "vegetable monstrosities".'

'That's a bit harsh, isn't it?'

He shrugged. 'There's always been a lot of snobbery in gardening. Plants come in and go out of fashion the same way colours and planting schemes do.'

'I've never understood that,' Anne Marie said. 'How can the colour of a beautiful flower suddenly be out of fashion?'

'Exactly. It's all a load of nonsense,' Cape declared. 'In my opinion, you either like something or you don't. That's what your gardening choices should be based on. You shouldn't be worrying about what somebody else might say if they happen to look around your garden.'

'Well, it seems as if the Mortons have always done exactly what they wanted.'

'I'm not so sure about that,' Cape said. 'I mean, the topiary and the maze weren't Emilia's choice, were they?'

'But she obviously liked them,' Anne Marie said.

'What makes you say that?'

'She hired you to keep them looking perfect.'

'But that doesn't mean she liked them. She might just have respected what her family had created.'

Anne Marie thought about this for a moment. It was an interesting point of view and she couldn't help thinking of her own situation at Garrard House. Nothing there was her choice, was it? She simply endured it to keep the peace. From the dull white dinner service to the magnolia walls, none of it was of her choosing.

'I think a lot of people live with the decisions of others,' she said at last.

'I wish I'd had the chance to talk to her,' Cape said. 'All I know is that she walked in the maze, but that doesn't really tell us anything, does it?'

'Maybe we'll find out more once we're allowed in the house,' Anne Marie said, and the two of them glanced up at the Gothic exterior.

'I wonder what secrets it holds,' Cape said.

'I can't wait to see it,' Anne Marie confessed.

'Did you get the email from Mr Mander? The first meeting is set for Monday evening.'

'Yes.'

'The great handover begins,' he said. 'After that, it sounds like it's up to us to organise things.' He took a deep breath. 'But let's not worry about that yet. I was going to show you around.'

He led the way through a long avenue of topiary hedges which seemed to reach to the very sky in happy spirals and joyful twists.

'You take care of this all on your own?' she asked him.

'Yep.'

'It's quite a job.'

'I wouldn't give it up for the world,' he told her. 'I love it here.'

They walked around in silence, their feet crunching over the frosty lawn. The air was cold and still and their breath misted the space around them.

'Did you want to go inside the maze?' he asked her as they reached one of the entrances.

Anne Marie had only ever seen photographs of the maze on the internet and had always been curious about it but, now that she was standing at its entrance, she wasn't at all sure.

'Well, maybe just a little way.'

Cape gave a laugh. 'You can't just go a *little* way into a maze!' he declared.

'Oh.'

Cape cocked his head to one side. 'We don't have to go in at all if you don't want to.'

'No, I want to.'

'Are you sure? Because you don't look sure.'

She took a deep breath. 'Let's do it,' she said with determination, taking the first step and entering the maze. 'You do know your way?'

'Yes, of course,' he said.

'Good. Did you want to lead?'

'Absolutely not,' he told her. 'You should experience it yourself. False turns, doubling back and everything.'

Anne Marie nodded. She could do this, she told herself and, although she felt horribly self-conscious with Cape so close behind watching every wrong move that she made, she also found that she soon fell into a strange rhythm. Her feet seemed to be taking on a life of their own.

Left feels good here. But right here. No, I've been here before. This isn't the way. I think I've seen that bend already so that means take a left now.

And on it went until she found the centre where a beautiful wrought-iron bench greeted her and she took a well-deserved sit down.

'Well done!' Cape said, clapping a hand on her shoulder.

She looked up at the sudden familiarity of the moment and he withdrew his hand quickly, taking a step away from her.

'Thank you,' she whispered.

'How do you feel?' he asked.

'It was the strangest sensation,' she told him. 'I had no thoughts in my head other than where I was going. It was wonderfully freeing.'

He nodded as if in recognition. 'Mazes and labyrinths were often used for meditation and spiritual journeys.'

'Really? I didn't know that.'

'But I think they're just for pleasure these days.'

'You said mazes *and* labyrinths,' she said. 'Aren't they the same thing?'

'No, they're not. A maze can have many entrances and exits and multiple dead-ends, but a labyrinth has a single direct route.'

'This is most definitely a maze,' she said, 'and I think I found all of the dead ends!'

He smiled. 'You did.'

'Can we get out of here now?'

He nodded. 'Want me to lead the way?'

'Yes please.'

She followed him and he made it look so very easy, turning left and right in exactly the correct places. She was quite sure that she would never have been able to do it in under an hour.

'That was fun,' she said. 'I can say that now that I'm out of there.'

'I remember the first time I went in. It took me forty minutes to find my way to the centre and then out again.'

'Do you ever get lost when you're trimming the hedges?'

'No. It's kind of like a second home to me now.'

'It's very special,' she said. 'But what are we going to do with it?'

'I think it's the rest of the garden we need to worry about first,' he said. 'Did you want to take a look?'

Anne Marie knew where they were going. Leaving the maze and the topiary garden, they rounded the house and walked towards the walled garden. The neat lawn was soon replaced by long grasses and clumps of nettles which rampaged along the brick wall that was happily crumbling into old age.

Reaching a wooden door that had long fallen off its hinges, they stood looking on in speechless wonder as a pair of rabbits scuttled into a thicket of brambles. There were thistles the size of full-grown men, there was broken glass everywhere and frost-cracked pots lay scattered around in terracotta graveyards. But Anne Marie's eyes also saw the enormous potential of a space that could bring people together and that they could use, though one question was foremost in her mind.

'Where on *earth* do we start?' she asked.

'We start with the people,' Cape said. 'We find out what everybody's skills are and assign jobs to them.'

'You make it sound so easy.'

'I don't think it will be if that's any consolation.'

'It isn't really,' she said, smiling up at him, but then she sighed. 'I don't know why I've been chosen for this. I don't think I have any skills. I'm an editor. What can I possibly bring to this project?'

'You said you loved the garden.'

'Yes.'

'Having a passion for something is half the battle, I find. It's a pretty good driving force to getting a job done.'

'Well, I would love to see all this restored.'

'There you go then. You're halfway there already!'

They laughed together.

'You know, I've been dying to get to work on this place,' Cape confessed to her. 'I was only ever contracted to take care of the maze and the hedges. I wasn't allowed to even come into this part of the garden.'

'Why do you think that was?' Anne Marie asked.

'Well, at first I thought it was a money issue, but it seems clear that there was always plenty of that.'

'Maybe Miss Morton didn't want to waste any money on a part of the garden she didn't use,' Anne Marie suggested as the two of them walked along an overgrown path strewn with broken snail shells.

'I once sneaked in here,' Cape said. 'I was curious to see if there were any old tools that could be rescued.'

'And were there?'

'There were a couple of nice pieces actually, but Mrs Beatty took them away. She occasionally pokes around the garden to see what I'm up to. I'm not sure what she did with the tools. Probably locked them away in a dark shed to rot.'

'Maybe we could look for them now that the garden is going to be restored.'

'Yes, I'd like that.'

They soon reached the other side of the walled garden and turned around to look at the waste ground before them.

'There's a lot to do here, isn't there?' Anne Marie said.

'And it isn't just the walled garden either. There are footpaths around it and statues everywhere which have been left to deteriorate. There are all sorts of areas between here and the topiary garden that need attention and we're starting at the ugliest time of year,' Cape pointed out, 'although, if we work hard, this part could be a really productive place come summer.'

Anne Marie looked at the space with fresh eyes, trying to imagine it on a perfect summer's day with raised beds full of beautiful produce, immaculate pathways linking the spaces between and a fully restored greenhouse full of ripening tomatoes and luscious vines. Perhaps all that wouldn't be achievable by the summer, but it was fun to dream and it was important to have a vision.

As they were walking back to the topiary garden they heard the sound of tyres on the gravel driveway and looked round to see a car leaving.

'That's Mrs Beatty,' Cape said. 'Looks like she's off early today. Mind you, she gets here at the crack of dawn.' His expression changed.

'What is it?' Anne Marie asked him.

'Mrs Beatty's gone.'

'Yes,' Anne Marie said, frowning.

'We could go in.'

'Inside the house?'

'Why not? We could take a look around.'

'Are we allowed to do that?'

'Well, it's kind of been left to us, hasn't it?'

'But shouldn't we wait for everyone else to join us next week?'

'You want to wait?' he asked her, a tiny grin hovering at the side of his mouth.

A little bubble of excitement rose in Anne Marie. 'Not really,' she confessed. 'But how exactly are we going to get inside?'

'Ah,' he said, 'I have a way. Come on.'

Anne Marie wasn't quite sure what he was up to, but she found herself following him, curious as to where he was going.

They soon reached a great wooden door at the side of the house.

'As the gardener here, I was given access to the cloakroom and kitchen on the ground floor so I could take a break when needed,' Cape said, producing a key from his trouser pocket and opening the door.

Anne Marie followed him inside and saw a stark kitchen with old-fashioned cupboards, a butler's sink and a small wooden table with a couple of chairs in the centre of the room. It was pretty basic, but everything looked clean and tidy.

'Can I get you a cup of tea?' he asked as she looked around.

'Oh, no thank you.'

'We'll continue then?' He left the room, entering a hallway with a quarry-tiled floor and passing a small cloakroom before starting up the stairs.

They were doing it. They were really venturing inside, Anne Marie thought, feeling a surge of excitement as well as a good dose of nerves. She'd so often wondered what the house looked like and couldn't quite believe she was going to find out right now.

'Are you *sure* we should be doing this?' she asked.

'You don't want to?' Cape asked, stopping on a landing and looking back at her.

'Oh, I want to do it, but . . . never mind – let's do it.'

He grinned and tried the door that led off the landing.

'Locked,' he said. 'I tried this one once before and couldn't get in this way.'

'Why were you trying to get in?'

'It was after I found a scarf in the maze and wanted to return it to Miss Morton in person. I found another door up the next flight. That one was open. Come on.'

He continued up the stairs and stopped at a second door.

'Mrs Beatty might have locked this one since my little visit,' he said, resting his hand on the doorknob for a moment.

'Go on, then,' Anne Marie pressed. 'I want to see what's on the other side!'

He smiled at her enthusiasm and turned the handle.

'It's not locked,' he said, pushing the door open and then walking out onto the landing.

For a few moments, they walked around the house in awed silence. Anne Marie had never seen anything like it. She didn't know where to look first: there was so much to take in, from the ornate ceilings to the art on the walls and the rich carpets beneath her feet. Her eyes darted around, finding it impossible to settle on any one thing.

At first, they peeped cautiously into the rooms they passed. Many were filled with white dust sheets so they couldn't see their contents.

'There's only Mrs Beatty to take care of everything,' Cape explained.

'Do you know anything about her?'

'She's a widow. That's all I know. She probably bossed her husband into an early grave.'

'Oh, look,' Anne Marie cried as she caught sight of the paintings on the landing. 'These are exquisite. Look at the colours. I've never seen anything like this in my life. At least not outside a museum. They're all Pre-Raphaelites.'

Cape frowned. 'I'm afraid I don't know much about them.'

'It's a movement of painting from the mid-nineteenth century. I think this one's Rossetti.'

'Was he famous?'

'Pretty famous.'

'I don't know a lot about painting.'

'Neither do I, but I became quite interested in the Pre-Raphaelites when I was doing my degree,' she told him. 'We spent a term learning about them – Rossetti was a poet as well as a painter, and the Pre-Raphaelites were drawn to poems by writers like Tennyson and Keats. So many of their paintings depicted women like the Lady of Shalott and Mariana, and Ophelia from *Hamlet*. Women who were trapped in a man's world – often physically trapped in a single room like the Lady of Shalott was.'

'Like this lady,' Cape said and the two of them studied a painting of a woman wearing a midnight-blue dress. She had a melancholic look on her face as she stared out of a mullioned window. 'It could be Miss Morton.'

'You think so?'

'Well, I never saw her, but I always imagined her trapped in this old place because I never saw her outside it.'

'Or inside it,' Anne Marie said. 'Maybe she didn't exist at all!'

'Now, there's a thought. Maybe Mrs Beatty made her up.'

'Except, I thought I saw her once – just briefly – at a window when I was leaving the garden.'

'You did?'

'I'm not sure, though. It could have been anyone, I suppose.'

'In all the years I've worked here, I've never caught more than a glimpse of her. The only people I've seen coming and going have been

Mrs Beatty, the window cleaner and the man who comes to sweep the chimneys once a year.'

Anne Marie looked up at the painting again. 'It can't be Miss Morton,' she said. 'Look at the dress. It's Victorian.'

'She's got long red hair like you,' Cape pointed out.

'It could be Elizabeth Siddal. She had red hair and was painted lots of times by Rossetti and Millais. Although I'm not sure,' Anne Marie added. 'There's something not quite . . .' She paused. 'I'm not sure about it. It looks Pre-Raphaelite. The colours are so rich and vibrant, like jewels, but something's not quite right about it.'

'Do you think it's valuable?'

'Well, if this is a real Rossetti, then yes. Enormously so. His paintings can sell for millions of pounds.'

Cape made a funny choking sound. '*Millions?*'

'Rossetti's very popular. But these aren't to be sold, remember?'

'You think I'd try to sell them?' he asked her and she turned to look at him.

'No, of course not,' she told him. 'You wouldn't, would you?' There was humour in her tone, but she was watching him carefully for his response.

'I could buy my dream garden with the proceeds of one of these,' he replied, 'so perhaps you'd better keep an eye on it.' He gave her a wink and she smiled.

They spent a little while longer looking around the rooms, barely daring to breathe as they entered them and making sure they didn't knock into anything.

They were at the front of the house and were just admiring the ornate plasterwork of the ceiling when they heard the sound of a car on the gravel driveway. Cape rushed over to the window.

'It's Mrs Beatty!' he cried.

'I thought she'd gone home!' Anne Marie said.

'We have to get out of here. Quick!' He grabbed her arm and the two of them flew along the landing towards the door that led to the servants' stairs.

'Leave it as you found it,' Anne Marie said and then cursed herself for sounding so bossy.

'The door wasn't locked,' Cape reminded her.

'Will she be mad if she sees us in here?'

'She won't see us. She never comes round to this part of the house.'

'Are you sure?'

'Trust me,' Cape said as they reached the bottom of the stairs.

'Oh my goodness! I haven't moved so fast in years! I'm actually out of breath.'

'Sorry about that!' Cape said.

'You weren't to know she'd come back.'

They looked at each other, huge smiles on their faces at their shared adventure.

'Can I get you a cup of tea now?' Cape asked.

'You know, I might just be ready for one.'

They were making their way into the kitchen when the door from the garden opened and Mrs Beatty entered.

'Ah, there you are,' she said, eyeing Cape suspiciously.

'Mrs Beatty – what a surprise,' Cape said. 'Are you well? I was just going to make Anne Marie a cup of tea. She's part of the—'

'Yes, I know who she is,' Mrs Beatty interrupted.

'It's good to meet you,' Anne Marie said, stepping forward and extending her right hand which Mrs Beatty shook perfunctorily. Her expression was stern and Anne Marie felt the full weight of her disapproval.

'The meeting of the group is on Monday evening,' she said.

'Yes, we know,' Cape said. 'Anne Marie's just been looking around the garden today.'

'And I really should get going,' Anne Marie said.

'Then I won't stop you,' Mrs Beatty said. 'I'll see you next week.'

Anne Marie and Cape exchanged glances and they all walked out into the garden together. Mrs Beatty followed them for a moment and then overtook them, turning around quickly and looking Cape directly in the eye.

'I noticed some weeds along the driveway as I drove in,' she said.

'I'll attend to those straight away,' he said.

She nodded and left them.

They waited a few seconds before speaking to be sure she was out of earshot.

'Is she always so friendly?' Anne Marie asked.

'No, usually she's *much* more abrupt,' Cape joked. 'God, I hope I haven't traumatised you with all this.'

Anne Marie shook her head. 'I've had a great time.'

'Really?'

'It's been . . . an adventure and I don't often have adventures.' She looked back up at the house and then out towards the topiary. 'I'm looking forward to – well – whatever happens next.'

'Yeah, me too,' Cape said.

'Well, I guess I'll see you on Monday.'

He gave her a nod. 'Thanks for coming today.'

'Thank you for inviting me.'

She turned to go.

'Hey!' he called after her. 'You can go down the main driveway.'

Anne Marie stopped and looked in its direction, but then shook her head. 'I like the church way,' she said, waving her hand at him in goodbye.

She'd just reached the bend in the path when she decided to turn back and look at the house. Cape was still standing there, that smile of his lighting up his face and she couldn't help looking forward to seeing him again.

Chapter 6

'I like your name,' Emilia told Jay Alexander. They were walking in the topiary garden, leaving Tobias to deal with a private phone call inside the house.

'I like yours,' Jay told Emilia. 'It's wonderfully old-fashioned.'

'Yes, our parents always liked old things. Their parents too. Apparently, Mum wanted to call us Toby and Emily, but Dad insisted on Tobias and Emilia. We all seem to be stuck in some sort of time warp here.'

'So that explains the dress?'

Emilia could feel herself blushing. 'It's Victorian.'

'Yes, I can see that. Why are you wearing it?'

She took a deep breath. How on earth was she going to explain the dress to an outsider? Honestly, she decided.

'Tobias likes me to,' she confessed, instantly feeling as if she'd betrayed some trust between herself and her brother.

Jay frowned. 'That sounds a bit . . .'

'Weird?'

'Yes.'

'I know. It is,' she said. 'It's *really* weird – I've been wearing the old dresses for a few days now and I've kind of grown to like them. But it's beautiful, isn't it? Nicer than jeans and a T-shirt.'

'Well, yes,' he admitted. 'I suppose it is.'

He smiled and she smiled back. She'd only known this man for half an hour and she already liked him immensely. He was tall with fair hair and brown eyes that crinkled at the edges when he smiled, which he seemed to do a lot. He was one of life's happy people and it was nice to have a little bit of happiness at Morton Hall – Tobias was always so serious about everything and it could weigh her down.

'Where did that smile go?' Jay asked her now.

'Sorry?'

'Your face clouded over there.'

'Did it?'

'Yes.'

She shrugged. 'It was nothing.'

'No? What were you thinking about?'

She bit her lip, wondering whether to answer. 'I – I was just thinking about Tobias.'

'And does your face always cloud over when you think about your brother?'

They stopped walking. They'd reached the west entrance of the maze and Emilia turned to face him.

'I was just thinking how easy it is to chat to you. I don't get to do that very often.'

'Tobias isn't the chatty sort?'

She gave a little smile at that. 'No, not exactly. He – well – he spends a lot of time alone.'

'Which means you spend a lot of time alone too?'

Emilia paused. There were too many questions coming at her now and she felt a little uncomfortable so she asked him one of her own.

'How did you meet Tobias? Only you don't strike me as somebody he'd really get on with.'

'Ah, you've found me out!' Jay said, holding his hands up as if in defeat. 'Would you hold it against me if I confessed something?'

'I'd have to hear it first,' she told him.

He leaned towards her, lowering his head conspiratorially. 'I heard your brother had a marvellous art collection here, which I was desperate to see!'

Emilia's eyes widened. 'Is that true?'

Jay nodded. 'I'm ashamed to say it is. I'm an artist, you see. I love paintings, especially portraits, and portraits in private collections – those hidden gems you don't normally get to see – are particularly interesting to me. I travel up and down the country cataloguing them.'

'Really?'

'I'm not talking about the big houses like Chatsworth or Hatfield where the collections are famous, but smaller houses like yours – where the owners were affluent enough to be collectors, but whose purchases aren't well known. That's what interests me.'

'So, have you seen the collection here?'

'Not yet,' he said. 'I got distracted by something more beautiful.'

Emilia could feel her face heating up at his declaration and by the way he was looking at her.

'Oh, you mean the maze?' She gestured to it. 'Yes, it is a bit special, isn't it?'

He held her gaze as she smiled at him and, when he spoke, his voice was deep and very calm.

'I wasn't talking about the maze.'

She swallowed hard. She'd never been the focus of a man's attention before. Well, not one that wasn't her father, her brother or a teacher. She wasn't sure how it made her feel. Fluttery inside, she thought, skittish, flirtatious. Happy. Yes, that was it. He made her feel happy.

'Have you seen the topiary?' she asked him.

'Only from the windows of the house. It's very impressive.'

'Let me show you.' She led the way before he could say any more.

'You know, I've just had the best idea ever,' he called after her.

'What's that?'

'I want to paint you. In that dress.'

'Don't be silly.' She stopped underneath the topiary peacock.

'Why's that being silly?'

'Because' – she stopped and frowned – 'because I'm not a model.'

'You don't have to be a model to be painted. I bet all of your ancestors were painted, weren't they? They wouldn't have been models.'

Emilia considered this. 'They were probably more patient than me. I'm a fidget. You'd get mad at me.'

'I promise I won't get mad at you and we'll take lots of breaks.'

'But I haven't said you can paint me yet.'

'Haven't you? I thought you had.' He was wearing a little smile which was really very hard to resist.

'No!' she said, trying desperately hard to be mad at him and failing.

'Listen, I really would like to paint you. That dress, that smile, that red hair. We'll be the Dante Gabriel Rossetti and Elizabeth Siddal of the 1980s.'

Emilia gave a snort. 'You're not painting me drowning in a bathtub!'

'So you know about Miss Siddal?'

'Of course. She posed as Ophelia for Millais and nearly died. We have a portrait of her here and at least one Rossetti and a Millais.'

Jay looked stunned by this. 'You do?'

'You didn't know?'

'Well, I was hoping, but one can never be sure.'

'You'll have to see them.'

'You'll have to show me.'

They walked around the topiary garden. 'This is better than anything in the house,' she told him, watching as he shielded his eyes from the brilliant-blue summer sky and studied the topiary beasts.

'They're pretty impressive,' he said, 'but they are only hedges.'

Emilia gasped in mock horror. 'How can you say such a thing? Just look at the little face on our dodo!' she said as they approached the odd-looking creature.

'I'm just saying that I get more from looking at a painting.'

'Yes, but just as much care and attention has gone into turning this heap of hedge into a living, breathing creature as anything put down on canvas,' she said. 'I'd say it was harder, actually.'

'Oh, now you're just being perverse,' he said, a twinkle in his eyes.

'I am not!' Her hands were on her hips. 'I think very highly of our topiary. It's some of the best in the country.'

'I don't doubt it,' he said, 'but I can't get all worked up about it the way you obviously do.'

'But just look at the contours of this dodo's face – the shape of the beak and the way he's holding his head ever so slightly off to one side. It's as if he's watching us. That's character.'

'He does have character,' Jay conceded. 'You have a very talented gardener.'

'We do.'

'Are you going to show me the maze, then?'

'You want to see it?'

'Sure.'

'Okay.' Emilia led the way across the lawn, passing a little knot garden stuffed full of rosemary, mint and thyme which was dancing with bees.

'There's so much space here,' he said. 'You're very lucky.'

'Do you have a garden?'

'I live in a second-floor flat in Oxford,' he told her. 'I don't even have a balcony. I've just got this depressing view of another block of flats.'

'You should move.'

He laughed. 'As simple as that?'

'Get somewhere with a garden.'

'Maybe I could move here? Live in the centre of your maze?'

'That might be nicer than a flat.'

They'd reached the west entrance of the maze again and that's when they heard Tobias calling from the topiary garden.

'Quick!'

Before she had time to think, Emilia had grabbed Jay's hand and had run into the maze.

'What are you doing?' Jay shouted after her.

'Quiet! He won't follow us in here. He hates the maze. He gets claustrophobic.'

'But why are we hiding from your brother?'

They turned to the left and ran down a long green corridor before turning right. Only then did Emilia stop running, dropping Jay's hand.

'Because, if he finds you, he'll take you away from me, or me away from you. He's very possessive like that. He doesn't like to share anybody.'

'And you don't want to share me?' Jay asked.

Emilia realised that she had given away a lot rather too soon, but what was the point of hiding anything?

'I like talking to you,' she confessed, surprising herself.

'I like talking to you too.'

They smiled at one another in understanding.

'Emmy?' Tobias shouted. 'Jay?'

Emilia's hand flew to Jay's face, covering his mouth and causing him to giggle.

'Shush!' she hushed, slowly removing her hand.

'Are you sure he won't come in after us?' Jay whispered.

She nodded.

'Come *on*!' Tobias cried from outside the maze. 'I know you're in there.'

Emilia and Jay stood perfectly still, their eyes upon each other as Tobias continued to call, his tone getting progressively angrier.

'He sounds pretty mad,' Jay said in a low voice.

'He likes to get his own way.'

'So I see.'

They were quiet for a moment longer. Tobias's cries were now receding.

'I think he's gone to the walled garden,' Emilia said.

'So we're safe?'

'For now.'

Jay shook his head. 'I didn't expect this today.'

'Expect what?'

'To be trapped in a maze with a beautiful woman.'

Emilia's mouth suddenly went dry as she looked into the brown eyes staring at her.

'We'll have to come out sooner or later,' he said.

'Later then,' she told him and that's when he moved forward, the golden gravel at the centre of the maze crunching softly under his feet. Emilia didn't dare move. She knew what was going to happen; she just couldn't believe that it was going to happen to her. How many times had she read about moments such as these in the slim romance novels that she and her friends had hidden under their pillows at boarding school, to be brought out and read secretly in huddles of giggling girls? How often had she visualised herself as one of those very heroines swept up into the arms of the hero? And now, here she was, in the heart of the maze with a handsome man who seemed intent on kissing her.

Slowly, oh so slowly, he lowered his lips until they touched her mouth. It felt as if the whole warmth of the summer was in that kiss – the blue of the sky, the cries of the swallows, the scent of the herbs and the deep secrecy of the maze. She knew she would never be able to see, hear or smell those things ever again without thinking of this man and this moment.

When their lips finally parted, Jay let out a long deep sigh.

'Was that too forward of me?' he asked, his mouth just a breath away from her own – ready, it seemed, to repeat the experience if she gave him the tiniest of encouragements.

'It might have been,' she told him.

He nodded and then rested his forehead against hers.

'It won't happen again.'

'No?' she said, unable to hide her disappointment, which made him smile.

'Well, maybe—'

Before he could finish his sentence, she'd kissed him.

'That was very forward of me too,' she told him a moment later.

'Yes, it was,' he replied, 'but I liked it.'

'Come on,' she said, turning away from him in a flounce of Victorian dress. 'We'd better go and find Tobias.'

'Already?'

'Before he rings the police!'

'Would he do that?'

'Very likely!'

Emilia led the way through the maze. Jay muttered something about being impressed that she knew her way, but she wasn't really listening to him because her mind was focussed on her brother. He'd sounded pretty mad when they'd been in the maze. She'd managed to tune him out, but she was growing more and more anxious about facing him now – he'd always been one to hold a grudge. Jay was his friend and not hers and she had heard the jealousy in his voice as he'd shouted to them across the garden.

'Hey – slow down!' Jay called behind her. 'What happened to *later rather than sooner*?'

But she didn't slow down, not until they reached the house.

They entered together, their footsteps sounding loudly on the slate floor of the hall. Emilia knew where her brother would be and entered the sitting room with a feeling of dread weighing her down. Sure enough, Tobias was slumped in an armchair in a dark corner of the room; his head was lowered, cradled in his hands as if he had a pain that only his clenched fists could prevent from splitting his skull in two. He was prone to headaches, although Emilia had her suspicions that he brought them on himself through whatever substances he had hidden in his bedroom. He spent such a long time in there with the door locked that she'd come to the conclusion he must be taking something. It would certainly go some way to explaining his tempestuous mood swings.

'Tobias?' Emilia called softly as they entered the room.

He looked up, his eyes glazed as if he had been sleeping.

'Where have you two been?' he asked.

'Just in the garden, Tobes,' Emilia said, doing her utmost to keep her tone light.

'But I walked all around the garden and couldn't find you. Didn't you hear me calling you?'

Emilia frowned. 'You were calling us?'

'Yes, Emilia, I was *calling* you.' His face was suddenly dark and morose, as though he knew she was lying to him.

'Oh, I didn't hear you.' She watched as her brother's gaze switched from her face to Jay's as if daring his friend to lie to him.

'Nope,' Jay said, shaking his head. 'Didn't hear you.'

They stood in silence. Tobias's disapproval was evident as he kept them waiting before he spoke again, controlling the silence as a headmaster might.

'I've had an idea,' Tobias said at last, standing up. 'Sit.' He motioned to the sofa opposite him and the two of them obediently sat down as Tobias began to pace the room.

'What is it?' Jay asked.

Tobias stopped by the window, looking out into the garden.

'I'd like you to paint Emilia,' he said at last, his eyes still fixed outside.

Emilia turned to Jay who looked as surprised as she felt.

'You'll start tomorrow,' Tobias told Jay, only now turning to face him. 'Unless you have any other plans and I don't think you do.'

'No other plans,' Jay confirmed.

'Good. Because this will be your priority. A commission.'

'I'm happy to accept,' Jay told him.

Tobias gave a little nod.

'Now, did you want to see these paintings of ours or not?' Tobias asked. 'That *is* what you came here for, isn't it?'

'Yes, of course,' Jay said, getting up to follow Tobias out of the room. Emilia watched them and, as Jay reached the door, he turned around and gave her the kind of smile that she knew would be her undoing.

Chapter 7

Cape was the first to arrive at Morton Hall on Monday evening. He parked his car in the usual spot and walked to the front door which had been left open. Mrs Beatty was there to greet him and did so with a little nod of her head.

'Good evening,' he said, nodding back.

She motioned to a room to the left of the hallway and Cape walked in to a great fire which was doing its best to keep the cold January night at bay. There were three large sofas and a coffee table in the middle which had been laid with cups, two teapots and a plate of biscuits.

It was the first time Cape had been in this part of the house and he looked around the room now, studying the landscape paintings on the wall, the large ornate mantel clock which ticked quietly, and the fat blue-and-white china bowls on a fancy sideboard. It was all so different from his own farmer's cottage with the simple pieces of furniture he'd inherited from his father, and he suddenly felt out of place. He was definitely more at home in the garden of Morton Hall, he reasoned, helping himself to a chocolate biscuit from the table.

Anne Marie was next to arrive and he was pleased to see her friendly face.

'How are you?' he asked her.

'I'm good.'

'Ready for all this?'

'I'm not sure what to expect,' she confessed.

'I don't think any of us are, but the chocolate biscuits are good.' He nodded towards the plate, but something else had caught Anne Marie's eye.

'Look at that painting,' she said.

'Oh, wow!' Cape said. He hadn't spotted it before. 'It's the maze.'

They crossed the room and stood looking at the beautifully framed watercolour which featured a young woman in a midnight-blue gown standing at the centre of the maze.

'It's the red-haired woman,' Anne Marie said. 'She's even wearing the same dress.'

'Like in the painting upstairs?'

Anne Marie gave him a nudge with her elbow as Mrs Beatty walked into the room.

'Mrs Beatty?' Cape said. 'Any idea how old this painting is?'

She frowned at being asked such a question. 'I'm a housekeeper not an art historian,' she told him and then left the room again as more people arrived.

Cape gave a disgruntled laugh. 'I was only asking.'

'Maybe she's not a fan of art,' Anne Marie said.

'Could you really work in a place like this and not be? I mean, she must dust these things. How could you not come to love them and know about them?'

'Well, there are quite a lot of things to dust in a place like this. I don't think you'd have time to coo over them all.'

'Good point,' Cape said, his eyes wandering around the room again.

'It's so beautiful, isn't it?' Anne Marie said. 'A real Arts and Crafts interior. Everything is handmade and individual. I love the tiles around the fireplace. I think they're William De Morgan.'

They walked back to the fireplace together and looked at the deep-blue flowers and rich-green leaves painted on the tiles that shimmered in the firelight.

'I think that's a De Morgan plate over there too,' Anne Marie told him. 'The one with the deep red-and-gold lustre and the curving dragon.'

'Wow, it's lovely,' he said, noticing it for the first time.

'I'd hate to be responsible for keeping all these treasures clean,' Anne Marie said. 'Mrs Beatty has a nerve-wracking job.'

'At least a hedge grows back if you cut into it too much,' Cape said.

The room was suddenly beginning to fill up as the rest of the guests assembled. Cape couldn't help wishing that he and Anne Marie could have it to themselves for a little while longer. He liked talking to her. She was one of those people who was easy to chat to and always had something interesting to say. He couldn't remember the last time he'd enjoyed talking to Renee and that made him feel just dreadful. They seemed to do nothing but fight these days or else talk *at* each other, never making a meaningful connection. It was sad and he couldn't help wondering when things had started to break down between them. Was it since they'd moved out to the cottage just five years ago?

Before that, they'd lived in Oxford in a small terrace with a court-yard garden. It had driven Cape nuts not having a decent-sized garden of his own and it had been his idea to move out of town and find something a bit bigger with room to breathe. Renee hadn't been keen. She'd liked being near the centre of everything but, with Poppy growing up, he'd managed to persuade Renee that a garden would be beneficial. She hadn't put up much of a fight, it had to be said, but she was spending more and more time in Oxford these days, hanging around after work to go to the pub with friends or venturing back into town during the evenings, leaving him to pick Poppy up from school and cook for her. Except tonight. When Cape had told Renee that he had a meeting at Morton Hall, she'd rolled her eyes at him.

'You're married to that place,' she told him. 'Perhaps I should have married you and then you'd spend more time with me.'

Her words struck him deeply as he remembered proposing to her when she discovered she was pregnant with Poppy. He'd been going to pop the question anyway, but the imminent arrival of their child had made him even more anxious to seal their union. But she'd said no. She hadn't wanted to get married. She wasn't the sort of girl to need a ring on her finger or a piece of paper to be filed away. Cape had been surprised. He was an old-fashioned guy, but there was no point trying to force her to do something she didn't want to do, and so the matter had been dropped between them. Poppy had been born and they'd seemed perfectly content. Until now. Until this California business which had really driven a wedge between them. But perhaps it was more than that. Perhaps California was just a symptom of something much bigger that was happening to them.

Cape tried to shake the matter from his head. This evening wasn't about him and Renee. It was about the future of Morton Hall and he wanted to concentrate on that. Indeed, it was a relief for him to be able to focus on something other than his disintegrating relationship.

As the room filled, Mrs Beatty took control, taking coats and guiding people towards the coffee table.

As in the solicitors' office in Henley-on-Thames, there were seven of them gathered and Cape watched his new companions. The man he remembered as Patrick Everard did not look happy. So no change there, Cape thought. The young blonde woman was staring around the room open-mouthed in wonder while the older man was nervously looking down at the boots he was wearing as if fearful they might damage the elaborately patterned rug they were all standing on. The two other women were making small talk as they poured their tea and Anne Marie was staring at another of the room's magnificent paintings. Everyone, it seemed, felt awkward about being there.

'Coming out on a cold winter's night after a long day's work is *not* my idea of fun,' Patrick announced to nobody in particular. He was now standing with his back to the fire and completely blocking it from everybody else. 'And I hope this isn't going to take long. I've left my boys with a bone-head of a babysitter who I'm sure was eyeing up my wine cabinet.'

Cape did his best to hide a smile because he couldn't tell if Patrick was trying to be amusing or not.

Mrs Beatty gave Mr Everard a glare which clearly told him his remarks weren't welcome and then cleared her throat, waiting until she was quite sure that she had everybody's attention.

'I'm Mrs Beatty,' she began. 'I'm the housekeeper here at Morton Hall and I thought it best if we met here tonight so you could all get to know each other and work out how you want to move forward. I don't have a lot to say, but I wanted to make it clear that I will be here at all times to keep an eye on everything. It's what Miss Morton wanted. I have been working for the family since 1980, taking care of the house, and that isn't going to change. I will not be playing an active role in the jobs you have to do here. I'll be more of an adviser, if you need one. Please help yourself to tea but, once those biscuits have gone, that's it.' She gave a little nod of her head as she left the room.

'Well,' Cape said, 'that's put us in our places, hasn't it?'

'A friendly soul, isn't she?' Patrick said.

'Shush! She'll hear you!' Anne Marie said.

'I reckon she's got this room bugged anyway so she can hear what we all talk about.'

'So, where do we begin, then?' the eldest woman in the group asked as everybody found a seat by the fire.

'I think we all need to introduce ourselves,' Cape suggested, 'and perhaps say a little about our backgrounds and what we all think we can bring to this project. Anyone want to start?'

The older man who'd been examining his boots before raised a hand. As well as his big workman's boots, he was wearing corduroy trousers and a tweed jacket. His dark hair was slightly silvered and he had the sort of face that looked as if it spent ninety per cent of its time in the great outdoors.

'I'll go first,' he said. 'I'm Mac Minter. Been a gardener all my life, working all over the Chilterns.'

Cape's eyebrows rose. 'I can't believe we've never met.'

'I don't advertise,' Mac said. 'Been word of mouth for the past twenty years.'

'So you'd be able to fit the garden here into your timetable?' Cape asked.

'Don't see why not,' Mac said. 'I can do the usual things in a garden. I've got access to a digger and I can do a bit of hard landscaping, but I'm not so good at all that designing stuff. Not my thing that.'

'Well, I think we're very lucky to have you on board, Mac,' Cape said, watching as Mac took a sip of his tea and looked down at his boots again. It was the older woman to his right who spoke next.

'I'm Dorothy Cloudsley and I really don't know why I'm here,' she said with a nervous laugh.

'Join the club,' Patrick said.

She smiled. She had a lovely open face with rosy cheeks and her hair was an astonishing silver-white, worn down to her shoulders.

'I've lived in Parvington all my life,' she went on. 'I was married to Derek Cloudsley whom some of you might know from the horticultural show. He used to win the Bower's cup most years for his garden box.'

'Oh, yes, I remember,' Anne Marie said. 'I was once silly enough to go up against him with my tomatoes. That taught me!'

Dorothy smiled at that. 'He died a couple of years ago.'

The group muttered its sympathies.

'And that's it, really. That's me. I have two grown-up daughters, but they both lead their own lives so it's just me most of the time. I love gardening and I'm happy to do anything I can here. My back's not what it once was, but I don't shirk from hard work.'

'Thanks, Dorothy, I'm sure you'll be a great help,' Cape said, nodding to the woman sitting next to her.

'Me?' she said in alarm, her hand flying to her chest. 'Okay. Well, I'm Kathleen Cardy. I used to run a bed and breakfast in the village. In the thatched cottage where the fire was.'

'That was your place?' Dorothy asked.

Kathleen nodded. 'I haven't managed to get the business up and running since the fire. I've kind of . . .' She paused. '. . . lost my way. So maybe this gardening thing will give me some sort of structure to my life again. I don't know. I might not see it through. I'm not very good with plants. I try to grow evergreens and other safe things. So I might be more of a hindrance here.'

'I'm sure you won't be,' Cape told her.

'I'm still a bit shocked by all of this,' she continued. 'I'm not really—'

'You're not the only one,' Patrick said, shaking his head, his expression still glum.

Kathleen glanced at him and frowned, obviously displeased at being interrupted.

Cape cleared his throat and turned to the other sofa where the youngest member of their group was sitting, her slender hands wrapped around her cup of tea. She was pretty with short blonde hair and large hazel eyes and was wearing a woollen jacket, a long scarf in pink-and-blue swirls and a large pair of silver hoop earrings.

'I'm Erin Hartley,' she began with a hesitant smile. 'I've just graduated. I've got a degree in art history.'

'Didn't I read about you in the local paper?' Dorothy asked.

'Yeah, you might have done,' Erin said. 'Mum kept ringing them up until they wrote about me.' A sweet blush coloured her face.

'Congratulations, my dear,' Dorothy said.

'Thank you.'

'And what have you been doing since graduating?' Cape asked.

'Well, I've been toying with taking a trip to Italy to see Florence and Rome, but it's a bit expensive really, so I've been doing volunteer work at the Ashmolean in Oxford and working part-time in the museum shop.'

'You've got a degree and you're working in a *shop*?' Patrick said.

Erin shrugged. 'It's experience. Nobody wants you without experience.'

Patrick shook his head as if in despair.

'We all need to start somewhere and you're in a really great place there,' Cape said, doing his best to quash Patrick's thoughtless remark.

'Well, I'm Patrick Everard,' Patrick said with a sigh as if it were a very great effort just to speak his name. 'And I've never gardened in my life.'

'Then it'll be a challenge,' Cape told him, 'but not an unpleasant one, I hope.'

'Yeah, well that remains to be seen.'

'And what do you do?' Dorothy asked him from the other sofa.

'I'm in IT at a company in Oxford. You won't have heard of them.'

'Oh,' Dorothy said. 'And you have a wife? Children?'

'Two boys. No wife. She – er – went.'

There was an uncomfortable silence in the room only broken by the crackle of a log on the fire.

'Well, I'm Anne Marie.'

Everybody turned to face her and Cape was glad she'd taken the initiative to draw attention away from Patrick, who was looking decidedly uncomfortable after his unexpected revelation.

'I'm a freelance editor,' Anne Marie went on. 'I work from home and I used to . . . that is . . .' She paused and looked at Cape.

'Tell them,' he said, immediately knowing what she was going to say.

Anne Marie took a deep breath. 'I used to walk around the gardens here. Well, the deserted part – the walled garden. I didn't think anyone would see me there, but Cape knew, didn't you?'

'I had an idea,' he said, giving her a smile for her bravery in confessing.

'I can't explain it, but I was drawn to this place. It made me feel calm. I love how a garden can do that – even one that's neglected and unloved. There's still something special about it. You don't have to do anything to it or in it. You just have to be still for a while and watch it, breathe it all in.' She stopped and then bit her lip. 'Sorry, I'm rambling.'

'Not at all!' Dorothy said, leaning forward on the sofa. 'That was so beautifully put. Inspiring too.'

'And she's right,' Cape said. 'Gardens are special places and the one here at Morton Hall is one of the most special I've ever seen. I really think we can make something of it.'

'And who are you?' Patrick asked.

'Ah, yes!' Cape said, suddenly realising that he hadn't introduced himself yet. 'I'm Cape Colman and I'm a gardener and garden designer. I've been working here at Morton Hall part-time for five years. I'm responsible for keeping the maze and the topiary in good condition and the borders and driveway at the front of the house. That's it really, but I love this place and will do everything I can to see that it's restored to its former glory. The walled garden desperately needs attention. It'll be a lot of work, but I think it's something that would be worthwhile for us and the community.'

'It seems we're lucky to have you on board,' Dorothy said. 'I think the rest of us are struggling to process all this and to know where to begin.'

'Well, it's not going to be easy,' Cape said. 'If we get a mild winter, which looks likely, we could make good progress. I think it's just a case of getting organised.'

'We need a spokesperson,' Kathleen said. 'Somebody to rally us.'

'I'm nominating Cape,' Dorothy said, gesturing towards him. 'He knows this garden. I think we'll be in safe hands if he's in charge and guides us through this.'

Several people nodded.

'Are you sure?' Cape said. 'I mean, I don't mind, but I'm happy to share the role or—'

'I think we need one person for this,' Dorothy said. 'Does anyone remember when we tried to set up a committee for the village show? The bickering and backstabbing it caused. In the end, Edwin Steer stepped forward, taking on the role all by himself and it's been running smoothly ever since. It's a lot of work, but he does it quietly and well. Committees cause chaos as far as I'm concerned.'

'Well, we will be a sort of committee here. We'll have to make decisions together,' Cape said.

'But we'll listen to you and your experience,' Dorothy said.

'I agree,' Kathleen said. 'My fingers are *so* not green. I wouldn't trust me to make any sort of big decision when it comes to gardening.'

'What about time? How are we going to decide who does what and when? I've not exactly got spare hours spilling out of my pockets,' Patrick told the group.

'Yes, of course,' Cape said. 'We're starting at the worst time of year with the shortest daylight hours which only really leaves weekends for those of us with full-time jobs, doesn't it?'

'Great,' Patrick said. 'Just what I want to be doing with my weekends – up to my knees in some cold muddy garden.'

Kathleen gasped at this statement. 'Why are you here?' she asked Patrick.

'Pardon?' he said.

'Why are you here when you've clearly no interest in this project at all?'

'Because I've been summoned, lady, that's why,' he said. 'I'm not here by choice!'

Cape raised a hand. He'd expected that a group of strangers might have disagreements over the course of this project, but he hadn't expected them to come so soon.

'This situation is going to take a bit of getting used to,' Cape said as calmly as he could. He wasn't used to managing people and was finding it an alarming experience, which was worrying considering he'd only been given the role five minutes ago. 'We need to establish who's available when, and who we'd like to work with, perhaps, and what our individual skills are. Maybe some of us would be best suited to certain jobs. We'll work all that out over the coming weeks. To begin with, I think it would be a good idea if there were at least two of us on site at any one time and, maybe over these next few wintry weeks, we could all arrange to come during the weekends.'

'That sounds good,' Dorothy said. 'Or any time really. I'm retired now so I'm free apart from Tuesday mornings when I attempt to keep fit in the village hall and Thursday evenings which is WI.'

Cape noticed that Patrick rolled his eyes at that comment.

'So we're all good for the weekends?'

Everybody nodded.

'Not too early, though!' Erin begged. 'Friday night is kind of – busy.'

'Ah, I remember those days of being young and carefree,' Patrick said. 'The biggest decision you'd have to make on a Friday night was which pub to go to next.'

Erin glared at him. 'Actually I babysit on a Friday night,' she said. 'For somebody else who likes to go to the pub.'

Kathleen giggled and Cape couldn't help grinning. Patrick seemed very good at riling people, Cape thought.

'I'd suggest what we need to do first is clear the walled garden,' Cape said. 'It's a big space and it's completely overgrown. We can't do anything until all the grass, weeds and thistles are gone.'

Mac Minter cleared his throat. 'I can bring a digger to clear the land.'

Cape's eyebrows rose. 'You can? This weekend?'

Mac nodded. 'No problem.'

'That would make a really good start.'

'Eight o'clock too early? I – er – get up early.'

'I'll see you then.'

'I can join you for about ten,' Erin said. 'If that's okay?'

'Can I bring my boys?' Patrick asked.

Cape was surprised by his question, but it didn't take him long to reply. 'I don't see why not. Any objections from anyone?'

'Not if they're able to help,' Mac said.

'I'd say, the more the merrier,' Dorothy said with an encouraging smile.

'How old are they?' Anne Marie asked.

'Matthew's twelve and Elliot's ten,' Patrick said. 'They're good lads. Most of the time.'

'I've got a ten-year-old daughter, Poppy,' Cape said. 'She'd love to come too.'

'This is going to be a very jolly party,' Dorothy said. 'More tea anyone?'

The group sat around for a while longer, chatting more easily amongst themselves now. At one point, Mac got up and chucked another log on the fire and Kathleen poured more tea.

It came as a genuine surprise when the mantel clock struck nine and Mrs Beatty entered the room once again.

'I trust you've all come to some sort of arrangement?' she asked, addressing her question to Cape as if instinctively knowing he was the spokesperson for the group.

'Yes, I believe so,' he told her, looking around at everyone who nodded in agreement.

'We're going to make a start this Saturday,' Erin said.

'Mrs Beatty?' Cape began. 'It is okay to bring children with us, isn't it?'

'Children?'

'Our children.'

She frowned. 'Not toddlers. It's too dangerous for toddlers.'

'No, no. Big children. Ten. Twelve. That sort of age.'

'They'd be able to help,' Erin said, as if knowing a sweetener was needed.

'And they are a part of the community,' Dorothy said. 'That is what this project is all about, isn't it?'

Mrs Beatty pursed her lips. 'We're not used to children here,' she told them. 'Mr Colman occasionally brings his daughter.'

'Once a month,' he chipped in.

'Yes. That's quite enough. This is a delicate place. It's not for running around and wrecking. I know what children can do. Picking up stones and throwing them into greenhouses.'

Cape shifted uneasily on the sofa. 'I can assure you, we'll keep an eye on the children,' he said. 'There won't be any damage to worry about.'

It was then that Erin raised a hand. 'Erm, payment was mentioned,' she said. 'I'm sorry to raise it but – if I'm working, I'll need to get paid. I've got student debts to clear.'

Mrs Beatty nodded. 'You will all be given forms to fill in at the end of each month. Keep a track of your hours and you'll then be paid for them.'

'And will we be able to see the house?' Erin asked, gazing around the room.

'No,' Mrs Beatty said. An uncomfortable silence greeted this declaration. 'At least not for a while,' she added. 'There are things to sort out first.'

'Oh,' Erin said, sounding disappointed. 'That's a shame.'

Patrick clapped his hands together and stood up. 'Right. If that's all sorted, I'm off.'

The others slowly stood up.

'So, we're all good for Saturday morning and seeing how things go from there?' Cape said.

Everyone nodded and said they'd see each other at various times during the morning, and the room slowly emptied. Only Cape and Anne Marie hung back.

'Patrick's as charming as ever,' Anne Marie whispered to Cape.

'Yes,' Cape said. 'He seems to have the knack of being able to upset everyone.'

'Did you see the way Kathleen was glaring at him?'

'I can't say I noticed.'

'I hope we're all going to be able to get along.'

'That's the beauty of gardening – there'll always be a job to do at the furthest corner of the property,' Cape said. 'If people don't get along, we'll simply keep them separate.'

Anne Marie smiled and he couldn't help thinking that he'd received more smiles from this new friend of his in the brief time he'd known her than from Renee in the whole of the last month. The thought of that made him sad. He couldn't help feeling that he'd somehow failed Renee if he could no longer make her smile.

'Dorothy seems lovely,' Anne Marie continued, 'and obviously lonely after losing her husband.'

'And Erin's a livewire.'

'What do you make of Mac?' Anne Marie asked.

'He seems pleasant enough, although he looked a little uncomfortable, didn't you think?'

'I think he looks like one of those people who's uncomfortable in rooms. He'll probably look less awkward when he's out in the garden.'

Cape nodded. 'That's a very wise thing to say. I kept looking at the way he was shifting his feet about like he was itching to get up and go. He didn't look right sitting on a sofa, did he?'

'He'll probably look much more at home sitting on his digger,' Anne Marie said.

Mrs Beatty was now fussing around with the cups and tray.

'Don't you two have homes to go to?' she asked, not bothering to look up at them both as she tidied away.

'Just on our way,' Cape said.

'Can I help you with those?' Anne Marie asked.

'I can manage. I've been managing here on my own all these years.'

Anne Marie and Cape exchanged a glance.

'Goodnight, then,' she said.

'Thank you for the tea and biscuits.'

'Crumbs everywhere,' Mrs Beatty muttered to herself as they moved out into the hallway.

Cape and Anne Marie stopped by the door and did up their coats.

'I don't think anyone's got anything in common,' he said. 'I mean other than being summoned here today and living in the same village.'

'Don't you think?'

'You do?' he asked her.

She nodded. 'Everybody here seems a little lost.'

Cape couldn't help frowning at that. 'What do you mean?'

'Well, there's Kathleen after her fire, Erin looking for her place in the world, Dorothy trying to stay busy, and Patrick . . .' She paused. 'Patrick seems lost in his own anger.'

'What about Mac?'

'I think Mac seems quite a content sort of person. I mean, he wasn't content sat in that room with us, but he didn't seem as lost as the rest of them.'

'And am I one of your lost souls?' he couldn't help asking.

She glanced up at him, suddenly looking shy. 'I don't think so. Well, maybe a little.'

'Really?'

'You seem more sad than lost.'

'I do?'

'Sorry,' she said, her hand reaching towards the front door. 'I shouldn't have said that.'

'No, no – I want to hear more. I'm finding this all fascinating.'

'Now you're making fun of me.'

'I'm not,' he said, following her out into the grand porch where a large moth was flying around the lamp which had been left on. 'I think it's really amazing how you've taken all this in. I just saw a bunch of nervous people in that room who'd rather not be there, but you saw something else entirely.'

She gave a little shrug. 'I guess I like watching people,' she said.

'And what about you?' he asked.

'What about me?'

'You were watching everyone else in that room, but were you amongst the lost souls in there?'

She looked at him, her eyes clouded with confusion. 'I – erm – I don't know.' She left the porch, beginning to walk down the long dark driveway.

'Anne Marie? I'm sorry. I didn't mean to upset you. It was just a silly question.'

'You didn't upset me. I'd just better get home.'

'Can I give you a lift?'

'No, thank you.'

'You're walking?'

'I like to walk.'

'Even in the dark?'

'I've got a torch.' Her hand dived into her pocket and came out a moment later with her torch.

'It's no trouble to drop you—'

'I'll be fine,' she told him. 'I'll see you on Saturday.'

He watched, puzzled and a little alarmed as she disappeared into the darkness. What had just happened back there? Why had she suddenly got spooked by his question? Had the phrase *lost soul* touched a nerve? She looked kind of lost to Cape and that made him feel intensely sad because she seemed like a really sweet person.

He sighed, his breath fogging the night air. He hoped he hadn't upset her. Maybe he'd get a chance to talk to her more at the weekend, he thought as he turned and headed towards his car. He did hope so.

The truth was, Anne Marie wasn't looking forward to getting home and, if she walked, it would delay her arrival just a little longer. She'd left the house only ten minutes into dinner which both Irma and Rebecca had deigned to sit down to along with their father. Anne Marie had been so surprised that it had thrown her for a moment because she had been going to sneak out of the house to go to the meeting at Morton Hall. She'd assumed nobody would be there to notice her departure. But they had been – *all* three of them.

She'd anxiously looked at the kitchen clock, hoping for a miracle. Maybe inspiration would suddenly clout Grant around the head and he'd rush off to his study, and Irma and Rebecca's phones would go off and they'd leave the table without explaining. Then Anne Marie could slip away unobserved. But miracles had been thin on the ground that evening and so, at the last possible moment, she'd got up.

'I'm just going to . . .' She'd let her sentence peter out as nobody seemed that interested anyway. She'd then walked through to the hall-way where she put on her coat and boots and had left the house as quietly as possible. Once outside, she turned her mobile off, her heart racing at the subterfuge. She really wasn't a natural when it came to hiding anything or sneaking out to places.

Now, as she reached the front door of Garrard House, she worried about the reception she'd receive on the other side. Maybe they'd all just gone about their evening as normal. Nobody would have questioned the strange disappearance of Anne Marie surely: the TV would have been switched on, music blasted and a whisky poured as yet another book was taken down from a shelf. Very likely, she would open the door and lock it behind her, take off her boots and coat and make herself a cup of tea in the kitchen without anybody knowing she had been anywhere at all.

She took a deep breath as she slid her key into the lock and entered.

'Where the hell did you go?' Grant exploded as soon as she'd shut the front door.

'Grant!' she cried in surprise. 'I've – I've just been at a meeting. Didn't I tell you?'

'No, you didn't!'

'Oh, I – well – it was just a meeting.'

'You got up in the middle of dinner and didn't come back again.'

'You noticed?'

'Of course I noticed! Why wouldn't I notice?'

She stared at his face. She'd never seen him look so worried. Or perhaps he was just angry.

'It's just you never normally notice,' she told him.

'What the hell does that mean?'

'Well, you're usually so wrapped up in your work, it doesn't matter how I spend my evenings.'

He shook his head. 'But we were all having dinner together.'

'Yes, I know. I'm sorry.'

'That was a very strange thing to do, Anne Marie. Where was this meeting anyway?'

She took a deep breath. It was time to tell him what had been going on.

'Miss Morton died and she's left rather an unusual will.'

'Miss Morton from Morton Hall?'

'Yes.'

'You were at Morton Hall this evening?'

She nodded and then briefly told him about the letter from the solicitor and the subsequent meetings.

'But why you?' Grant asked.

Anne Marie had known he would ask that very question and who could blame him? She'd asked it herself enough times already.

'I don't know,' she told him honestly.

'You don't know?' His brow furrowed and his mouth flattened into a thin line which happened when he was displeased. She'd seen that look countless times in his lectures when a student wasn't paying attention. She'd used to think it funny, but it wasn't so funny when it was directed towards her.

She watched as he turned and stalked into his study, glad that the questioning had been brief.

She was just heading into the kitchen when Irma ran down the stairs. 'Where've you been? Dad was *furious!*'

Anne Marie was about to tell her, but she waltzed through to the living room and, a second later, the television was blaring. And that was fine. She could hear music coming from Rebecca's room upstairs, and Grant was safely ensconced in his study, which meant that she could make a cup of tea and settle down in her own study, undisturbed for a while, and just think.

Her husband might be angry about her involvement in the Morton Hall project and her step-daughters might not care, but Anne Marie couldn't help feeling excited by it all.

Chapter 8

Being painted was a new experience for Emilia and one that she didn't altogether object to. It gave her time to think and that wasn't always possible living with Tobias because he was always giving her things to *do* and was forever checking up on her. It was always, *Emmy – did you do this?* Or *Emmy – did you do that?* He treated her like a personal servant rather than a human being in her own right. Heavens, she'd only been home for a month and he was already driving her crazy. Thank goodness Jay Alexander had turned up when he had, she thought. He'd breezed into her life and made her feel alive again – and it was so good to have somebody to talk to. *Really* talk to. Tobias had always been the talker in their relationship and Emilia the listener. But Jay not only listened to her – he also asked her questions. He was genuinely interested in what she had to say and that was a very heady experience. Only, there wasn't any talking while he was painting. He'd made that quite clear. He liked to work in silence and she respected that.

Being the subject of a portrait had made Emilia aware that she was the sole focus of the attention of the man she was becoming increasingly fond of, she thought as she continued to look out of the window at nothing in particular. *Fond.* She dismissed the word, knowing that it fell far too short of the emotions she felt for him. How quickly they had crept up on her. From the magical moment in the maze when they'd kissed, he had filled her every waking thought – and a fair few of her sleeping ones too. She wondered if he felt the same way about her and thought about sneaking a peek at him.

The problem with being painted was that it didn't give her a chance to observe Jay. While he spent hour upon hour observing her, she was forced to gaze out of the mullioned window and down onto the garden. It was nice as views went, but she would rather be looking at him.

She sighed, rolling her shoulders back in an attempt to relieve her stiffness.

'You're right,' he said at last.

'What?'

'You *are* a fidget!'

'I did warn you.' She turned to face him and then laughed.

'What are you laughing at?'

'You look slightly demented,' she told him.

His fair hair had taken on a life of its own, dancing around his face in mad waves as his brushes moved across the canvas.

'Pardon?'

'Your hair.'

'Ah, well, you're not meant to be looking at me.'

'But I like looking at you,' she said, crossing the room, her hand reaching out to straighten his locks.

He shook his head and put his brushes down. 'Let's have a break.'

'Can we?'

'I think you've earned it.'

'Shall we go into the garden?'

'Good idea.'

After he washed his hands, they walked out into the bright sunshine together. The garden was looking glorious. The herbaceous borders were filled with summer beauties like peonies and roses, and the scent of the lavender that lined the path was wonderfully heady.

'Did you want to get changed?' he asked her.

'We're going to continue, aren't we?'

'Yes, but wouldn't you be more comfortable having a break from that dress?'

Emilia's hands caressed the midnight-blue dress and she shook her head.

'I like it.'

'You're a strange one.'

'I know.'

Emilia had grown used to walking through the gardens wearing the Victorian dresses that Tobias had forced upon her. She liked the feel of them, the sound they made on the gravel paths and the way they moved as she walked up the stairs. They made her feel feminine in a way that her usual garb of jeans and jumpers never could. If that made her strange, then so be it. Perhaps she'd been born in the wrong century. The thought had never occurred to her until she'd started trying on the dresses, but they'd given her a strange connection to the past, a fabric portal into the lives of her ancestors.

Jay had even made a small watercolour painting of her in the maze while she'd been wearing the blue dress. Tobias had framed it immediately and it now hung in the main sitting room.

'You know, you looked very thoughtful when you were looking out of the window,' Jay told her. 'A little melancholic.'

'Aren't most portraits unsmiling?'

'Yes. It's pretty hard to keep a smile in place for the entire length of a portrait.'

'Well then.'

'What were you thinking about?'

They'd reached the west entrance of the maze. It was funny but, over the last few weeks since he'd been painting her, they usually found their way here.

'What was I thinking about? You, me, Tobias. I was wondering what would happen when you finish the portrait.'

'Oh, there's weeks of work left on it.'

'Really?'

'I'll make sure of it.'

She smiled and he winked at her.

'You know,' he continued, 'you really do have that whole Pre-Raphaelite look going on.'

'Have I?'

'Yes. The red hair, the pale skin, that wistful look in the eyes.'

'Being trapped in a house by a tyrant of a brother,' she added.

Jay frowned and reached out to touch her arm. 'Emilia?'

'I'm just joking!' she said quickly.

'Are you?'

'Yes.' She held his gaze. 'Tobias can just be a bit of a bully, that's all.'

'That's not exactly a virtue,' Jay pointed out. 'I worry about you being here with him when I'm not around. I wish he'd let me stay, but he made it clear I was only welcome for a few days. But I worry about you when I'm not here.'

'Don't be so dramatic.'

'No, I really do. You're all alone in this big old house that, quite frankly, looks like something out of a film you wouldn't want to watch late at night on your own.'

She laughed at that.

'And then there's your brother,' he went on. 'I think I'd rather be holed up with Dracula.'

'Oh, you're being silly. Tobias is all right. He just gets a bit glum.'

'What do you mean by glum? You've used that word before.'

They had neared the centre of the maze now. Just a few more turns and they'd be there.

'Well, he can get a bit down, you know?'

'No, I don't know. The Tobias I knew at Oxford was always hyper.'

'Yes, there's that side of him too. He can swing from being really high on life and enthusiastic about everything to being really introverted.

He'll lock himself in his bedroom for hours. Days sometimes. I worry about him in there.'

'Do you think he's on something?'

'I've wondered about that too, but I think he's really good at hiding it if he is. I think he sleeps a lot. He's always very quiet. I did have a poke around his room once, but I couldn't find anything obvious. But he's always been rather morose. Even when he was a small boy, he could sulk and pout like nobody else.'

They reached the centre of the maze and sat down on the bench there. The sun was hot above them and a pigeon cooed from the high branches of a tree.

'You should have a parasol with that outfit,' Jay said. 'Then you'd look like a heroine from a Monet painting.'

'I thought you said I was a Pre-Raphaelite.'

'You're both.'

'You're fickle.'

He grinned and then he took her right hand in both of his. 'Seriously,' he said, 'I worry about you here. You're so isolated.'

'Stop worrying. I'm absolutely fine. This is my home.'

Jay shook his head. 'You know, you're the most unusual person.'

'Is that a compliment or an insult?' Emilia asked. 'Because I'm really not sure.'

'Oh, it's a compliment,' he told her. 'I've never met anyone like you before and I've met a lot of women.'

'Do I want to hear this?' she asked with a little laugh.

'I don't know, do you?'

Emilia wrinkled her nose. 'I'm not sure,' she said slowly.

Still with her hand in his, he looked directly at her. 'I just mean that you're different. In a really *good* way. You're not loud or brash. You're not into playing games.'

'Women play games?'

'Oh, yeah!'

'What sort of games?'

Jay shrugged. 'Just silly mind games. But not you. You're open and honest and—'

'You're going to make me blush!'

'*And* you blush! Most of the girls I've dated wouldn't recognise a natural blush if it hit them in the face!'

Emilia giggled.

'You're really sweet and innocent and that's so refreshing.' He tutted and suddenly looked annoyed. 'God, I'm sounding horribly condescending now.'

'No, you're not.'

'I just want you to know that you're special.'

Emilia grimaced. 'Now *that* sounds condescending.'

Jay cursed. 'I'm sorry!'

'I'm just teasing!'

There was a pause during which Jay's head lowered towards hers and she wondered if he was going to kiss her, but they were interrupted by a strange sound.

'What the hell is that?' Jay asked, looking around.

Emilia bit back a smile. 'It's Tobias. He's teaching himself the violin.'

'Heaven preserve us that's *awful*!'

'I know, and he insists on playing it by an open window so there's no escape if you're in the garden.'

'Is he doing that on purpose because he knows we're out here?'

'Very likely.'

'I think my eardrums are bleeding!'

Emilia laughed. 'He'll get better, I'm sure.'

'Will it be quieter in the house?'

'We can go and find out.'

'Come on then,' Jay said, her hand still in his.

He led the way out of the maze. He knew it well now and rarely made a mistake.

'Hey, the violin's stopped,' he said just as they were about to exit the maze.

'It didn't last long.'

'No, thank goodness. Maybe his own ears were bleeding.'

'I don't know why he's suddenly taken it up. He was poking around the attics and found it. I think it's quite an old violin. It's probably worth a lot of money.'

'And he's sawing away on it like a piece of timber.'

'I think it's nice that he's showing an interest in music.'

'Does he have a tutor?'

Emilia shook her head. 'He wouldn't tolerate one. He's teaching himself.'

'Isn't that difficult?'

'I guess.'

'He doesn't do things by halves, your brother, does he?'

'No, he's into full immersion,' Emilia agreed. 'You should have seen him when he found it. He was so excited – just like a kid at Christmas. He was practically leaping up and down. But he wouldn't let me near it.'

'Why not?'

'It's his. He's very protective of it.'

Jay grimaced. 'The more you talk about your brother, the odder he sounds.'

'He's just a little . . .' She paused. 'Unusual. That's all.'

'No, *you're* unusual and that's a good thing, but your brother—'

'What?'

Jay took a deep breath. 'I'm not so sure,' he told her. 'I think there's something off with him.'

'What do you mean, *off?*'

'Something not quite switched on. Not right. Do you know what I mean?'

'No.'

'Well, you see him as normal because you grew up with him. Anything a child grows up with seems normal. But you did admit he's always been morose and I think you see it now, don't you? How he's not like other people. He never was at college. He was popular, but there was always something aloof about him. Something odd.'

'How can you say that? You're his friend.'

'We're not really friends. We just inhabited the same lecture theatres for three years.'

'And you used that connection to come and see the art collection here,' Emilia said, remembering what he'd told her before.

'I know. It was a bit mean of me, but I got to meet you, didn't I?'

'So I shouldn't reprimand you, is that what you're saying?'

He stopped walking and pulled her closer towards him. 'I'd rather be kissed than reprimanded,' he said, but she put her hands out to stop him as he inched closer.

'I think we'd better get back to work, don't you?' she said.

'Spoilsport,' he said as they made their way out of the maze.

'Ah, there you are!' Tobias said, almost crashing into them as they exited.

The first thought to fly through Emilia's brain was just how much of their conversation her brother had heard. She could feel her face heating in anxiety.

'What are you doing?' she asked him.

'Wondering where you two were. I went into Clarissa's room and you weren't there. I thought you were working?'

'We were just taking a break,' Jay said. 'We were both getting a bit stiff.'

Tobias eyed them both and gave an indecipherable nod. 'How's it going?'

'Very well,' Jay told him.

'Can I see it?'

'Not yet,' Jay said. 'It's too early. It would spoil things.'

Tobias nodded, but he didn't look convinced by this argument. 'I want to see it soon. I need to see what I'm paying for.'

'Of course.'

An uneasy silence descended between the three of them.

'Well, I'll leave you to get back to work,' Tobias said at last and he returned to the house.

'Is your brother always so bossy?' Jay asked once he was out of earshot.

'Always!'

'How do you put up with it?'

'I try to zone him out whenever I can.'

'And does that work?'

'Not really. He's very persistent.'

'Do you think he heard us?'

'In the maze? I was wondering that too,' Emilia said.

'God, was he hanging around listening to us?'

'I don't know.'

'That's so weird,' Jay said. 'He's so weird.'

'Don't keep saying that.'

'I'm sorry. I don't mean to upset you. I'm just . . .'

'What?'

'Worried about you.'

'Well, don't be. I'm a big girl and I can take care of myself,' she insisted, but the look she saw in Jay's eyes told her that he wasn't at all convinced.

Chapter 9

For the first time since Cape had started at Morton Hall, there was another gardener working alongside him. Not only that, but Mac had arrived that Saturday morning before Cape, his digger already positioned at the entrance to the walled garden.

'You don't hang around, do you?' Cape said, waving a hand as he approached. He was pleased to see him there, but he couldn't help feeling a little bit threatened by this other man's presence. The garden had been his domain, his responsibility, and now he was expected to share it – not just with Mac but with a whole group of strangers. He definitely had mixed feelings about the whole thing but it was for the greater good, as he kept reminding himself, and he couldn't help but be excited by the thought of restoring the garden to its former glory.

'I thought I'd make an early start and pace the garden out,' Mac said, removing his woolly cap and running a hand through his thick, dark hair.

'Anyone else here yet?' Cape asked.

'Nope. You're the first. Well, second,' Mac said. 'Not got your daughter with you?'

'Dance class,' Cape explained. He'd been looking forward to Poppy's company, hoping he could have her with him for the whole day, but Renee had reminded him that a new dance class was beginning. 'Another time.'

'Good to get them into gardening early,' Mac said.

'Absolutely. I'm all for that.'

'So, are you happy if I make a start?'

'Please,' Cape said. 'There's a lot to do.'

Mac nodded and Cape watched as he hopped onto the digger and drove it into the walled garden.

From previous wanderings around this space, Cape knew that there was a lot of rubbish to clear. Mrs Beatty had said that a skip would be arriving at some point, but Cape wanted to make a start piling it all together. He'd brought all the pairs of tough gardening gloves he could round up at his place, and he put a pair on now and walked across the overgrown expanse towards the long lean-to greenhouse. It was a magnificent structure with its huge lead-weights pulley system which opened the windows. But many of them were damaged now and broken glass lay around in great shards. He'd make a start clearing those up, not wanting to leave that unpleasant job for anybody else.

His booted feet trod carefully over the ground as he began to clear this first patch of land. What an enormous task it all seemed, he thought. But with the seven of them, plus various children coming and going, the job was definitely achievable. Cape had spent the previous night trying to visualise how the garden would have looked one hundred and fifty years ago. How he wished he could get a glimpse of the garden when it was first being designed and laid out, when the yew hedges of the maze were being planted and the great topiary shapes had first been dreamt up. The walled garden must have been a paradise of produce, with a whole team of gardeners employed to keep it all running. Had they loved it as much as he did now, he wondered? Did they stride around that little bit of earth with the same sense of pride and enjoyment? He felt quite sure that they had, for gardeners were almost always people with a passion for what they did.

It was a rare gardener who was just going through the motions, working the nine till five. Gardening was a vocation. It was what got you out of bed on the cold, dark winter mornings when you knew that the sun would never show itself and a day of numb fingers and frozen toes lay ahead of you. It was what kept you going when a crop failed or a pest struck. It gave you a resilience against rain, frost and snow, because a gardener knows that those days will pass and all of your hard work will pay off when the first green shoots force their way up through the soil, their leaves and blooms unfurling. Yes, he thought: gardening was the only job for him.

He turned to see how Mac was getting on. He'd made good progress digging up some of the nettles and brambles and was just turning the machine around when he stopped and hopped out to examine the ground. Cape watched.

'Hey!' Mac shouted over a moment later, waving to him.

'What is it?' Cape asked, crossing the space quickly. Was there a hoard of Saxon treasure? A Viking longboat?

'Is that what I think it is?' Cape asked, peering into the half-opened black case. A moment later, he let out a laugh. 'It's a violin.'

Mac shook his head in bemusement. 'What on *earth* is that doing here?'

'I have absolutely no idea.'

Mac took off his cap and scratched his head. 'It's amazing what you find in gardens,' he said. 'You know, I once found an engagement ring.'

'Really?'

He nodded. 'Big fat ruby. Lovely thing once I'd washed all the muck off it. Been in the ground a good old while, I reckon.'

'What did you do with it?'

'I took it to the owner. A Mr Phillips, I think it was. He'd lived in that place all his life and looked puzzled when I presented him with the ring. But then he recognised it and his eyes went all misty like.' Mac smiled at the memory. 'Told me he'd proposed to a sweet slip of a girl there several decades before, but she'd turned him down and he'd flung the ring in the herbaceous border in frustration and had forgotten about it. Well, he snatched it out of my hand after telling me that just as *Mrs Phillips* showed up, asking what we were talking about. My theory is that she had no idea about that sweet slip of a girl her husband had proposed to before her.'

Cape laughed. 'I once found a vase. Beautiful. I wiped away a section of dirt on it and read the word *Ming*.'

'Ming?' Mac said. 'I've heard of that. Wouldn't that be worth a bit?'

'Absolutely,' Cape said, 'only, when I wiped a bit more of the dirt away, I saw that it read Bir*ming*ham.'

Mac grinned. 'Bad luck.'

'Yeah, I know.'

'So what do we do with this violin?' Mac asked.

Cape looked thoughtful for a moment. 'I guess we take it up to the house.'

Anne Marie wasn't going to make it to Morton Hall until later in the day. First, she had to pay a visit to her mother. She hadn't been officially invited to visit, but her mother had left a number of messages on Anne Marie's answer machine while she'd been working. They were the usual passive-aggressive messages like, 'I hardly ever see you these days, but don't go worrying. The last thing I want you to do is worry.'

Anne Marie would ignore such a message at her peril. She once had and the accumulated grief that descended upon her the next time she saw her mother had not been worth it.

Janet Lattimore lived in the sort of Thames Valley village that was frequently used as a location in films. With its close proximity to London and its pretty brick-and-flint cottages and rolling countryside, it was a favourite with directors and would pop up as a backdrop in everything from cosy crimes to the latest blockbuster. She'd moved there after losing her husband three years ago. Anne Marie's father had been a director at a bank in Oxford, and the family home had been in the leafy suburbs. After he'd died, the three-storey house had been sold for a ridiculous sum and Janet had moved into a tiny two-bedroom house in the Chiltern village. It seemed like a horribly quiet existence after the bustle of Oxford and Anne Marie couldn't help but wonder what her mother did there all day. Janet was sixty-seven now, having retired from teaching five years earlier. She still went into Oxford from time to time and had joined a few local groups. Still, Anne Marie worried about her being on her own.

Parking outside the cottage now, she took a deep breath.

I am not going to let her rile me, she told herself. Grant and his daughters had already done a pretty good job of that this morning.

'You're going to Morton Hall *again?*' Grant had complained.

'Yes. I'll be going there every week from now on.'

She'd surprised herself by her confident tone and had had to hide a smile as Grant had skulked back to his study. Irma and Rebecca had been in their bedrooms on their respective phones and had barely glanced up at her as she'd poked her head around the doors.

'I'm going to see Grandma Janet,' she told Rebecca. 'Do you want to come too?'

'She's not *my* grandma,' Rebecca told her. She always said it and it wounded Anne Marie every single time.

Banishing all thoughts of her step-daughters, she got out of the car, picking up the bunch of flowers she'd bought for her mother from a florist en route. Her mother knew the difference between flowers from a florist and those bought in a supermarket or petrol station. Anne Marie remembered the scene her mother had once made when she'd been handed a bunch of flowers from the local Co-op.

'Is this all I'm worth to you? Your sister would never have bought flowers like these.'

It baffled Anne Marie how anybody could complain about being bought flowers, but her mother had a knack for turning anything into a heated battle.

Opening the green-painted gate and walking up the neat brick path, Anne Marie took a moment to compose herself before knocking on the door. Her mother answered a moment later.

'Hello, Mum. I brought you these,' Anne Marie said, presenting the bunch of flowers. She watched as her mother examined them, sniffing the sweet perfume and then examining the wrapping as if she might find a clue to just how much her daughter valued her. It was ever the way, Anne Marie thought as she followed her mother into the cottage. She'd lost count of the number of times she'd had to apologise for gifts because they didn't please her mother or else return them because they were unsatisfactory.

Her mother went through to the kitchen where she made a great fuss about trying to find a vase for the bouquet.

'No, this one is *much* too big,' she said as she pulled a glass vase out from a cupboard under the sink.

Anne Marie bit her lip, determined not to show her pain.

After tea was made, they walked through to the tiny living room that overlooked the village green. It was a pretty room with a beautiful fireplace above which was a mantelpiece full of photographs. Of Anne. The beloved daughter. The magnificent firstborn. The perfect one.

But somebody else had joined Anne on the mantelpiece of memories: her father. It was funny, but Anne Marie couldn't remember seeing any photographs of her father while he was alive: death had given his memory the glow of a saint and he was now worthy of a silver frame.

Anne Marie couldn't help noticing that there weren't any photographs of her on the mantelpiece. She would have to die before she was adored and talked well of.

'So, I take it you've been busy,' her mother began, implying that Anne Marie had been lax in not returning her phone calls.

'Yes. Work's as busy as ever and I'm doing voluntary work in a garden.'

'A garden?'

'Morton Hall.'

Her mother's face blanched. 'What are you doing going there?'

'There's a group of us. Seven. For some reason, Miss Morton chose us to restore the gardens. She's left her estate to the village on the condition that the group restores the garden.'

'Why on earth would she do that?'

'I don't know,' Anne Marie said honestly. 'Nobody seems to know.'

Her mother shifted in her chair. 'I never liked that place.'

'You've been there?' This was news to Anne Marie.

'Once. Your father had some business there and I accompanied him.'

'Really?'

'Spooky-looking place. All Gothic towers and dark windows.'

'Yes, it's not the bonniest of houses, but the garden is very beautiful.'

'I don't like you going there, Anne Marie.'

Anne Marie frowned. 'It's only for a few hours a week.'

'It's unhealthy.'

'What do you mean?'

'That family. The Morton family. They weren't right.'

'What do you know about them?'

'Only that,' her mother said curtly. 'The way they locked themselves away there and had nothing to do with anyone. There were stories about them. Rumours.'

'What sort of rumours?'

'That he wasn't right. That he kept his sister under lock and key.'

'I didn't know you knew anything about them.'

'I don't. Only that. Only stories I heard. But you shouldn't get muddled up in it all.'

'But the family has all gone now,' Anne Marie said.

'It's not a healthy environment.'

Anne Marie thought about the time she'd spent there, sitting on the bench and soaking in the calm of the wild walled garden, and how it had helped to restore a little bit of peace in her life.

'I think it's one of the healthiest places I've ever been,' she told her mother. 'The garden at least. I've only seen a bit of the house.'

'When did you go into the house?'

'For the meeting with Mrs Beatty, the housekeeper.' She didn't divulge the other secret trip made with Cape.

'You shouldn't have anything to do with that place.'

'It's too late for that. I'm committed now and I'm going there today.' She watched her mother's face as it turned even more sour. 'Anyway, I want to go,' she added.

Her mother shook her head. 'You're so unlike your sister,' she said. 'If your sister were alive, she would have listened to me, but you've always been headstrong.'

Anne Marie almost gasped at the outright lie. Her – *headstrong!* It was ridiculous. She'd never been given a chance to be headstrong either in her family or in her marriage. And, once again, the familiar refrain: *If your sister were alive.* How many times did Anne Marie want to shout, 'But she isn't! She's dead.' It seemed absurd to assume what Anne would have been like or how she would have responded or what she would have said in any given situation, but that's what her mother always did.

It had always perplexed Anne Marie that her mother had chosen to use her dead child's name as part of her second child's. Wasn't that a recipe for sorrow? Surely every time she spoke her second child's name, a little piece of her would tear inside as she remembered that precious first child whom she'd lost.

'I've got to go, Mum,' she said, standing up.

'But you only just got here.' Suddenly, her mother was all contrition.

'I'm sorry – I've got to get to Morton Hall.'

The scowl was instantly back in place. 'You shouldn't go there.'

Anne Marie had reached the front door. 'I'll call you next week, okay?' She leaned forward to kiss her cheek.

'Anne Marie!'

Stopping by the garden gate, she turned around.

'What is it?' she asked. Her mother's mouth dropped open as if she was about to say something. But, just as quickly, it clamped shut again and she shook her head before disappearing inside the cottage and closing the door behind her.

Once in her car, Anne Marie stared out of the windscreen and yet saw nothing. What possible objection could her mother have for her working in the garden? It was absurd and just another example of how she could never hope to please her. No matter what she did, it would always be wrong, and it would always be compared to what her dead sister might have done in the same circumstances.

Anne. Anne Marie. Would she never be free to be herself?

Chapter 10

Anne Marie parked her car outside Garrard House, but didn't go back inside for fear of Grant complaining about what she was doing again. She'd had her fill of that today. Instead, she opened the boot and reached in for a pair of wellies, taking off her shoes and pulling on a thick pair of woolly socks. She was actually quite excited by the idea of getting stuck in. They had such a tiny garden at Garrard House and there really wasn't very much to it other than a lawn, a laurel hedge and a couple of nondescript conifers in pots. She had once made the suggestion of sowing a wildflower area. Actually, she had been hoping to dig up the whole boring lawn and turn it over to poppies, cornflowers and daisies. Grant had looked at her in horror. She'd have thought that a man so in tune with the beauty of classic novels and poetry would have welcomed the romance of a meadow, but he was very attached to that little piece of lawn, mowing it in neat stripes and sitting out on it briefly a few times a year with his gin and tonic and a newspaper.

As she walked to Morton Hall, Anne Marie wondered what kind of garden Cape had. She couldn't imagine him being happy with a lawn and a laurel hedge. She visualised grand herbaceous borders and pots overflowing with colour.

'Anne Marie!'

Cape was striding across the driveway towards her. He was wearing a tartan cap and a wax jacket and his cheeks blazed red from being out in the cold.

'You walked up the driveway!'

'Yes, I thought I'd give it a go.'

'Come and see what we've found,' he said.

'What is it?'

'Wait and see.'

Mac was at the far end of the walled garden in the digger when they entered. Anne Marie sent him a wave and he returned it. She followed Cape over the uneven ground and stopped just outside the greenhouse.

'It's a violin!' Anne Marie said, quite unnecessarily, when she saw the black case.

'I know!' Cape laughed as he opened it up.

'Was it here in the garden?'

'Just over there,' Cape said, pointing to an area of ground that had now been cleared. 'Amongst the brambles.'

'Why would someone leave a violin in a garden?'

'Do you think they threw it out on purpose or left it accidentally?'

'I don't know,' Anne Marie said. 'How long's it been out here?'

'There's moss on the case,' Cape said.

'It's lucky the instrument isn't damaged. Well, not superficially at least.'

'Maybe Mrs Beatty will know something about it.'

Anne Marie smiled. 'Yes! We could ask her.'

'Just what we thought, and it would be a good excuse to see the house again.'

'If she lets us in.'

'She couldn't *not* on a day like today,' Cape said, glancing up at the grey sky that was threatening rain.

'Shall we go?' Anne Marie asked and Cape grinned and nodded, fastening the violin case and motioning to Mac in the digger.

'Anyone else turn up yet?'

'Not yet,' Cape said as they left the walled garden. 'I wanted to come earlier, but I had to go and see my mother.'

'She lives locally?'

'Yes.'

'That's nice.'

Anne Marie didn't say anything.

'Isn't it?' Cape prodded.

'Isn't it what?' Anne Marie said, deliberately evading his question.

'Nice. I mean, you're lucky to have your mother nearby.'

'Oh, I see. Well, of course. I don't have to travel far.' She was all too aware that Cape's eyes were upon her. 'What?'

He shrugged. 'You tell me.'

'Tell you what?'

'You're all prickly.'

'No, I'm not.'

'Are you okay?'

'I'm fine.' She quickened her pace and, with relief, reached the front door of the house where she turned to face Cape. He was carrying the violin and leaned forward and rang the doorbell.

It was a moment or two before the door was opened by Mrs Beatty, who greeted them with a frown.

'Is everything all right?' she asked them, her tone suggesting she didn't care either way.

Cape cleared his throat and lifted up the violin case for her to see. Her face immediately blanched.

'Where did you find that?'

'In the walled garden near the greenhouse.'

'Give it to me.'

'Who did it belong to?' Cape asked.

'It belongs to the house,' Mrs Beatty said as she took the violin from him.

Anne Marie could see that her hand now clasping the violin case was shaking.

'Was it Miss Morton's?' she asked.

Mrs Beatty didn't say anything, but she was looking down at the violin case as if she didn't quite believe what she was seeing.

Anne Marie felt Cape nudging her arm with his elbow as if to alert her to Mrs Beatty's reaction.

'We'd better get back to the garden,' he said, though they both waited a moment longer in case Mrs Beatty decided to say something else. But she didn't. Instead she did a funny sort of shuffling reverse and closed the door to them.

'Well,' Cape said, 'we didn't get invited in.'

'She looked really shocked.'

'You don't think the violin was hers, do you?'

Anne Marie shook her head. 'Her hand was shaking.'

'Yes.'

'I wish she'd talk to us. She doesn't seem to want to share anything about the house with us at all.'

'Give it a few weeks. Who knows, she might don a pair of wellies and join us in the garden sometime.'

Anne Marie smiled. 'I can't quite see that myself.'

It wasn't until after lunch that the rest of the group turned up to help. Cape, Mac and Anne Marie had eaten their packed lunches in the kitchen. The three of them had chatted amiably enough, speculating on the violin and wondering what else they might dig up in the garden during its restoration.

Now, back outside, Cape watched Anne Marie as she worked. She was talking to Kathleen while Dorothy, Erin, Patrick and his two sons were working on the other side of the garden, throwing broken pots, old bricks and other debris into a wheelbarrow. He felt strangely drawn to Anne Marie. What was her story? He kept getting little hints of it: the step-daughters who didn't want to spend time with her, and the mother who appeared to make Anne Marie reticent at best and miserable at worst. She seemed to be sad and yet there were glimpses of such joy within her. He loved to see her smile. She was smiling now at something Kathleen had said and, looking up suddenly, she caught his eye and he smiled back.

He walked across to join them.

'Everything okay?' he asked.

'Good,' Kathleen said.

'Kath was just telling me about a few of her gardening disasters,' Anne Marie said.

'I mistakenly thought I might be able to grow things,' she said. 'But I stick to fake flowers in the house these days.'

Cape grimaced at the thought. 'I see we'll have to restore not only this garden, but your faith in gardening too.'

'Could take a lot of work,' she warned him.

'I've never been one to shy away from work,' Cape said. 'What kind of jobs do you think you'd get on best with?'

Kathleen looked thoughtful. 'Well, I don't want to risk killing anything so don't put me in charge of tending anything delicate.'

'Duly noted.'

'Maybe I could be a general dogsbody, and I don't mind a bit of weeding.'

'Really?' Anne Marie said. 'That's my least favourite job.'

'I actually quite like it,' Kathleen said. 'I find it a good stress buster.'

'Well, we've got plenty of weeds here,' Cape said, 'and it'll be an ongoing job once we start planting up the vegetable garden.'

'Then I'm your woman,' Kathleen told him.

'Good,' Cape said, turning around as Mac approached in his digger.

'Going to need to clear this area,' he told them as he hopped out onto the ground.

'Sure thing,' Cape said. 'We'll make ourselves scarce.'

Cape walked across to where the rest of them were working.

'We're going to need to move on for a bit,' he told them.

'Oh, what a shame,' Dorothy said. 'I was just finding my rhythm in here.'

'Dorothy's shifted most of those bricks by herself,' Erin said with a grin, nodding to the wheelbarrow.

'Don't do yourself a mischief on day one,' Cape warned her.

'I've never felt fitter,' she said. 'Getting out in the fresh air suits me. Are you sure we have to move?'

'Just for a bit while Mac clears the ground.'

'So what can we do?' Kathleen asked. She and Anne Marie had joined them now.

'I think we could start by clearing a few of the paths around the garden,' Cape told them. 'There are some really lovely red-brick ones that have been lost over the years. I'll occasionally catch a glimpse of one and it would be nice to restore them.'

'Great!' Kathleen said.

'I'd start by shifting all the dead leaves. There are old plastic sacks over there that Mac brought with him. If we fill those with the leaves and pop a few holes in the bottom, they'll make pretty good compost for future years.'

'I'm impressed,' Dorothy said. 'You're thinking ahead.'

'It was Mac's idea,' Cape said. He'd been impressed by Mac's foresight too. Compost was the foundation of every good garden. It was a natural product that was easy to come by and would save the estate money. 'There are some rakes over there and a couple of brooms.'

Everybody went and grabbed an implement and followed Cape out of the walled garden.

'How are your boys getting on?' Cape asked Patrick as they fell into step together.

'They're not used to being outdoors,' Patrick said with a weary sigh. 'Mind you, neither am I. I think we all spend an unhealthy amount of time at our computers.'

'That's the modern world, isn't it?'

'They looked at me as if I was mad when I told them about this project,' Patrick went on. '"It's winter," they kept saying, but they don't go out in the summer either.' He sighed. 'Are you sure this is a good idea?'

'What do you mean?'

'This whole gardening thing? I mean, we're a bunch of old folks and kids who know next to nothing.'

Cape frowned. 'That's not true. Mac and I—'

'Yeah, I know you guys know what you're doing, but what use are the rest of us?'

'That's what we're trying to establish here,' Cape told him. 'But I'm really confident everyone can play an important role.'

'Well, you've got more optimism than I have,' Patrick confessed.

'And we're hardly old,' Cape said, picking up on his earlier comment.

'Oh, come on – that Dorothy woman?'

'She's coping okay, isn't she?'

'Maybe for now, but *I* don't want to be responsible if she keels over and has a heart attack.'

Cape almost choked in shock at the comment and Dorothy must have heard it too, because she turned around and glared at him.

'I beg your pardon?' she said, her face clouding over.

Patrick wiped his hands on the front of his jeans. 'Look, lady – all I meant was that you're no spring chicken.'

There was a sharp intake of breath from Dorothy. 'I'll have you know that I have absolutely *no* intention of keeling over and, if I do, I'll make sure it's as far away from you as possible!'

Cape did his best to hide his amusement at this as he turned to face Patrick, who had the good grace to look a little shamefaced.

'I didn't mean—' Patrick began.

'Dorothy's *more* than pulling her weight,' Erin said. 'Have you seen the amount of bricks she's moved today? And she did it all with a smile on her face, which is more than some people can manage around here.'

'Okay, okay!' Patrick said in defeat.

'I think you might owe Dorothy an apology,' Cape whispered.

He noticed that Patrick's two boys were lagging behind the group. The older one, Matthew, was shuffling his feet along the ground while Elliot, a couple of years younger, had picked up a stick and was thrashing the hedge with it. Kathleen was watching in obvious disapproval.

'How about I give them something really fun to do?' Cape said.

'Like what?' Patrick asked.

'There's a yew bush that's been growing in a pot for a while. It's been kind of an experiment of mine. I haven't been able to make up my mind what to do with it. Your boys could practise on it if they want.'

'Practise what exactly?'

'Topiary. Clipping.'

'And you're sure they can't do any damage?' Patrick asked.

'They'll only be using secateurs,' Cape assured him.

'No, I didn't mean damage to themselves, I meant to the yew bush.'

'Oh, right. No. It's pretty indestructible.'

'Well, if you're sure.'

'I think it might get them interested, you know?'

Patrick gave a snort. 'You reckon?'

'Got to be worth a try, hasn't it?' Cape said, trying not to be discouraged by Patrick's response.

'I guess,' Patrick said.

'Right, boys!' Cape clapped his hands together in enthusiasm as he turned towards Matthew and Elliot. 'Have you ever heard of topiary?'

They both looked up at him with bored, sulky expressions on their faces.

'No? Well, it's a way of clipping hedges into shapes. You can make anything from animals to crowns. The only thing limiting you is your own imagination.'

The spark that Cape had hoped to ignite remained unlit.

'Come with me,' Cape said, leading them across the lawn towards the topiary garden.

'What do you think of these, then?' he asked as the boys stared up at the strange shapes above and around them.

'They're weird,' Matthew announced.

'Kind of freaky,' Elliot declared.

'I think they're kind of cool,' Cape said.

'Why are you showing them to us?' Matthew asked in suspicion.

'Because I think you can have a good go at making one of these yourselves.'

'Seriously?' Matthew said.

'Seriously. See that pot over there?'

The boys nodded.

'It's yours. It's a yew bush. A lot of topiary is made out of yew. It's easy to work with.' He reached into one of his jacket pockets and brought out two small pairs of secateurs and handed one each to the boys before giving them the world's quickest lesson in topiary shaping.

'So, we can make anything?' Matthew asked once he'd finished.

'Anything you like.'

'A football?' Elliot suggested.

'That's a good idea, although round shapes can be deceptively hard to get absolutely perfect,' Cape warned them.

'I'm going to make a dragon,' Matthew announced, enthusiasm showing at last.

'I wouldn't be too ambitious either,' Cape warned. 'Maybe something in between a football and a dragon.'

'Or a dragon kicking a football!' Matthew said.

Cape laughed. 'One day. But perhaps not today.' He paused and then clapped his hands together. 'Right, I'll leave you to it. We'll be just round the corner so holler if you need any help.'

Cape left, but couldn't help turning to take one last look at the boys who were standing examining the potted yew bush as if it were an alien life form. He grinned. They'd soon get stuck in. Now it was his turn – clearing one of the beautiful brick pathways that lay hidden under years of fallen leaves, moss and general debris.

He was thrilled to see that his fellow gardeners had taken the initiative and made a start with the rakes and brooms; a section of the path had already come to life, waking up after its slumber, ready to be admired and used once again.

It was good, satisfying work, which quickly built up the body's temperature so that you forgot just how cold the January afternoon was. He noticed that Patrick was keeping his distance from Dorothy, but that the women were working well together. He walked towards them.

'Dorothy?' he said. 'Can I have a word?'

The old lady looked up and nodded. 'Everything okay?'

They walked down the path out of earshot of the group.

'I was just making sure you're all right. After Patrick's comments, I mean.'

Dorothy glanced over to where Patrick was raking leaves and took a deep breath as if fortifying herself.

'If he thinks he can turf me out of this project then he's wrong!' she declared. 'I might be old, but I'm not dead yet!'

Cape grinned. 'That's the spirit.'

'In fact, I've never felt more alive,' she went on. 'I might move slightly slower than you young ones, but I hope I can be of some use to you all.'

'But you are,' Cape assured her.

'Well, that's good to hear,' she said, 'and, if I feel any keeling over coming on, I'll let you know.' She gave Cape a little wink and they returned to the group.

'Hey, Cape – we could have a bonfire with all these leaves,' Patrick suggested.

'I think Cape wants them for compost,' Anne Marie said.

Cape thought for a moment and came to a decision. 'I think a bonfire to round our first day off would be a great idea,' he said. 'There'll be plenty more leaves to collect in the garden for compost and these are good and dry so will make a nice fire to warm us up. Your boys will like that too, won't they?'

Patrick shrugged. 'They might. Or they might think it's really lame. Everything's really lame to them at the moment.'

'Oh, dear,' Dorothy said, compassion flooding her face. 'It sounds like you've got a battle on your hands.'

'You're telling me. Everything I say or do is wrong, and they're not even teenagers yet. I hate to think what happens when that stage kicks in.'

'They're probably just rebelling a bit since their mother . . .' Kathleen began.

'It's okay. You can say it.'

'I just meant—'

'Since she walked out and hasn't been in touch?' Patrick said, suddenly full of fury. 'I suppose that would screw you up pretty good as a kid, wouldn't it?'

Dorothy, who was standing next to him, reached out and touched his shoulder. 'These things take time,' she said. 'They're finding their way in a new and difficult world.'

'Aren't we all?' Patrick said with a derisive sort of snort.

'When I lost my husband, I didn't know what to do with myself. I felt sad and mad all at once. It took me ages to even want to leave the house. I felt as if everybody was staring at me, waiting to see if I'd crumble.'

Everybody had stopped working now and was listening to Dorothy. 'That's so sad,' Erin said.

'I know it's not the same,' Dorothy said, 'but your boys are probably grieving in a similar way. They need time and love and support. They'll get through it.'

Cape had been watching Patrick's response to Dorothy's words and could see that he felt deeply uneasy. He had cast his eyes down to the ground to avoid eye contact and was doing a funny sort of shuffle with his feet. Perhaps he was regretting his earlier words to her, especially now that she was showing such kindness towards him.

'Something else they'll benefit from is fresh air and plenty of exercise,' Cape added to lighten the mood a little. 'That'll do them the power of good.'

'I'm not sure It's doing *me* the power of good,' Kathleen said. 'I've just broken a nail.' Her tone was more amused than annoyed though.

'You're not wearing the gloves I gave you,' Cape said. 'They'll save you from a dozen different mishaps in the garden.'

She nodded and walked across to the dilapidated bench where she'd left them. Patrick's gaze followed her, but he quickly withdrew it when she turned around and came back, the gloves now firmly on.

Work resumed and the beautiful red-brick path continued to reveal itself to the gardeners.

'Just look at the colour of these bricks,' Dorothy enthused. 'I wonder who the last person was to walk down this path.'

'I often wonder that when I'm in the garden,' Cape confessed. 'I sometimes think I've caught a glimpse of somebody just walking into the shadows or around the corner. It makes you wonder if the ghosts of gardeners past are here.'

'Oh, don't!' Erin said. 'That's spooky.'

'Can gardens be haunted? Isn't it just houses?' Dorothy asked.

'I don't see why they can't be,' Kathleen said. 'If somebody spends a long enough time in one place, they're bound to leave a little bit of themselves behind.'

'Maybe we'll all leave a little bit of ourselves behind here,' Cape suggested.

'But this project only goes on for a year, doesn't it?' Patrick was quick to point out.

'Initially,' Cape said. 'We'll have to find a way of maintaining the gardens once they're restored.'

'Won't that be somebody else's job?' Patrick asked.

'I don't know,' Cape said honestly. 'I thought maybe some of us would want to continue here.'

The group didn't say anything. They still obviously had reservations about the amount of time they were willing to donate to this project.

'I'd like to stay on,' Anne Marie said.

Cape glanced her way and smiled. 'Good.'

'I might,' Erin said. 'Unless someone buys me a month's holiday in Italy or I'm given my dream job in a museum or gallery.'

They continued work on the path for a while, but the light was beginning to fade. The sky had turned an eerie shade of sepia and the temperature had dropped. Mac emerged from the walled garden and stood admiring the path that had been unearthed.

'Nice,' he said, nodding in appreciation.

'A pretty good first day's work,' Kathleen said.

'Hey, I'd better see how your boys are getting on with that yew,' Cape told Patrick who nodded, but didn't offer to go with him.

Cape made his way to the topiary garden and instantly came to a standstill at the sight that greeted him. It was an evergreen apocalypse. Years of patient growth had been mercilessly hacked away in less than an hour, the devastation littering the ground around the terracotta pot. Cape cursed under his breath and looked around for the boys who were nowhere to be seen.

'Boys?' Cape shouted. 'Matthew? Elliot? Where are you?' He stood still, his head cocked to one side as he thought he heard voices. 'Boys?'

'We're in the maze!' a voice shouted back through the half-light of dusk.

It was then that Patrick joined him.

'Where are the boys?' he asked, looking around.

'They're in the maze,' Cape said.

'Dad?' a voice yelled.

'Elliot?'

'We're lost, Dad!'

Patrick gave a tiny grin. 'Were they meant to go in the maze?'

'I didn't exactly give them permission,' Cape confessed.

'I see. And how did they get on with the—' Patrick stopped, his mouth suddenly dropping open. 'Bloody hell! Is that the plant you gave them?'

Cape rubbed his chin. 'Erm, yeah.'

'I'm guessing it shouldn't look like that.'

'Not in an ideal world.'

'Little blighters,' Patrick said.

'I should have supervised them.'

Patrick shook his head. 'This would still have happened. The minute your back was turned.'

'I'll go and get them out of the maze.'

'Leave them in there,' Patrick said.

'But it'll be getting dark soon,' Cape pointed out.

'Serve them right.'

Cape frowned, half amused, half appalled. 'Are you sure?'

Patrick looked a little uneasy and then cleared his throat. 'Well, just for a few more minutes.'

Cape nodded. 'You got it.'

The cries from the maze continued.

'Dad? Dad? Are you there? We can't get out! Daaaaaad!'

Cape waited in a sort of agony. His instinct was to rush into action and head into the maze, but he couldn't exactly defy Patrick's wish, could he? He looked at him now as the daylight began to fade. There wasn't that much time. He'd have to get a torch out if they left it much longer.

'Erm, Patrick?' he tried. 'What do you want to do?'

The boys' shouts from the maze had caused the others in the group to gather round.

'What's going on?' Erin asked.

'The boys are in the maze,' Cape told them.

'I take it they're lost?' Anne Marie said.

'It sure sounds like they are,' Mac said as the cries from the maze continued.

'Shouldn't someone go in after them?' Dorothy said, looking from Cape to Patrick and back again.

Patrick held up a hand for a moment, his head nodding a little as if he was counting.

'All right. In you go,' he said to Cape.

Cape breathed a sigh of relief and took off at a cracking pace.

'It's all right, boys!' he called. 'Stay where you are and I'll have you out in no time.'

Cape had never negotiated the maze so fast, not even the time Poppy had run off and got herself lost, though she hadn't been so anxious – she'd simply laughed. He remembered the day so clearly. He'd followed that laugh until he'd found her, scooping her up in his arms and peppering her flushed cheek with kisses. He had a feeling that Matthew and Elliot were more likely to be peppered with reprimands than kisses when their father got hold of them.

'There you are!' Cape said a moment later as he rounded a corner and found the boys.

'This place sucks!' Matthew said.

'It's freaky,' Elliot said. 'Can we go home now?'

'You sure can,' Cape said. 'Follow me and *don't* get lost again.'

'I'm not planning to,' Matthew said in all seriousness, making Cape smile. He had a feeling these boys had learned a rather valuable lesson.

At last they reached the exit and Patrick was there to leap upon them.

'What the hell do you think you were doing?' he shouted, causing Dorothy and Anne Marie to flinch. Erin raised her eyebrows and Mac and Kathleen looked on in alarm.

'We're sorry,' Matthew said. 'We just wanted to have a look.'

'I don't mean the *maze*. I mean that yew bush!' Patrick cried, pointing to the bare stump that was left in the pot.

The boys looked guiltily towards the mess they'd made.

'How do you explain that, eh?' Patrick demanded.

'We didn't know when to stop,' Matthew said, his voice small.

'Didn't know when to stop!' Patrick shook his head. 'You need to apologise to Mr Colman *right now!*'

The boys turned to Cape.

'Sorry,' Matthew said.

'Sorry,' Elliot echoed.

'That took years to grow,' Cape told them. 'We can't have that sort of damage done to the garden if you're to continue coming here.'

'You're inviting them back?' Patrick asked in surprise.

'Of course. They've got to learn and this is just their first day, but we'll keep them under closer supervision, okay?'

'Thank Mr Colman,' Patrick told them.

'Thank you, Mr Colman,' the boys said in unison.

'Right, let's get you home before you do any more damage.' Patrick raised a hand in farewell to the group. 'We'll see you tomorrow morning.'

The group muttered its goodbyes as he disappeared down the driveway with his boys.

'What a very odd thing to do,' Dorothy said. 'I couldn't have let those boys cry all that time in the maze if they'd been mine.'

'What is wrong with that man?' Kathleen asked.

'I think the boys try him quite hard,' Cape said in Patrick's defence.

'But to leave them like that,' Dorothy said. 'That just wasn't right.'

'He's going through a tough time himself,' Anne Marie pointed out.

'That's no excuse to take it out on those poor boys,' Dorothy said. 'Not after what they've been through.'

'We just have to hope that Patrick gets lost in the maze at some point,' Kathleen said. 'Then we can let *him* stew in there for a bit.'

Dorothy chuckled at that.

'Right, gotta go,' Mac said. 'I'll be here first thing tomorrow.'

'Good job today,' Cape said and Mac gave a nod.

'Yes, better head back before it's too dark to see,' Dorothy said.

'I'll walk with you,' Kathleen said. 'This driveway gives me the creeps in the dark.'

'Me too,' Erin said. 'Anne Marie?'

'I'll be right with you,' she said.

Everybody said their goodbyes, promising to return the next day.

'You okay?' Cape said as he was left standing alone with Anne Marie.

'I just wanted to apologise,' she said.

'Apologise? What for?'

'When I arrived today,' she said, sinking her hands in the pockets of her coat. 'I was a bit grumpy.'

'Were you?' Cape said.

'A bit. Maybe.'

Cape studied her, watching her face as a look of regret passed over it. 'Well, maybe just a *little*.'

She nodded. 'Sorry. I'd – erm – just got back from visiting my mum.'

'Yes, you said.'

'She can . . .' She paused. '. . . try a person.'

'Like Patrick's boys?'

Anne Marie gave a little smile. 'Something like that.'

'I'm sorry to hear that.'

'It's okay. I'm kind of used to it now although it's harder since my dad died. She seems to be getting worse.'

'Worse – how?'

'She's never happy.' Anne Marie took a deep breath. 'I took her some flowers and she made this big show about the bouquet not being big enough.'

'Really?'

'She's never satisfied.'

Cape couldn't be sure because of the fading light, but there seemed to be tears in Anne Marie's eyes.

'It makes me so cross that she can still upset me like this. I'm a grown woman, for goodness' sake.'

'Hey,' he said, reaching a hand out to squeeze her shoulder. 'Parents are great at riling kids. It's all part of the job description.'

'Do your parents still rile you?'

'I'm afraid I've lost both my parents.'

'Oh, I'm sorry.'

He shrugged. 'It was a long time ago. My mum died when I was seven and my dad died a few years ago. He used to rib me all the time, though.'

'I don't think my mum's ever ribbed me,' Anne Marie said. 'She's rubbed me up the wrong way – a lot!'

Cape laughed and Anne Marie joined in.

'Sorry, I shouldn't laugh,' he said.

'It's okay. I needed to.'

'But you've had a good day here?'

'I've had a brilliant day.'

'Work in the garden can alleviate all sorts of trouble, I find. Everything just falls away as you focus on the job in hand. It's like being in a gym with a therapist.'

Anne Marie laughed again.

'I just hope Patrick manages to find his stride,' Cape said.

'He's still riling everyone.'

'Yes. It seems to be his default setting, but let's see how things go, eh? It's early days.'

Anne Marie nodded. 'Right, I'd better get going,' she said.

'Let me give you a lift.'

'It's okay.'

'It's dark now.'

Anne Marie looked up at the inky sky as if needing confirmation. 'Well, okay.'

She followed him as they walked to his car. 'Sorry about the mess. I shifted some compost the other day and it's still pretty grim in here.' He did his best to wipe the passenger seat down and the two of them got in. 'Whereabouts are you?'

'On the other side of the village.'

They drove the short distance. Parvington was short on street lighting, but the cottage windows were all ablaze.

'Here,' Anne Marie said a moment later.

'On the left?'

'Yes. Thank you.'

Cape cut the engine and waited. Anne Marie didn't move. 'You okay?'

'Yes.'

'You going home?'

She nodded.

He frowned. 'Anne Marie?'

'Yes?'

'Are you all right? Because there's no rush,' he added. 'I can sit here a while longer if you want.'

'No, I'm good,' she said, suddenly springing up and opening the car door. 'Thank you.'

'No problem.'

'I mean for today. For listening to me prattling on,' she said.

'It was my pleasure and you weren't prattling.'

'I'll see you tomorrow, okay?'

'You bet.'

He paused for a moment, watching as she walked up the path to the imposing mock Georgian frontage of her house. The porch light was on and he waited for her to get her key out and let herself in, but she didn't. She paused, seemingly searching the contents of her handbag. Had she lost her key? If so, why didn't she just ring the bell? There were plenty of lights on so surely somebody was home. No, she had the keys in her hands, he saw. So what was she doing?

At that moment, she turned around and saw that he was still there and gave a funny little wave, seemingly embarrassed at having been caught doing whatever she was doing. Cape waved back and started his engine and left. As he drove out of the village towards his own home in the Thames Valley, he had the strange feeling that Anne Marie would still be loitering on her porch.

Chapter 11

The bare hedgerows of the Thames Valley lit up in Cape's headlights as he drove along the winding roads home. Recent rain made the roads treacherous and had turned the lane to his cottage into a river. He slowed down, inching his way through the water and avoiding the potholes he knew lurked to either side of him. He'd once thought about updating his old car but, with the mass of tools he had to take everywhere and the state of the lanes in winter, it really wasn't worth it. Plus there was the issue of money. He couldn't justify spending on a newer vehicle.

Pulling up to his home, he saw the lights were on, but the curtains hadn't yet been drawn. He smiled as he saw Poppy skipping into the living room. He loved that she still skipped at ten years old. He watched her for a moment before getting out of the car and going inside.

'Daddy's home!' Poppy shouted, skipping down the hallway to greet him.

'Well, hello there!' he said with a laugh, kissing the top of her head and smelling the delicious strawberry-scented shampoo she adored.

'Come and see this,' she said, taking his hand and tugging him into the living room.

'What is it?'

'Wait and *see!*'

A moment later, Poppy was holding a book up to him.

'It's a colouring book. I didn't think you liked those anymore?'

'Well, I prefer making my own drawings,' she agreed, 'but this is different. Look.'

Cape flipped through the pages. 'They're all gardens,' he said, looking at the illustrations.

'And there's one that's just like our garden, Daddy.'

'Our back garden?'

'No, silly! Morton Hall. Look.' She took the book from him and turned to the page, presenting it to him proudly as if she'd unearthed a great treasure.

'Ah, topiary!' he said.

'They're not as good as when you draw your topiary animals, but they're still pretty good.'

It was then that Renee came into the room.

'It's spaghetti for tea, okay?' she said.

'Sounds great,' Cape said. After nothing but a limp sandwich and an apple for lunch, he didn't really mind what Renee was making for tea. 'You okay? Had a good day?'

'Yes, fine. You?'

'Really good.' He was just going to share his day with her – to tell her about Mac and his digger, finding the violin, the desecration of the yew bush and Patrick's more punishment – when she left the room.

'So, how did dance class go?' he asked Poppy.

Poppy frowned at him. 'When?'

'Today.'

'But I didn't have dance today.'

'You didn't?'

'Miss Powell told us last week that the studio had to be fixed. I think the floor's wonky or something.'

It was Cape's turn to frown. Had he got it wrong? He wouldn't be surprised, but he was sure Renee had told him she was taking Poppy to dance today.

He was just about to shout through to Renee when he decided to try something else first. 'What did you get up to, then, you and Mum?'

'We went shopping.'

'Did you? Where?'

'Henley.'

'Oh, nice.'

'Mum wanted a new suitcase. She said her old one wouldn't make a trip to the supermarket let alone—'

'Poppy? Have you washed your hands?' Renee shouted through from the kitchen.

'They're clean!' Poppy shouted back.

'That wasn't the question, was it?'

Poppy puffed her cheeks out. 'I'd better wash them. I've got a bit of blue pen on my little finger anyway.'

'Poppy?' Cape said as she reached the door. 'What did Mum say about her suitcase?'

'She told me not to tell you,' Poppy said.

Cape swallowed hard. 'But your mummy and I don't have secrets.'

'She bought me my own case too. Said it was my special gift for keeping quiet.'

Cape nodded. 'I see.'

'Don't tell her I said anything, will you?' Poppy said, her forehead creasing in anxiety.

'I won't,' he promised.

Sitting around the kitchen table eating their spaghetti later that evening, Cape was finding it hard to make small talk or follow what Renee was saying about some problem with local road works.

'I swear they're always digging that road up. Why can't they get it right the first time?'

Cape wasn't really listening. He could hear that she was talking, but the words meant nothing to him. The only thing he could think of was the fact that she'd lied to him. Was it the first time? Probably not. Would it be the last? He doubted it. A dark chasm was opening up inside him. He was living with a woman he couldn't trust and she was plotting to leave him and take his daughter with her, he suddenly felt quite sure of that.

'You're not going,' he suddenly blurted.

'Pardon?'

'You're not going to America.'

Renee clattered her knife and fork down. 'What are you talking about?'

Cape sighed. Wishing she'd just level with him. 'I know about the suitcases, Renee.'

Renee immediately glared at Poppy. 'Did you tell Daddy about the suitcases?'

'She didn't *need* to tell me,' Cape said, covering for his daughter.

'It just slipped out, Mummy. I'm sorry.'

'It's not her fault. I asked what she did when she told me she hadn't been to dance class.'

'I told you not to say anything,' Renee continued.

'I don't think that's the issue here,' Cape pointed out.

'Does this mean I don't get to keep my suitcase?'

'Poppy, sweetheart, why don't you go up to your room?' Cape said. 'Take your colouring book with you and show me one of the gardens you've done later, okay?'

She nodded, her face sombre.

'And you can keep your suitcase. Don't worry about that,' he added.

They both waited for Poppy to leave the room, listening to her as she collected some of her things from the living room before heading upstairs to her bedroom.

'Are you going to send me to my room now?' Renee asked him, standing up to clear the table.

'No, of course not. But I'd like an explanation.'

'About what?' she asked, taking his plate from him and heading towards the kitchen counter.

'About why you lied to me.' She paused for a moment. 'Renee? We need to talk about this.'

She moved over to the sink and clattered the plates into it. Cape got up from the table and joined her.

'You give me no choice,' she said.

'What do you mean?'

'You won't discuss this with me so I'm getting on with it on my own.'

'But we have discussed it,' he protested. 'It's just that I'm not giving you the answers you want to hear.'

He could see the tension in her shoulders and the sadness in her eyes and suddenly felt an overwhelming urge to hug her. He couldn't remember the last time they'd hugged. They hadn't been physically close for some time and that upset him greatly, but it was more upsetting to see her like this now.

'Renee, I know this means a lot to you, but you can't just go behind my back like this and organise something I'm not happy with.'

'I don't see why I can't go ahead.'

He frowned. 'Because we're a family. We do things together. Or, at least, we should.'

'But you don't want to go,' she reminded him. 'You keep saying that to me.'

'I'm just being honest and I'm really sorry that I can't be more enthusiastic about going because it obviously means so much to you.'

She turned away from him, pressing her hands against the kitchen counter. 'So, what do we do, Cape?'

He took a deep breath and moved towards her, reaching a hand out but stopping short of her shoulder before withdrawing.

'Why don't we wait until a time when we can all go?' Cape suggested. 'For a visit, I mean – to see Martina.'

'A visit?'

'Of course. Don't you think you'll want to visit first before making such a momentous decision? We can see how we feel about it then, okay?'

'You can't keep stalling this, Cape. I will go there.'

'I'm not stalling. I'm trying to come up with a reasonable compromise that we're all happy with, that's all. I'm not trying to thwart you, Renee. Really I'm not.'

She turned back round to him and he could see that there were tears glittering in her eyes.

'Come here,' he said, opening his arms to her, but she shook her head and left the room.

Later that night, after Renee had gone to bed and he was quite sure she was asleep, Cape took the two new suitcases up into the loft. A kind person would have said that he was merely protecting his family by hiding the suitcases. But someone else might have pointed out that Renee hated the loft and never went up there because of her intense fear of spiders and that Cape's move had accounted for that.

As he climbed back down the ladder and shut the loft door, Cape paused by Poppy's bedroom door and peered inside at the sleeping figure of his daughter, thinking of that tiny suitcase up in the loft. If he'd had his own way, he would have taken both suitcases back to the shop for a refund or had a bonfire when Renee was out at work. But the loft would have to do for now.

Sunday was brighter but colder than Saturday. After an uneasy breakfast, Cape had persuaded Renee to let him take Poppy with him. Perhaps Renee thought this gesture would help Cape forget about the suitcase business. He had no intention of mentioning it again. It was obviously impossible for them to have a proper conversation about that particular subject.

Indeed, he and Renee hadn't spoken much about anything over breakfast. She hadn't shown any interest in what he might be doing at Morton Hall that day and, when he'd asked about her day, she'd shrugged her shoulders and not said anything. More than ever he could feel the rift between them widening and he had no idea what was going to happen next. All he knew was that his home no longer felt like a home. There was always an uneasy tension in the air as if they were on the verge of something monumental, something final. Up until now, he hadn't wanted to push things to discover exactly what Renee was thinking or planning, but he had a feeling he was going to find out pretty soon. She'd lied to him: he felt he could no longer trust her, and it broke his heart to admit that he wasn't sure that this was something they could fix. She was the mother of his daughter, but she no longer felt like his partner. A partner didn't go behind your back. A partner didn't lie to you. And a partner shouldn't turn away when you tried to reach out to them.

He turned to look at Poppy now as she worked quietly alongside him in the garden. He had given her a pair of secateurs and she was wearing her very own pair of stout gardening gloves while she trimmed back a section of ivy from a wall.

He cleared his throat.

'Pops?' he began.

'Yes?'

'That suitcase business.'

'Am I still in trouble?'

'No! You were *never* in trouble.' He reached out and squeezed her shoulder. 'I – erm – well I want you to tell me if your mum ever talks to you about leaving, okay?'

'You mean going to California?'

Cape scratched his jaw. 'Does she talk to you about it?'

Poppy nodded. 'A bit. She says I'd love it over there. I'd get my own swimming pool and it's warm and sunny all the time, not like the bloody Thames Valley.'

'Poppy!'

'I'm just saying what she said.'

Cape bit back a smile. 'I know.' He'd recognised Renee's voice through his daughter, but it had still been a shock to hear her swear.

'So, you'll tell me, will you? I mean if she ever mentions going.'

'But we'd all be going together, wouldn't we?' Poppy asked.

Cape smiled. He had to try to make light of this. 'Well, you know – just in case she forgets to mention it to me.'

'She wouldn't forget, silly!'

Cape looked into the innocent eyes of his daughter. She was so trusting and so unsuspecting, wasn't she?

'No,' he said at last. 'Of course she wouldn't.'

She smiled up at him and then continued with her work. She was making good progress too, better progress than Patrick's boys, that was for sure. They were dawdling about, picking up stones and chucking balls of moss at each other.

'Pack that in, you two,' Patrick warned them. Along with the others, he was continuing to clear the path they'd begun the day before.

'Can't you keep those boys under control?' Kathleen asked. 'They're going to damage something.'

'Feel free to lend a hand,' Patrick said.

Kathleen glared at him. 'They're not really my responsibility, are they?'

Patrick guffawed. 'And here I was thinking we were a team.'

'Well, I didn't sign up for child-minding duties,' Kathleen said.

'And I didn't sign up for crotchety middle-aged-woman duties,' Patrick retorted.

Kathleen gasped, her mouth falling open in horror. '*What* did you call me?'

Patrick's face had reddened. 'I didn't mean to say that . . .'

Kathleen placed her hands on her hips. 'You seem *very* good at saying things you don't mean to say,' she pointed out before moving swiftly away from him.

'Kathleen – I really didn't . . .' He stopped, knowing the battle was lost.

Everybody looked on in silence, passing shocked glances to each other, and it took a moment for the group to stop staring at Patrick and Kathleen and continue with the job in hand.

'I thought we'd done this path-clearing job,' Erin said.

'I'm afraid the path goes right around the garden,' Cape told her.

'Ah!' Erin said.

'Not bored already, I hope?' Cape said.

'Oh, no!' Erin exclaimed. 'I just like to know what's ahead of me.'

'That's the thing – we're not really going to know until we start uncovering things,' Cape confessed.

'It's more like archaeology than gardening,' Dorothy said.

'We need that team off the television,' Kathleen said.

'But don't they only have three days to unearth things?' Erin asked.

'And we've got just a year,' Dorothy said. 'Do you think that's going to be long enough, Cape? Especially as we're all middle-aged or old and decrepit!'

Kathleen laughed but Patrick just shook his head.

'Seriously, Cape,' Dorothy continued, 'what do you think? Is a year enough time to really make a difference?'

Cape stopped work for a moment and pondered this. 'It's hard to say, but we'll give it our best shot and do what we can.'

'Is somebody going to inspect what we've done in that time?' Kathleen asked. 'Are we going to be graded or something?'

'I don't think so,' Cape said. 'From what I understand, we need to show our commitment to this place. I don't think we're going to be judged on how much we achieve, just that we've really put our hearts into it.'

'And our backs,' Mac added.

Everybody laughed.

'It's all going to look so different,' Anne Marie said.

'Of course,' Cape agreed.

'I mean; I'm going to miss it.'

'Miss what?' Kathleen asked.

'The romance of it.'

'What are you talking about?' Patrick said, his eyes narrowing at her.

'The overgrown garden. The briars, the long grasses, the tangles of nettles and the great swathes of ivy. I'm going to miss all that. It was beautiful.'

Patrick snorted.

'She's right,' Dorothy said. 'I'm going to miss the wildness too. There was something rather magical about it.'

Cape looked at Anne Marie, understanding her completely. She was losing a little piece of herself, he realised: the special place she'd come to sit was now being ripped away by Mac and his digger.

'A neglected garden can be a beautiful thing,' Cape said. 'It can be a place to dream as well as a habitat for wildlife.'

'So why are we working our fingers to the bone restoring this place?' Patrick asked.

'Because it was a little too neglected,' Cape said. 'It'd become unsafe, unusable.'

'We're breathing new life into it,' Dorothy said with a smile.

And that's when they heard the shatter of broken glass.

Patrick threw down his fork and took off into the walled garden while the rest them stood absolutely still, listening to the tirade he rained down upon his two boys.

'They went off,' Poppy told them.

'We've got to keep a better eye on them,' Dorothy said.

'They're Patrick's responsibility,' Kathleen said. 'We shouldn't have to babysit them.'

'But, if this garden is to be for the community, we'll have to learn to share it with children,' Cape pointed out.

Kathleen didn't look at all pleased by this and pushed her broom along the path with renewed vigour.

Patrick emerged from the walled garden, a hand firmly placed on each of his boys' shoulders. The others quickly got back to work, avoiding eye contact and thus embarrassment.

Cape walked towards Anne Marie. 'I'm sorry you're losing your sanctuary,' he told her.

'Yes, I hadn't realised until this morning,' she said. 'It looks so barren in the walled garden now.'

'But we'll plant it all up. It's going to be beautiful,' Cape said.

She nodded, looking as if she was going to say something else. 'Last night,' she began after a pause, 'it wasn't what you thought.'

'What do you mean?'

'When you were watching me.'

'I didn't think anything,' he said, although it had baffled him why she'd been dawdling before opening the front door.

'I needed a moment to gather my thoughts. That's all.'

'You don't need to explain,' he said. 'It's really none of my business.'

'I must have looked odd.' She gave a nervous laugh.

'No,' he assured her.

She looked down at the newly revealed path beneath her feet. 'Well, that's all I wanted to say really.' She turned to go.

'Anne Marie?'

'Yes?'

He cleared his throat and lowered his voice so that the others wouldn't hear. 'You know you can talk to me. About anything.'

She looked at him, her eyes seemingly full of emotion.

'I'm a good listener,' he went on, giving her a smile. 'If you want to talk, I mean.'

They held each other's gaze and then she nodded and turned away.

It wasn't until lunchtime that he got a chance to speak to her again. He instinctively knew where she'd be. While the others were doing their best to keep warm in the kitchen, Anne Marie was nowhere to be seen. He asked Dorothy to keep an eye on Poppy while he went in search of her. Sure enough, she was sitting on her bench in the walled garden. Mac had moved it to clear the space around it and now it stood in the middle of the freshly turned earth. She was wearing a thick winter coat, a green-and-blue scarf that had snaked its way around her neck and fingerless gloves while she ate a sandwich.

'I thought you might be here,' he said.

'I couldn't resist. Just for old times' sake.'

'Aren't you cold?'

'A little.'

'The others are in the kitchen. Mrs Beatty's put a heater in there, but it's still not very warm. Patrick says he's going to buy thermals as his unmentionables have turned to ice.'

'He said that out loud?'

'Yep.'

'In front of his boys? And Dorothy?'

'Everybody.'

Anne Marie bit her lip, but couldn't stop the laughter from bubbling out of her. 'I've never met anybody like him before.'

'Thank your lucky stars!' Cape said.

'You mean you have?'

'One or two.'

'I hope his boys settle into things. They don't seem happy to be here.'

'Yeah, that's putting it mildly,' Cape said. 'I wonder if there's a special project we can get them on – something Patrick can work on with them.'

'Maybe they could grow something together,' Anne Marie suggested. 'If the boys are encouraged to plant seeds and see them grow, that might get them excited about gardening.'

'Hey, that's a great idea!'

'And weren't we going to have a bonfire yesterday?'

'Ah, yes. That kind of got forgotten when the boys got lost in the maze, didn't it? But we could definitely set that up for this afternoon. It would be a nice way to round the weekend off.'

'And a good way to warm up!'

'Nothing better than a bonfire on a cold winter's day.'

A robin flew down from the wall and landed on a sod of earth, its head cocked to one side as it searched for worms.

'It's not the same,' Anne Marie suddenly said. 'This place.'

Cape looked around at the vast area of the walled garden that Mac had cleared. 'I know.'

'I'm going to miss that messy wilderness.'

'It's a different kind of wilderness now, isn't it?' Cape said. 'A wilderness of possibilities.'

She smiled. 'I like that. Gardeners are dreamers, aren't they?'

'Yep.'

'Do you go around the county looking at people's gardens and thinking what you'd do with them if they were yours?'

'Occupational hazard,' he confessed. 'It's impossible to pass a garden without wanting to plant something in it or take something out of it.'

'And I bet your own garden is amazing.'

'It's rather on the small side to be amazing,' Cape said. 'It's more practical. You know – a lawn for Poppy and the washing line, a tiny greenhouse and a couple of raised beds.' He laughed.

'What?'

'I'm just thinking of when we first moved there and I explained the importance of compost bays to Renee and how much space they'd take up. She didn't speak to me for days. Made me fence them off too.'

'But you got them?'

'Fuel for the garden. Nothing can work efficiently without fuel.'

They sat for a while longer, finishing their sandwiches and watching a flock of fieldfares fly over.

'I'm sorry you can't hide away on your bench anymore,' he said.

She turned to face him. 'Is that what you think I was doing – hiding away?'

'Weren't you?' He watched closely for her response.

'Of course I was,' she whispered, looking down at the ground.

Cape took a deep breath, fogging the air as he breathed out. 'I'm sorry you're not happy.'

'What?' She looked up at him, a flash of fear in her brown eyes. He held her gaze and watched a kaleidoscope of emotions dance over her face and then she sighed. 'I'm in a strange place at the moment. You'll have to forgive me if I brood a bit.'

'You're not brooding,' he insisted. 'Tell me what's going on.'

'You've said you're a good listener,' she reminded him.

'I am.'

She smiled. 'But if I start talking about all this, I might not stop,' she warned him.

'That's a chance I'm willing to take.'

'Are you sure? You might unleash a beast here! You see, I don't normally get to talk to anyone about any of this.'

'I'm happy to listen – really I am. If you want to talk, that is,' he said, holding his hands out, palms upwards as if in invitation.

Anne Marie gazed out across the walled garden. The robin was still hopping around and had been joined by a blackbird, who was moving with intent across the bare earth.

'Grant – my husband – doesn't like me being here,' she began. 'He doesn't like anything much, actually. Except his books. He loves his books. It's hard to compete with them and I've tried. For years, I've tried, but I don't really feel I'm there when I'm talking to him. I feel like I could be talking about anything: it doesn't matter *what* because he's not really paying attention.'

'He's an academic?'

'Yes. He's a lecturer at St Bridget's in Oxford. Literature. He specialises in Romantic poetry and he's writing a book.'

'Oh, wow. That's interesting.'

'You'd think so,' Anne Marie agreed, 'but he's writing about this obscure poet and – this is going to sound mean – but his poems aren't that good.'

'And that's the reason he's obscure, you think?'

'I do, but Grant won't hear my opinion about it, and I feel he's wasting such an enormous amount of time on this.'

'You've told him what you think?'

Anne Marie nodded. 'But I'm not an academic. I mean, I have a degree. Grant was my lecturer actually.'

'So he should value your opinion.'

She frowned. 'I've never thought of it like that before.'

'He's missing out if he doesn't talk things through with you.'

'You think so?' She sounded surprised by this declaration.

'Of course he is. You're smart, Anne Marie.'

'Really?'

'You don't think so?'

She threw out a laugh. 'I – well – I have a degree.'

Cape shook his head. 'That's all well and good, but you've got something more than a degree.'

'What?'

'Emotional intelligence,' he said. 'I've seen the way you work with the others here. You're really great with people. You know how to talk to them and, crucially, when *not* to talk to them – when to just listen.' He paused, wondering whether to go on and deciding that he would because it seemed obvious to him that this fragile woman really needed to hear his words.

'I overheard part of your conversation with Dorothy earlier,' he told her. 'You knew all the right things to say when she was talking about losing her husband. It was obvious that she needed to talk to someone and the look of joy on her face when she was sharing with you was really something. Your husband's a fool if he doesn't listen to you. Your step-daughters too. They're really missing out.'

Cape leaned forward to look at Anne Marie's face. She'd turned away from him and now he knew why.

'Oh, God – I've made you cry! Anne Marie – I'm so sorry. What an *idiot* I am!'

'No, no.' She gave a big sniff. 'I'm being silly, that's all. It's just that nobody's ever talked to me this way before. Nobody's ever—' she stopped.

'What? What did I say?' He rested a hand on hers.

When she looked at him, her big brown eyes were shining with tears. 'Nobody's ever praised me before.'

He frowned. Had he heard her right?

'You can't mean that,' he said.

She sniffed and then reached for a tissue from her pocket and blew her nose. 'Sorry,' she said.

'Don't apologise. I said you could talk to me, didn't I?'

'Yes, but I didn't mean to spill all this out on you.'

'It's okay,' he assured her. 'It's just that I'm sorry it's made you sad.'

'I'll be okay in a minute.'

He nodded.

'It's just an odd time for me at the moment. I feel like I'm moving through some strange twilight world where nothing's really happening.

It's like I'm watching everything from a distance. Except here. *This* is real. This place. This work. I really need this in my life at the moment.'

'And we need you,' he said.

She smiled. 'It's nice to be needed. I don't get that at home.'

Cape shook his head. 'That has to be one of the saddest things I've ever heard. God, Anne Marie – how can you live like that?'

She gave a little shrug. 'I don't know. I've just been floating along, I think, trying to get by.'

'That doesn't sound like much fun to me.'

'It isn't.'

'So you used to come here to think things through?'

She nodded. 'This place is such a wonderful escape. I think I would have gone a bit crazy if I hadn't been able to come here.'

'Does your husband know you used to come here?'

'No, he never knew.'

'You never told him?'

'I never needed to. He never noticed I'd gone.'

'He didn't notice?'

'When he isn't teaching, he's always in his study. He shuts himself away in there for hours.'

'And he's always done that?'

'Ever since I've been married to him and probably before,' Anne Marie said. 'He lost his first wife some years ago. I'm his second wife. The second wife and the second daughter.'

'Pardon?'

Anne Marie gave a tight smile. 'Just my little joke. I'm always second.'

Cape was about to ask her more when Poppy ran into the walled garden.

'There you are!' she cried. 'Elliot broke the toilet chain and his dad's furious with him. Apparently, he tried to swing on it like Tarzan.'

'He's lucky the whole thing didn't come crashing down on top of him,' Cape said, thinking of the high-flush toilet.

'That's what his dad said.'

Cape shook his head. 'I think we'd better find a really interesting job for those boys so they don't get themselves into any more mischief.'

As soon as Patrick appeared with his sons, Cape took him to one side and mentioned his idea of a special project for them.

'Sounds good,' Patrick said.

'You can make a start by gathering as many pots and containers as you can from around the garden. There are stacks of terracotta ones around the greenhouse. They'll need cleaning so get a bucket of water from the kitchen. I've got some brushes you can use.'

Patrick nodded. 'Hear that, boys? Get to it, then!'

They all worked for another hour after lunch and then they started making preparations for the bonfire, collecting leaves, twigs and branches and piling them up in the centre of the walled garden. Once it was lit, they all gathered around it, toasting their hands and smiling into the flames. Only Kathleen didn't look happy.

'You okay?' Cape asked her.

Kathleen gazed into the orange flames. 'I wasn't sure if I'd be able to look at a fire again,' she told him.

'Do they know what caused your fire?' Patrick asked.

'They've said it was an electrical fault. Some connection that wasn't working properly.'

'At least it wasn't your fault,' he said.

'It might have helped if it was,' she said.

'How come?'

'Because I've got all this rage inside me that I can't direct at anything in particular. At least I could have blamed myself if I'd caused it.'

Patrick looked at her as if she was a crazy woman. 'That doesn't make any sense.'

'I can't rant at a piece of faulty electric when I think of all my photo albums that were destroyed. All those precious pictures of my family, my parents and grandparents. All my letters and diaries and scrapbooks. My pictures and my novels. My clothes and other bits and pieces I'd collected over the years. Things I'd kept around me for so many years that they'd become a part of me.'

Erin, who was standing on the other side of Kathleen, reached out a hand and rubbed her shoulder.

'That's horrible,' she said. 'I can only imagine what that feels like.'

'Everything gone within hours. A whole lifetime.'

'But you're alive, my dear. You're still here,' Dorothy said.

Kathleen nodded. 'I know,' she whispered. 'I know.'

They all gazed into the fire, the darkening sky making the flames seem even brighter.

'I can't remember the last time I had a bonfire,' Dorothy said. 'We used to have them at our last house. We had a big garden and there was always something to burn. We used to have a permanent place where we'd heap cuttings from the garden and, every so often, we'd have a big fire. We'd invite neighbours and friends and cook baked potatoes in the embers.'

'Sounds wonderful,' Erin said.

'Oh, it was,' Dorothy said. 'You know, I haven't thought about that in ages.' Her eyes misted over as she gazed into the flames and remembered the past.

'Always check for hedgehogs,' Mac suddenly blurted.

'Pardon?' Dorothy said.

'Hedgehogs like to burrow into bonfires. If you've made a big heap in advance of your fire, it's advisable to move it all in case a hedgehog has made a home there.'

'Oh, I see,' Dorothy said.

'Right!' Patrick said, clapping his hands together. 'Best get back home.'

'Aw, Dad!' Elliot groaned. 'Do we have to? I want to watch the fire.'

'Me too,' Matthew said.

Patrick looked puzzled by this outburst. 'Well, okay,' he said, scratching his chin. 'I guess we can stay a bit longer.'

'Can we bake potatoes like Dorothy said?' Matthew asked.

Dorothy laughed. 'Well, I don't have any potatoes on me at the moment, but I'm sure that could be arranged some time.'

'Really?' Matthew said.

'Absolutely.'

Patrick nodded towards Dorothy and she nodded back at him.

Cape glanced at Anne Marie and they exchanged smiles. The group, it seemed, was going to get along just fine.

Chapter 12

'Who's Angela?' Tobias demanded.

They were standing in the living room where Emilia had been rearranging the furniture. She wasn't allowed to redecorate, but at least she could assert herself by moving a few pieces around. It drove Tobias mad.

'Put that bloody chair back, will you? And tell me who this Angela is.'

'I've told you. She's a friend from university.'

'And why's she coming here?'

'Because I've been home for weeks now and I've seen nobody but you, Jay and Mrs Beatty.'

'And what's wrong with that?'

'Nothing. It's just that I'd like bit of female conversation. With a friend.'

'But *I'm* your friend.'

Emilia took a deep breath, trying to keep calm. 'Yes, but you're my brother.'

'What does that mean?'

'It means that I can't talk to you about everything.'

This, she quickly realised, had been exactly the wrong thing to say.

'You *should* talk to me about everything,' Tobias said. 'I don't want you hiding things from me, Emilia.'

'I'm not hiding things from you.'

'What aren't you telling me then?'

'Nothing! It's just different talking to a girlfriend.' She sighed and reached across to hug him. He was dangerous when he got sulky. Most people could bounce back from the sulks, but Tobias could make them last for days, weeks even, and she didn't want that with Angela arriving. It would be just like him to make her friend's visit all about him, dominating the house with his brooding presence and creating an unpleasant atmosphere.

'She'll want you to show her around,' Emilia went on, releasing her brother from her hug. 'I've told her you give a mean tour.' She hadn't, but she thought this would please him.

'I'll have to see what sort of a person she is before I take her around the house,' Tobias told her. 'We have a special collection here.'

'I know we do. Angela will love it.'

'Because you can't take just anybody round this house.'

'Quite right, but Angela adores art. She'll be very appreciative. Like your friend Jay,' she said, careful to stress that Jay was *his* friend.

'And where's he gone by the way?'

'He had to go up to Scotland,' Emilia said. 'A prior engagement with a gallery in Edinburgh.'

'And he's still nowhere near finishing your portrait?'

'I think there's still a lot of work to do on it,' Emilia told him. What she didn't say was that Jay had been making several other sketches of Emilia, filling sketchpad after sketchpad just so they could be in each other's company for as long as possible. He could have finished the portrait long ago, but he hadn't told Tobias that.

'It's a very large portrait,' Emilia added. 'I think you'll be thrilled with the result. It'll be worth the wait.'

'It better had, otherwise I won't pay him,' Tobias declared. It was then that he noticed something. 'Why are you wearing those horrible jeans?'

'Because it would be a bit odd if I met Angela in Oxford wearing a nineteenth-century gown. I doubt I could even get in the car wearing one, let alone drive!'

He seemed to consider this for a moment and then nodded. 'I don't like it when people come here.'

'I know you don't.'

'I like being just us.'

'That isn't very healthy, is it?'

'Why not?'

'Because you need friends, Tobias. Don't you ever want to talk to anybody?'

'No, I don't.'

'Well, *I* do. Anyway, I'm sure you'll like Angela. She's fun.'

'I don't need fun in my life.'

Emilia shook her head in despair.

'Just keep her visit as short as possible,' Tobias warned.

'She's coming for a week,' Emilia announced and then bit her lip, thinking it best to get things over and done with as quickly as possible. 'And she's staying here.'

'What?'

'She's coming down from York, Tobias.'

'What's that got to do with anything? Why can't she stay in a hotel like a normal person?'

'Because we've got all these rooms doing nothing.'

'That's how I like them.'

'But it's such a waste.'

'They're my rooms, Emilia.'

'*Our* rooms. And it's only for a week. It'll fly by. You'll see.'

Angela Godfrey was such a wonderful breath of fresh air that just seeing her joyous face made Emilia happy. With her short blonde curly hair, which bounced around her face, her pink lipgloss and blue eyeshadow, she looked like a flower personified, and Emilia adored her.

'Emmy!' Angela cried as she caught sight of her outside Oxford train station.

'Angie!'

They threw themselves at each other, hugging and kissing each other's cheeks.

'God, I've missed you!'

'I've missed you too!' Emilia said, suddenly realising how very long she'd been without female companionship. After all, Mrs Beatty wasn't exactly the sort you would confide in about the new love of your life. 'Come on, let's get home. Tobias is anxious to get his car back in one piece.'

They chatted non-stop on the journey back to Parvington. Angela had never been to Oxfordshire before and commented on the prettiness of the villages they drove through. It was a gentler landscape than that of North Yorkshire. Her home was on the edge of a village overlooking a windswept moor. It sounded very romantic to Emilia – very *Wuthering Heights* – but Angela soon put her right, telling her that there was nothing romantic about knotted hair and a wind-chapped face.

Turning into the driveway of Morton Hall, Emilia awaited her friend's response and it wasn't long before it came.

'Blimey, this is your home?'

'It is.'

'It looks like a museum.'

Emilia laughed. 'It's Victorian Gothic. Not everybody likes that style.'

'It's a bit—'

'Austere?' Emilia suggested.

'Yes.'

'It's more beautiful inside. Wait until you see the paintings and the furnishings.'

It was a sad fact that Emilia hadn't had many friends visit her home over the years. Her mother had once given her and her brother permission to have a birthday party each when Emilia was six years old. She had invited a few friends from the local primary school and Joanna Morton had almost swooned with exhaustion by the end of the day, fanning herself with a copy of *Country Life* and declaring that she was very glad that the whole business was over. Emilia couldn't remember much about her brother's party. He'd been ten or eleven and she'd spent most of it outside, away from the noise that the boys were making. Other than those two parties, she could count the number of visitors on one hand, and her brother seemed intent on keeping it that way. But she was determined to defy him in this.

She parked her brother's car and helped Angela with her luggage, entering the hall a moment later.

'This really *is* like a museum!' Angela cried as she looked at the impressive hallway and the sweep of stairs.

'Wait until you see your bedroom.'

Emilia led the way, listening to Angela's low whistles as she took in the many portraits that lined the gallery.

'Are all these your relatives?'

'Every single one.'

'Wow, you know I don't even know who my dad is,' Angela reminded her. 'Mum's got her suspicions it was somebody she met at a pop concert, but she doesn't really remember.'

Emilia grinned. 'We can go back six generations quite easily.' She stopped outside a bedroom and opened the door, motioning to Angela to go in first.

'Emmy! This is like a hotel!'

'I hope not. Tobias would hate that.'

'A film set, then. Something from a wildly romantic film where the heroine floats around in a dress the colour of moonbeams.'

Emilia laughed.

'My own four-poster bed! Really?'

'Bought specially for you!'

'No!'

Emilia smiled. 'No – it's been here as long as the house.'

'And nobody sleeps in it?'

'Not very often.'

'It's not haunted, is it?'

'Probably!'

'I don't care,' Angela declared, flopping down onto the embroidered counterpane. 'It'll be worth being haunted by ghosts to sleep in a room like this.'

'I'll leave you to settle in, then,' Emilia said. 'You've got a bathroom through there with fresh towels, but call if you need anything else.'

'Do I get my own butler?'

'I'm afraid not. There's only Mrs Beatty.'

'Oh. I was kind of imagining some gorgeous young man in black and white.'

'Sorry to disappoint.'

'But I'm not disappointed. Emmy, this is amazing. I can't believe anyone still lives in houses like this. I thought they were all destroyed after the war or turned into hotels or country clubs.'

'A lot of them were.'

'It certainly beats our stone semi.'

'I bet your stone semi is perfect,' Emilia said. 'I bet you don't have trouble getting warm in your home, or getting to one end of it and then realising that the very thing you most want is about half a mile away at the other end.'

Angela laughed. 'No chance! It's absolutely tiny. If you sneeze in one room, the next one shakes.'

Emilia smiled. 'Come downstairs when you're ready and we can have some tea in the garden.'

'Sounds heavenly!'

Emilia left her, a huge smile on her face. It was so good to have her friend there. The house suddenly seemed full of light and happiness and she was looking forward to the next few days.

Passing Tobias's room, Emilia stopped, wondering whether she should let him know that Angela had arrived. He must have heard them coming up the stairs. Indeed, she'd half expected him to show his face. She had to admit to being relieved when he hadn't made an appearance because she wanted to keep her light-hearted mood for a little longer and she had a feeling that Tobias would spoil that. He would speak to them in that condescending way of his, believing himself to be the adult and the two of them children, frowning at them and disapproving of everything they did and said. She couldn't face that yet and so she walked on past his room and went downstairs into the kitchen to make the tea.

A little while later, Emilia and Angela were sitting out in the garden drinking tea and eating cake.

'This is the life,' Angela said, gazing across the garden at the giant topiary beasts. 'I could get used to this. Mind if I move in full-time?'

'I wouldn't mind at all,' Emilia said. 'But somebody else might.'

'Tobias?'

Emilia nodded.

'I have yet to meet this mysterious brother of yours.'

'Don't be in a rush to.'

Angela pointed a finger at her. 'You see, it's remarks like that that make me curious about him.' She paused. 'Tell me what he's like.'

Emilia took a deep breath. 'How to describe Tobias,' she began. 'He's serious to the point of being dour. He's intense. He's passionate about this place and the family history. He's protective and . . .' She paused.

'What?'

She shook her head. 'Nothing.'

'*Nothing?*'

Emilia bit her lip. She was going to say that her brother was strange, but that was going too far. She was desperate to be honest and to talk, to really talk to her friend but, when it came down to it, she found that she couldn't.

'He's Tobias,' she finished, giving a little laugh that sounded false even to her own ears.

They sat contentedly for a few moments, enjoying the warmth of the summer sunshine.

'So, what do you do here all day?' Angela asked.

'Well, I take care of the house.'

'Isn't that what Mrs Beatty does?'

'It is, but I supervise. I tell her what needs doing. And I've been going through all the family archives recently. It's fascinating stuff. The Mortons never threw anything away. I'm finding all sorts of marvellous things like shopping lists from the 1880s and a diary my great-grandmother kept.'

'But to spend all your days here,' Angela said. 'I mean, don't get me wrong, this is a beautiful house, in an eerie kind of way, but I think I'd go mad if I stayed here all the time.'

'I thought I would too. I mean, I do get a little bored. Sometimes. That's why I'm so excited you're here. But this place has a strange effect on you. You find yourself slowing down and living with the rhythms of the house. It's hard to explain. Maybe it will be easier if I show you.'

'Where are we going?' Angela asked as Emilia got up from the bench.

'To a very special room, but we'll have to be quiet.'

'Why?'

'Because we don't want Tobias finding out. Or Mrs Beatty for that matter.'

'Oooooh, I love a bit of subterfuge!'

'Come on.'

They took their cups and plates to the kitchen and then climbed the staircase once more.

'This house really is amazing,' Angela said as they rushed down the landing together. 'I still feel as if I'm going to bump into the ghost of Queen Victoria any moment.'

They came to a stop beside a door, Emilia turning to face her. 'This is it.'

'What?'

Emilia opened the door into the room and Angela charged inside. 'Wow! This is the best yet!' she cried.

'This was Clarissa Morton's room. She was the first lady of Morton Hall,' Emilia told her friend, but she wasn't sure if she was listening.

'Look at the paintings on this bed,' Angela said, moving forward to admire the Pre-Raphaelite beauties on the panels. 'And the stained glass and the tiles around the fireplace. Are they De Morgan?'

Emilia nodded proudly.

'This is amazing.'

'Wait until you see the clothes.'

Emilia walked across the handwoven carpet and opened the wardrobe, smiling as she heard Angela's gasp of delight.

'Are these all – you know – original?' she asked as she came forward.

'Of course they are. Everything in this house comes straight from the Victorians. You know, we don't even have a television? I think Tobias has got a radio, but everything else is at least a hundred years old.'

Angela shoved her head into the wardrobe, her fingers hovering over the clothes encased in their wrappings. 'These are beautiful, and there are so many of them.'

'Everything was kept. I don't think they threw anything away,' Emilia explained. 'Let's get some of them out, shall we? You can't really see them properly in there and you're going to want to see the detail, I promise you. Give me a hand.'

'Can I? Can I really?'

'Of course you can. Only don't let Tobias know. He's a bit possessive of these. Well, he's possessive of everything really. He only lets me
wear the dresses he chooses each day.'

Angela's head snapped around and she stared at her friend. 'Wait a
minute. You *wear* these dresses?'

Emilia nodded. 'All the time. It was strange at first, but I soon got
used to it.'

Angela reached a hand out and took hold of Emilia's arm. 'Am I
getting this right? You wear them like they're everyday clothes?'

'Yes.' Emilia grinned. 'I know, that must sound weird.'

'Erm, yeah! Just a bit.'

'But it isn't really. The clothes are here and they're beautiful. Why
shouldn't I wear them?'

Angela's frown had deepened, but then she laughed. 'You're crazy,
you know that? Do you also go around speaking like a heroine from a
Tennyson poem when nobody else is here?'

'No, of course not. And don't look at me like that. I'm not crazy.'

'Well, you're eccentric or something then.'

'You'll see what I mean in a moment.'

'What do you mean?'

'We'll both try some dresses on together. There's still a few here I
haven't worn yet.'

'You're kidding? I can try these on?'

Emilia smiled. 'You won't ever want to wear jeans again!'

For the next half hour, the two young women laid out dress after
dress on the bed, gasping and giggling. It was as if they were children
and had been given free rein with the largest dressing-up box in the
world.

'Look at this one!' Angela cried as she held up an emerald gown in
the finest of satins.

'And this,' Emilia said, stroking one made from amethyst velvet.

'The beading on this one is exquisite.'

'And the lace on this one.'

They cooed over the rainbow array of materials and then the real fun began as they shed their twentieth-century clothes and cautiously stepped into the dresses that transported them back to the nineteenth century.

'Oh, my god – look at you!' Angela screamed.

'Look at *you*!' Emilia echoed. 'You look amazing!'

Angela turned around, discovering the large mirror on the other side of the room.

'Wow!' she said a moment later and then turned back to Emilia. 'Lady Emilia, I presume?'

'Why, yes, Countess Godfrey!'

They did a funny little curtsy at each other and then laughed.

'Quick – I want to try that amazing red one on next,' Angela said.

'That's one of my favourites although Tobias has told me I should never wear it.'

'And you do *everything* your brother says?'

'No, of course not,' Emilia said, 'it's just there's no point upsetting him if I don't have to. He takes things to heart and it isn't worth the stress.'

'Well, I think you should wear it right now,' Angela said, handing her the red dress.

Emilia could feel the temptation racing around her body like some kind of mad energy.

'I don't think I should,' she said, shaking her head and trying not to look at the beautiful dress.

'Don't you want to?' Angela asked.

'Oh, I want to all right!'

'Well, go on, then!' Angela thrust the dress towards her and Emilia could do nothing but take hold of it.

'This is just wrong.'

'Why? It's no different from the other dresses, surely?'

'But Tobias said—'

'What? What right does he have to tell you what you can and can't do? Anyway, I don't see him here so where's the harm?'

Emilia looked up at her friend. 'You're worse than a devil sitting on my shoulder and whispering in my ear.'

'Go on – I want to see that dress on you *now*! And I'm going to try on that emerald one.'

A few silent minutes passed as the two of them changed dresses and then the miraculous moment of transformation occurred and they stood side by side, staring at their reflections in the mirror.

'No wonder you just stay home playing dress-up all day. I would too if I lived here!'

'I told you you'd be hooked.'

'This dress feels amazing. It's like a great big beautiful comfort blanket.'

'That's probably because we're not strapped in with corsets.'

'So, you wear these with your normal knickers and bras?' Angela asked.

'Absolutely.'

'I don't suppose I could take some of these home with me.'

'What, to walk around the Yorkshire Dales in?' Emilia asked.

'Yes, that would look a bit odd in Upper Wharfedale! Hopping over stiles and scaring the sheep in a Victorian gown.'

They both laughed and soon found they couldn't stop. It was one of those wonderfully rare moments when laughter just takes over, bubbling up from inside you in an unstoppable flow. Emilia could feel actual tears coursing down her face and she knew that they were making too much noise – *way* too much noise – but she couldn't help it. She hadn't laughed so much in ages. She couldn't remember the last time, in fact. Perhaps that's why she couldn't stop now.

'What the *hell* is going on in here?'

Their laughter stopped and Emilia looked up to see a red-faced Tobias standing in the doorway.

'Tobias!' she said, swallowing hard and wiping the tears from her cheeks. 'Were we making too much noise? I'm sorry.'

'What are you doing in here?' he asked. 'You know you shouldn't be in here unsupervised.'

Emilia could feel the weight of Angela's gaze upon her.

'I'm sorry. I thought it would be all right to show Angela.'

'And that dress! I've told you I don't want you wearing that one. It's obscene – take it off!'

'But it's just a dress like the others.'

'It's the dress of a Jezebel.'

Angela spluttered. 'A Jezebel? Who says stuff like that anymore?'

Emilia's eyes widened as she saw the look of disapproval on her brother's face. She wasn't sure what had upset him the most: her own disobedience or Angela's impertinence.

'Tobias?' she quickly intercepted. 'This is my friend, Angela.'

Angela stepped forward and, before Tobias could say anything, had leaned forward and kissed his cheek. He looked so shocked by this that Emilia felt sure he was going to explode.

'I'm *so* pleased to meet you!' Angela blurted. 'You're very bossy, aren't you?'

A look of pure shock landed square on Tobias's face as if he'd never been confronted by such a woman in his life, which he probably hadn't.

'I beg your pardon?' he said.

'I said, you're very bossy,' Angela repeated. 'Look, we were just being silly and trying on a few clothes. It's what girls do.'

'Maybe, but not with these sorts of clothes,' he said, walking towards the bed where the heaps of gowns lay. 'These are special. They're valuable. One of a kind. They're not toys to be played with.' His right hand reached out to them, but didn't quite touch them, his fingers hovering over them with a kind of painful possession.

'We were being very careful with them,' Emilia told him, 'and we were going to put them back right away.'

'No we weren't,' Angela said. 'We were going to waltz around the house and garden in them, weren't we, Emmy?'

Emilia's mouth dropped open in horror as Tobias's stare moved from Angela to her.

'You were what?'

'Angela's just messing with you.'

Now it was Angela's turn to stare at her and she did so with her hands on her hips.

'We thought you'd like it,' Angela continued. 'We thought you might join us and wear something too. Not a dress, obviously.' She gave bright laugh. 'But surely there are some men's clothes from the same period?'

Emilia watched her brother's reaction. She'd never seen him looking so baffled.

'Look – I'd really rather you didn't—'

'I think you'd look splendid as a Victorian gentleman. You have that kind of timeless face, don't you think, Emmy?'

'Well, I . . .'

'Maybe we can find you something to wear in one of the other rooms. After all, it's a bit odd to expect Emmy to dress up when you don't join in too, don't you think? I'd say there was something a bit suspicious about that.'

Emilia watched as Angela walked towards her brother and linked her arm through his.

'Emilia said you'd give me a tour of the house,' she went on. 'I'd like that. Can I keep this dress on while you show me around? I'd very much like to.'

Tobias studied her face for a moment and then gave a little nod.

'Excellent!' Angela said and Emilia watched dumbstruck as, arm in arm, they left the room together.

Chapter 13

The cold, dark days of January finally came to an end and were replaced by the more hopeful month of February with its noticeably longer days and much-anticipated pops of colour from the crocuses. It was wonderful to be able to work in the garden until five o'clock, and the team made the most of it. Cape remembered the protests at the beginning of the project and how many of their team had said that they could only give the minimum five hours each week, but that had changed and all seven of them could be found in the garden on both Saturdays and Sundays, sometimes for the entire duration of the day, and very often during the week too.

Mac had taken delivery of a lorryload of well-rotted manure, which was now being wheelbarrowed into the walled garden and heaped into the raised beds that had been newly made by Patrick and his sons.

'We'll take care of that,' Patrick had declared as soon as he'd seen it, surprising everyone as he flashed a smile at the group.

'He's changed his tune,' Kathleen said.

'He's officially in charge of the veg beds,' Cape said. 'Him, Matthew and Elliot.'

Dorothy looked impressed. 'Good for them. And what are the rest of us in charge of?'

'Any special requests?' Cape asked.

'I wouldn't mind unearthing some of those statues that you mentioned were hiding around the garden,' Dorothy said.

'Be my guest,' Cape said with a happy gesture of his hand. 'Kath?'

'Oh, I'm easy. Point me anywhere you need help – as long as it isn't green or fragile, that is.'

'I don't mind either,' Erin said.

'Neither do I,' Anne Marie agreed. 'I'll go where I'm needed.'

'Actually, I'll help Dorothy with the statues,' Erin added and Dorothy smiled. The two of them seemed to have formed a special relationship, Anne Marie thought. It was as if Dorothy had adopted Erin as a surrogate daughter – perhaps in place of her two daughters whom she'd mentioned led their own very separate lives.

And so they all found their personal rhythm. Cape and Mac were gentle directors, always making sure that everybody was happy with the chores assigned to them. Anne Marie was particularly impressed by Cape's patience, especially when he had his daughter with him. What an angel she was, Anne Marie thought. She'd been instantly charmed by the young girl, and Poppy appeared to like her too, which made Anne Marie both happy and wistful. Growing up, Anne Marie had always imagined that she would have children of her own one day and, when she'd met Grant, the subject had never come up. She knew he had two daughters and had assumed he'd be happy to have more children. It wasn't until a year into their marriage that he broke the news.

'I have my family,' he'd said. 'I can't be disturbed at this stage in my career by babies.'

Anne Marie had been dumbfounded. He hadn't considered her needs and desires at all. There'd been one time, shortly after he told her this, that she'd thought she'd been pregnant. For two whole weeks, her emotions had been out of control, swinging from secret elation at the idea of being a mother to terrible nervousness at the thought of telling Grant the news. How would he take it? Would he think she'd tricked him? The thought had occurred to her, but she would never have done that.

She remembered the precise moment she'd found out it was a false alarm. It'd been a good job that she'd been working at home on her own that day for she hadn't been able to control her disappointment. By the time Irma and Rebecca arrived home from school, all her tears had been dried, her face washed and calmed and her disappointment locked deep inside her where nobody had ever thought to look for it.

Now, watching Poppy with Cape, she couldn't help but long for that most delicious of relationships. She'd never have it with Irma or Rebecca. They would forever remain hostile towards her, she knew that.

'Hey there,' Cape said, sneaking up on her as she stuck her spade deep into the earth. 'You doing okay?'

'Good.'

'Yeah?' He didn't sound convinced and she leaned forward on her spade and looked at him. 'Poppy said you looked sad so I thought I'd come over and see if you're okay.'

'She said that?'

'She did.' Cape glanced over at his daughter who was wrestling with a very large weed. 'She's very good at picking up on moods.'

'It's funny she should pick up on this one because I was thinking about her.'

'Were you?'

She nodded. 'You're so lucky to have her.'

'Oh, I know.' Cape smiled. 'I don't know what I'd do without her. You know, I never imagined myself as a father. Some people always know they're going to have a family, don't they? They have this little scene in their head of what the future will be like, but I never had that. I mean, other than becoming a gardener. But, now that I have Poppy, I can't imagine any other way of life.'

She looked at the tender expression on his face and something inside her seemed to melt. Never, not once, had she seen Grant look at his daughters that way. Had he ever, she wondered? Perhaps when they were little, they'd been closer. Perhaps things had changed for them all after Lucinda had died. But she'd never heard him praise them or seen him admire them.

'You have two step-daughters, right?' Cape said.

'They're not mine,' Anne Marie blurted. 'I mean, I'll never be close to them. Not like you with Poppy.'

Cape frowned. 'That's a shame. They're missing out on a pretty amazing step-mother.'

Anne Marie laughed at that. 'I doubt they'd see it that way.'

'And you've tried to get close to them?'

Anne Marie swallowed. 'I've tried.' Her mind flipped back over the years, remembering one particular incident and wondering if she dared to share it.

'I once took the girls out to a stately home. It wasn't a grand one like Blenheim Palace. It was smaller, more intimate, and famous for its dolls' houses, which I thought might be of interest to them. I was really looking forward to the day. I'd got up early to make packed lunches, careful of the girls' likes and dislikes, and off we went. I remember they weren't very chatty in the car. In fact, I don't think they spoke at all. I didn't worry at first, but it soon became uncomfortable and I realised that they'd made a pact to freeze me out with silence.'

'That's awful!'

'I'd never experienced anything like it,' Anne Marie confessed. 'I tried to ignore it at first – pretend that it wasn't happening. I'd ask them questions and then end up answering them myself. As the day went on, I felt sure Rebecca – the youngest – would crack. I could see her mind working overtime, but Irma would give her these warning looks.'

'So they didn't say a thing?'

'Not a single word. We walked around the house and garden together and I swear I could feel myself almost breaking into a sweat like I was about to have a panic attack. It was the most horrible feeling.

I didn't know what to do. Should I confront them, shout at them, shake them by the shoulders until the words were forced out of them?'

'What did you do?'

'I took the coward's way out and did nothing but be nice to them. I bought them ice cream and then took them round the gift shop where I bought them both a little book about dolls' houses. I thought there might be trouble if I just bought one so I was careful to make sure they had one each.'

'That's very thoughtful of you, especially considering how they treated you.'

'I wish I hadn't now. When we got outside the shop, Irma opened her book up and spat inside it.'

'You're kidding!'

'I'm afraid not,' Anne Marie said. 'Rebecca looked genuinely shocked at first, but then she followed her sister's lead and spat on hers too. I asked them both what their father would say about their actions.'

'And what did they say?'

'Nothing. Irma just laughed.'

Cape shook his head, a disgusted look on his face. 'Did you tell your husband?'

'God, no. I doubt he would have believed me anyway.'

Cape rubbed his chin. 'Anne Marie, I have to say that I've never heard anything like this in my life. How do you cope with it?'

She gave a little shrug. 'I – I don't know.'

'Because I seriously wouldn't put up with behaviour like that,' he told her. 'Tell me it's got better since then.'

She shook her head. 'I can't, because it hasn't.'

'But they speak to you at least?'

'Monosyllabic answers and groans of protest.'

'And how long have you been living like this?'

'Grant and I got married four years ago.'

'And he has no idea that his daughters treat you like this?'

Anne Marie didn't answer for a moment. 'No.'

'Then he sounds like a big part of the problem,' Cape said. 'You need to tell him, Anne Marie. You can't be expected to share your home, your *life* with these bullies. And that's what they are – make no mistake. They might only be children, but they're bullies and that's totally unacceptable.'

Anne Marie stared at him, hearing his words, but unable to respond for a moment. 'But they lost their mother when they were so young,' she said at last.

'That isn't an excuse to treat you the way they do.'

Anne Marie sighed. She'd reached out to the girls so many times, trying to understand how they must feel to have a new mother figure. It must have been so hard for them, but Cape was right: that didn't give them an excuse to treat her so badly.

'I mean, I can't tell you what to do here,' Cape continued. 'It isn't my place, but I hate to think of you so unhappy. You deserve better than that.'

She nodded, thinking how kind he was and realising that she'd been more honest and open with this man in the brief space of time that she'd known him than she had with her husband over the course of their marriage.

'Promise me you'll at least say something,' Cape said, reaching out and taking her cold hand in his warm one and squeezing gently. 'I can't believe your husband hasn't noticed you're unhappy.'

'I'm very good at hiding it.'

'But you shouldn't have to hide.' Cape cocked his head to one side to try to catch her eye. 'You know that, don't you?'

It was then that Poppy ran up to them. 'Look at this, Daddy!' She was holding a massive weed in her tiny fists and didn't notice her father quickly dropping Anne Marie's hand.

'Did you pull that up yourself?'

'Of course!'

'Wow! My strong girl. You'll get big muscles.'

'I hope not,' she declared. 'Muscles wouldn't look nice in my tutu.'

They watched as she skipped away, intent on pulling up even more weeds.

'She's wonderful,' Anne Marie said.

'Yep.'

They watched Poppy for a moment and then Cape turned to Anne Marie again.

'You will think about what I've said, won't you?'

'I will,' she promised.

He gave her a smile and she found herself smiling back.

She spent the rest of the day thinking about what Cape had said to her and how he'd made her promise to do something about her situation, to *say* something to Grant. The more she thought about it, the angrier she became with herself. What was wrong with her? She'd spent the last few years living like some kind of slave, moving to the beat of somebody else's drum. She had made no protest, had never stood her ground and had turned into a kind of nonperson. Perhaps one of the problems had been that she'd never really had anybody to talk to. All of her friends had families and problems of their own and it wasn't in her nature to bother them.

She couldn't talk to her mother and, even if she did broach the subject, her mother wouldn't believe anything was wrong because she adored Grant. To her mind, he was just the sort of respectable husband Anne Marie should be with. Marrying Grant was one of the few things Anne Marie had managed to do right as far as her mother was concerned. And she couldn't exactly confide in her clients. She could just imagine how that would go.

Please find attached my notes on your manuscript. Now, I'd like to tell you a bit about my dysfunctional family.

She wasn't sure how she got through the rest of the day in the garden. Now that Cape had planted the idea in her head, she could think of nothing else. Suddenly, all the years of subservience, of being nothing more to the Keely family than a personal punchbag, came rolling forward to taunt her. How had she let things go on like this for so long?

She managed to work until four o'clock before nearly self-combusting with her emotions. It was no good – she had to get home.

'Cape?' she said, walking up to where he was doing his best to get a rotten fence post out of the earth.

'Hey – you all right?'

'I'm fine. Okay if I leave a bit earlier today?'

'Sure. Whenever you like.'

'I feel bad because there's still a good hour of daylight left, but there's something I've got to sort out.'

'No worries,' he told her.

'I'll see you bright and early tomorrow. Bye, Poppy.'

'Bye, Anne Marie!' Poppy chimed, looking up from the patch of earth that she'd successfully cleared all on her own.

'You off, my dear?' Dorothy said, raising her head from a tangle of ivy she was trimming as Anne Marie walked by.

'Got something to deal with that can't wait a moment longer.'

'Sounds ominous,' Dorothy said.

'It is,' Anne Marie said and, because she really couldn't wait, she forewent her usual route through the church and walked straight down the main driveway.

Once home, she tapped on Grant's study door.

'I'm back!'

She heard a grunt of acknowledgement from within the depths of the room and sighed. Her husband really should be called *Grunt* rather than Grant, she thought with a mutinous grin. It fitted him perfectly.

She went upstairs. The thump of an obnoxious bass was coming from Irma's room and she could hear Rebecca humming to herself which probably meant that she was plugged into something.

Anne Marie went into the bedroom, taking off her earth-encrusted clothes and having a quick shower before putting on a fresh pair of trousers and a clean jumper. She knew what she was going to do. She'd been thinking about it all afternoon, though having it planned out in her head wasn't keeping the nerves at bay.

She took a deep breath and walked downstairs and into the kitchen where she made a cup of tea which she took through to the living room. As usual, she watched the clock on the mantelpiece, waiting for the second hand to reach five. When it did, she gave a little nod, only this time, for the first time ever, she wasn't going to walk through to her husband's study with the cup of tea. This time, she went and sat on the sofa, picking up a book from the coffee table and drinking the cup of tea herself. She felt a mixture of nerves and wonderful rebellion, wondering when Grant would notice that she hadn't come in with his five o'clock cup of tea.

It didn't take long. It was about eight minutes past five when she heard his study door open.

'Anne Marie?' he called.

She waited a moment before responding. 'Yes?'

'Where are you?'

'I'm in the living room.'

He appeared in the doorway with a frown on his face.

'What are you doing?'

'What does it look like I'm doing? I'm reading a book.'

'But it's after five o'clock.'

'Yes,' she said matter-of-factly.

'You didn't bring me my tea.'

'Didn't I?'

'No,' he said, his tone perplexed, almost angry. 'What's going on?'

'Nothing's going on.'

'But you've got a cup of tea.'

'Yes.'

He scratched his head. 'But you always make *me* a cup of tea at five o'clock.'

'Exactly.'

'Eh?'

'I'm trying something different today: making *myself* a cup of tea. You should try that, you know.'

'But I'm working.'

'And I've been working too.'

'At the garden?'

'Yes.' She waited for him to ask her more. Maybe he'd ask about the progress of the walled garden or how the group was getting along. But he didn't. He merely shook his head and left the room. A moment later, she heard him clattering about in the kitchen, obviously making himself a cup of tea.

I'm going to sit here and do nothing, she told herself, although every bone in her body was urging her to go through and help him, but only because that was what she was used to doing. She had been conditioned to do that and she never got any thanks for it. Not that she did it because she expected to be thanked. But she did expect to be loved. That was the thing that was missing here. A lot could be overlooked if you knew somebody loved you. You wouldn't mind the tedious repetition of chores if you received a gentle squeeze or a sweet kiss every so often. But to give so much of oneself and not receive anything – that wasn't a good deal. She was empty with the lack of love she received from the Keely family. She felt wrung dry by it and she knew she had to end it.

When had the end truly begun, she wondered? When had Grant turned his attention so resolutely away from her and into his books? Anne Marie thought that it was little by little. It must surely have been or else she would have noticed, wouldn't she? When had she stopped being the very centre of his attention? When had she morphed from lover to housekeeper?

She glanced at the photograph of the two of them taken at Ullswater on their honeymoon. That week in the Lake District was still so fresh in her mind. They'd visited the haunts of Wordsworth and Grant had quoted *Lyrical Ballads* at every opportunity. They'd sat on great boulders overlooking deep waters, strode across high fells hand in hand and spent cosy evenings in local pubs talking and talking. Why didn't they talk anymore? Where had that love gone, she wondered?

But, perhaps the biggest question of all was, why had she accepted things for so long? How had she taken on this role that Grant had given to her? It made her so mad now that she thought about it. She'd allowed herself to be used like this, to turn away from all the hopes and dreams she'd once had.

More clattering was heard from the kitchen and then she heard him return to his study, the door closing behind him a little louder than normal. His way of a protest. Anne Marie couldn't help feeling disappointed, but what had she expected? Had she imagined that realisation would dawn on Grant? That he'd instinctively know that her not making him a cup of tea was symptomatic of something that ran much deeper? No. He probably just thought that she was being odd and that the moment would no doubt pass.

But it wouldn't, would it? The moment she was now living in meant that she could never go back. By listening to Cape and acknowledging all she had been slowly coming to realise over the past few months, she had set herself on a course that meant that her future might be uncertain, but she was heading straight towards it with eyes wide open.

Anne Marie wasn't aware that she'd been sitting on the sofa thinking and reading for so long until Irma's voice pierced her ears.

'I'm hungry,' she complained. 'What's for tea?'

Was it seven o'clock already? She looked at the clock. No. It was half past seven. Late enough for Irma to realise that something was amiss.

'I said, what's for tea?' Irma repeated.

Anne Marie shrugged. She felt very silly pretending to be petulant, but there was also something wonderfully freeing about it.

'Have whatever you want,' she told her step-daughter.

'What do you mean?'

'I mean, you're a fifteen-year-old girl. You should be able to fix yourself something for tea by now.'

Irma frowned, looking a lot like her father as she did so. 'But you always make tea.' She sounded like him too.

'Yes, but not anymore.'

'Are you on strike?'

'Maybe.'

Irma stared at her and Anne Marie thought that she saw something approaching respect in the girl's eyes, but the moment was interrupted as her sister came into the room.

'What's going on?' Rebecca asked. 'Where's tea?'

'She hasn't made any,' Irma said.

'Why not?'

'Why not?' Anne Marie said. 'Because half the time you two don't want any or only eat half of it or sulk over it. I simply thought, why bother? I'm done with tea.'

Rebecca looked shocked. She'd obviously never been challenged in such a way before.

'You're being silly,' Rebecca announced.

'She's on strike,' Irma said. 'We'd better have toast.'

The two girls left the room and Anne Marie almost had to sit on her hands to prevent herself from getting up and helping them find something to eat. It was ridiculous. She never got any thanks and yet she felt this compulsion to take care of them all. What was that about? How long had she been a doormat? Grant and his daughters were perfectly capable of taking care of themselves. They could all cook, clean and tidy up and yet they seemed to have happily forgotten these skills the moment she walked into their lives.

It was after nine that night when she dared to knock on Grant's study door.

'Come in,' he called back gruffly, looking up when she approached his desk.

'Hello,' she said, suddenly feeling intensely shy.

'No dinner tonight?' he asked.

'No,' she said.

He didn't question her and she bit her lip, feeling that she'd been childish and mean in not making them dinner. But then she took a deep breath, refusing to let Grant make her feel like that anymore.

'I thought *you* might want to make dinner for a change?'

He frowned. 'I'm writing a book.'

'Yes, but you're always writing a book. You can't not eat whenever you're writing a book.'

'But you always make din—'

'Grant,' she interrupted, 'we need to talk.'

He looked confused by this declaration. 'Well, I'm busy.'

'You're always busy.'

'Yes. I know.'

'And we never talk anymore. Haven't you realised that?'

'What do you mean?'

'I mean,' she turned around looking for a chair to perch on, but there wasn't one. The last thing Grant would want would be anybody else sitting down in his study. 'I mean, we never spend any real time with each other and just talk. You're always working and I'm always – well – working around you working.'

'What do you want to talk about?' he asked, removing his glasses and gazing at her and, for a brief moment, she thought she glimpsed the man she'd fallen in love with. 'Because I'm really making good progress with this and want to get back to it.'

And there it was, she thought. That's where she stood with him.

'It doesn't matter,' she said.

'It'll wait?' he asked.

'Yes. It'll wait.'

That night, Anne Marie found it difficult to sleep. She lay awake in the dark bedroom, Grant tossing and turning beside her. He wasn't happy. Like his daughters, he was used to getting his own way and she had challenged that. She smiled, wondering what Cape would say when she told him what she'd done. It was funny how often she thought of him and she couldn't wait to see his face when she recounted her evening. She could imagine him smiling, perhaps even laughing. Maybe he would even take her hand in his again. She caught her breath at the thought of it. There was something about Cape that made her feel so very safe, which was a feeling she hadn't had in a long time. He made her want to be honest, to speak the truth about what she was thinking and feeling. He also made her realise that somebody did care about her and that it wasn't her husband.

But the glow from her brief victory soon faded as she remembered the scene in the study and how Grant had made her feel so worthless with the utterance of just those two words, 'It'll wait?'

She stared at the ceiling for a bit before reaching her hand across the bed to touch Grant's shoulder.

'Grant?' she whispered into the dark. 'Are you awake?'

He mumbled something incoherent.

'I really need to talk to you.'

He mumbled something else that sounded suspiciously like a string of curse words.

'It's important,' she tried again, waiting for a moment in the hope that he would rouse himself. 'Grant?'

There was no response and she soon heard the soft regular sound of his snores.

The next morning, she got up while it was still dark. Grant was asleep, his bare back facing her, exposed. She paused a moment and then reached across the bed, pulling the duvet up so that it gently covered him. The so-familiar shape of him brought tears to her eyes because she knew this was the last time she would look at him that way, with this closeness and intimacy. But the man she'd been sharing her bed with, her life with, didn't really notice her or even take the time to talk to her. She truly felt that she could have been anybody. It didn't matter to him who cooked his meals and kept his house and slept alongside him. *She* didn't matter.

She picked up a small suitcase and quickly packed a few things, and then went to retrieve her laptop from her study. She'd come back for her few other personal possessions another time when she wasn't feeling so emotional. For now, she just had to get out of there.

It was too early to go to Morton Hall so she drove around the country lanes for a bit, parking in a village she'd always adored and taking a footpath that led up to the Ridgeway. She'd grabbed a blueberry muffin from the kitchen before leaving and she ate that now as she walked up a steep hill, passing the sleeping thatched cottages and breathing in the icy February air. Snowdrops shivered in the frosty shadows and she spied a pair of red kites circling in the pale blue sky.

The ground was iron-hard beneath her feet, but she kept walking, soon getting into a happy stride that helped to clear her head. She needed this, she thought. Before she joined the group at Morton Hall, she needed to be on her own for a while.

Never did she imagine that she would be in the position she was in now. When she'd married Grant, she'd thought it would be forever.

She'd happily taken on the mantle of step-mother to Irma and Rebecca, knowing that it wouldn't be easy. She knew she'd never be able to replace their mother, and she'd known that there was a great resistance to the girls welcoming her, but she'd imagined that things would ease over time and that the two girls would come to accept her. They might never love her as a mother, but they might at least come to respect her, like her even, share confidences and ask for advice. But that had never happened and it wasn't likely to now, was it?

Annoyingly, there was a little part of her that was anxious about what Grant would do without her. How would he cope with teaching, writing his book and taking care of his two daughters? Well, whatever he'd done before she'd entered his life, he'd have to do again, wouldn't he? He'd probably hate her for walking out. He'd blame her for disrupting his studies, she was sure of that. Anne Marie had given him the great gift of time by taking care of everything for him, but it had been at her own expense and she'd received no thanks for that service.

She stopped where the path split by a wood and turned around, viewing the landscape below her. The hill she had climbed afforded her a fine view of the Chiltern village below. Woodsmoke was rising from some of the chimneys as people awoke to start the day. It was still early and so Anne Marie continued walking, telling herself that everything was going to be all right. The long days of insecurity and isolation were over and she promised herself that nobody would ever make her feel so completely ignored again.

It was just after ten o'clock when she arrived at Morton Hall. She hadn't realised she'd walked so far along the Ridgeway, but she felt so much better for the exercise and the freedom that the countryside had provided her with that morning. She hadn't made her mind up whether to tell the group what had happened. It was all so fresh and raw that she didn't trust herself not to burst into tears but, as soon as she saw Cape's friendly smile, she knew she couldn't hide the truth.

'Hey, you!' he called as she approached him. 'I wasn't sure if you were coming today.'

She took a deep breath and looked him square in the eye.

'What's wrong?' he asked.

'I think I've left my husband,' she told him.

Cape was pacing up and down the path, trying to catch Anne Marie before she left for the day. A sudden downpour had stopped the group from completing a full day's work and it was decided that it would be best to down tools.

Cape watched as Patrick and his sons left. They were closely followed by Dorothy and Erin. Mac was next, leaving just Anne Marie and Kathleen. They were in the kitchen together. He hadn't had a chance to speak to Anne Marie since she'd dropped her bombshell because she'd deliberately made herself scarce by choosing to work in a quiet corner of the garden whereas Cape had been busy with Mac, sawing down some of the more dangerous branches of a walnut tree in the nuttery. He'd been anxious to speak to her, but hadn't had a chance. Until now.

As he walked into the kitchen, Kathleen was wiping down the kitchen table while Anne Marie was drying the mugs before putting them away in a cupboard. He cleared his throat.

'Okay?' he asked her.

'Yes, it's been a good day,' Anne Marie said.

'I saw you working with Patrick and his boys,' Cape said, addressing Kathleen.

She nodded. 'I'm kind of warming to them,' she confessed. 'We actually had a conversation that didn't involve insulting one another too.'

'That's certainly progress,' Cape said.

'He was telling me a little bit about his wife. She sounds like a piece of work. He thinks she might have left with an old boyfriend of hers and he believes that she was still seeing him throughout their entire marriage.'

'Really?'

'He found one of her old phones and – well – there were messages. The sort of messages you don't expect your wife to be sending or receiving from somebody else.'

'Poor Patrick,' Anne Marie said.

'And poor boys. I can't imagine a mother walking out on her own children,' Cape said.

'Yes, I think that's the thing that's shaken Patrick up the most.' Kathleen finished wiping the table and rinsed the cloth at the sink. 'But I think this time with his boys is really making a difference. He told me that they just shut themselves away at home. You know what kids are like these days – glued to their computers or tablets – and Patrick's struggled to know how to reach them. But being here with none of those distractions, he said he's really beginning to connect with them.'

Cape grinned. 'That's good.'

'Isn't it?' Kathleen said.

'Kath,' Cape said after a pause, 'would you mind if I have a word with Anne Marie?'

'Of course not,' Kathleen said. 'Anne Marie? I'll wait for you outside, okay? There's something I want to run by you.'

Cape shuffled his feet uneasily as he waited for Kathleen to leave.

'Is everything okay?' Anne Marie asked him.

'No. I've been frantic about you all day.'

'You have?'

'Of course I have. One day I'm giving you a bit of friendly advice and then the very next day you tell me you've left your husband.'

She smiled.

'It's not funny,' he told her.

'I'm not laughing.'

'Are you going to tell me what's going on?'

'I told you. I've left him.'

'So I gather.' He pulled a chair out from the table and sat down and Anne Marie did the same thing. 'I feel dreadful,' he said. 'Was I the reason this happened?'

Anne Marie gave him a comforting smile. 'Oh, Cape! Have you been worrying about that all day?'

'Yeah, of course I have!'

'But this has been coming on for some time now. Don't blame yourself. You just helped me to see things clearly.'

'I can't believe you've really done it.'

'Neither can I, but I have.'

'And you're okay?'

She nodded. 'I think so, yes.'

He watched her closely, checking to see if there was a flicker of indecision in her answer, but there didn't seem to be.

'What did he say when you told him?'

She bit her lip.

'What?' he asked.

'I didn't exactly tell him.'

'You *didn't* tell him you were leaving?'

'Not exactly.'

'What do you mean? Either you did or you didn't.'

'Okay,' she said. 'I didn't.'

Cape shook his head. 'You've got to talk to him.'

'I know. But not now. Not yet. I need some time to be alone and think things through. I can't do that in that house. I can't breathe in there, let alone think.'

'But won't he be worried?'

'I doubt it. He'll just think I'm here for the day. He won't notice that I've packed anything. I only took the bare essentials.'

'And tonight? He'll notice then, surely?'

She didn't say anything for a moment but then nodded. 'He might notice.'

'I think he will unless he's a total fool.'

'I doubt he'll notice until tea time and he might not even notice then because I didn't make it last night. He'll just think I'm going through a funny phase and give me a wide berth. He doesn't like confrontation. He'll immerse himself in his books. But he might realise something's up at bedtime.'

Cape felt astounded by what she was telling him. 'He *might* notice at bedtime?'

She shrugged. 'Or he might be so tired, he'll think I went to bed after him and got up before him. He might not realise for days.'

'Are you kidding me?'

'We're not like normal couples, Cape. We don't talk. We work. Separately. We share the same house, but he never asks me how I'm feeling. He doesn't seem to see me at all. I couldn't take that anymore.'

'I know,' he said gently, his hand reaching out and covering hers. 'Have you anywhere to go?'

She shook her head. 'I hadn't really thought about that. My mission had been to get out of the house and I didn't think what I was going to do after that.'

'Have you family you could stay with?'

'I could go to my mother's, but her home's a bit on the small side. Anyway, I couldn't bear to hear what she'd say about what I've done.'

'She can stay with me,' Kathleen suddenly piped up as she walked into the kitchen. 'I didn't mean to earwig, but – well – I guess I was. But you could stay at mine, Anne Marie. There's plenty of room and I'm not opening up for guests until Easter so I've got three rooms you can choose from.'

'Oh, Kath, that's so kind, but I couldn't put you out.'

'You won't be. It'll be nice to have somebody to share the house with again.'

'Really? You're not just saying that?'

'I'm honestly not.'

Anne Marie stood up and Cape watched as she walked over to Kathleen and gave her a big hug.

'Thank you!' she said. 'You're a life-saver.'

Cape followed them outside.

'You'll be okay?' he asked Anne Marie.

'I'll be fine.'

'You call me if you need anything,' he told her and then wondered what Renee would make of him receiving phone calls from a woman who'd just left her husband after he'd had a chat with her.

'Thanks, Cape. You've been wonderful.'

He smiled, but he didn't feel very wonderful. He felt anxious, perplexed and deeply concerned for the new friend he was beginning to feel very fond of.

***

It was strange to leave Morton Hall and not go back to her own home, Anne Marie thought. Kathleen hopped into her car and the two of them set off for the recently rethatched bed and breakfast in the heart of the village.

'It's a bit of a shell at the moment, I'm afraid,' Kathleen said as Anne Marie parked her car outside.

'I'm sure it will be wonderful,' Anne Marie told her.

'It really will be nice to have some company,' Kathleen said. 'If I'm honest, it's been a bit lonely since the fire.'

'You must let me know what I owe you for the room.'

Kathleen batted a hand in the air. 'No, no. I wouldn't hear of it.'

'But I insist on paying my way,' Anne Marie told her as they got out of the car. She grabbed her suitcase and laptop and Kathleen opened the little white gate that led into her front garden.

'I'll tell you what – help me out with a bit of decorating and we'll call it quits. I can't stand painting walls!'

'You're on!' Anne Marie said.

Kathleen hadn't been exaggerating when she'd said that her home was a bit of a shell. It was all bare walls and floors with the sparsest of furniture in each room, but it was such a warm and welcoming sight that Anne Marie immediately fell in love with the place and could easily imagine how delightful it would be once everything was up and running again.

'It's taking an age to sort things out with the insurance,' Kathleen informed her. 'I've managed to redecorate most of upstairs, but I'm living with the bare essentials downstairs and putting everything I buy on credit cards.'

'It must be really difficult for you.'

'It's not been easy, that's for sure. It's so silly, but you totally take everything for granted, don't you? I mean, I had this funny old armchair for years. It was one of the first things I bought when I left home and got my own place. It seemed terribly expensive at the time even though it was in the sale, but it was so sweet and comfortable. I loved that chair and I know I'll never find its like again. Silly, isn't it?'

'No, not at all,' Anne Marie insisted.

'And a cute little wooden stool which my house rabbit had partially chewed. That was a part of my personal history. You can never get things like that back, can you?'

She led her up the stairs and turned right onto a narrow landing.

'I think this is the nicest room,' she said a moment later, opening a door into a bedroom. 'It gets the morning sun and is lovely and light. It's not much to look at, but you should be comfortable.'

Anne Marie took in the double bed and single wardrobe and the small bedside table on which sat a lamp. The floral fabric of the curtains and bedding made the simple room both pretty and feminine.

'Oh, it's lovely, Kath. Thank you.'

'There's a small en suite through that door. I'll let you settle in. Come downstairs when you're ready and I'll make us some tea.'

Kathleen left the room and Anne Marie sat down on the bed. The enormity of what she had done hit her again. She'd left her husband, her step-daughters, her home.

She reached for her mobile and switched it on. It had been off while she'd worked at Morton Hall and now she checked to see if there were any messages. There weren't. Had Grant even noticed that she wasn't home?

She took a deep breath and quickly texted him.

I won't be coming home. AM.

He'd probably think nothing of it. He might simply imagine that she was spending some time with her mother. She waited a few moments to see if a reply came, but wasn't at all surprised when there was none.

Chapter 14

Cape took a deep breath of icy air as he stopped digging for a moment, looking down the great sweep of lawn which ended at the River Thames just outside Medmenham. The house, a Palladian manor in red brick with huge sash windows across three floors and great columns either side of the front door, belonged to his favourite clients, Colonel and Mrs Shelton. They'd asked him to create some more flower beds and redefine the existing ones. It was hard work, but it was a very good way to keep warm. It also gave him time to think about what had happened the day before.

He still couldn't believe it. Anne Marie had left her husband, and she'd sworn that it had nothing to do with the conversation they'd had. But that seemed a bit of a coincidence, didn't it? He was quite sure there was no way she'd have done that if he hadn't given her the idea of speaking to her husband and standing up for herself. Or would she? He was beginning to realise that there was much more to Anne Marie than he'd ever imagined.

The temptation to ring her had almost got the better of him several times the night before. He'd paced the kitchen, his mobile in his hand, wondering if he should reach out and make sure she was okay. It would be another week before he saw her again at Morton Hall. She'd proved herself quite capable of taking care of things, but there was something about her that brought out the protective side of him and, more than anything else, he wanted to check up on her.

He gazed out across the silvery-blue of the river, but all he could see was Anne Marie's face: beautiful, solemn and framed by that lovely red hair. He swallowed hard, acknowledging the fact that he was teetering on the precipice of something very dangerous. Anne Marie might have left her family home, but she was still very much married, and Cape was as good as married too although Renee was as distant and as irritable as ever.

Cape shook his head as he remembered the most recent incident. He'd offered to take them all out for fish and chips on Saturday night and she'd told him not to be silly. What was silly about fish and chips? They'd done that all the time when they'd first met, chatting and giggling together as the car fogged up with steam. Was a portion of vinegar-soaked chips in the car not good enough for her anymore? Was it not *California*-enough for her?

As soon as the thought entered his head, he felt mean for having it. He of all people knew what it was to have a dream. His dream might have been simple enough: to become a gardener – and with the love and support of his father he had achieved that dream. But Renee's was now threatening his own. That was the heart of the problem, wasn't it? They wanted different things and he didn't know what to do about it.

He picked up his spade again and pushed it hard into the ground. He really wasn't sure what was going to happen to his little family unit, but he had a feeling that the decision wasn't going to be his to make. He truly felt that Renee was slipping away from him and the worst thing about it was that he wasn't even sure that he wanted to stop her.

Anne Marie had woken up on that Monday morning to a room flooded with winter sunshine. Kathleen hadn't been exaggerating when she'd said the room got the morning sun, and Anne Marie was delighted to have such a comforting start to her day.

Kathleen had been a total sweetheart, making them both a slap-up breakfast and clearing a small table for Anne Marie to use as a makeshift office for her editing work. Kathleen had left after breakfast. While the bed and breakfast was undergoing renovations, she had taken a part-time job on the reception of a nearby hotel, so Anne Marie had been told that she had the place to herself each morning: she aimed to do the bulk of her work during that time, leaving her afternoons free to help Kathleen.

But that first morning's work had been interrupted. She'd just made herself a cup of tea, fired up her laptop and got comfortable when her mobile rang. It was Grant. She looked at his name flashing up, wondering whether to answer or leave it to go to voicemail, but that would just be delaying the inevitable, wouldn't it? So she took his call.

'Where the hell are you?' he shouted down the phone. 'You didn't come home last night, did you?'

Had he only just noticed?

'Anne Marie?'

She hung up on him. She couldn't talk to him when he was in that kind of a mood because it would be all about him and he simply wouldn't hear her.

It was pretty hard to concentrate on her work after that, but she refused to let Grant get the better of her. She wasn't going to have him speak to her like that ever again.

By lunch time, she felt brave enough to switch her phone back on. There were five messages.

Anne Marie? I said, where the hell are you?

She pressed delete.

Look, this isn't funny, Anne Marie. I demand you—

Delete.

This is getting serious, now. I'm not able to work for worrying about you. It's really selfish of you to—

Delete.

Hello? Anne Marie?

Her finger hovered over the delete. It wasn't Grant: it was Cape.

I'm just wondering how you are. Hope you're okay. Give me a call if you need to talk, all right? Okay, then. I'll – erm – see you around. Bye.

She took a deep breath. He'd sounded truly anxious about her, which was more than could be said for her husband. She played the fifth and final message.

That's it, Anne Marie. I'm not going to keep calling you if you're simply going to bugg—

She pressed delete and made herself some lunch.

By Thursday, Anne Marie felt it was time to confront Grant and sort things out. It seemed strange that he hadn't worked out that she was actually still in Parvington. If he'd taken a simple walk through the village, he would have spotted her car parked outside Kathleen's. But the only time Grant left the house was to go to work and that meant him leaving from the other side of the village. The girls caught their bus from that side too. Anne Marie was only a short walk away from them, but they had absolutely no idea.

After consulting his timetable, she drove the short distance to Garrard House late that morning when she knew he would be teaching. Walking through the front door knowing that she would never live there again was a strange experience; she had to suppress the lump in her throat as she entered the bedroom and caught sight of their wedding photograph on the dresser. How long ago that day seemed now. She barely recognised the smiling woman she'd been back then. Where had she vanished? Where had all that sparkle gone?

Looking up into the mirror behind the photograph, she saw the pale-faced woman she'd turned into, the woman who didn't laugh much anymore, the woman who found it hard to even have a conversation. But there was a determination in the large brown eyes staring back at her. She hadn't given up completely. She still had a life to live and she was determined to make it a good one, and so she got to work, hauling her biggest suitcase out from under the bed and packing the rest of her clothes. She then ventured up into the loft where a supply of boxes was kept and filled them with her books and the few pieces of crockery from the kitchen that belonged to her. It pained her to leave the photo albums, but she was only a small part of them. Instead, she took one of the smaller framed photos of their wedding. Grant would be sure to notice if she touched any of the thousands of books in his library, but she felt quite sure that he wouldn't miss this photo.

Packing her car with her things, she promised herself that she would return later that evening. It wouldn't be easy and she was absolutely dreading it, but she would be a coward if she didn't face things head on and Grant deserved to know what was happening.

Anne Marie recognised Kathleen's car parked outside her bed and breakfast when she got back, but she frowned when she saw another vehicle alongside it. It looked like Cape's car, but what would he be doing here?

She got out, grabbing one of her boxes of books, and walked up the path. The front door was already open, saving her the trouble of finding the key Kathleen had lent her, and there stood Cape.

'What are you doing here?' she asked in surprise.

'I was worried about you,' he said.

'You don't need to be worried about me.'

'Maybe not, but I can't help it. Are you okay? Here – let me.' He reached out to take the box from her.

'I'm fine. Kathleen's taking good care of me.'

'I'm sure she is.'

'You really came over to see how I am?' She smiled as Kathleen appeared in the hallway.

'Cape's here. Well, you can see that. Isn't he sweet?'

'Yes,' Anne Marie said. 'But you should have just rung me. You didn't need to come all the way out here.'

'It's no bother, really.'

'I've put the kettle on for you both,' Kathleen said. 'I'm nipping out to the shop for a paper.' And she was gone before anybody could question her. Anne Marie wasn't sure she liked the implication of that. Surely Kathleen didn't think there was anything going on between her and Cape, did she?

Cape cleared his throat, suddenly looking awkward at being there.

'I'll make us some tea,' Anne Marie said, and Cape followed her through to the kitchen.

'Has Grant been to see you?' he asked.

'Here? No! He doesn't know where I am.'

'Really?'

'I'm going to see him tonight,' she explained. 'I've just been to collect some of my things.'

'So you're serious about this? You've really left him?'

Anne Marie got two mugs from the cupboard and made the tea. 'I wouldn't have walked out if I hadn't been serious.'

'Of course not.'

They walked through to the living room and sat down on the sofa together as it was the only place for them both to sit.

'Kathleen's getting her place back bit by bit,' she told him.

'She's amazing.'

'She is, isn't she?'

'But not as amazing as you.'

Anne Marie caught her breath at his declaration. 'I'm not amazing.'

Cape smiled. 'No? What would you say you were then? Brave? Courageous?'

She shook her head. 'I've just been a fool not to have acted sooner. But you helped me to see that the time had come.'

Cape swallowed hard. 'I feel really bad about that.'

'Don't,' she told him. 'Please don't.'

'I can't help it. I feel like I might have pushed you into doing that.'

'But it was *my* decision,' she assured him, 'and it needed to be made.'

Cape took a long slow sip of his tea.

'I needed to do it, Cape,' she whispered. 'I needed to leave him.'

He nodded and sighed. 'I know,' he said at last.

'He'd never do this.'

'Do what?' he asked.

'Just sit and talk like we're doing now. I think we'd have been all right if he paid me even the smallest attention.' She paused and then continued. 'I remember there was this one bad day I was having. A real stinker. I'd been doing some editing for a small publisher I'd really loved working with the authors, but the publisher refused to pay me for the work I'd done – which was pretty considerable – until the book was on sale and earning. I was fuming. I'd put so much time and energy into it. Anyway, I tried to talk to Grant about it, and you know what he said?'

'What?'

'He said, "You'll sort it out" and then shut himself in his study. *You'll sort it out.*'

'In other words, *he* didn't want to help you sort it out?'

'Exactly.'

'Maybe he had complete faith in you.'

'Or maybe he just wasn't interested in anything that was going on in my life,' Anne Marie said. 'That's what it felt like.'

Cape put his empty mug on the table in front of him.

'Do you mind me asking why you married him?'

Anne Marie gave a little laugh at that and then she sighed, her mind flying back to those early heady days when she'd been a student of Dr Keely's at St Bridget's College in Oxford.

'He was handsome, smart and witty,' she said, 'and he used to pay me attention. We'd talk too – walking around the quad after lectures, discussing poetry and all the great nineteenth-century novelists we loved. I thought I was in love and that it would last forever, but there wasn't anything beyond those conversations. He never really wanted to get to know *me*.' She looked down at her hands, her fingers knotting themselves together. 'He just wanted a like-minded person to share the load with. I think he might have picked any of the students in my class and been happy.'

'I don't believe that,' Cape said. 'He chose you because you're special.'

'Really? I think he chose me because I don't fight back. At least, I never have until now. He got the measure of me pretty quickly. He knew I'd always try to do what was right and that I wouldn't make a scene.'

'I'm sure there was more to it than that. He must have known how wonderful you are.'

'It's kind of you to say that, but he never made me feel very wonderful.' She paused again. 'I'm sorry, I didn't mean to go on like that.'

'Hey, I asked you, didn't I?'

'Yes, you did,' she said, 'and I bet you won't ever make that mistake again!'

They exchanged awkward smiles.

'How are you? How's Poppy?' Anne Marie asked.

Cape visibly relaxed. 'She's good. She talks about Morton constantly.'

'Patrick's boys seem to be enjoying it now too.'

'Yeah, it's great how Patrick's motivated them.'

'I think you helped a lot with that.'

Cape shrugged. 'I just pointed them in the right direction.'

She smiled. She loved his modesty. 'I think everyone's getting a lot out of the garden. You know, I was wondering if that might have been Miss Morton's intention.'

'What do you mean?'

Anne Marie took a sip of tea. 'I keep thinking about our little group and why she picked us all. Did she know what was going on in our lives? Like Kathleen who suffered this awful fire, and Dorothy who lost her husband. Miss Morton couldn't just have randomly plucked our names out of a hat. I think we might have been specially chosen.'

'You mean like charity cases?'

'Perhaps,' Anne Marie said. 'Maybe she thought we all needed the release that gardening brings.'

Cape looked thoughtful. 'I like it. I've always thought of gardening as a release too. A kind of therapy.'

'And she knew that it would do us good.'

'You think she knew about your marriage?' Cape asked.

'I don't see how she could, but I think she was aware that I visited the garden.'

Cape nodded. 'I wish we knew more about her.'

'Erin said Mrs Beatty took her to one side on Sunday just before she left and asked if she'd be up for working in the house.'

'We're going to lose her help in the garden?'

'I don't know. But we might find out more about Miss Morton if Erin works in the house.'

'She's got a degree in art history, hasn't she? Maybe that's why Miss Morton chose her for this project.'

Anne Marie felt excited by this. 'You think so? That never occurred to me, but it makes total sense.' She smiled at him, but a shadow seemed to have passed over his face.

'Cape? What is it?'

He shook his head. 'Nothing. I was just thinking.'

'What about?'

'I don't want to bother you with all this.'

'But you've just been listening to all my woes,' she reminded him.

He gave a little smile. 'I was just wishing that I could persuade Renee to join our group.'

'Your partner?'

He nodded. 'I've never been able to get her into gardening, but I'm pretty sure it would help us come together again. Like it's helping Patrick and his sons. I've mentioned the project to her a couple of times, but she isn't interested.'

'Are things difficult at the moment?'

'That's the understatement of the year.'

'I'm sorry.'

'Yeah, so am I. I don't know what's gone wrong. One minute, everything was good. We'd found our home, we had Poppy, our jobs were going well . . .' His voice petered out. 'What the hell happened? I thought we wanted the same things but, now, I'm not so sure. I think she's using what we have as some kind of stepping stone whereas I'm content with where we are. We've got a good life. It's comfortable. Happy. Well, that's what I thought.'

'And what does she want?'

'America.'

'Really?'

He nodded. 'Her sister's in California and Renee's got this absolute conviction that life's better over there.'

'And you don't believe that?'

'It might be a bit warmer,' he said, 'but I don't imagine it's that much different from here.'

'So, if it's not that different, why don't you want to go?'

He gave a chuckle. 'Ah!' he said. 'Good point. Because I love it here. Because I can't imagine life away from the green fields and woods of Oxfordshire.'

'That's a problem.'

'You're telling me,' he said. 'I've asked her if she'll wait a while. She knows about the garden at Morton Hall and how passionate I am about this project, but she told me that there'll never be a right time because I'm always into one project or another.'

'And is she right about that?'

He grinned. 'Pretty much. I guess I've been a bit selfish when it comes to my career, but it's just because I love my job so much. Is that so wrong of me?'

Anne Marie sighed. 'It's hard to compromise when you're so passionate about something.'

'Like Grant and his work, you mean?'

She nodded.

'He didn't compromise and you left him.'

Anne Marie frowned. 'You think Renee will leave you?'

'It's certainly crossed my mind and she has mentioned it.'

'Really?'

'She said she'd take Poppy too.'

'Oh, Cape!'

'I don't think it'll come to that. But I'm – I don't know – permanently on edge.'

'I'm not surprised.' She gave him a sympathetic smile. 'Do you think she's changed since you met her?'

'I'm not sure,' he said after a pause. 'I don't think people change so much as our perceptions of them do. I think I kind of only saw a part of her when we got together and now I'm discovering all these other sides to her.'

Anne Marie nodded. 'That's how I feel about Grant. It was like he was showing me only the charming parts – the parts that would reel me in.'

'It's hard to keep up that kind of charade after a few years of co-habiting, isn't it?' He looked down at the floorboards, his shoulders seeming to sag as he gave a weary sigh. 'I can't help wondering if I could have changed anything or if it was inevitable that we would end up like this. But there's a part of me that thinks it would have all ended between us years ago if it hadn't been for Poppy.'

'Really?'

'I think she's held us together these last couple of years. I really do.'

They sat quietly for a moment before Cape spoke. 'Listen, I'd better get going.'

They stood up and walked to the front door. Anne Marie couldn't help feeling disappointed that he was leaving. She'd really enjoyed talking to him.

'Thanks for coming over,' she said, opening the door.

'No problem,' he told her. 'You'll tell me if you need – well – anything, won't you?'

Her mouth dropped open, surprised by his offer. 'I'll be fine.'

'I know you will.'

'And you – I hope things are okay with Renee.'

'Yeah, well . . .' He shrugged. 'I'll see you at the weekend.'

'You bet!' Anne Marie said as he left.

Kathleen arrived back a couple of minutes later.

'Cape gone, has he? Nice of him to pop round, wasn't it?' she said.

'And unexpected,' Anne Marie said.

'Was it?'

'Yes, he shouldn't have gone to that trouble.'

'But it's obvious why he did.'

'What do you mean?' Anne Marie felt confused.

'He likes you,' Kathleen told her.

'*What?*'

She smiled. 'You must know that.'

'Well, he's kind to me. But he's kind to everyone. He's one of those people who likes taking care of others.'

'I don't mean *that*. I mean, he *likes* you likes you.'

Anne Marie walked through to the living room and picked up her and Cape's mugs before going into the kitchen, noting that Kathleen was following her.

'I'm married,' she stated, 'and Cape has Poppy's mother.'

'That might be so,' Kathleen said, 'but he still likes you.'

She turned to face her new landlady. 'We're friends and new friends at that.'

'Of course,' Kathleen said, seemingly reading that Anne Marie wanted this particular conversation to end.

It was evening when Anne Marie left Kathleen's. She'd chosen to walk through the village rather than driving the short distance. She felt inexplicably nervous as she returned to Garrard House, but she knew she couldn't put it off any longer. It would just become more and more difficult as time went on.

She fished in her handbag for the front door key, then, taking a deep breath that fogged the night air as she exhaled, she entered.

It was quiet but, once she'd stood for a moment in the hallway, she could hear the regular thump thump from a bass upstairs. Nobody, it seemed, had heard her come in. Steeling herself, she approached Grant's study and tapped quietly on the door. Predictably, there was no reply, so she knocked louder.

'What is it?' he barked from the other side. He must think it was one of the girls daring to bother him while he was working.

'It's your wife,' Anne Marie barked in return. She immediately heard his chair scrape the floor and the door was opened a moment later.

'You're back!' he stated, taking his glasses off and rubbing his eyes as if he didn't quite believe what he was seeing.

'We need to talk.'

'Where have you been?'

'I'm staying at Kath's.'

He frowned. 'Kath?'

'She owns the thatched bed and breakfast in the village. The one that had the fire.'

'You've been *right here* in the village?'

She nodded. 'Kath's part of the team at Morton Hall.'

'I don't give a damn who Kath is,' he blurted. 'What the hell are you doing moving in with her?'

Anger flared up in her. 'If you're going to be rude, there's no point in us talking.' She turned to leave, but he caught her arm.

'Anne Marie – don't go!' There was desperation in his voice. 'Please.'

She looked down at the hand that was still clutching her arm like some kind of mad claw and he relinquished his hold.

'I'll make us some tea,' he said, and she watched as he headed into the kitchen. It was the first time in their marriage that he'd offered to make her a cup.

She walked through to the living room and took her coat off, placing it on the sofa before sitting down. Grant joined her a few minutes later.

'One sugar, right?'

'Yes.'

That he had to ask just reaffirmed that she was making the right decision.

He took a deep breath and sat down next to her. 'The girls were worried about you,' he said.

'No, they weren't. They were probably just anxious about who would make their meals and clean their clothes.'

'When are you coming back?'

She frowned. 'Grant, I'm not coming back.'

'What do you mean?'

'I'm leaving for good. I thought you understood that.'

'You thought I understood – how the hell could I have understood that when we haven't talked about it? I'm not a mind reader, Annie!'

'Yes, well that's why I'm here now – to talk.'

He shook his head. 'You've lost your mind.'

'What?' She couldn't quite believe the accusation fired at her. Not only was it incredibly rude but it was so arrogant of him to assume that only an insane person would want to leave him.

'You've got everything here. *Everything.* A beautiful home, two loving daughters and a husband who adores you.'

A laugh exploded from her quite involuntarily, which surprised both her and him.

'Were you just describing my life? Because I really didn't recognise it.'

'Didn't recognise—'

'You don't love me, Grant,' she interrupted. 'You never have. Not really. You're married to your work. I was just convenient to have around.'

'How can you say that?'

'Because one of us has to and you don't have the courage to admit the truth. And as for your girls, they've openly disliked me from day one. You've never noticed, have you? You're so tied up that you never see or hear how rude they are to me and how much they upset me. I've taken it for as long as I can. You say this is my home, but it never has been. It's yours. It was your wife's. It's your daughters'. But it's never been mine. I simply held it together while you all got on with your lives. But it could have been anyone here in my place. It didn't matter that it was me because none of you really got to know me. I've never even had one conversation with Irma or Rebecca. Not one – in all these years. I've been grunted at and complained to, and I've even had things thrown at me. Did you know about that? Did you know about the time I went into Irma's room to check for laundry and she threw a pair of jeans at me? She's a pretty good shot, your daughter, because the belt was still threaded through and the buckle hit me square in the face. You never noticed that bruise, did you? You never noticed it and she never apologised for it.'

'That must have been an accident,' he said. 'She wasn't thinking.'

'Grant, that's just one small incident. There are dozens of them, *hundreds* of them. I feel as if I'm being abused every single day of my life and I'm not going to allow that to go on, do you understand?'

She stood up, her cup of tea with one sugar untouched.

'I'm leaving you all. I've never been more unhappy in my life than I have living here.'

'Annie! We can talk about this. We can make things right. I'll get the girls and we can make time and sit down and talk about this properly.'

She shook her head. 'No. You say you'll talk about it but, if I agreed to that, you'd be straight back in your study with the door closed.'

'This isn't fair. You're not giving us a chance here.'

Her eyes widened in disbelief. 'How can you say that? I've given you all four years of my life, Grant. I don't want to keep score here, but this is the first cup of tea you've ever made me, and the girls have never once acknowledged my birthday.'

'Rubbish!'

'It's true. You just don't want to believe it. They don't even give me a card. They add their name to the one from you when they know you're not looking.'

Grant looked totally perplexed by this admission.

'Listen,' she said, 'we have to admit that this hasn't worked. We should never have been together, you and I.'

'Don't say that—'

She paused before continuing, suddenly feeling very tired with it all and knowing that the finishing line was up ahead; she just had to reach it.

'I idolised you when I was a student, I really did. I loved talking to you so much and I was flattered when I thought you liked talking to me.'

'But I did—'

'No, you didn't. You would have been happy talking to anyone, Grant. I just happened to be the one who lingered a little after class. That's all.'

She waited a moment, as if to give him a chance to process this and defend himself, but he didn't. He seemed to realise that they'd come to an end and that any argument he might put forward was hopeless.

She picked up her coat and put it on and walked into the hallway. He didn't follow her. She stood by the front door and took her keys out of her handbag, placing them on the table by the coat stand. She wouldn't need them anymore.

When she returned to the bed and breakfast, Kathleen appeared in the hallway.

'You've been to see him, haven't you?'

Anne Marie nodded. She didn't have the energy for anything else.

'Want to talk?'

'I don't think I can talk anymore tonight. But thanks.'

Kathleen nodded and Anne Marie made her way to her bedroom and switched on her bedside lamp before drawing the curtains against the cold night.

A great weight of sadness filled her as she sat down on the bed. She hadn't been sure what she'd feel after confronting Grant. Relief perhaps, but not this intense sadness. Did she still love him? It was something that she hadn't asked herself for some time now, but she was quite sure that there would always be a little corner of her heart that loved her husband in spite of everything. She knew that she'd always carry with her those sweet early days when they had first found each other.

Chapter 15

Emilia was excited by the prospect of a meal with guests. Never before had she cooked for anyone at home other than herself, but there were two visitors at Morton Hall and that was cause for celebration.

Emilia smiled to herself when she thought about her brother's initial resistance to her friend Angela staying. He hadn't made any further noises about her leaving, she mused. Emilia might not have seen a lot of them because they were spending so much time together but, when she had, Tobias had definitely been in a better mood than usual and that was all down to Angela.

For a moment, Emilia tried to imagine what it would be like to have a dozen Angelas staying with them. How wonderful it would be to shock the empty bedrooms into life and to fill the place with joy. Perhaps there was still time to do that. Perhaps today was just the first day in a whole new life for Morton Hall.

With Mrs Beatty's help, Emilia set the dining room table with a beautiful red linen tablecloth, laid out white china plates and silver cutlery and the prettiest crystal glasses. It was probably a little over the top for a weekday lunch, but she believed in grabbing the opportunity while everybody was together.

Jay was sketching in the garden. They'd been working on the portrait all morning and he was now taking a break while she prepared lunch. Tobias and Angela were somewhere in the house. She'd heard them laughing together and had sent Mrs Beatty to tell them that lunch would be served at one o'clock.

As Mrs Beatty had left the dining room, Emilia took a moment to look around her. It was rare that she and Tobias ever sat down to eat together. More often than not, they would grab something independently of one another. They were, she thought, turning into their parents – leading separate lives under the same beautiful roof.

Her parents had never entertained at the hall. To them, the house was a very private place. It seemed crazy to Emilia. Why have such a beautiful home filled with wonderful things if you weren't going to share it with others? Surely you'd want to show it off a bit? But, no, that wasn't the point of the Morton collection. Her grandparents had been the same, she'd heard, and their parents before them. But, just organising this simple lunch was giving Emilia so much pleasure and she couldn't understand why her relatives had never done the same.

However, once she was in the kitchen trying to organise all the dishes, she began to realise the work involved in catering for four people.

'Don't panic,' Mrs Beatty told her as Emilia fussed over the dishes. 'It all looks splendid.'

But Emilia was beginning to have misgivings.

'Is it too unsophisticated?' she asked. She'd chosen a buffet-style spread, which included quiches, ham and salads and, as pretty as it looked to her eyes, she was worried that it wasn't – well – elegant enough.

'What are you talking about? Everyone will love it.'

'Maybe I should have made a proper three-course meal,' Emilia said, twisting her fingers into knots. But she knew that slaving over a recipe with upwards of a dozen different ingredients wasn't her. Whenever she'd shown the slightest interest in the kitchen, Tobias had been quick to remind her that she was the lady of the house and that was what they had Mrs Beatty for, and so Emilia's cooking skills were limited.

'Come on, now – let's gather the troops and get this on its way to the dining room,' Mrs Beatty said.

A few minutes later and everybody was assembled, their plates stacked high. Emilia sat next to Jay on one side of the long table and Tobias sat next to Angela. Both the women were wearing Victorian dresses. Emilia had changed out of the midnight-blue portrait dress she'd been wearing earlier that morning and had chosen a violet-coloured gown, and Angela was wearing a crimson one with lacy sleeves.

'Emmy – this looks amazing!' Angela said as she began to eat.

'Thank you.'

Tobias frowned. 'You made all this?'

'Yes. Well, the quiche bases were bought but, other than that, yes.'

Angela laughed at Tobias's expression. 'You look so shocked!'

'Yes, he does,' Emilia agreed, 'which is rather insulting. You know I *can* do more than sit and have my portrait painted, you know, or float around the house giving orders to Mrs Beatty.'

'But your place—'

'Oh, listen to him!' Angela chided, leaning towards him and slapping his wrist. 'You sound like an old Victorian. You should grow a twirly moustache to complete the package.'

'I'm just saying that my sister shouldn't be—'

'You have *got* to lighten up, Tobias!' Angela interrupted before starting to laugh and, to Emilia's astonishment, Tobias joined in too. Emilia stole a glance at Jay and he looked as surprised as she felt. Angela, she thought, was good for her brother. Well, she was good for him when he was in this sort of a mood.

She watched for the rest of the meal as the two of them flirted together. At one point, her brother picked Angela's hand up and kissed the inside of her wrist.

'Jay,' Tobias said at last, 'tell me about my investment.'

'Your investment?'

'The painting, you idiot! The reason you're still here and eating my food.'

'Ah, yes.'

'Well, how's it going?'

'Good. It's coming along.'

'Yes, you keep telling me this, but I've yet to see the evidence.'

'You've got to be patient, Tobias,' Emilia told him. 'These things take time and I don't think you'll be disappointed with the result.'

'Have you seen it?' Tobias asked, turning to Angela.

'No, I haven't.'

'Are you sure Emmy's not sneaked you in to have a look when my back's turned?'

'I don't think anybody's allowed in that room while they're working,' Angela said. 'If that *is* what they're actually doing in there.'

'What do you mean?' Tobias's face darkened in an instant.

'I'm just teasing,' Angela said, but Emilia could see the suspicion in her brother's eyes as he turned his attention first to her and then to Jay.

Jay cleared his throat. 'I'm a professional artist and, when I say I'm working, I'm working.'

'I'm sure you are,' Angela said. 'I was just being silly.' She caught Emilia's eye and her smile vanished as she no doubt realised the implications of her teasing. 'Anyway, what's wrong if your sister has a little romance in her life?'

'Angela!' Emilia cried in warning, appalled at the openness of her friend's conversation.

'What? Aren't we allowed to talk about it? I mean, you two *are* a couple, aren't you?'

Jay cleared his throat.

'I mean, *we* are, aren't we?' Angela said, turning to Tobias.

Tobias reached across the table and took Angela's hand again.

'Ouch!' she cried. 'Not so rough. You'll leave bruises if you grab like that.'

'You want to be a couple?' he asked her, his voice sounding steely to Emilia.

'Yes, but you've got to be gentler,' she told him.

Emilia watched them with an appalled sort of fascination and was heartily relieved when the meal soon came to an end.

'Angela, will you help me?' Emilia asked, eager to get away before Angela or Tobias thought to ask any more probing questions about her and Jay.

Tobias didn't look happy at this. 'Isn't that Mrs Beatty's job?'

'I've given her the afternoon off,' Emilia told him.

'What?'

'Tobias, you keep telling me that it's my job to run the house and make decisions concerning the staff, so I am.'

'And you're doing a brilliant job,' Angela said as she left the table. 'Isn't she?' She turned to look at Tobias who simply glared back at her.

The two of them quickly cleared the table. Jay got up to help too while Tobias sat back and watched them as if they were fools.

Reaching the kitchen, Emilia turned to Jay.

'I'll meet you upstairs in a little while, okay?'

'You don't want a hand in here?' he asked.

'No, I'd like to speak to Angela if that's okay.'

Jay nodded and left the room.

Once she was quite certain Jay was out of earshot, she turned to her friend.

'God, Angela, I've hardly seen you! What have you been up to?'

'Do you really need to ask?' Angela said as she placed her stack of plates by the sink.

'I mistakenly thought you came here to see me,' Emilia said, and she was only half teasing. She placed her own stack of plates down and that's when she saw the red marks around Angela's wrist.

Angela immediately saw what she was looking at and endeavoured to pull down the lace around her sleeve to cover the marks.

'Angela – listen to me – there's something I need to tell you.'

'Angela?' Tobias's voice called through.

'I'm in the kitchen,' Angela called back.

'Yes,' Tobias said as he came into the room, 'and you really shouldn't be.'

'Oh, listen to him!' Angela teased. 'You really should have words with him, Emmy.'

Emilia was about to say that she'd love to have words with both of them, but that she just hadn't been given the chance when, sure enough, Tobias took hold of Angela's hand and Emilia was left watching in bemusement as her friend left the kitchen with her brother.

'You look pensive,' Jay said, putting his brushes down. 'Want to tell me what's on your mind?'

'Not really,' Emilia said, although she had to admit to herself that she hadn't been able to stop thinking about Angela since she'd seen the marks on her wrist and the fact that she hadn't seen her for two whole days since their shared lunch.

'Well, I can't paint you when you're scowling like that.'

'I'm not scowling.'

'Oh, yes you are.'

She turned away from the window and sighed. 'I'm worried about Angela.'

'Is she still here?'

'Yes.'

'I thought she was meant to be leaving soon?'

'So did I,' Emilia told him. 'She was only meant to be here for a week, but I think she's really fallen under the spell of Tobias.'

Jay laughed.

'It's not funny,' Emilia told him. 'I'm worried about her.'

'Why?'

'Because he's – he's not for everyone.'

'What do you mean?'

'You know what I mean. He's tricky. He's hard to handle and I don't . . .' She paused.

'Don't what?'

'I don't trust him to be kind to her.' She shook her head. 'Isn't it awful to say that about my own brother?'

'Have you told Angela how you feel?'

'I've tried, but I haven't really had a chance to get her on her own. Tobias is always hanging around. Anyway, I'm not sure she'd listen to me. I think she's really smitten.'

'Then just leave things as they are. Let her find her own way through this.'

'Really?'

'You might be pleasantly surprised at the result. It could be the making of Tobias. To fall in love.'

Emilia thought this over for a moment. She'd never known her brother to be in love before. Was it even possible for him to experience that emotion?

'I don't know,' she said at last. 'I'm not sure my brother's capable of a pure emotion like love. I think he's got some sort of ulterior motive with Angela.'

'How do you mean?'

'Just a feeling I've got.' She paused, wondering whether to confess more. 'I was watching him during lunch and he kept giving me these little sideways glances – like he was checking that I was noticing him making a fuss of Angela.'

'Trying to make you jealous, you mean? Why would he do that?'

Emilia held his gaze. 'Because he's jealous of me and you.'

Jay put his paintbrush down, giving her his full attention now. 'Really? That's what you're thinking?'

Emilia shrugged. 'I just felt it was a kind of one-upmanship thing with him. I don't really believe he has any feelings for her and, if he doesn't, I think she should know that.'

Jay seemed to weigh her words and then nodded.

'Want to take a break?' he asked.

'I think I do.'

'Good, let's grab a couple of cans and go into the garden.'

As soon as they were outside, Jay took Emilia's hand in his and they headed towards the maze. It was a routine of theirs now – to escape into the leafy depths where they knew they wouldn't be disturbed but, before they could make it to the west entrance, Emilia spotted Angela sitting on a bench under the cedar tree.

'Jay, would you mind if I went and spoke to her?'

'Alone?'

'Yes.'

'Of course not,' he said.

She gave him a kiss. 'Thank you,' she said. 'I'll see you back inside in a few minutes, okay?'

He nodded and took himself off into the maze.

'Hello stranger,' Emilia said as she approached her friend. She was wearing a teal-green gown she'd come to favour. Tobias had long since stopped complaining about Angela wearing the Victorian clothes and Emilia suspected that he had come to like it.

Angela looked up and beamed her a smile.

'Come and sit here!'

Emilia took a seat on the bench beside her and opened her can of drink, passing it to Angela to share a moment later.

'Watch the dress!' she warned.

'Oh, I spend my whole days watching these dresses. How did the Victorians cope? I'm a nervous wreck although I've come to love the feel of them.'

'I love them too but I like the option of knowing I can slip on a pair of jeans anytime I want.'

Angela laughed. 'Agreed!'

'Tobias would probably make a fuss if I suddenly started wearing jeans again.'

'Yes, I think he likes a woman to look like a woman,' Angela said.

They sat for a few minutes, gazing across the garden. Angela was the first to speak.

'You're in love with him, aren't you?'

Emilia's head snapped around to look at her friend. 'What?'

'That painter guy – Jay? I notice you're keeping him all to yourself.'

'We're working together.'

'And is that all?' Angela gave her a little nudge with her elbow which almost had her spilling her drink down her dress.

'Careful!'

'Sorry! The dress!' Angela said, her hands up in a surrendering pose. 'So, come on – tell me about Jay the painter. We didn't really get a chance to talk the other day at lunch and I'm sorry if I embarrassed you. I didn't mean to.'

'It's okay.'

'So, go on – tell me everything!'

Emilia took a deep breath. She couldn't keep the smile from her face a moment longer. 'I think I'm in love.'

'I *knew* it!' Angela cried. 'I knew the minute I saw you in Oxford that there was something different about you.'

'Really?'

'Absolutely. You looked . . .' She paused. '. . . happy.'

Emilia smiled. 'I am. I'm *really* happy.'

'Good – you deserve it.' Angela gave her a hug. 'So, tell me all about him.'

'Well, we've not known each other long, but he's one of those peo-ple you feel comfortable with right away, you know? We can talk for hours and we both love the garden here. We've practically moved into the maze!'

Angela giggled. 'Been up to anything else in there?'

Emilia's mouth dropped open. 'Angela!'

'Oh, come on – you can tell me!'

Emilia could feel her cheeks heating up at her friend's questioning but, as embarrassed as she was, she was also desperate to share her joy with her friend.

'Well, there have been one or two *amazing* experiences in there,' she said.

They laughed together.

'Hey, I have a bone to pick with you, sister,' Angela went on.

'What?'

'You never told me your brother was so handsome.'

'It's not exactly something I'd go around saying.'

'I guess not.'

Emilia took a sip from her can, summoning up the courage to say what was on her mind.

'Angela?'

'Yes?'

'I feel like I should warn you.'

'Warn me? About what?'

'Tobias.'

'What about him?'

'He's – well, he seems to be in one of his good moods at the moment.'

She frowned. 'You mean he isn't always?'

'He has mood swings. You should be careful around him.'

Angela's sunny smile vanished. 'Careful?'

'You mustn't . . .'

'What?'

'This is really hard for me to say.'

'What is? Tell me, Emmy. You're scaring me.'

Emilia took a deep breath. 'I don't think it's a good idea for you to get involved with him.'

There was a pause between the two women.

'Are you serious?'

'I wouldn't be saying this if I wasn't serious.'

'But what business is it of yours?'

'What business?' Emilia was a little taken aback by this question. 'Because he's my brother and you're my best friend and – forgive me for saying this, but you came here to visit me, didn't you? And you've been spending far more time with Tobias than you have me.'

'That's not fair!'

'Isn't it?' Emilia took a deep breath. 'Look, I don't want to argue with you – really I don't. I just wanted to let you know. Tobias is . . . well, he's different.'

Angela frowned. 'I know. He's special. I've never met anyone like him. He's so clever and witty and—'

'I know. He's all those things and more. A lot more. I just don't want to see you get hurt, Angie.'

'What are you talking about? I won't get hurt.'

'You don't know him. Not really. He's not so much fun to be around when he's in one of his black moods.'

'Black moods! You make him sound like Heathcliff. Does he howl like a wolf and bash his head against tree trunks?'

'Not far off.'

Angela studied her. 'You're messing with me, aren't you?'

'I wish I was.' Emilia swallowed hard. 'Look, I don't know how close you two have got, but I guess it's pretty close. I just thought you should know.' She reached out to touch Angela's hand, but her friend stood up.

'I thought there was something weird going on between you and your brother.'

'*What?*'

'The way he talks to you and treats you and the way you respond. You don't want to let anybody else in, do you? You want to keep him all to yourself.'

'No, it's not like that.'

'You like being the centre of his attention, don't you? You don't want anybody coming between you and him.'

'Angie – you're being silly.'

'Am I? Then why would you say something like that about Tobias? He's been nothing but sweet to me. I think he's really beginning to care about me, Emmy.'

'Are you? Are you really sure about that?'

'And you're trying to spoil something that's really special.'

'I'm not – I *promise* you I'm not. You're my best friend and I . . .'

Angela stood up, flushed and agitated. 'Just leave us alone, will you?'

'Oh, Angie – don't go like this!' Emilia called after her as she ran across the lawn towards the house. But it was no use – she wasn't going to listen.

It came to a head in the middle of the night just two days later. Emilia had been sleeping with her windows open as the air was unbearably hot even after the sun had set. She'd been dozing in fits and starts, her bedding twisting around her body as she'd tried to get comfortable, and then she'd heard the raised voices coming from along the landing. Tobias's room.

She sat bolt upright in bed, adrenaline coursing through her. She hadn't heard raised voices since the row between her parents when her father had told her mother to give up her work, but she'd never forgotten how that had made her feel. Now, knowing that it was her brother and her best friend fighting, she felt just as anxious and she sprang out of bed and grabbed a cardigan from a chair, stuffing her feet into her slippers and running out of her room.

Tobias was at the head of the stairs when she came out, but Angela was nowhere to be seen.

'Angela?' Emilia called. Her brother turned to face her, his expression dark.

'She's gone.'

'What? Where's she gone?'

'She's left.'

'But she doesn't have a car. She can't just walk back to Yorkshire with her suitcase.'

'I've called a taxi. It'll pick her up at the end of the driveway. Or somewhere between the driveway and Oxford depending how fast she's moving.'

Emilia was dumbfounded. Was her brother serious?

'You didn't even offer to drive her into Oxford?'

'It's the middle of the night.'

'Exactly! You can't just throw somebody out in the dark!'

'I didn't. She's the one who left, Emilia.'

'What the hell happened anyway? I heard you both shouting.'

'I don't know what happened.'

'Well, what did you say to her?'

He glowered at her and shrugged his shoulders.

'Tobias! What did you say to her?'

He ran a hand through his red hair. 'I told her not to be so clingy.'

'Clingy? What do you mean?'

'I mean she was getting all intense on me. I couldn't breathe.'

'And what did she say?'

'She said some stuff, okay?'

'No, it's not okay!' Emilia cried. 'First of all, I invited Angela down to see me – *me*! She's my best friend and then you and she hide away all day and all night and I don't get to see either of you.'

'You mean while you spend all your time with Jay? How's that any different?'

'Because Jay and I are still talking to each other. We're not screaming the house down in the middle of the night.'

'Oh, aren't you just the perfect couple?'

Emilia looked at her brother and a feeling of pity overcame her. 'That's what this has all been about, isn't it?'

'What do you mean?'

'You don't like the idea of me and Jay together.'

'Shut up, Emmy.'

'You don't like the thought that I might be a grown-up woman and want to have a normal relationship with a man. That's it, isn't it? You think you can keep me here in this house forever. Well you can't, Tobias. That's *not* going to happen.'

He held his hands up like an unbreachable barrier between them. 'You know, I've had enough. I'm going to bed.'

'Don't you walk away from me! I'm not done with you.'

'Yeah? Well, I'm done with you. With all of you!'

Emilia watched as he strode down the landing and slammed his bedroom door behind him. She had a feeling he'd be in there for days.

'He's out of control, Emmy,' Jay said, putting his paintbrush down.

'No he isn't. He's just sunk into one of his moods after I shouted at him a bit.'

Jay shook his head, obviously exasperated by her explanation. It was funny but Emilia found herself defending her brother whenever Jay criticised him. Maybe that was only natural because Tobias was the only family Emilia had left now. But everything Jay had been saying over the past two weeks since Tobias had shut himself away was true. Tobias was controlling, bad-tempered and – yes – a little bit strange, and he seemed to be getting worse. He was spending more and more time in that room of his. Either he was screeching on the violin, which at least told Emilia that he was conscious, or else it was deadly silent on the other side of the door.

'Tobes?' she'd call through, gently knocking on the dark wood. 'Are you okay? Can I get you anything?'

No matter how many times she called, there would never be a response. She sometimes wished that he'd bellow at her to leave him alone just so she knew for sure that he was still there. She'd even tried to reach him from outside, throwing little stones up at the mullioned window, but the thick curtains had been drawn against the summer light and he hadn't come to the window. Emilia knew he was eating because she found the evidence in the kitchen in the mornings. Mrs Beatty would shake her head.

'Who made this mess in the middle of the night?'

But Emilia knew that Mrs Beatty was fully aware of what was going on.

As wonderful as it was to be able to spend uninterrupted time with Jay, Emilia couldn't help but worry about her brother. She was also still worrying about Angela. After she'd left, Emilia had called her home number endlessly, but there'd been no reply. Then, finally, when Angela did answer, Emilia had received a torrent of abuse and had been accused of coming between her friend and Tobias. It had taken over an hour to calm Angela down.

'It's not natural,' she kept saying.

'What isn't?'

'He kept talking about you, Emmy. All the time. It was driving me crazy! And when I told him how weird that was, he – he . . .'

'What?' Emilia asked. 'What did he say?'

'He didn't say anything. He just grabbed me by the wrists with this wild look in his eyes like he wanted to kill me.'

Emilia had seen that look too. Tobias was scary when he was like that, flying from love to hate in a heartbeat.

Thinking of that now made her blood run cold. She hadn't told Jay about her conversation with her friend, but he seemed to understand the gist of it.

'Want some lunch?' he asked her now, interrupting her thoughts. 'We could eat outside.'

She nodded. It would be good to feel the sun on her skin. She felt as if she'd been indoors forever even though it was only for the space of a morning. Being painted, she thought, could do that to a person. It sort of trapped you in time, denying you physical movement while allowing the mind to float free. Well, she'd had way too much time focussing on negative things that morning and was glad when she and Jay made it out into the garden with their lunch, choosing the deeply shaded corner where the picnic table was.

'I hate to say it, but we're nearly done with the portrait,' he told her after they'd finished eating. 'I'm not sure how long we can keep up the charade of painting.'

'Maybe we could start another one,' Emilia suggested. 'Maybe Tobias could commission you to paint the house or garden.'

He shook his head. 'Not really me, that. I like painting people. I like painting *you*.'

'But I can't be your only subject.'

'Why not? Lots of artists have muses.'

'That wouldn't be very interesting, though, would it?'

'You mean you don't want to pose for me all day?' The question was asked in a light-hearted manner, but she could tell there was an edge of seriousness about it.

She reached across the table and placed her hand on his.

'I'd like to be with you all day,' she whispered.

225

His expression softened and she could feel her heart race at the intensity of the moment.

'Emmy, why don't we get out of here?' Jay said.

'You mean go to the maze?'

'No – get out of *here* – Morton Hall.'

'What, a day out?' Emilia said. She couldn't remember the last time she'd had one of those.

Jay shook his head. 'No, silly! I mean we should go. Really go!'

'But I can't do that,' she said, shocked by his suggestion.

'Why not?'

'I couldn't leave my brother.'

Jay sighed. 'He's a grown man. He'll be fine without you.'

'But this is my home.'

'Yes, I know, but you just said you wanted to be with me all day. Don't you want to make a life with me some day? A life just for us?'

'Well, I—'

'I mean . . .' He paused, squeezing her hand in his. '. . . I think you and I might be heading towards something rather wonderful.'

She smiled at him. 'Me too,' she whispered.

'And that something rather wonderful – well – I don't want to do that here under your brother's nose.'

Emilia laughed. 'No, you're right.'

'Then you'll think about it at least?'

She took a deep breath. 'It's just that I've never thought about leaving here,' she confessed. 'I mean, it's crossed my mind that I might have to one day if Tobias gets married, but I've never really imagined a life outside Morton Hall.'

Jay held her gaze. 'Well, I think it's time you started to imagine.'

Chapter 16

The brief winter flurry of snow in February was overtaken by a mild March. Daffodils gilded the edges of the garden, replacing the army of snowdrops and crocuses. There were also hyacinths blooming amongst the winter leaves that were still to be cleared. It was, Cape said, 'a good start on the bulb front', and Anne Marie had spotted the fresh leaves of bluebells flourishing in the nuttery.

The days were now lengthening and that meant more time could be spent in the garden. A few members of the group had been coming during the week as well as the weekends and the results were visible. Mac had managed to clear a path on the other side of the walled garden and had done a fantastic job pruning some of the old trees there. Dorothy and Erin had joined forces to clear a wild area to the west of the house using a scythe that Mac had found in one of the old sheds. Erin had once taken a summer course in scything and had been tutoring Dorothy in how to use the traditional garden tool. The two women worked incredibly well together and had also scrubbed a mountain of terracotta pots ready to use for planting.

All of the raised beds had been made in the walled garden and a delivery of topsoil had filled them all. The long greenhouse had been cleared and repaired, its new windows looking splendid, and the group was suitably excited as to what could be achieved in the new space.

It was on a Saturday in March when Patrick was in the greenhouse with Kathleen, Cape and Anne Marie. Patrick's boys were spending the day with their grandparents, but had sent some seedlings they'd been growing on a windowsill at home.

Anne Marie and Cape were at one end of the greenhouse, pushing a couple of workbenches together, when the row began.

'I don't know why you came to Morton Hall!' Kathleen yelled at Patrick. 'You're always in a bad mood and you're always complaining.'

'Hey – you're the one who's complaining, lady!' Patrick pointed out.

'Don't call me *lady*.'

'Yeah, my mistake,' he said.

'Why you—'

For one dreadful moment, Anne Marie was quite sure that Kathleen was going to fly at Patrick and she ran towards her, stopping her, but Kathleen had taken her gardening gloves off and thrown them at Patrick's face.

'I'll slap you properly next time,' she told him.

'What the hell did I do?'

Cape joined them. 'Come on, you two. I thought you were getting along all right now,' he said.

'Yeah, well, he's been grouching at me all morning,' Kathleen said.

'Are you kidding?' Patrick said. '*You've* been on at *me*.'

'Only because you keep taking my tools.'

Cape looked at Anne Marie and she shrugged. She'd been aware that there'd been some sort of discord between Kathleen and Patrick initially but, like Cape, she'd thought it was a thing of the past.

'Let's take a break, okay?' Cape said.

'Fine!' Kathleen said, stalking out of the greenhouse.

'I'll go with her,' Anne Marie said, following her towards the communal kitchen.

By the time she got there, Kathleen was slamming her way around the cupboards.

'Are you okay?' Anne Marie asked.

'That man is impossible!'

Anne Marie did her best to bite back a smile because Patrick had truly improved over the last few weeks. He could still be a tad sardonic, but he was really throwing himself into the work and had made excellent progress with the vegetable garden, which was to be planted out once the risk of frost was over.

'He's making a real effort to get on with everyone now, though,' Anne Marie said.

'Except me. He hates me.'

'He doesn't hate you!'

'Then why is he always teasing me?'

'Because he likes you best of all?' Anne Marie suggested.

'You're kidding me.'

'I'm not,' she said. 'I really think he likes you, and don't forget the way he's opened up to you about his wife. I'd say he has a soft spot for you, for sure.'

Kathleen shook her head. 'He's the last person I'd want to get involved with. The *last*! I've not waited this long for some moody grouch like Patrick.'

Anne Marie reached for the tin of biscuits which Dorothy had kindly brought in for the weekend. If there was ever a time for a sugary shortbread, it was now.

'I'm a patient woman,' Kathleen said. 'I've dated a lot of wrong'uns and I can spot them at fifty paces – and that's exactly what Patrick is.'

Anne Marie gave her a sympathetic smile. One evening a few weeks ago, her new friend had opened up to her about her romantic history – or rather her *un*romantic history. Now in her early forties, she'd declared that she still believed in true love, but she'd never found the right man for her. Anne Marie suspected that her standards were very high, but Kathleen insisted that she wouldn't give up her independence for any old man.

They drank their tea together and munched on a couple of shortbread fingers.

'I've really seen a change in Patrick,' Anne Marie ventured. 'His sons too.'

'I like his boys,' Kathleen said, 'and I never thought I'd say that after my first encounter with them.'

'Yes, they were a little bit wild when they first arrived,' Anne Marie agreed. 'But maybe Patrick will follow suit. Maybe you'll grow to like him as much as you like his boys.'

'Huh!' she snorted. 'I wouldn't count on it.'

Anne Marie grinned. 'Come on, let's get back to it before Cape sends out a search party for us.'

Kathleen and Patrick might have been at odds, but other friendships were being forged in the garden. Dorothy and Erin seemed to have gravitated towards one another and spent a lot of time working together, teaming up during the week when other people couldn't make it to the garden and sneaking off for tea breaks in the kitchen.

It was the next day when the two women came running into the walled garden.

'Cape!' Dorothy shouted. 'I think you should come and see this.'

Everybody downed tools and ran to where Dorothy and Erin had been working on a sheltered path on the way to the nuttery.

'What is it, Dorothy?' Cape asked. 'What have you found?'

'I think it's another statue,' Dorothy said.

'How exciting!' Kathleen said. 'It's all very Howard Carter, isn't it?'

'Who's he?' Matthew asked.

'He was the man who discovered the tomb of Tutankhamun,' Kathleen informed him.

'Wow! You mean there's an Egyptian tomb here?' Matthew said.

'Cool!' Elliot said.

'Erm, let's not get too excited,' Cape said.

The group looked at the great plinth which had been cleared of a swathe of ivy and brambles.

'We didn't want to uncover any more without you guys here,' Erin said.

'Are those feet?' Mac asked, peering closer.

'They sure look like feet,' Cape said. 'Go on, then – let's find out what's under all that ivy.'

Dorothy and Erin exchanged glances.

'Go on – you do it, my dear,' Dorothy told her young friend.

'Okay!' Erin said, taking a deep breath and grabbing hold of a handful of ivy and chopping into it.

'They're definitely feet!' Patrick said.

'And legs!' Elliot cried a moment later.

Erin continued to hack away at the ivy, clearing it inch by over-grown inch, revealing a pair of mossy knees and then . . .

'Oh, my god!' Cape exclaimed.

Kathleen burst into laughter as the virile stone appendage greeted the group's eyes.

'He's – erm – ready for action it would seem!' Patrick said.

'Perhaps we should cover him up again,' Dorothy suggested, a pretty blush colouring her cheeks.

'Oh, no!' Erin said. 'He's much too handsome.'

'How do you know that? You haven't seen his face yet!' Kathleen teased.

Erin started to laugh and, soon, the others were all joining in.

'Boys,' Patrick began, 'look away!'

'We know what it is, Dad!' Matthew said in a world-weary tone as he rolled his eyes.

'I'm just glad Poppy isn't here to see it,' Cape said.

'Or Mrs Beatty,' Anne Marie said. 'Do you think she's seen it?'

'It's a beautiful work of art. Everybody should see it,' Erin said as she cleared the rest of the ivy away to reveal what had once been a very handsome face.

'Oh, dear,' Dorothy said. 'He's missing his nose.'

'His other bit more than makes up for it!' Kathleen said and the laughter began again. 'I don't think anybody will be looking at his nose.'

The group worked until the sun began to set. The March days were still bitterly cold, especially once the light began to fail, and the team were good and prompt when it came to packing up to go home.

'Have you heard from Grant?' Cape asked Anne Marie after the others had departed. She was cleaning one of the old spades they'd found behind an ancient shed. It had a split handle, but there was still a good bit of life in it yet.

'Not since I told him I wasn't coming back,' Anne Marie told him.

'He's not contacted you at all?'

'Well, he did text to tell me he was throwing out some of my old university essays he'd found. I went to collect them when he was out. He'd left them on the doorstep underneath a pair of my shoes that I'd forgotten.'

'Nice of him.'

'Yes, it had been raining and everything was soaked.'

'What a jerk,' Cape said. 'Sorry.'

'It's okay. He is a jerk.' She gave a tiny smile. It had taken her years to gain the confidence to call her husband that and she'd quite enjoyed the experience.

The spade clean, Anne Marie popped it into a shed which Cape locked.

'That's another weekend, then,' he said and the two of them left the walled garden together.

'Patrick's boys are still here,' Anne Marie said a moment later as they rounded the corner and saw the two of them chasing each other around the topiary garden.

'Matthew? Elliot?' Cape called. 'Where's your dad?'

'In the kitchen,' Matthew said. 'He told us to wait out here. He's in there with Kathleen.'

Cape and Anne Marie exchanged glances.

'I thought they'd left.'

'Yes, Kath said she had to get back and I told her not to worry because I fancied a walk anyway.'

They waited, wondering what was going on in the kitchen and hoping that it wasn't another slanging match. Kathleen was the first to emerge.

'He's impossible!' she declared, shaking her head.

'Patrick?' Cape asked.

'Who else?' Kathleen said. 'I'll see you later, Annie?'

'Yes. See you.'

They watched as she walked to her car and sped down the driveway, spraying gravel in her haste to get away.

A moment later, Patrick emerged from the kitchen, his face flushed. But what was even more striking was the fact that his mouth was also a deep red – a red which perfectly matched the colour of Kathleen's lipstick.

Chapter 17

March blew in and out in a flurry of showers and it was a great relief when April arrived with a balmy kiss. Jackets were shed as the team worked in the garden. Great slabs arrived and new paths were made. Benches were bought and then, one wondrous morning, a lorry laden with plants was delivered. The garden was really beginning to take shape.

Relationships were beginning to take shape too, Cape had noticed, watching as Kathleen and Patrick worked side by side with his boys. They certainly kept everyone guessing, he thought. A few of the group had been wondering whether something was brewing between them, and Anne Marie and Cape were never really certain if the tempestuous pair were going to trade insults or kisses next. But Kathleen's relationship with his boys had definitely changed for the better. She genuinely seemed to care about them now whereas, before, she'd merely tolerated them.

Then there was Dorothy and Erin. Just that morning, he'd watched as Erin helped Dorothy move one of the large terracotta pots they'd uncovered in the nuttery. They had become a natural pair, making tea for everybody together and chatting amiably in corners of the garden.

Just like him and Mac, Cape thought with a smile. That had been one of the biggest surprises to come out of this project. Mac Minter was slowly beginning to come out of his shell, and Cape was enjoying getting to know the older man. They'd been sharing their love for gardening, and Cape had told Mac about his father and how passionate he'd been about it, while Mac, in turn, had told Cape about his grandfather. He'd been the one to encourage Mac to become a gardener; his father had been an accountant.

'I took one look at that line of work to know it wasn't for me,' Mac had confided. 'My dad was always pale-faced and stressed and had this hunched look about him. Came from decades at a desk. The human body isn't meant to sit down all day.'

'I agree,' Cape had said.

'But he didn't believe in my dream,' Mac had gone on. 'He never supported it. I was on my own.'

Well, Mac wasn't on his own now. He was surrounded by a group of fellow dreamers and Cape couldn't have been happier with their progress in the garden.

If only things could have been going as smoothly at home, Cape thought. Renee seemed more distant than ever, finding excuses to be out in the evenings and, whenever they did happen to be home at the same time, she would feign tiredness to avoid conversation. Cape felt relieved and would move through to his study, throwing himself into his work. It made him think about Anne Marie and Grant. Hadn't he hidden away in his study? And look how that had ended. But then he'd shake his head. Different situation, he assured himself. Grant had pushed Anne Marie away, resolutely shutting her out from his life, whereas Renee had forced Cape to find sanctuary in his work.

Now that spring had arrived, his workload had increased. Everybody, it seemed, had discovered they had a garden that needed work. Not that he was complaining; he was happy to fill his hours and was working on several exciting new projects that took him all over the Chilterns and beyond. How he loved getting out into the countryside, discovering the hidden gardens of England behind the cottages and the hedgerows. One never knew what one was going to come across, from the tiny spaces behind the traditional thatched cottages to the great rolling lawns behind the mansions in the Thames Valley.

Perhaps he shouldn't have worked quite so hard. Perhaps he might have been able to prevent what had happened if he'd been around more, if he'd made an effort. But somehow, he doubted it.

It was at the end of one of those perfect spring days when the blue sky had been filled with friendly white clouds and the celandine had shone like golden pennies along the lanes. He pulled up outside their cottage, his limbs aching from a good day's work. He noticed that the house was dark and, when he went inside, it felt cold and empty.

'Renee?' he called, instinctively knowing that nobody was home. 'Poppy?'

It was late. Poppy usually had dance class on a Thursday after school, but they should have been home well before now. He checked his phone, but there were no messages. He rang Renee's mobile, but there was no answer.

He didn't begin to panic until an hour later. He'd made himself some tea and toast before going upstairs. That's when he realised that something was seriously wrong. The wardrobe door was open and all Renee's cosmetics were missing from the bathroom. She hadn't even tried to disguise the fact that she'd left.

Cape ran into Poppy's room and noticed a hurricane of clothes on the bed as if her little wardrobe had been completely emptied and a few things chosen to take. He looked around. Her favourite teddy was gone and the doll with the loose right arm, and the poster of her favourite girl band had been taken down. Cape swallowed hard, suddenly feeling hot. You didn't take posters on holiday with you.

He sat down on the edge of Poppy's bed, looking at the little lamp with the tutu shade. He saw the ropes of pretty beads on her dressing table and her collection of miniature ballerinas. Again, the favourite was missing – the one she called Miss Twirl.

Getting up, he walked out onto the landing and opened the loft door, pulled down the ladder and climbed in. Sure enough, the suitcases were gone. Renee had done it, hadn't she? Hiding the suitcases hadn't stopped her.

She'd left him and she'd taken Poppy with her.

The curtains had been drawn for the night at Kathleen's and Anne Marie was sitting on the sofa having just cooked pasta for the two of them. How quickly she'd got used to her new friend. They were really beginning to feel like roommates and had developed a nice easy relationship. After her years with Grant and his daughters, Anne Marie found it a novel experience to actually talk to the person you lived with and how wonderful it was to pass the time drifting from subject to subject. There was no uneasy tension between them. She didn't fear a flare-up of emotions; she wasn't going to be ignored, bullied or moaned about. Her company truly seemed to be appreciated.

Anne Marie had confided in Kathleen about her failed marriage and had found a sympathetic ear.

'Marriage is highly overrated,' Kath had said. '*Men* are highly overrated.'

Anne Marie had had to agree with her, though she couldn't help wondering if, at some point, the subject of Patrick would surface. But Kath never spoke about him and no reference was made to the two of them emerging from the kitchen with *her* lipstick on *his* mouth.

They were just finishing their dinner when Anne Marie's mobile rang.

'Anne Marie? I didn't know who to call.'

'Cape? Are you okay?'

'No! No, I'm not okay. Renee's gone and she's taken Poppy with her.'

'What?'

'They've gone. They've really gone. All their stuff too.'

Anne Marie gasped. 'Cape – is there anything I can do?'

There was a pause.

'Do you want to come over?' she asked. 'I'm at Kath's. We can talk about it. Cape?'

'Yes, yes,' he said as if he'd been thrown a lifeline. 'I'll come over.'

She hung up.

'What did he say?' Kathleen asked.

'It's his partner,' Anne Marie said. 'She's left and taken Poppy with her.'

Cape was with them in less than half an hour, looking pale and shaken. Kathleen made him a cup of tea and Anne Marie tried to get him to sit down on the sofa, but he couldn't.

'America?' Kathleen cried when he told her. 'Are you *sure*?'

'Absolutely sure. She's been planning this for months or at least talking about it and her passport's gone.' He gave a strange laugh. 'Talking about it, but I never thought she'd do it. Not really. I mean, she threatened to. But a threat's just that, right? You don't really take your child away from her father and get on a plane to another continent, do you?'

'How are you going to find out?' Anne Marie asked.

'She'll ring, won't she?' Cape said. 'She's got to at some point.'

'Of course she'll ring,' Kathleen said. 'She's not a complete monster, is she?'

There was a pause.

'*Is* she?' Kathleen repeated.

Cape was pacing so much that Anne Marie felt sure he'd wear a trench in Kathleen's beautiful new carpet.

'Cape – let's walk, shall we?'

He nodded, but he looked as though he would have nodded at anything she might have said.

'Come on.' She reached out to guide him into the hallway where she grabbed her coat and boots. It was dark but still quite mild outside and the two of them fell into step, heading into the heart of the village. She hoped that the exercise and the fresh air might do him good. A walk always helped her to think and she had the feeling that Cape was the sort of person who needed to walk when his mind was full of demons.

They soon found their way to Morton Hall. The moon was almost full and very bright, lighting their way as they edged around the house towards the topiary garden. How wonderful the beasts looked in the silvery light. It was as if they were bathed in magic and might come to life at any moment.

Their feet were silent on the grass as they walked towards the maze. It somehow seemed inevitable that they would end up there. Anne Marie couldn't really explain why, but she felt herself drawn to it that night.

Cape led the way and they found themselves in the centre just a few minutes later, sitting down on the bench together. Neither spoke, but that was fine. Cape seemed to need the silence and Anne Marie was happy with that.

They looked up into the heavens. The sky was packed with stars and they filled their eyes with them.

'Do you think she's up there?' Cape asked after a moment. 'Do you think my little girl is up in the sky flying far away from me?'

Anne Marie wasn't sure what to say to that, but reached out and touched his hand, letting him know that she was there and that she could feel his pain.

'I don't want to believe she's done this,' he said a few minutes later. 'I want to go home and find them both there.' He shook his head. 'No, I don't. I want to find *Poppy* there. Is that awful?'

Anne Marie squeezed his hand. 'Not after what Renee's done to you.'

'How could she do that? How could she go out and buy suitcases knowing that she was planning to take my daughter away from me? Do you think she felt guilty at all? Do you think she might have paused while packing and thought, hey, this is a *really* bad thing to do?'

'I'm not sure,' Anne Marie said, not knowing what else to say to him.

'You know I hid them?'

'Hid what?'

'The suitcases Renee had bought.' He gave a hollow-sounding laugh. 'I put them in the loft because she's scared to go up there. I stupidly thought that might stop her, but it didn't. I don't think anything would have.'

'Oh, Cape! I'm so sorry.'

'I just can't get into the mind of the person who'd do that. I never realised she was so totally selfish and that she could do something like this to me. Just take Poppy away when I'm out of the house. God! How long has she been planning this for?'

Anne Marie squeezed his hand and they sat quietly for a minute or two.

'I'm sorry,' Cape said at last. 'I shouldn't be burdening you with all this.'

'You're not burdening me,' she told him honestly. 'Anyway, even if you were, I think I owe you after you listened to all my worries. I just wish I could be of more help. I wish I could swap places with you.'

'What do you mean?'

'It seems a bit twisted, but I would have welcomed Grant leaving and taking my step-daughters away. So it seems unfair that it's happened to you. I know how close you are to Poppy. If they'd been taken from me, I doubt very much that I'd have complained. Isn't that terrible?'

'Not at all. Not after the things they've said and done to you.'

'If I could take this pain away from you, I would. I really would,' she told him.

He turned to face her and gave her a smile. 'You're so sweet,' he said. 'Sweet and kind. And beautiful.'

Before she knew what was happening, he'd leaned towards her, his mouth finding hers in the gentlest of kisses. She was surprised for a moment, but the kiss felt so natural and so good that she didn't protest. Perhaps they'd been moving towards this for a while – she leaving Grant and Cape feeling increasingly isolated from Renee. They'd shared so much over the past few months and the feeling of intimacy between them had been growing. Perhaps a kiss was the next step.

'I'm sorry,' he said. 'I shouldn't have . . .' His words petered out. 'I mean, I've wanted to for a long time, but – well – I'm a mess.'

'*You're* a mess?' she said with a light laugh. 'Have you taken a look at my life recently?'

He laughed. 'We're two messes in a maze.'

'Yes!'

'What if we walked out of here and none of this had happened?' he asked.

'You mean the kiss?'

'No. What if I went home to find Renee was there and you went home to Grant.'

Anne Marie swallowed hard. 'I don't want to go home to Grant.'

'And I don't want Renee in my home anymore.' He sighed. 'We might be in a mess, but we're moving in the right direction, aren't we? I mean, if I could just get my Poppy back.'

'You'll get her back,' she said.

'You sound a lot more confident than I feel.'

'She's your daughter, Cape. You'll find a way.'

He stood up and held his hand out to her, helping her off the bench. She wondered if they were going to kiss again, and half hoped that they would, but his mind seemed to be elsewhere now as he looked up into the stars. Was he still imagining his daughter flying somewhere up there in the inky darkness? Or was he still thinking about what had just happened between them as she was?

They walked back to Kathleen's in silence. Cape had put his hands in his pockets and she took that to mean that he was still thinking about Poppy.

'Thank you,' he said as they reached the bed and breakfast.

'For what?'

'For helping to calm me down tonight. I don't know what I'd have done without you.'

'I'm glad if I've helped in any way.'

'You have. You really have.'

'Good.'

He nodded. 'And – erm . . .'

'It's okay,' she interrupted.

'What's okay?'

'The kiss – you don't need to worry about me making a big thing out of it. It was – well – of the moment, wasn't it?'

He cocked his head to one side. 'What do you mean?'

'I mean, your head's full and mine is too. We don't need to complicate things between us.'

'Oh,' he said. 'I see.'

She swallowed hard, knowing that she had to be firm about this. 'It was nice – don't get me wrong.'

'Yes,' he agreed. 'It was very nice.'

'But we're both in strange places at the moment.' She bit her lip, not quite sure how to continue, only knowing that she must.

'Look,' he said, 'I like you, Anne Marie. I can't pretend that I don't. But I don't want to put any pressure on you.'

'I'm . . . we're . . .'

'You don't have to say anything. It's fine.'

'I like you too, Cape.'

He smiled. 'Good. I'll see you at the garden, okay?'

'Absolutely.'

He leaned forward and kissed her on the cheek and Anne Marie silently cursed herself for having pushed him away.

The Thames Valley police weren't very helpful nor were they terribly sympathetic.

'It's been twenty-four hours!' Cape had cried. 'She's got my daughter with her. My ten-year-old daughter!'

'If your daughter's with her mother then she should be safe,' the officer had told him.

Cape hadn't been placated. He'd been told not to panic, but to wait at home for news which would no doubt come in the next few hours, the officer assured him. If his daughter was with her mother, it was a domestic issue.

After leaving the police station, Cape had dithered about, lost in his own confusion, and then a thought occurred to him. The salon. He rarely visited Renee's work, but he headed there now, parking across the street and startling an old woman having a perm when he charged inside.

'Cape?' Renee's friend and colleague, Helena, looked up from the head full of curlers.

'You need to tell me everything,' he said.

She looked confused for a moment, but then nodded. 'Bella? Can you take over here?' Helena asked a young woman. 'You'd better come with me.' She guided Cape into a room at the back of the salon. 'Can I get you a tea or coffee?'

'No. You can tell me where Renee is.'

Helena pushed her fair hair out of her face and sighed. 'I don't know what to tell you, Cape.'

'All of it – everything you know.'

She leant against a table and crossed her arms over her chest.

'She's my best mate,' she told him.

'That's why I came to you. I'm betting you'll know more than me about all this.'

'You're putting me in a very awkward situation.'

'And what kind of a situation do you think *I'm* in?' he asked gruffly. He took a deep breath. 'Please, Helena – just tell me what you know. I'm tearing my hair out not knowing what's going on. What's she said to you?'

Helena fiddled with her nails for a moment before speaking. 'How much do you know?'

'That she's disappeared. That she's taken my daughter with her.'

'She's in America,' Helena said.

Cape closed his eyes and nodded. 'Yes. I thought she might be.'

'She's been planning it for weeks. *Months*. It's all she ever talked about. She even got herself a nickname from the customers. *USA-Renee*!'

Cape flopped down into a chair. 'I was kind of hoping you'd say she was hiding out at yours.'

'I'm afraid not.'

'No. I see that now. I've just been trying to tell myself that she wouldn't really do this.'

'She really did it, Cape. I'm sorry.'

'I wish you'd given me the heads-up.'

Helena frowned. 'You know I couldn't do that.'

'No, I know.' He paused before asking the question he'd been dreading asking. 'Did she say anything about how long she's going to be there for?'

Helena looked puzzled by his question. 'What do you mean? She's gone for good,' she told him. 'That was her plan. Surely you knew that?'

'Helena?' Bella's voice shouted through from the shop.

'Look, I'd better get back and supervise that perm. Bella's a bit of a catastrophe when it comes to curls.' She paused. 'I'm really sorry I can't be any real help.'

'No, you have been,' Cape said, getting up to leave.

'You're a good guy, Cape. This shouldn't have happened to you.'

Now, back at home, sitting on the sofa with his head in his hands, Cape felt totally helpless. Renee still wasn't answering her phone and there were no missed calls, texts or emails from her. Anger and frustration coursed through him, but what could he do except wait?

It wasn't until the next day that Cape finally received a message from Renee. It was left on the home answering machine so she wouldn't have to talk to him directly, which was frustrating for him but at least it was contact.

You left me no choice, Cape, she told him. *I begged you and you didn't listen. I had to do this and I had to have Poppy with me.*

There was no apology and no invitation for him to join them.

He sank down onto the sofa, his shoulders sagging as if in defeat. He'd never felt more helpless in his life.

Chapter 18

It was one of those glorious hot summer days that get British people through the long, dark days of winter. The sky was a blinding blue and the garden had a sort of reverent hush about it that demanded you turn your own volume down and just sit and observe the beauty around you.

It was too hot to paint. The bedroom had been stifling and Emilia and Jay had simply given up. Now they were lying on a rug under the shade of the cedar tree, one of its glorious branches acting like a massive green parasol above them.

Emilia had taken the midnight-blue gown off and was now wearing a white cotton dress of her own. She'd almost forgotten what it was like to wear twentieth-century clothes. The fabric was so light and she almost felt naked wearing it, and she was slightly self-conscious at how pale her arms and legs looked. Jay had told her he loved her skin. He called her his 'porcelain beauty' and said that Rossetti would have forsaken all his other muses to paint her. Emilia wasn't sure about that, but it was fun to be flattered.

'It's going to be another hot evening,' Jay complained. 'My flat's like an oven and I hate opening the window onto the noisy road.' He gave a weary sigh as he gazed up into the cedar tree.

'I can't bear to think of you there,' Emilia said, trying to imagine his tiny Oxford home. 'Hey – why don't you sleep out in the garden tonight?'

Jay turned over and pushed himself up onto his elbows to look at her. 'Here?'

'No, one of the gardens in the village,' she said with a laugh. 'Of *course* here! I could sneak out some blankets and an old rug. It'd be much cooler than your flat. We could set you up a little bed in the centre of the maze. Tobias wouldn't have a clue. I don't know why we haven't thought of it sooner. We could even have a midnight feast.'

'Would you stay with me, then?' he asked, reaching out and catching her hand in his. 'I mean, beyond this midnight feast?'

Her lips parted and she didn't answer for a moment.

'Just imagine it, Emmy,' Jay continued, his voice fuelled with excitement. 'A whole night under the stars in the middle of the maze. I can't think of anything more romantic.'

It was two weeks after the night in the maze and Emilia was walking down the stairs when she heard her brother calling.

'Emmy?'

'Yes?'

'Come in here.'

She entered the living room. Tobias was standing by the fireplace, his hands clasped behind his back like a stiff Victorian gentleman. Where had he learned to pose like that, she wondered? Did he secretly practise? Angela would have no doubt laughed at him had she still been a part of things at Morton Hall, and the notion amused Emilia now, but the reality of her brother standing there scared her a little too.

'What is it?' she asked him.

'Sit down.'

She did as she was told. She was wearing an emerald gown, which was a favourite of Tobias's, and he smiled at it now.

'You look nice,' he told her.

247

'Thank you,' she said, wishing he'd get on with whatever it was he wanted to say.

'How's the portrait going?'

'Good. It's nearly finished. I think you'll be able to see it soon.'

'Good. That's good.' He cleared his throat. 'And you've been happy with Jay painting you?'

'Yes, of course. Why wouldn't I have been?'

'I just wanted to make sure.'

'I'm really happy. Was that all?'

'What's your hurry?'

'No hurry.'

'Then sit and talk to me,' he said.

'All right then.'

He sat on the sofa beside her and she heard him sigh.

'Have you been in touch with Angela?' she dared to ask.

He looked puzzled. 'No. Why would you ask that?'

'Oh, I don't know – because you two were close for a while?'

'She means nothing to me,' he said bluntly. 'She wasn't like you.'

'She's not meant to be like me,' Emilia said. 'She's Angela. I'm your sister.'

Tobias shook his head. 'We don't need anyone else, you and I.'

She swallowed. She didn't like it when Tobias talked this way. It scared her.

'Yes, we do. We should have people in our lives, Tobias. *Other* people. It's healthy. It's good for us.'

'No, it's not. It's bad. It upsets things. I like things the way they are when it's just you and me.'

'I know you do,' she said, keeping her voice calm and trying not to flinch as he picked up her hand. 'But you enjoyed being around Angela, didn't you?'

'No.'

'Come on, Tobes – you did. I know you did.'

A dark expression passed over his face. 'Maybe in the beginning.'

'There, you see? And I think you could have made things work too. You just need to be a little more patient with people and a little bit freer with yourself.'

He gave a derisive laugh.

'You need to give things time.' She could feel her heart thudding as his grip on her hand tightened. 'I really think you should let more people into your life.'

'I invited Jay here.'

'Yes, and that's good.'

'Is it?'

'Of course it is. Why would you ask that?'

'Because I'm not happy with you spending so much time with him.'

'I have to. He's painting me.'

'But I've seen you in the garden together.'

'We're just talking.'

'Don't lie to me, Emmy. I can always tell when you're lying.'

'What do you want me to say?'

'I want to know the truth.'

'About what?'

'What's going on with you?'

She gently removed her hand from his – a move that didn't go unnoticed by him. He frowned at her.

'Tell me what's going on.'

'We've become friends,' she said at last.

'It's more than that.'

'If you know what's going on, why are you asking me all these questions?' She made to stand up, but Tobias grasped her hand and forced her down again. 'Tobias!'

'Tell me the truth!'

'Let go of me.'

'Not until you're honest with me.'

She glared at him.

'You think you're in love with this man,' he continued, 'but you're not. He's just the first man you've ever really spent time with.'

'And whose fault is that? I've spent my whole life in this house. Then I was sent to an all-girls' school. The only time I got to meet men was at university and you were always so careful to remind me that I was there to study and not to fall in love, remember? I think you'd rather I didn't meet anyone at all, wouldn't you?'

'That's right.'

'Well, that's not normal!' she cried.

'Don't you dare tell me what's normal and what isn't.'

'*Somebody* needs to tell you and I'm the only one who dares!'

They faced each other, eyes blazing in defiance. Tobias was the first to speak.

'Go to your room, Emilia.'

'You can't treat me like a child.'

'Go to your room.'

She stood up and turned her back on him.

'I said—'

'I'm going!' she shouted at him. 'Not because you tell me to, but so I can lock myself in it away from you!'

When she reached her room and had bolted the door, she sank down heavily on the bed. She hated fighting with her brother. *Hated* it. But there seemed to be no other way with him sometimes.

When he'd asked her to sit with him and talk to her, a little part of her had hoped that they really *could* talk, because she'd wanted to tell him something important.

She'd wanted to tell him that she believed she was pregnant and that it was time for her to make a life away from Morton Hall.

'Have you ever been married, Mac?' Cape asked as the two of them shifted a half-rotten beech branch from a flower bed to a wildlife area. In the three months in which the group had been working together, Mac was the person Cape felt most intrigued by, other than Anne Marie, of course. They'd had a few personal conversations, which he'd enjoyed immensely, but he felt like there was much more to find out about the older man.

Mac took his cap off and ran a hand through his thick hair. 'Married?'

'You don't mind me asking?' Cape said. 'I mean, tell me if I'm being nosy.'

Mac shook his head. 'I haven't had time to get married,' he said. 'Time or inclination.'

Cape grinned. 'Married to your gardens?'

'Yep. Although there was a woman once. Just once. Thought it might work out, but it wasn't meant to be. She was allergic to flowers. Can you imagine that? How could I marry someone allergic to flowers? Got to have flowers about me. You can't make a garden or a home without them.'

'Did you love her?' Cape asked.

'For a while. But I guess I loved my work more.'

Cape nodded.

'I think about her every so often,' Mac continued, 'and I've been out with a few other women, but they pass like the seasons.'

Cape couldn't help smiling at his philosophical take on things. He truly didn't seem to mind being on his own.

'I take it you've not heard from her again, then,' Mac said, obviously referring to Renee. Cape had told him about what had happened the week before. It had just come pouring out of him in an angry torrent and Mac had been there for him.

'Not since the message she left last week.' Cape took his own cap off and scratched his head, mirroring Mac's movement a few moments earlier. 'It's driving me crazy. I've phoned and I've emailed. I've used every social media platform available and she still doesn't get back to me, and her sister's not replied to the emails I've sent either.'

'Have you been back to the police?' Mac asked.

'It's crossed my mind, but what would they be able to do? They'll just say there's been contact and it's a domestic problem.'

'Maybe you should go over there.'

'Yeah, maybe I should. But guess what? I don't have her sister's address. Isn't that crazy? I've no idea how to find Renee even if I did go out there.'

'What about her parents? Would they know?'

'Her mother died years ago and she doesn't really talk to her father so I'm guessing he won't be much help, and her friend Helena's told me all she knows.'

'I'd say you're stuffed, then.'

'Thanks.'

Mac bent down and picked up a rogue terracotta tile that was resting on a bed of leaves.

'You know,' he said, jabbing the tile in the air towards him, 'I thought you and that nice Anne Marie were getting close.'

'Did you?' Cape was surprised. Had it been that obvious to the group, he wondered?

'You mean you aren't?'

For a moment, Cape wondered whether to confide in Mac about the kiss he'd shared with Anne Marie in the maze, but there was no telling where Mac might stand on Cape getting involved with a married woman. And that was exactly what Anne Marie was. She might have left her husband, but she was still wearing her ring, he'd noticed. She'd also given him a gentle nudge to back off and he had to respect that. Besides, didn't he have enough problems to be dealing with in his life?

The truth was, his head was full of Poppy at the moment. He'd barely slept since she and Renee had left. The house felt empty without them and he carried an appalling kind of anxiety around with him as he paced the rooms where his daughter no longer played. Every move, every action seemed abnormal and torturous without her. Fixing breakfast without reaching for her favourite glass and bowl was wrong, and leaving the house without first claiming a sweet kiss on his cheek was dreadful to him.

He remembered the day that Renee had told him she was pregnant. He'd walked around in a daze for weeks afterwards. He wasn't ready to be a father, he kept thinking. He wasn't up to the job. Now, he couldn't bear the thought of not having Poppy in his life. She was so much a part of him that being separated from her was eating him up inside.

'You like her, don't you?' Mac asked, breaking into Cape's thoughts.

'Pardon?'

'Anne Marie.'

Cape took a moment to switch his focus from Poppy to Anne Marie. 'Oh, yeah, I like her,' he confessed, thinking of their kiss in the maze.

'Can't say I blame you. She's a sweet soul.'

'She is, isn't she? I don't think I've met a sweeter woman in my life.'

'Good worker too,' Mac observed.

'Where is she?' Cape looked across the garden, but couldn't see any sign of Anne Marie.

'Keeping away from you by the looks of things.'

Cape glanced at Mac as if for confirmation of this. 'You might be right about that.'

The truth was, Anne Marie had been doing her best to avoid Cape. She felt awful, but she wanted to keep her head down, do her time in the garden and go home. Things had been moving far too quickly between them and her head was spinning with it all. She liked him and she couldn't deny that there was a connection between them but, as much as she'd loved their kiss in the maze, she needed to get through the mess of her separation first. She didn't dare allow herself a glimpse of even the tiniest romance in her future.

Kathleen had been a godsend. She'd told Anne Marie she could stay with her for as long as she liked, which really took the pressure off. The last thing Anne Marie wanted to do was begin looking for accommodation and facing her life as a single woman. Being welcomed into Kathleen's home and talking to her each day was really helping her through this whole miserable process.

She was just pulling up a large thistle when Erin ran across the lawn towards her.

'Hey, Erin!'

'Mrs Beatty wants you. Us,' Erin said between great pants of breath.

'Me? Us?'

'Come on.'

Anne Marie put the thistle down and removed her gloves.

'Where are we going?' she asked.

'Into the house – at *last*!'

Anne Marie smiled at Erin's enthusiasm, knowing that she'd been dying to see the house and its collection.

'Slow down!' Anne Marie called after her, struggling to keep up with the young woman as she raced across the lawn. 'Did she say what she wanted us to do?'

'Not yet, but I'm hoping she'll give us a tour at least.'

Anne Marie wasn't as hopeful. If she knew Mrs Beatty, there'd be some kind of hard graft involved in their trip to the house.

Unsurprisingly, Mrs Beatty didn't look pleased to see Anne Marie or Erin even though she'd summoned them.

'You will remove your boots and coats and wash your hands in the cloakroom,' she said, nodding to a door off the hallway.

Removing their boots, they trotted off to the cloakroom – a pretty little space hung with tiles depicting dragonesque creatures. They took it in turn to wash their hands and returned to the hall. For a minute, Anne Marie was quite convinced that Mrs Beatty was actually going to ask them both to show her their hands to check that they'd washed them to her satisfaction. But she refrained.

'Come with me,' she commanded, and the two of them followed her down a hallway, turning left at the end into a large room that seemed to be some kind of office. Like all the rooms Anne Marie had seen so far, it was beautiful, with wood-panelled walls and a large mullioned window. But it wasn't the beauty of the room they were staring at now; it was the heaps of papers, files and books everywhere.

Mrs Beatty cleared her throat. 'It needs a little organising,' she conceded.

'A little?' Erin said, her face registering her shock.

'The Mortons didn't like people,' Mrs Beatty said, and then paused. Anne Marie had heard the same rumours so wasn't surprised by this.

'I mean,' Mrs Beatty continued, 'they didn't like people poking around. Old Mr Morton did his best with the paperwork, but I fear it got the better of him, and young Tobias was – well – he never was one for that side of things.'

'You want us to do the filing?' Erin said, clearly disappointed.

'To begin with, yes. This place needs to be sorted out just as much as the garden does. If not more. It shouldn't take too long.'

'Really?' Erin didn't sound convinced by this.

'And then we can move onto the art collection – cataloguing that. It's never been done, you see.'

Erin's expression changed and Anne Marie realised that Mrs Beatty was dangling the art collection as a particularly juicy carrot for Erin. *You can catalogue that later, but the filing must be done first.*

'I think if we separate all the official things like bills, invoices, statements, et cetera and then collate the more personal items like letters, shopping lists—'

'Shopping lists?' Anne Marie queried.

'All here,' Mrs Beatty said. 'The Mortons never threw anything away.'

'But this will take decades,' Erin exclaimed.

'I've put some new box files out for your use. Divide things up as you go. You don't need to worry about date order. We can come back to that later. There's a kitchen down the corridor with a kettle if you need to take a break in, say . . .' She checked her watch. '. . . two hours or so.'

Erin's mouth dropped open and Anne Marie swallowed hard. In essence, they were being told that they were to endure two hours of filing before taking an official break. Part of her wanted to laugh at Mrs Beatty's nerve, but part of her rather admired her. She knew what she wanted and how to get it.

'This is a dreary place,' Erin said as soon as Mrs Beatty had left them. 'I've been dying to get in here all this time and now I think I'd rather be out in the garden.'

'But it will lead to other things,' Anne Marie suggested. 'Mrs Beatty said so.'

Erin looked thoughtful. 'Yes! Maybe this is a test and, if I pass, I'll be allowed to poke around the attics and curate some kind of exhibition or something.'

'Well, she said that the art collection needed cataloguing.'

Erin nodded.

'Was it my imagination or was Mrs Beatty really staring at me?' Anne Marie asked Erin.

'When?'

'Just now. The whole time.'

'I didn't notice,' Erin said.

'I don't have mud on my face or anything, do I?' Anne Marie said, giving her nose a stroke with anxious fingers.

'No.'

'I got the weirdest feeling when she was looking at me. Like she was trying to work me out.'

But Erin wasn't really listening to her. She'd spotted a portrait hanging above the desk and walked across the room to examine it.

'Look at him. That's the sternest-looking moustache I've ever seen.'

Anne Marie joined her and looked up into the grim Victorian face. 'You wouldn't want to cross him, would you?'

'I wonder who he was.'

'A Morton.'

'One of the ones who didn't bother with filing?' Erin tutted.

'Probably,' Anne Marie said. 'Come on. Let's make a start.'

It was dusty, dirty work, but not without its pleasures.

'Look at this receipt,' Erin cried with joy after they'd been at it for a good half-hour. 'It's for a Burne-Jones stained-glass window bought at auction.'

Anne Marie took a look at it and spluttered at the amount paid, which was eye-watering even back in the 1970s.

'Each member of the family kept adding to the collection, it seems,' Erin said, clearly fascinated.

It was a few minutes later when Anne Marie found a newspaper clipping from the 1980s.

'Tobias Morton found dead in his bedroom,' she read.

'Oh, let's see!' Erin grabbed the piece of paper from her and examined it. 'He was handsome, wasn't he?'

'I suppose,' Anne Marie said, looking over Erin's shoulder and studying the pale face that stared back out at her from the newspaper.

'What did it say he died of?'

'Suspected drug overdose,' Anne Marie read. 'So sad.'

'Why is it that so many rich people get themselves into trouble with drink and drugs? I mean, why would you do that to yourself if you owned this amazing house?'

'I don't think it's as simple as that. A beautiful house doesn't necessarily make you happy.'

'So he was Miss Morton's brother?' Erin asked.

'Yes. It says here that she was the one to find his body.'

'But there's no photo of her.'

'No, it's only a brief story. That's a bit strange, isn't it?'

'From what I've heard, nobody knew much about the family here,' Erin said, handing the clipping back to Anne Marie who placed it in a box file.

For some reason, the story in the newspaper had made Anne Marie intensely sad. There was something about the idea of Miss Morton on her own, finding the dead body of her brother, that touched her deeply. What must that have been like, she wondered? She couldn't even begin to imagine. And where had Mrs Beatty been? What had she made of it all? She wasn't the sort of person one felt you could ask about such things, but she must have felt something towards her previous employer.

'And now they're both gone.'

'Pardon?' Erin said, looking up from the pile of papers she was sorting through.

'Tobias and Emilia. The last of the Mortons.'

'That's why we're here.'

'Don't you think that's sad? Not to have anyone to leave your home to?' Anne Marie said.

'But they did – they left it to us.'

'I know, but not to have *family*.'

'I guess.'

Anne Marie swallowed, suddenly realising what she'd just said. She didn't have family, did she? Other than her mother, that was. But, when her mother died, Anne Marie would be the last one, wouldn't she?

'Are you all right?' Erin asked.

'What?' She looked up. 'Oh, I'm fine.'

'You'd rather be out in the garden too, wouldn't you?'

Anne Marie fixed her attention on the view from the mullioned window. 'No,' she said a moment later. 'I rather like it in here. I feel strangely at home.'

Chapter 19

Jay looked pensive.

'What is it?' Emilia asked, turning around from the window.

'It's done.'

'What is?'

'The painting.'

'Really?'

He looked at her and nodded, a sad smile on his face.

'Can I see it?'

'Of course.'

She left the window where she had been standing for the last hour and a half and walked towards the easel.

'It's funny,' she said with a small laugh, 'but I'm actually nervous.'

'But you've seen it before.'

'Yes, but that was a while ago now.'

'Well, if you'd rather not see it . . .' Jay said, blocking her way.

'Silly!' she said, batting his arm and then pushing him firmly aside before taking a look at the canvas. She tipped her head first one way and then the other.

'Well?' Jay said, seemingly impatient for her response.

'You've made me look like . . . like . . .'

'An angel?'

'I don't know about that. An angel in the house, perhaps.'

'What?'

'The angel in the house,' she said again. 'It was the Victorian notion of the ideal woman – one who was submissive to the men around her, who knew her place in the patriarchal world. The term comes from a poem by Coventry Patmore, but you'll be more familiar with her portrayal in the art of the time. A lot of the Pre-Raphaelite artists portrayed her trapped in a room or framed by a window. That's what you've done to me here.'

Jay took a step towards her.

'Yes, but you're looking outside, aren't you? You're looking *out* of the window and beyond the garden walls.'

Emilia looked at the portrait again, at the slightly melancholic look on her face, but also at the dazzling light he'd caught in her eyes. Was it the light of optimism, perhaps, as if she was looking into her own future and a life outside Morton Hall? A life that saw her as Jay's wife and a mother?

Instinctively, her hand flew to her stomach, reminding her that she hadn't yet told Jay that she was pregnant. Today, she told herself. She would tell him today.

'So, do you like it?' Jay whispered in her ear. 'Because I think my heart would break if you didn't.'

She smiled at him. 'I love it,' she said.

'Yeah?'

'Yes.'

He leaned forward and kissed her.

'The question is, will Tobias like it?' she said.

'Only one way to find out. I'll go and get him.'

'Want me to come with you?'

'No. You wait here,' he said.

'You know which his room is?'

'The one with the locked door? I know it.'

'Or he might be in the study downstairs.'

'I'll check both.'

Emilia walked over to the window as Jay left. It would be strange not to have to stand there anymore, looking out. They'd spent so many hours in this space together in companionable silence as Jay had worked and now that was over. The painting was done and she would no longer have to wear the beautiful midnight-blue dress.

'Well, you've taken your time about it,' Tobias said as he came into the room a moment later.

'As you'll see, it's life-size, as requested.'

Emilia turned around as her brother took in the portrait for the first time, his dark eyes narrowed. She swallowed hard as he looked up from the canvas to where she was standing by the window.

'You've caught her,' he said, his eyes glancing down at the painting again. 'Absolutely.'

'Good. Good,' Jay said, nodding. 'Then, you're pleased with it?'

There was a pause and Emilia looked at Jay's face as he awaited the approval of his patron. She'd never seen him anything but confident, yet here he was – the anxious artist, worrying that his work might not be good enough.

'I am.'

Emilia watched as her brother held out a folded cheque to Jay.

'Wow!' Jay said with undisguised glee as he looked at it. 'This is more than we agreed.'

Tobias nodded. 'You've done a good job.'

'But you wrote this out before you'd seen the portrait.'

'I trusted you.'

The two men stared at one another and Emilia wondered if Tobias would shake his hand, perhaps, or offer him a drink. Maybe they'd become friends – *real* friends this time – and then she could tell him, tell them *both*, about the baby. They could become a family together and fill Morton Hall with—

Before she could finish her flight of fantasy, Tobias cleared his throat.

'You'd better say your goodbyes. I expect you'll want an hour or so to get your things together and have a spot of tea before your journey home.' Tobias's eyebrows rose in question, but Jay just frowned at him.

'Yes,' Emilia said quickly, catching Jay's eye before he had the chance to cause a scene. 'That's a lovely idea.'

'Good,' Tobias said and he gave a funny sort of nod before leaving the room.

Jay cursed under his breath.

'Shush!' Emilia warned.

'A spot of tea?' Jay said. 'He thinks I'll leave quietly after a spot of bloody tea?'

Emilia reached towards him, placing her hands on his shoulders. 'Calm down.'

'How can I be calm? Your brother's throwing me out or hadn't you noticed?' He shook his head. 'Emmy, I don't know why we keep delaying this. We should just go. Both of us – now.'

'What?'

'I mean, what's keeping you here? It's crazy to want to stay.'

'But I'm not ready.'

'What do you mean?'

'I don't want to leave Tobias just yet.'

'You want to invite him with us? Would that make you happy?'

'Don't be silly.'

'Because I'm beginning to feel jealous of your brother. He sees more of you than I do.'

'He won't be happy if I just up and leave.'

'He's got your portrait to keep him company.'

Emilia's fingers bunched into fists. How could she explain this to Jay?

'It's just, I've got a bad feeling about this.'

'What bad feeling?' he asked. 'You're not making any sense here. I thought you wanted to get away from this place. I thought you wanted to be with me.'

'I *do*, Jay.'

He picked up her left hand and turned it over to kiss the delicate skin of her wrist and that's when he saw the bruises.

'Jesus, Emmy. Did *he* do that to you?'

She pulled her hand away from him. She'd forgotten about the angry purple marks.

'It's nothing. It doesn't even hurt anymore.'

Jay wasn't appeased. 'I want to kill him!'

'Don't say that.'

'I can't help it. It's how he makes me feel. We've got to leave,' he told her. 'We can't keep putting it off.'

'I know,' she said, 'and we will.'

'When?'

'Soon.'

'Give me a date, Emilia. *Soon* isn't good enough.'

She swallowed hard. 'I don't know.'

'Friday. We're leaving Friday.'

'Jay – that's not enough time!'

He took her hands gently in his once again. 'I want to be with you. I *need* to be with you.'

Something in her heart melted at his desperate tone and she nodded. Perhaps that would be the night to tell him her news, she thought. Yes, she'd tell him then.

'All right. Friday it is.'

He kissed her. 'We'll meet in the maze at midnight.'

'Oh, Jay!'

He grinned. 'It'll be the romantic adventure of your life!'

Meeting in the maze at midnight might have seemed like a wildly romantic thing to do, but the reality of it was quite different, Emilia thought as she opened her bedroom door a crack and listened. She couldn't tell if Tobias was still up or not.

She checked her suitcase again. She'd packed only the essentials. Jay had recently bought himself a second-hand car, but it wasn't very big. Emilia wasn't even sure where they were going. They hadn't talked anything through other than getting away from Morton Hall.

Tiptoeing out of her room, Emilia made her way slowly down the stairs, unbolting the great front door and letting herself out into the garden. The moon was bright and the romance of the moment got the better of her, banishing her fears and putting Tobias out of her mind as she focussed on finding Jay.

She left her suitcase outside the west entrance of the maze and ventured inside. She'd been in the maze before at night, loving the deep darkness of the place, but she knew this time would be her last at Morton Hall. She hadn't really thought about that until now. She'd never see the maze again, would she? For she instinctively knew that Tobias would want nothing more to do with her after she left like this.

Her footsteps were light and her speed picked up as she neared the centre of the maze. She could feel her heart racing and was tempted to call Jay's name, but thought it was better to be cautious. She would be with him soon enough.

One more left and one more right and she would be in the centre: she felt sure that Jay was already there, waiting for her.

But it wasn't Jay who was there. It was Tobias.

Cape was out in his garden one Friday afternoon pulling down a length of old trellis when he heard the phone ring from the house. At first, he thought about ignoring it, but he really couldn't take that chance with

Poppy gone and so he ran inside, grabbing the phone before the caller rang off.

It was Helena.

She cleared her throat and then said, 'I have a message from Renee. Poppy's flying home today.'

'What?' Cape blurted.

'Renee asked me to tell you to meet her at the airport.'

'Airport?'

'She's coming into Heathrow,' Helena told him, giving him the time and details of the flight.

'Is Renee not with her?'

There was a pause. 'No.'

'What do you mean, *no*?'

'Renee's in America. She's staying.'

'Wait a minute,' Cape said. 'Are you telling me she sent my daughter home alone? She's flying across an ocean *on her own*?'

'It's all done properly, Cape. They have people to look out for kids on planes and in airports.'

He couldn't quite believe what he was hearing. 'But this is my kid! Nobody puts *my* kid on a plane on her own! For God's sake!'

'Don't yell at me,' Helena warned. 'I'm just the mug passing on the message.'

'I'm sorry,' he said quickly. 'This is just a bit of a shock.'

He heard her exhale. 'I know.'

'What did Renee say?'

'Not a lot. It was more a series of instructions. She sounded stressed and I didn't want to make things more difficult than they were.'

Cape cursed. What had Renee been thinking? Couldn't she just have come home or, at the very least, accompanied Poppy back before returning herself? Was that really too much to ask?

'And she said nothing else?'

'No, nothing.'

There was an awkward silence as if they were both realising the strangeness of the situation they now found themselves in.

'I'm on my way,' he told her. 'And Helena?'

'Yes?'

'Thanks.'

Cape wasn't surprised that Poppy fell asleep in the car on the way home. She looked exhausted, her face drained of all colour. He'd never forget the intense anxiety he'd felt as he'd waited for her arrival at the airport, checking his watch and phone endlessly in case she was trying to call him, and keeping an eye on the predicted arrival time of her plane in case it was delayed. He'd paced the concourse, unable to sit still for even a minute. Then there was the moment when he'd seen her. He'd never forget it. How small she'd looked standing there with her brand-new suitcase. He'd run towards her, shouting her name across the crowds and scooping her up in his arms.

Now, driving across the Thames, he wanted to chuck that suitcase into the dark water. He shook his head, trying to banish the feelings of anger that were threatening to spill over. He had his girl back and that was what mattered. She was safe and he was damned sure he was going to keep her safe from now on – whatever that took.

Arriving home, he turned the engine off and turned to face her in the passenger seat.

'Hey, Poppy Poppet,' he said, using the nickname he'd given her when she was tiny. 'We're home.'

She yawned and then beamed him a smile that warmed his heart. He opened her door and took her suitcase and the two of them went inside.

'Is it too late for tea?' she asked.

'Of course not. You can have whatever you want, darling.'

'Toast with peanut butter?'

'Coming right up.'

He watched as she climbed the stairs and he swallowed hard as the emotion he'd been bottling up threatened to surface again. Busy. He had to keep busy, and so he prepared his little girl her tea, choosing her favourite plate, which was covered in vibrant poppies, and filling a pink glass with orange juice.

'Poppy?' he called a few minutes later. 'Your toast is ready.'

There was no reply so he went up the stairs, knocking gently on the bedroom door which was ajar.

'Hey!' he said as he saw her lying on the bed, her face hiding in a large teddy bear. 'What's wrong, sweetheart?'

She sniffed and pushed her hair out of her eyes before looking up.

'I missed my room,' she whispered. 'I didn't think I'd see it again.'

'Oh, my Poppy!' he said.

'We were staying in this funny place that smelt bad.'

'It smelt bad?'

'But it had a pool.'

'And did you swim in it?'

'No. It was dirty all the time so I was told not to. I wasn't even allowed to put my feet in it just a little bit.'

Cape gave a short laugh. So much for the Californian dream.

'I kept crying, Daddy! I told Mummy I didn't want to be there.'

'You made her life hell, eh, baby?'

'I think so. I wanted to be home. I missed you and I told Mummy she was mean to leave without you and that it was wrong.' She threw her skinny arms around his neck and he buried his face in her hair, smelling that sweet smell he couldn't live without.

'Nothing can keep us apart anymore, I promise you,' he told her.

She nodded, her head knocking against his neck.

A few moments passed before she spoke again.

'She's not coming home, is she?'

'I don't think so, Poppet,' he said, and the realisation that Renee would rather give up her own daughter than her dream hit him again. 'It's just the two of us.'

Poppy gave a little sniff. 'That's all right though, isn't it?'

'Yes,' he said. 'That's all right. Now, come on downstairs for some tea.'

After she'd eaten and had returned to her room, he opened her suitcase, looking forward to putting all of her things back where they belonged. But he didn't get that far because there was an envelope on the top of Poppy's clothes.

Cape, it read. He picked it up and opened it.

Sending Poppy home is the hardest thing I'll ever have to do, Renee had written. She'd still managed to do it, though, he thought bitterly.

He read on.

But I'm not going to apologise for taking her. I believe it was the right thing to do. Only, it turned out to be all wrong for Poppy. She was miserable from the moment we left home and I realised how much she is like you. She's your girl, Cape, and she should be with you. R.

And that was it. There was no official goodbye. No explanation as to whether she'd ever return to England or if she expected or even wanted him and Poppy to join her at a later date. There was no message of love or regret over her leaving her family behind and no good wishes for their future. But what had he been expecting? Renee had never been one to explain herself – she just did whatever suited her and expected the world to move along with her. Well, he was personally glad if she was out of their lives for good now, although he was anxious and sad for the disruption it would cause Poppy. He'd known that his relationship with Renee had been failing for some time, but it seemed strange to think that he might never hear from her again. After being a part of each other's lives for so many years, it was remarkable to him that he felt so calm about it all.

It was a blessed relief to take Poppy with him to Morton Hall the next day. Everybody was delighted to see her. News had spread amongst the group of Poppy's disappearance and everyone gave her a hug and welcomed her back.

It wasn't until after lunch that Cape got to speak to Anne Marie on her own.

'Hey,' he said.

'Hi. How are you?'

'Good,' he said. 'Exhausted.'

'It's so great that Poppy's back. What a relief for you.'

'I picked her up at the airport yesterday.'

'So Renee's back?'

'Erm, no.'

'No?' Anne Marie blurted. 'What do you mean?'

'Poppy came back on her own.' He watched as Anne Marie's forehead crinkled in bewilderment.

'She flew home alone?'

'Yep.'

'You're kidding me?'

'I wish I was.'

'Renee put her on a plane and—'

'I *still* can't believe she did that.'

'Cape! You must've been furious.'

'I went through every emotion in the book and then some.'

'I can imagine.' She reached out and touched his arm and their eyes met. He saw Anne Marie bite her lip as she withdrew her hand a moment later. 'I'm so glad she's back.'

She turned to go.

'Anne Marie?'

'Yes?'

'Everything okay with you?'

She paused before answering. 'Yes.'

'Because we haven't had much of a chance to talk,' he went on. 'Not since the night in the maze.'

'No,' she said, the word coming quickly and sounding sharp. 'I mean, no, we haven't,' she added, a little more gently.

'Then you're good?'

She nodded and made a little sound in the affirmative and he watched as she walked away. He was just about to go after her and ask her more when Poppy ran across the garden towards him.

'Daddy! Come and see the mess Matthew and Elliot have made in the greenhouse. There's compost and gravel *everywhere* and Patrick's gone all red in the face!'

Chapter 20

The shock of seeing Tobias standing in the middle of the maze hit Emilia like a physical blow.

'What are you doing here?' she demanded.

'I might ask you the same thing.'

They stood staring at each other as if weighing one another's next move.

'He's gone, Emilia.'

'What?'

'You won't be seeing him again.'

'What do you mean?'

'We had a talk, Jay and I, and let me tell you, he understood me perfectly.'

Emilia looked around in panic, swallowing hard as she wondered whether to call out his name.

'I made it worth his while,' Tobias added. 'I can be very persuasive when I want to be. Or rather, *money* can be very persuasive.'

'You didn't! I don't believe you.'

'Oh, I did.'

'Jay wouldn't have left. It wasn't about money.'

'It's *always* about money. You saw his face when I gave him the cheque for the portrait. He couldn't believe his luck. Well, you should have seen it when I gave him the one tonight.'

Emilia shook her head. 'You're lying. I *know* you're lying! We're in love. Don't you understand that?'

'Love! You're too greedy, Emilia. You have all the love you need right here.'

She looked at him aghast. 'What?'

He took her hands in his. 'Why do you need anybody else?'

'Get off me!' She tried to wrench her hands free and he let go of her and it was then that she saw the blood on his knuckles.

'Oh, my god! What did you do to him? *What did you do?*'

She beat her hands against his chest and wailed like a mad woman.

'Come inside,' he told her, trying to catch hold of her, but she pulled away from him.

'I'm not going back inside with you.'

'No? And what are you going to do? Run after him? He's long gone, Emilia, and he isn't coming back.'

She started to run out of the maze now.

'Jay!' she cried into the night. 'JAY?'

She could hear Tobias's footsteps behind her, but she didn't stop. She had to find Jay. Tobias was lying. He was always lying or trying to manipulate her. He thought he could control her and now he believed that he could control Jay too, but he couldn't. She wouldn't let him. He'd never be able to come between them.

She'd just made it out of the maze when she felt the blow to the back of her head and the world turned black.

Emilia came round in her bedroom. Somebody had undressed her and put her to bed and she had the feeling that it wasn't Mrs Beatty. She jumped out of bed and ran to her door. It was locked. Panic gripped her as she ran to the window. It was still dark. She checked her clock. It was just after one. Had she been unconscious for nearly an hour? Her head was throbbing and hot tears began to fall as she remembered the encounter in the maze. Tobias, who'd always been afraid of the maze, had overcome his fear to prevent her from leaving him. At that realisation, her heart turned to stone. She had no more love for her brother. She could never forgive him for what he'd done.

Spring could be a fraught time for a gardener. Seedlings were growing, demanding to be planted out, but the weatherman might still be warning of late frosts. Patrick and his sons had been making excellent progress in the greenhouse, and the workbenches were full of trays of plants desperate to be allowed to grow and romp in the rich soil of the raised beds.

Both Cape and Mac had warned them not to be too eager to plant out. The safest measure would be to pot up some of the more vigorous plants. It was a time-consuming job, but one which everybody got involved with, glad to shelter from the spring wind in the comparative cosiness of the long Victorian greenhouse.

Anne Marie was enjoying the work. She and Erin had fallen into a routine of helping out in the garden for the first part of the morning and then going inside for the rest of the day to work in the study. It broke things up a bit. Erin was becoming more and more anxious to do some 'real work' with the collection, but Mrs Beatty insisted on them making progress in the study first.

She looked up from the bench where she, Erin and Kathleen were planting up the impressive squash plants while the others were working on various other plants on another bench. Cape was chatting to Dorothy and Mac while Patrick was giving his boys instructions.

It was when Kathleen took a tray of finished plants to the other side of the greenhouse that Patrick took his younger son, Elliot, to one side and whispered something in his ear before giving him a little push.

Anne Marie watched as the boy started to walk across the greenhouse towards Kathleen, but then stopped, looking back at his father who waved his hand in encouragement. The boy grimaced and Anne Marie continued watching as he walked a bit further, digging his hands into the pockets of his jeans and stopping just short of where Kathleen was.

'Dad wants to know if you'll come to dinner tonight,' Elliot bellowed, his voice reverberating around the greenhouse, causing everybody to look up from their tasks. Kathleen turned bright red, but it was nothing compared to the look of annoyance on Patrick's face. He'd obviously intended the message to be relayed more privately than that.

Anne Marie grinned and caught Cape's eye. He was smiling and she watched as he put down the pot he was holding, wiped his hands on the front of his jeans and walked towards her.

'Got a minute?'

She nodded, wiping her own hands down her trousers and following him out of the greenhouse. It was a crisp, clear spring day with a beautiful lilac-blue sky. The garden was heaving with irises and bluebells and there was the most delicate of white blossoms on the plum trees they'd planted in the walled garden. It truly was a blessed time of year.

'Everyone really seems to be enjoying things now,' Anne Marie said as they walked around the walled garden together. 'Remember when we first met?'

Cape chuckled. 'I'll never forget Patrick's outrage that he should be involved in a project like this!'

'He's really mellowed, hasn't he?'

'Gardens are good for people,' Cape said. 'The creation of them, the maintenance of them, the dreaming about what's possible in them.'

'And the boys too. I actually think you might have two budding gardeners there.'

'And a new couple.'

'Yes!' Anne Marie said. 'I'd never have put Patrick and Kath together.'

'I think they've surprised everyone, including themselves.'

They walked for a little longer. Anne Marie wondered why he'd pulled her from the group, but didn't want to prod him. Maybe he had a special job in mind for her.

'There's a meteor shower tonight,' he suddenly said.

'Pardon?'

'A meteor shower. Have you heard?'

'No. No I haven't.'

'We could watch it right here from the walled garden.'

'What, all the group?' Anne Marie asked.

Cape cleared his throat. 'I was thinking of just you and me.'

'Oh.'

He continued. 'The meteor, well it's pieces of comet – comet debris if you like – which pass through the earth's atmosphere.'

'You seem to know a lot about it.'

'Not really. Just what I heard on the radio. But I thought it would be cool to see it. There'll be hundreds of them passing over the next three days. This would be the perfect place to see them from with no light pollution and a good view of the sky and, apparently, it's going to be clear tonight.'

'I see.'

He stopped walking and looked at her.

'And, well, we haven't talked much since Poppy came back and since . . .' He paused. '. . . the maze.'

Anne Marie felt a flutter of nerves at thinking of their kiss in the maze.

'I guess I wanted to make sure that we were still friends,' he added.

'Of *course* we're still friends,' she told him.

A look of relief passed over his face. 'Then you'll meet me here? Tonight at nine?'

'Will Poppy be joining us?' she asked.

'No, she's having a sleep-over at a friend's house.'
'Will it be cold?'
'A clear night in April? I'd say it will be freezing!'
She laughed and then nodded. 'I'll wear my warmest clothes.'

Anne Marie wasn't the only one going out that night. Kathleen was buzzing around upstairs, a hairbrush in one hand and an anxious expression on her face.

'What should I wear? What should I wear?' she called as Anne Marie passed her on the landing.

'You're going to his house, right?'

'Right.'

'I'd keep it casual then.'

'But I want to wear something pretty. He's only ever seen me in jeans, wellies and old jumpers.'

'Good point. Have you got a suitable dress?'

'I can't remember the last time I wore a dress,' Kathleen confessed. 'Since the fire, I've been living in nothing but trousers and jumpers as I've been trying to put things back together again. But my sister brought me some things. I haven't really looked at them.'

Anne Marie followed Kathleen into her bedroom and watched as she opened the wardrobe door.

'Here,' she said, pulling out a pretty dress in a deep red. 'Do you think this will do?'

'I think you'll blow him away if you wear that.'

'Really?'

'Do you want to blow him away?'

Kathleen gave a naughty little smile. 'Yes. I think I do.'

Anne Marie didn't have the luxury of choosing a dress that evening. Instead, she wore her warmest trousers and put on several thick layers before leaving the house to join Cape at the garden at nine o'clock.

She couldn't help feeling a little anxious about meeting him there. After their last venture into the garden at night, she'd promised herself that she would focus on sorting out the mess that was her life rather than jumping headlong into another one. After all, any sort of relationship between her and Cape could be nothing but a mess because they were still involved with other people. She might have left Grant, and Renee might have left Cape, but things were by no means settled.

But surely she was worrying unnecessarily because she and Cape were just friends, weren't they?

Friends who were meeting in a darkened garden on their own to look at the stars.

She tried to banish the voice inside her head. She wasn't going to pay it any attention because, although there was an undeniable attraction between her and Cape, it wasn't going to go anywhere. She wasn't going to let it.

'We're friends,' she told herself as she walked up the driveway. '*Just* friends.'

How magical it was to wander around Morton Hall's garden at night. The dark shadows lent it an ethereal quality and the topiary looked more alive than ever in the thin beam of light from her torch.

Cape was waiting to meet her at the cedar tree, his own torch in his hand.

'Hey,' he said.

'Hello.'

'I've brought a flask of tea,' he told her.

'I brought some chocolate.'

'Excellent.'

They walked through to the walled garden, Cape leading the way to the old bench where Anne Marie used to sit on her own. It was already quite cold and Anne Marie was glad she'd thought to bring a woollen blanket with her, spreading it over their knees, and then pulling her hat down as far as it would go.

'Have you seen anything yet?' she asked him.

'Nothing but a couple of planes,' he replied. 'You don't think I'm crazy, do you?'

'No,' she said. 'Well, maybe a little.'

He laughed. 'My dad used to take me out at night sometimes. We'd visit gardens he was working on and stand and stare up at the sky. He loved the stars. He knew quite a bit about them too and would point them out, telling me their names.'

'It sounds like you had a lovely relationship with him.'

'Oh, I did,' Cape said. 'I was lucky.'

Anne Marie smiled in the darkness. 'I wish I'd been close to my father,' she said. 'I wish I was closer to my mother.'

'Is that something you can work on?' Cape asked gently.

Anne Marie pulled the blanket a little closer. 'I'm not sure,' she said honestly. 'I don't think my mum really wants to be close to me.' She could see Cape was staring at her, but she kept her focus on the sky above. 'I don't think we've ever had a normal conversation. Whenever we talk, she always brings up my sister.'

'Your sister who died?'

'Yes. Anne. She was the first-born, you see. It must have hurt Mum so much when Anne died. She was just seven years old too when pneumonia took her. I can't even imagine what that feels like – to lose a daughter. My parents never really got over her death.'

'But that was a long time ago,' Cape pointed out.

'I know, but I've never been allowed to forget it. Anne was the golden child. The first. The best. I was the second child. The second-best child. I was always made to remember that. My mother was always comparing me to her. *Anne wouldn't do that if she was alive*, she'd tell me, or, *Your sister would have done a better job than you.* I felt it was impossible to live up to this paragon who was no longer here.'

'Your mother shouldn't have done that to you.'

'Maybe it was her way of coping. I don't know.'

She felt Cape lift the blanket and reach for her hand which was hiding underneath its warmth. How comforting it was, she thought, just to have your hand held by a person who cared about you. She blinked away the tears that were threatening to spill. Where had all this emotion come from all of a sudden? How silly she was being. She took a deep breath and gazed into the inky sky.

'Looking at stars can make you philosophical,' Cape whispered.

'It certainly makes you feel small and unimportant.'

'Hey, you're not unimportant.'

'It sure feels like it sometimes.'

He squeezed her hands again.

'Kath mentioned your birthday's coming up soon,' he said.

'She did?' Anne Marie said in surprise.

'We should celebrate,' he suggested.

'I don't feel very much like celebrating this year.'

'That's what Kath said,' Cape told her. 'She sounded worried about you. Said you were feeling a bit low.'

'It's hard not to with all that's going on,' she confessed. 'But Kath shouldn't be worrying about me.'

There was a pause before Cape spoke again.

'So what's happening with you and Grant?'

'He emailed me this week. Said he doesn't want to involve solicitors.'

'Well, that sounds positive.'

'It's not out of any sort of compassion, though,' Anne Marie said. 'It's just because he's too tight with his money.'

Cape gave a little chuckle.

'But we'll be getting a divorce at some point although he hasn't mentioned that word yet.'

'And you're okay with that?'

'I think it's the only sane way forward,' she told him. 'It's sad. I don't think anybody ever gets married without wanting it to last forever, but . . .'

'What?'

'I think I'm beginning to find myself again,' she confessed to him. 'I've started writing.'

'Really?'

She nodded. 'The other night. I found one of my old notebooks. I hadn't touched it for years and I was flipping through it, reading all these random jottings from my student days when I'd been dreaming of being a writer. It was like travelling back in time and visiting that other version of myself – the one who'd got lost along the way.'

'But you've found her now,' Cape told her, 'and she's going to be a bestselling writer.'

'Well, I don't know,' she said with a little laugh, 'but I'm going to give it a try.'

They sat for a while longer.

'Are you cold?' Cape asked at last.

'A little,' she admitted.

Her neck was beginning to ache too and she couldn't help thinking about her warm bed back at Kathleen's and how cosy it would be to climb into it with a hot-water bottle and a cup of cocoa.

'Snuggle up,' Cape said.

'What?'

'Snuggle up next to me.'

They both shuffled a little closer until their shoulders and arms were up against each other.

'Better?' he asked.

'I think so.'

Friends, she whispered to herself. *They were just friends snuggling together for warmth.*

'No meteors yet,' he said.

'You didn't just make them up, did you?'

'What do you mean?'

'I mean, you didn't spin me some line about a meteor shower just to get me alone on a bench in the dark, did you?' She swallowed hard. What had made her say that? Surely she didn't want to draw attention to their current snuggly situation?

He laughed and she couldn't help acknowledging how much she loved the sound. It was so full of life and joy.

'You've found me out!' he said.

'I thought so.'

They laughed together and then silence consumed them once more.

It was very hard for Anne Marie to be sitting so close in the dark with Cape without remembering that other time they'd been alone in the garden at night together: the night they'd kissed in the maze. She wondered if he was thinking about it too. If *she* was, she supposed it was very likely that he might be too.

She turned to glance at him, but it was hard to make out his features clearly in the darkness even though her eyes had adjusted now and could trace the outline of the wall that surrounded the garden and the dark shapes of the fruit trees at the far end.

'Look!' Cape suddenly shouted.

Anne Marie looked up into the sky and saw a bright light shooting across it.

'Did you see it?'

'Yes!' she cried.

'Wow!'

'Was it—'

'Yes!'

'Amazing.'

'We've seen one!'

'Will there be more?' she asked, feeling like a meteor addict who hadn't quite had her fill yet and was now hooked.

'Let's wait and see.'

She felt him squeeze her hand under the blanket and she squeezed right back. It felt as if there was nothing else in the world but the two of them and this moment. There they were, safely cocooned in the walled garden, gazing up into the magical world of the sky and, for a few blissful moments, Anne Marie was able to forget the fact that she was the second-best second daughter, and a failed second wife. Sitting there with Cape, she felt nothing but the best.

They waited for what seemed like an eternity, but was, in fact, only another forty minutes.

'I don't think we're going to get lucky again,' Anne Marie said.

'Oh, I don't know,' Cape said. 'I feel pretty lucky sitting here with you.'

She turned to face him and felt the sweet heat of his mouth upon hers.

'I know you don't want to go anywhere with this,' he whispered.

'Did I say that?'

'I think you did.'

'I might have been mistaken,' she confessed.

'Yeah?'

'Might have.' She pressed her forehead against his and then they both turned to look at the sky again, just as a second meteor shot across the star-studded darkness.

'I think that means we've got heaven's blessing,' Cape whispered.

Cape dropped Anne Marie outside the bed and breakfast just after half past ten, leaning across the car to kiss her again.

'You okay?' he asked.

'Yes. You?'

'Never better.'

'Thanks for this evening.'

'Maybe one day we'll go out somewhere that isn't a freezing cold garden in the middle of the night,' he said.

'That would be different.'

They laughed.

'Will you be at the garden during the week?' he asked.

'I'm going to try to pop by and water the greenhouse.'

'Yes, Patrick said he and the boys like to do that after school now that it's lighter.'

They paused, neither of them seeming to want to say goodnight.

'I'd better go,' Anne Marie said at last.

'I'd better let you go,' Cape said, picking up her hand and leaning forward to kiss her again.

'Good night,' she managed at last, getting out of the car and finding her key to let herself in to the bed and breakfast.

***

'Oh, you're back!' Anne Marie said when she saw Kathleen. 'How did it go at Patrick's?'

Kathleen nodded. 'Yeah, good.'

'Just good?'

'All right then, *very* good. He can cook.'

'Well, that's always a bonus.'

'I don't know why I thought he'd call out for pizza or something, but he really surprised me. The boys too – they'd made chocolate mousse for dessert. It was exceptionally good!'

'And?'

'And what?'

'When he dropped you home?'

'We walked home. The boys came too.'

'Oh,' Anne Marie said and then saw a little smile spread across Kathleen's face.

'And Patrick made them turn their backs as we reached the gate here.' She paused.

'Go on! You're killing me!'

'And we might have had a little kiss.'

Anne Marie beamed her a smile. She could still feel Cape's kiss on her own lips. 'Good for you!'

Of course, Anne Marie hadn't needed to be told that Kathleen and Patrick had shared a kiss. The minute she'd seen her friend, she'd noticed that her trademark red lipstick had disappeared.

Saying goodnight and walking upstairs to her bedroom, Anne Marie looked down at the thin gold wedding band and the tiny garnet of her engagement ring. She remembered the day Grant had presented her with it. She'd always loved garnets and it was sweet of him to remember that, but it had been hard not to be just a little disappointed with the size of the stone. Perhaps he'd subconsciously known that their union wouldn't last and had been loath to spend any more on it than he had.

Sitting down on her bed, Anne Marie knew that it was time to take the rings off and she did so now, using a little force to pull them over her knuckles for they'd remained on her fingers since their wedding day. The skin underneath the rings was pale, deprived of sunshine for over four years. And how very bare she felt without them on. They'd become so much a part of her; she'd never even taken them off for cooking or gardening or any other chore.

'But not any longer,' she told herself, opening the small jewellery box she'd placed on the bedside table and putting the rings inside it.

Chapter 21

'I think we should protest,' Erin told Anne Marie one Saturday in May.

'What about?'

'About being locked away in this dungeon all day!'

'It's hardly a dungeon,' Anne Marie pointed out, looking around the glorious study with its panelled walls and mullioned window.

'Well, it feels like one to me.'

'Maybe you should rethink wanting to work in a museum, then,' Anne Marie warned her. 'You're very likely to end up in some dusty office somewhere.'

'But at least I'd be doing something *wonderful*,' Erin said. 'We're just filing here.'

She had a point, Anne Marie conceded. It didn't bother her so much, but Erin was obviously raring to get stuck in to some really exciting work.

'I guess I'd rather be outside today too,' she went on. 'It's such a gorgeous day.'

Anne Marie looked out of the window. Suddenly, everything had taken on that wonderful green of spring. Mac had assured them that the last frost was over and that it would be safe to start planting out. The team were starting work on a new area of land adjacent to the walled garden. It was an exciting time of year.

Still, there was work to be done in the study as well as the garden. They'd cleared so much space already, utilising three brand-new filing cabinets which had been brought especially for them to use, and Mrs Beatty had made noises that their job there would soon be done.

Perhaps it was Anne Marie's imagination, but she thought that Mrs Beatty was beginning to soften towards them all. There'd even been a hint of a smile on her face when Anne Marie had asked about a beautiful old fountain pen she'd found in the study.

'That was Miss Morton's,' Mrs Beatty told her, opening her palm to take the pen and handling it as if it was the most precious thing in the world. 'Emilia used to write me letters when she went away to university. She had the most beautiful flowing handwriting.'

Anne Marie had listened as Mrs Beatty's eyes took on a faraway look. She then cleared her throat and looked at Anne Marie.

'Here,' she said, holding the pen out to her.

'Where shall I put it?' Anne Marie asked. 'In one of the desk drawers?'

'No, no. It's for you. Keep it.'

Anne Marie was so baffled by this that she didn't know what to say. 'But I can't,' she managed at last.

'It's of no use to anyone in here. Take it,' Mrs Beatty insisted, that hint of a smile warming her face again.

'Thank you,' Anne Marie said, holding the silver pen with reverence. 'I'll take good care of it.'

'I know you will,' Mrs Beatty said before leaving the room.

Now Anne Marie returned to the pile of papers and receipts she'd assigned herself that morning. They were simple enough to process, but one of them caught her eye. She held it up to the light to look at it properly, scanning the writing three, four times to make sure she'd read it properly.

'Oh, my god,' she said at last.

Erin looked up from a pile of letters she was sorting through. 'Have you found something?'

'I – er – I don't know.'

Erin got up from her chair and looked over Anne Marie's shoulder. 'What is it?'

'It's a cheque written by my father.'

'Really?'

'There's his name. Andrew Lattimore.'

'Are you sure it's him?'

'I recognise the handwriting.'

Erin gasped. 'Have you seen the amount it's written for?'

Anne Marie nodded. She'd seen and she'd done a double-take. Her father had always been on good money as a director at a bank, but this amount was at least a year's salary even by his standards.

'Why's that in there?'

'I have no idea,' Anne Marie said honestly.

'It's written to Tobias Morton. Perhaps he sold your father a painting or something,' Erin suggested.

'Perhaps. But the Mortons never parted with anything, did they?'

'And they didn't here – the cheque's not been cashed. Why do you think that is?'

Anne Marie studied it again. 'Where did we file that newspaper clipping?'

'Which one?'

'The one about Tobias Morton's death?'

Erin looked towards the filing cabinets. 'Top right one, I think. Do you want me to find it?'

Anne Marie nodded and watched as Erin retrieved the clipping.

'Here.' She handed it to her and Anne Marie nodded.

'I thought so. Look – Tobias Morton died just a week after the cheque was written. He never got a chance to cash it. Look at the date.'

'But what about his sister? She could have cashed it,' Erin pointed out.

'Not unless she didn't know about it.'

'How could you *not* know about such a huge sum? Surely if your only relative was selling something so valuable, you'd know about it.'

'Everything all right in here?' Mrs Beatty's voice startled them as she stepped into the room eyeing them both warily.

'Yes!' Anne Marie said quickly. 'Fine.' She surreptitiously slid the cheque underneath another paper.

'Actually,' Erin said, clearing her throat, 'it's not fine.'

'*Not* fine?' Mrs Beatty repeated.

'That's right. We're not happy.'

Mrs Beatty glowered at them. 'And why would that be?'

Erin looked at Anne Marie as if for backup. 'I think we've done all we can here. I think we'd be more use to you—'

'Back in the garden?' Mrs Beatty suggested, a wry light shining in her eyes.

'No!' Erin said quickly.

Anne Marie could feel the young woman's pain. She'd made it into the house and didn't want to be ejected now.

'I agree with Erin,' Anne Marie piped up in support of her friend. 'Perhaps there's something else we can do to help you. We've made good headway with the study here and you did say that we could—'

'Tomorrow,' Mrs Beatty said.

'Tomorrow?'

'Tomorrow you will begin work upstairs. On the collection.'

Erin's bright eyes widened at this news. 'Do you promise?' she asked like an excited child.

'I'll meet you in the hall. Don't go upstairs unsupervised,' Mrs Beatty said before leaving the room.

Erin turned to Anne Marie.

'Can you believe it?'

'Well, it's what you've been waiting for.'

'We're going to see the collection!' Erin cried.

Anne Marie smiled and watched as Erin got her phone out and began texting someone. Anne Marie took the opportunity to retrieve the cheque written by her father, then folded it in half and placed it in the pocket of her jeans.

When Mrs Beatty opened the door to them on the Sunday morning, she looked slightly less stony-faced than normal.

'This way,' she said, leading them both upstairs.

Erin was fit to burst, her eyes darting around her as she took in the treasures.

'Look at that stained glass,' she said as they passed a window, 'and that tapestry.'

They reached a landing lined with portraits. Anne Marie instantly recognised where they were because she'd been there before. She glanced around, hoping for another glimpse of the portrait of the beautiful woman in the midnight-blue dress that she'd seen when she'd sneaked into the house with Cape. She was quite sure it had been hanging just where they were standing now, but it was no longer there. She looked around to see if it had simply been moved, but could see no sign of it.

She was about to ask Mrs Beatty about it, but realised – just in time – that she shouldn't have any knowledge of the painting because she hadn't officially been in this part of the house, had she? Strange that it would have been moved, though, wasn't it? It was a large portrait too and would have been tricky for Mrs Beatty to take off the wall on her own. But perhaps it was out for cleaning, she thought. There was probably some simple explanation for it.

Mrs Beatty gave them a brief history of the collection, pointing out the most important paintings and textiles.

'Our records of the collection are incomplete and need bringing into the twenty-first century. You'll find record cards for most of the pieces in this room here. What I need you to do is to make sure we have as much information as possible about each item in the collection. There are sales catalogues and all the original receipts which you've already filed away downstairs, but we have an extensive library too so you should be able to find anything else you need in there, such as information about the artists. Enter as much as you can on each index card and then copy that information onto the computer database.'

'We can handle the pieces ourselves?' Erin asked.

'Gloves will be provided for the more delicate pieces,' Mrs Beatty said, 'but don't attempt to move any of the larger pieces on your own. They're very valuable.'

'Of course.'

Mrs Beatty led them into a room off the landing. It looked suspiciously like a smaller version of the study downstairs with heaps of papers on two small tables in the centre of the room.

'Don't worry yourself with the papers. You'll be working with the index cards in those boxes there.' She pointed to a bench at the side of the room on which sat at least a dozen small wooden boxes. They were works of art in themselves and Anne Marie couldn't help but marvel at the fact that even items as mundane as index cards were housed in something so beautiful.

'I'll let you get acclimatised. The library is housed in the long gallery opposite. The art books are to the right of the door. You'll find the computer in the library too. I've left all the passwords for you to get in and I've set up a basic spreadsheet for you to enter the index cards on.' She paused and eyed them. 'Do you have any questions?'

Anne Marie was sorely tempted to ask the whereabouts of the painting of the lady in the blue dress, but thought better of it. Maybe she and Erin would find it together as they catalogued the collection.

'Where should we start?' Erin asked. 'I mean, is there somewhere you'd like us to begin – a room, perhaps, or a particular artist?'

'If I were you, I'd start on the landing and work your way around the rooms clockwise so that you don't get lost or in a muddle.'

'Would it be okay to photograph the items to help us?' Erin said.

'As long as it's only for your own records. We can't have photographs uploaded to those dreadful social sites that the whole world has access to.'

'Of course not,' Erin added, suitably warned.

'I'll leave you to it,' Mrs Beatty said, pausing for a moment as if she wanted to say something else. 'You'll be using the same kitchen and facilities as before on the ground floor. Let me know if you need anything.'

Anne Marie blinked at the offer of assistance and smiled as Mrs Beatty nodded towards her. They watched as she left and then Anne Marie turned to Erin whose face broke into the largest smile imaginable.

'Oh, my god! I'm so excited. Where's my phone?'

'Who are you going to call?'

'Nobody! I'm going to start taking photos and uploading them to my Instagram.'

'Don't even joke about that!' Anne Marie said.

Erin winked at her. 'Come on, let's go on a treasure hunt!'

The next few hours passed in a blur of excitement as they viewed the paintings, ceramics and tapestries along the landing. They familiarised themselves with the index cards, doing their best to decipher the crabby handwriting of whoever had made them, and cranked the old computer up. All the time, Anne Marie kept her eyes open for the portrait of the woman in the blue dress, without any luck. She felt pretty sure the subject was the same as the little watercolour of the lady in the maze that she'd noticed on the night when the group had first met, though she didn't get a chance to look at that again either.

When they joined the others for lunch, Cape approached her.

'You're beaming!' he said.

'You should see the collection in there, Cape, it's incredible,' she told him. 'I've never seen so many wonderful paintings in my life. Not outside an art gallery anyway. Erin's beside herself with excitement.'

'She's been waiting for this a long time.'

'She's a natural too. You can tell she's going to make a career in curating. She's totally in her element.'

'And you?' he asked. 'How do you feel?'

Anne Marie thought for a moment. 'I don't know.'

'What do you mean?'

She wasn't quite sure how to explain it to him. 'I've got a funny feeling in the house. I love it, but there's an atmosphere that isn't quite comfortable somehow. It's oppressive.'

'Yes, I felt that the day we went upstairs.'

'Did you?'

He nodded. 'Maybe it's just all that dark wood and those big old paintings.'

'I'm not sure. It feels like more than that to me.'

'You think the place is haunted?'

'No!' She laughed off his suggestion. 'But there's a mood about it.' She ran a hand through her red hair. 'I'm not explaining it very well.'

'You'd rather be out in the garden?'

'Oh, no. I'm happy to be in the house. I don't know. I guess I'll get used to it. Maybe I'm just not used to being around old things.'

'Hey, you missed out on the fun in the walled garden today,' he told her, taking her to one side so they could speak more privately.

'I thought you were all working in the new part?'

'We were. We are. But I had to go back and get some tools and that's when I saw them.'

'Who?'

'Patrick and Kathleen.'

Anne Marie smiled. 'Are you going to finish this story or keep me dangling?'

Cape smirked. 'I'm kind of enjoying keeping you dangling.'

She play-punched him in the arm.

'All right, all right!' Cape paused, obviously believing he was building the tension. 'They were kissing. Like *movie star* kissing. I kind of expected a director to yell "Cut!" at any moment.'

'Oh, Cape – that's old news! They've been kissing for weeks.'

'What?'

'They're going out, Cape. Didn't you know?'

'No! Why does nobody tell me these things?'

'I thought you must have realised.'

'No! I mean, I heard him ask her to dinner. Well, I heard *Elliot* ask her.'

'Yes, that was so funny,' Anne Marie said. 'And that's the night it all started. Although there was that time Patrick came out of the kitchen with red lipstick on his mouth, remember.'

'Of course!' Cape said. 'Our first Morton Hall gardeners' romance.'

Anne Marie put her hands on her hips. 'Really?'

Cape lowered his mouth to hers in a kiss that made her feel as though she might melt right away.

'All right then. Second,' he said.

'There must be something in the air,' she told him.

'Or the soil.'

'Or both.'

'Very likely,' he agreed.

When Anne Marie returned to her work inside after lunch, she felt a lightness of mood from her brief time in Cape's company, but it couldn't completely distract her from the strange atmosphere of the hall. She looked across the room to where Erin was examining a beautiful ceramic vase with a green-and-blue lustre glaze. Erin didn't seem at all bothered by her surroundings, so what was it that perturbed her so much, she wondered? Was the old place haunted? No, she didn't believe in ghosts, and yet there was something intensely sad about the building, as if there were memories still lingering in the shadowy corners, memories that weren't altogether happy.

Mrs Beatty rounded them up sharply at five o'clock.

'Oh, I'm happy to stay a while longer,' Erin assured her.

'I'm leaving so you will too,' Mrs Beatty told her matter-of-factly, and they were ushered down the stairs and out of the house, the door closing very firmly behind them.

Erin was smiling. 'I think I'm in love.'

'Really? Cape and I were just talking about all the romances going on around here.'

'Not with a person, silly,' Erin said. 'With this *house*! It's far better than any man. Give me an art collection over a boyfriend any time.'

Anne Marie shook her head. 'You obviously haven't found the right person yet.'

'The man who could rival this house hasn't been born and I doubt he ever will be.'

They said their goodbyes and Anne Marie walked home with a big smile on her face. Cape had texted her earlier to say he was leaving at four to pick Poppy up from a friend's and Kathleen said she was going home with Patrick and his boys.

It wasn't until she was back at Kathleen's that she remembered the cheque she'd pocketed from the study. She took it out and looked at it again. It was so strange to see her father's signature: that bold black swirl, and the eye-wateringly large amount he'd signed over to Tobias Morton.

But what was even stranger was the date. She hadn't noticed before, but it struck her now. The cheque had been written the month after she'd been born.

Chapter 22

Anne Marie sat in her car for a full five minutes before mustering the courage to get out and knock on her mother's front door. Even after a restless night's sleep, during which she could think of nothing but that cheque, she still didn't know what she was going to say or how her mother would react. Would she know anything about it and, even if she did, would she enlighten Anne Marie? There was no way of knowing but there was only one way to find out.

'Hi, Mum,' she managed as Janet Lattimore opened the front door with a frown on her face.

'Was I expecting you?' she asked.

'Not exactly.'

'Oh. Well, you'd better come in, I suppose.'

Anne Marie followed her through to the kitchen where her mother switched on the kettle and made them both a cup of tea.

'I'd have got more milk in if I'd known you were coming. I'm running low, you know.'

'Sorry.'

Her mother gave a world-weary sigh. 'What's all this about anyway?'

Anne Marie swallowed hard. 'I've got something to show you.'

'What?'

'Shall we sit down?'

'This is all very mysterious,' her mother said as they went through to the living room and sat on the sofa, placing their cups of tea on the table before them.

Anne Marie opened her handbag and took the cheque out, handing it to her mother.

'What is it?' she asked, reaching for her reading glasses.

'It's a cheque.'

'Well, I can see that.'

'It's a cheque I found at Morton Hall.'

Her mother looked nonplussed, but then squinted at it more closely. Was it Anne Marie's imagination or did her mother's face really drain of colour? Her lips tightened, she was sure of that, and she wore the pinched look she always got when she was angry.

'Why have you brought this to me?'

'Because I want to know why Dad wrote a cheque to Tobias Morton. That's a huge sum of money, but it was never cashed. Do you know anything about it?'

Her mother shook her head, her response quick. Perhaps a little too quick to be convincing.

'You *do* know something, don't you?'

'I don't know anything about this.'

'*Please*, Mum, think. Look at the date on it.' She leaned forward and pointed to it. 'It's written just a month after I was born. Does that mean anything to you?'

Her mother stood up abruptly. 'You shouldn't mess with the past, Anne Marie.'

'But why was Dad handing over this sum of money? Was he going to buy a painting? An antique? Was he going into business with Mr Morton or investing in something?'

'This was your father's business.'

'I know it was.'

'It's got nothing to do with you,' her mother said, but Anne Marie couldn't help feeling that it *had* got something to do with her, and that her mother knew exactly what too.

Anne Marie walked into the walled garden, opening the greenhouse door, the warmth embracing her immediately. She needed the peace of the garden after her visit to her mother's, and it seemed as if Dorothy was seeking refuge too because she was sitting on the bench at the far side of the garden. They waved to each other and Anne Marie got on with watering the plants that were doing so well under the care of Patrick and his sons.

Her mind had been racing since confronting her mother about the cheque. She had completely shut down and had refused to say anything more and Anne Marie had thought it best to leave. It was all she'd been able to do to get the cheque back from her mother. It was in her pocket now and she would never forget the look on her mother's face as she'd taken it from her.

'Don't,' she'd said.

'I have to return it,' Anne Marie had said.

She wondered if she should ask Mrs Beatty for an explanation. After all, it had been her who'd given them the job of filing so surely she'd know something about this cheque. Or maybe she wouldn't. Maybe she would have as few answers for her as her mother.

Perhaps her mother was right: perhaps she shouldn't mess with the past, but the past was pretty hard to avoid when you were working at Morton Hall.

'I thought I'd pop my head in and see how you were!' a voice chimed.

Anne Marie leapt, the watering can in her hand. 'Oh, you gave me a shock.'

'You were miles away, my dear.'

Anne Marie smiled at Dorothy. 'How are you, Dorothy?'

'How are *you*?'

'Oh, you know.'

Dorothy shook her head. 'Tell me anyway.'

Anne Marie put the watering can down. 'It's just some stuff up at the hall.'

'And how's it going up there?'

'Good.'

'Erin was telling me about it last night.'

'She was?'

'She came round for dinner. She said she wanted to see my old wedding photos, can you believe it?' Dorothy said. 'She's got the bug for the past, that one. She manages to make me feel old and young at the same time.' She chuckled. 'But she's obviously enjoying the work now. I could see she was getting a little bit impatient with all that filing. An active mind like hers needs more.'

'Oh, yes,' Anne Marie agreed.

Dorothy smiled. 'I can't tell you how good it is to talk to a young person. My two daughters never got married or expressed an interest in having a family and I can't help feeling I've missed the whole grandmother thing. I suppose that's why I'm enjoying being here so much, talking to Erin and watching the antics of Patrick's boys.'

Anne Marie nodded and then smiled. It was so lovely that Erin and Dorothy had adopted one another.

'And how about you? It seems you're not enjoying things quite as much as Erin.'

There was no point in trying to deny it.

'It's not that I'm not enjoying it,' Anne Marie began. 'It's more a feeling I get when I'm in there.'

'What kind of feeling?'

'Sadness.'

Dorothy frowned. 'The place makes you feel sad?'

'Not exactly. But I can feel sadness there. Is that odd?'

'No. Not at all,' Dorothy told her. 'I believe places can hold onto feelings just as people do.'

'You do?'

'Oh, yes. I once lived in a house out on the Ridgeway. A charming house. Like a doll's house. One of the prettiest I've ever seen, but I couldn't live there for more than a year.'

'Really?'

'My husband thought I was crazy. Told me to pull myself together and stop reading M. R. James.' She gave a wry smile. 'But it wasn't the M. R. James – it was the place. There was something in its air.' Dorothy sighed. 'It was three years after we moved from there that I found a reference to the house in a library book. The family that had lived there in the 1840s had all died bar one within six months of each other. Mother first, then three of the children and then the father. Only one of the daughters survived.'

'And was that what you felt, do you think? The sadness of the surviving daughter?'

'Who knows?' Dorothy said. 'But there was definitely something about that place that didn't sit well with me.'

'So you think Morton Hall is the same? Do you think the recent death of Emilia Morton is still present?'

'Maybe. What do you think?'

'I'm not sure what to think.'

'Maybe you should try to find out a bit more about the place. About Emilia,' Dorothy suggested.

'I've thought about trying to ask Mrs Beatty.'

'Ah,' Dorothy said, 'I'm not sure that's likely to help.'

'Yes, I thought as much.' They exchanged smiles.

'Although . . .'

'What?' Dorothy asked.

'I get the feeling she's warming to us.'

'She is? I hadn't noticed,' Dorothy said with a chuckle.

'I think she's finally getting used to having us around,' Anne Marie explained. 'It must be strange for her. I mean, she must have been so used to it just being her and Miss Morton here.'

'It's a strange place, isn't it?' Dorothy went on. 'I've always thought it's a lonely house. Whenever I walked by the drive, I'd look down and glimpse those twisted brick chimneys and wonder about the people living here.'

'You never met the Mortons?'

'Gracious, no!' Dorothy exclaimed. 'They didn't have anything to do with the villagers. They kept themselves to themselves. That's why it was such a surprise to hear that Emilia Morton had left the place to us all.'

'Yes,' Anne Marie agreed. 'That seems so odd, doesn't it?'

'Do you think we'll find out the reason?'

'I hope so.'

'Let me know if you discover anything, won't you?'

'I will.'

'And don't worry yourself. These things have a way of working themselves out. Just you wait and see.'

'Thank you.'

Dorothy nodded. 'Right, best get off. Mac's picking me up for lunch with his uncle. Between you and me, I think Mac's trying to match-make us!' She gave Anne Marie a wink and then left.

Anne Marie watched her go, smiling at the thought of Dorothy going on a lunch date with Mac's uncle. It had been good to talk to her about the way she'd been feeling about the hall and, although her mind wasn't completely at ease, Dorothy's words had comforted her a little.

These things have a way of working themselves out.

Leaving the greenhouse, she glanced up at Morton Hall, focussing her gaze on the window where she'd seen the woman that day as she'd left the walled garden. Had that been Emilia Morton looking down at her? Was it *her* presence, her sadness, Anne Marie could feel in the hall? Anne Marie wondered if she'd ever find out.

Emilia Morton stared out of her bedroom window at the spring garden below. She longed to be out in it, walking through the flowers, inhaling their scents and enjoying their colour. Instead, she was stuck in her bedroom, waiting, waiting.

'You should be in bed,' Mrs Beatty told her as she came into the room. 'Come on – it's not going to be long now.'

'Isn't it?'

'No. Now get back to bed. You know the doctor told you to rest.'

Emilia manoeuvred herself as best as she could. 'I feel like I've been in here for days. *Weeks!*'

'It'll all be over soon enough and then you'll be able to get out and about again. But, in the meantime, *rest!*'

'You've done this before, haven't you?' she asked.

'Yes,' Mrs Beatty told her.

'That's good to know.'

'Both my sisters and a neighbour. All home births.'

Emilia nodded, feeling comforted. It was a Morton tradition that the women in the family gave birth at home. At first, she'd protested but, as the months had worn on, she'd got used to the idea of staying at home with all her familiar things around her.

'It's so good to have you here,' she told her.

'Now, where else would I be?' Mrs Beatty asked.

Emilia smiled. 'I remember when you first came to Morton. I know I was eighteen and you were only – how old was it?'

'Twenty-four.'

'Yes, you were only six years older than I was, but I was scared of you all the same.'

Mrs Beatty shook her head. 'What was there to be scared of?'

'I don't know – your brusqueness?'

Mrs Beatty tutted. 'Not brusqueness – *efficiency*.'

'Oh, is that what it was?' Emilia laughed. 'Well, I don't know what we'd have done without you all these years.'

'You're not the only one,' Mrs Beatty confessed.

'What do you mean?'

'I mean, I needed you as much as you needed me. Your brother appointed me just after my husband died.'

'A car accident, wasn't it?'

'That's right.'

Emilia thought about this, trying to imagine how it must have felt for Mrs Beatty to lose her husband. She'd never really thought about her loss before, but, having fallen in love herself now, she began to realise what Mrs Beatty must have gone through.

'You became my family after that,' Mrs Beatty told her. 'I had a responsibility to you both.'

'And you've never let us down.'

The two women exchanged smiles.

'Where's Tobias?' Emilia asked after a moment.

'In the study.'

'I don't want to see him.'

'I've told him to keep busy and mind his own business.'

Emilia rested back on the bed. 'You won't leave me, will you?'

'I'm not going anywhere.'

'And it'll be all right.'

'The doctor said you're in perfect health. There shouldn't be any complications.'

'Oh, God! Don't even *say* that word!'

The last few months had been an agony for Emilia. She had never told her brother she was pregnant. She had simply got bigger in front of his eyes. She wasn't even sure of the moment he realised. She didn't care. It had been a strange time with the two of them living under the same roof, but leading separate lives. He'd become more withdrawn than ever and Emilia had been thankful for it.

Lying back on the bed now, her mind drifted over the last few months. Not a single day, not a single hour, had passed when she hadn't thought of Jay. She'd waited for him to come back to her. She'd written letter after letter, but all had gone unanswered. Even when she'd told him about the baby, she hadn't heard a word from him. She thought, as the weeks had elapsed, that the sting of Tobias's words to Jay – whatever he might have said, she could only imagine – would have lost their potency and that he would come back for her. But he hadn't and that made her question everything. Had he ever really loved her? Had it only really been a summer romance? If they'd managed to run away together that night, would it all have ended? Would she have found her way back to Morton Hall? Would she still have been alone in this bedroom about to give birth?

But she didn't have time to dwell on it any longer anyway.

'Mrs Beatty?'

'Yes?'

'I think my waters have just broken.'

Chapter 23

It was Saturday lunchtime, the week after Anne Marie had found the cheque written by her father, when another discovery was made.

'Anne Marie – come and see what I've found,' Erin cried, her eyes sparkling with excitement.

Anne Marie joined her, watching as she removed a white sheet from a painting which had been leaning against the wall of one of the bedrooms.

'It's the Victorian portrait.'

'You recognise it?' Erin asked.

'Cape and I saw this once before.' Anne Marie bit her lip as Erin gave her a puzzled look. 'We sneaked into the house when Mrs Beatty was out.'

'And you didn't tell me?'

'It was before the group began work here. We were desperate to see inside so came in when we were sure the coast was clear. We didn't get long before Mrs Beatty returned, but I'll never forget seeing this.'

'So it was hanging up when you last saw it?'

Anne Marie nodded. 'I noticed it was missing when Mrs Beatty brought us upstairs, but I couldn't say anything.'

'Why do you think she moved it?'

'I've no idea.'

'It's far too beautiful to have hidden away,' Erin said.

'I wonder who it's of,' Anne Marie said. 'Perhaps we could look at the family tree.'

'What made you say it's Victorian?' Erin asked.

'What do you mean?'

'The painting. You said it's Victorian, but it's modern.'

Anne Marie frowned. 'But look at the dress she's wearing.'

'Well, there's no denying that the dress is Victorian,' Erin said, 'but look – it's dated.'

'Oh, wow!' Anne Marie said as she saw the handwritten date on the back of the painting.

'It's got the artist's name too. Jay Alexander,' Erin pointed out.

'Have you heard of him?'

'No.'

'So, if that was painted in 1983, that must be—'

'Emilia Morton,' Erin finished.

Anne Marie gasped. '*That's* Emilia Morton?'

'I guess so. We could always ask Mrs Beatty.'

Anne Marie took a moment to consider this and then nodded. 'Yes. Let's do that.'

'Hey, she's got the same red hair as you,' Erin pointed out. Cape had said that too.

'Her skin's like yours as well,' Erin added.

'I'm afraid us redheads are cursed with pale skin.'

'No, it's more than that – look at the hue. It's not *pale* pale. There's this lovely fresh shell-pink colour.'

Anne Marie looked closer. 'Is mine that colour?'

'Yes. Your eyes are the same brown too.'

Anne Marie looked again. Although Emilia Morton was in profile as she looked out of the window, it was clear that her eyes were the same colour as Anne Marie's.

'This could almost be a portrait of you, Annie.'

Anne Marie laughed at the notion, but her eyes were fixed upon the face in the painting as if in a trance. It was as though the past was trying to reach out and tell her something.

'Maybe it is,' she said.

'What?' Erin said.

'The past.'

'What about it?'

'I'm not sure, but I'm going to find out.'

Emilia lay back on the bed, drenched in sweat.

'You have a beautiful daughter, Emilia.' Mrs Beatty handed the baby to her.

'Oh! Look at her!' Emilia cried.

'She's perfect.'

'I've never seen anything so beautiful. Look at her little mouth.'

'I am looking!'

'And she has red hair. Just coming through. Can you see it?'

'Oh, yes. I can see it. She's a Morton all right.'

Emilia leaned forward and kissed the perfect peachy skin of her newborn.

The two women stared at the baby in wonderment. They barely registered Tobias standing at the door until it creaked as he pushed it. Emilia glanced up from her daughter and smiled at her brother. They might not have spoken for an age and she might never forgive him for what he'd done, but her heart swelled with the love of the moment and she invited him in.

'Do you want to meet your niece?' she asked him.

Tobias hovered for a moment as if unsure. Finally, he stepped into the room, and made his way towards the bed.

'You can hold her if you like?' Emilia told him after he'd stood there wordlessly for a good few minutes.

Tobias shook his head. He was pale, paler than normal, she noticed, and she could clearly smell alcohol on him. Perhaps it was better he didn't hold the baby, she thought, relieved that he'd declined the offer.

'What do you think of her?' she asked, trying to coax a response from him.

He shrugged. 'She's a baby.'

'Well, yes.'

'I hope she won't make too much noise.' And, with that, he left the room.

Nobody could have predicted what Tobias would do next, but one thing Emilia was sure of – he must have been planning it for months.

It was just three weeks after Emilia had given birth. She'd been taking a walk around the garden as her baby had been sleeping. It had been so good to get out and to breathe in that fresh May air. But, when she'd returned, her baby wasn't in her cot. Emilia thought Mrs Beatty must have her and went in search of her.

The look on Mrs Beatty's face when she asked where her daughter was told Emilia all she needed to know. Her baby was gone.

Anne Marie turned away from Erin and went downstairs.

'Where are you going?' Erin asked, following her.

'To find Mrs Beatty.'

'Shall I come with you? Annie?'

Anne Marie was already downstairs and searching the rooms for the housekeeper.

'Mrs Beatty?' she called, going from room to room, opening doors she hadn't been invited to open yet. 'Mrs Beatty?'

'Anne Marie?' Mrs Beatty's voice came from behind her as she entered the dining room.

Anne Marie turned around to face her and the two women just stared at each other.

'You found it, didn't you?' Mrs Beatty said. 'I could tell the other day although you didn't say anything.'

Anne Marie swallowed hard. 'I found a cheque,' she said, her voice unsteady.

Mrs Beatty nodded. 'Yes.'

'Written by my father to Tobias Morton.' She paused, waiting for Mrs Beatty to speak. When she didn't, Anne Marie continued. 'Why didn't you tell me about it if you knew it was there?'

'I thought the time would come when you'd be ready and I think that time is now.'

'Ready for what?'

'To hear the truth. You've been putting the pieces of the puzzle together, haven't you?'

'I'm not sure. Have I?'

'What is it you want to know?' Mrs Beatty asked.

'What do you want to tell me?'

It was then that Erin appeared at the door of the dining room.

'Is everything okay, Annie?' she asked.

'I'm going to have a talk with Anne Marie,' Mrs Beatty announced.

'Okay,' Erin said, her tone cautious. 'Anne Marie? Do you want me with you?'

'Erin, I think you have work to do, don't you?' Mrs Beatty pressed.

'Well, yes.'

'It's okay, Erin. I'll be up in a minute.'

'It might take slightly longer than that,' Mrs Beatty announced as Erin left.

'What's going on? Are you going to tell me what business my father had with Tobias Morton?'

'Let's sit down, shall we?' Mrs Beatty said, stretching out a hand to guide her.

Anne Marie took a few deep breaths, trying to calm herself as she pulled out one of the dining chairs. She realised that she was shaking.

'This feels strange,' she said, taking the chair opposite Mrs Beatty. 'Me sitting here in this room.' She gave a nervous laugh.

'Not *so* odd,' Mrs Beatty said.

Anne Marie frowned. 'What is it you have to tell me? Tell me quickly because I don't think I can bear waiting any longer.'

Mrs Beatty looked down at the table, her forehead crinkling as she stared at its shiny surface. Then she looked back up at Anne Marie and something in her face had softened.

'You're the baby,' she said.

The words hung in the air for a few moments.

'What baby?' Anne Marie said.

'You're Emilia's little girl.'

Anne Marie could feel her pulse quickening, but she couldn't quite believe what she'd heard.

'I don't understand. What do you mean?'

'Emilia had a baby girl. On 19th April 1984.'

Anne Marie gasped. That was her birthday. 'But my parents—'

'Bought you.'

'What do you mean? I don't understand.'

'The cheque from your father. It was for you,' Mrs Beatty said. 'Tobias died before he could cash it.'

'No. I don't believe . . . why . . . why are you telling me this?'

'You're adopted, Anne Marie,' Mrs Beatty stated clearly and calmly. 'You were Emilia's daughter and Tobias took you from her. He found your parents, the Lattimores – I really don't know how – and made a deal with them. You were just three weeks old when you left here, but you're a Morton.'

Hot tears rose in Anne Marie's eyes. What was Mrs Beatty saying? That she was Emilia's daughter? She thought about the portrait and how very like her it looked. But that was just a coincidence, wasn't it?

'You're playing with me, right?' she asked, her voice a tiny squeak.

'No, my dear,' Mrs Beatty said. 'I'd never do that to you. But I thought you'd need time here before I told you. That's why I hid the portrait for a while. I wanted you to get to know this place, maybe even to fall in love with it a little bit.'

Anne Marie's hands were trembling in her lap. 'I need to talk to my mother.'

'Of course you do.'

'I need to hear this from her.'

'Yes.'

'Have you spoken to her?' Anne Marie asked.

'No. Never.'

Silence enveloped them for a few moments.

'I don't understand,' Anne Marie said at last. 'If Emilia knew about the cheque not being cashed after her brother had died, why didn't she fight to get me?'

'She didn't know about the cheque,' Mrs Beatty told her. 'Not at first. She never went into the study. I did a bit of light dusting, but the cheque was hidden away. We had no idea it was there. But I'll never forget the day Emilia found it. I thought she was going to tear it up, but she didn't. She said she wanted to keep it as a reminder of who her brother truly was – so that her feelings towards him wouldn't soften over time and she'd never forget the cruelty he was capable of.'

'When was that?'

'About eleven years after you'd left.'

'And she never tried to find me in all that time?'

'She was unwell. She slipped into a deep depression after you were taken from her. She didn't know what to do. Tobias wouldn't talk to her and he certainly wouldn't talk to me. He just locked himself in his study and sank deeper into himself.' She sighed wearily. 'I always felt so awkward around Tobias. We were of a similar age, you see, but we never had any sort of relationship as employer and employee. Not like Emilia and me.' She smiled then. 'And do you know what Emilia did?' Mrs Beatty went on. 'Do you know what she did to Tobias? She took his violin. It was the most precious thing of Tobias's she could think of. I saw her leaving the house with it and I didn't stop her. It was out there in the walled garden until the day you found it.'

Anne Marie remembered the day she and Cape had walked back to the hall with the violin. She'd never imagined that the discarded instrument had had something to do with her.

'She loved you so much,' Mrs Beatty said. 'She'd never have given you up.'

A tear rolled down Anne Marie's cheek. Her mind was racing wildly, trying to take it all in.

'And my father?'

'Jay Alexander.'

Anne Marie frowned. 'The artist of the portrait?'

Mrs Beatty nodded. 'Yes. He spent a summer here painting Emilia. He was a friend of Tobias's. Well, they knew each other at university. I don't think Tobias ever had any real friends.'

'What happened to him?'

'Jay? We don't really know, but I have a feeling that Tobias must have threatened him. Tobias didn't want to lose his sister, you see. He was so possessive of her. He didn't want her to have friends let alone a boyfriend or husband. A husband would have taken her away from here and he couldn't bear not to have Emilia all to himself.'

'But didn't Jay Alexander ever get in touch? Did he know about me?'

'He completely disappeared. Your mother did her best to find him, but he just seemed to vanish.'

Anne Marie took a moment to absorb this. 'Do you think he ever really loved her?'

'Oh, yes. I'm sure of it.'

'And he didn't try to come back after Tobias died?'

'No. Emilia thought he would, but she never heard from him.'

'You think he's still out there?'

'He might be.'

Anne Marie shook her head. 'I can't take all this in.'

'Don't be in a hurry to,' Mrs Beatty said.

'So Tobias Morton was my uncle?'

'That's right.'

'We found a newspaper clipping about his death.'

'Yes. Your uncle overdosed. He'd been abusing his body for years and had poured more substances into it than it could take. Perhaps it was through remorse at what he'd done, but I somehow doubt it.'

'But didn't my father, Mr Lattimore, want to know why the cheque was never cashed?'

'To my knowledge, he never got in touch. But would you?' Mrs Beatty gave a sigh. 'I don't mean to sound cynical, but he had both his money and his daughter.'

Anne Marie didn't know what to say. She couldn't imagine what her father must have been thinking. How much did her mother know? When Anne Marie had shown her the cheque, she'd shut down completely which indicated that she must know something about it.

'Anne Marie? Is there anything you want to ask me? Anything at all? I know this must be a shock for you and I realise that you're going to have all sorts of questions. I just want you to know that I'm here for you. Just as I was always here for your mother.'

This was a totally new Mrs Beatty she was seeing, she couldn't help thinking. The housekeeper had been so brusque with her before.

Perhaps it was her way of testing her out or seeing if she was worthy enough to be told she was a Morton. Perhaps Mrs Beatty had been safeguarding the truth to see if Anne Marie would be able to cope with it, if she was suited to the role. But then she remembered the way she'd caught the housekeeper looking at her that time, almost studying her. Then there'd been the gift of the pen. Now, Anne Marie could see its true significance and why Mrs Beatty had wanted her to have it.

'So, I'm the last surviving Morton?' she managed to ask at last.

'Yes. And I know what you're thinking. You're wondering why you weren't left the estate.'

'I wasn't thinking that.'

'It was something your mother thought long and hard about. But it had been such a burden to her. She wasn't always . . .' Mrs Beatty paused. '. . . *happy* here. I think she didn't want that pressure, that oppression, passed onto any one individual, least of all you. She knew the effect this place could have on someone.'

Anne Marie nodded to say that she understood.

'I – erm – I . . .'

'What is it?' Mrs Beatty asked.

Anne Marie cleared her throat. 'Did she – did she give me a name?'

Mrs Beatty held her gaze and nodded. 'Yes.'

'What? What did she call me?'

Anne Marie swore she could hear her heart beating.

'Anne Marie.'

'Yes?'

'That was it,' Mrs Beatty said. 'She called you Anne Marie.'

Anne Marie frowned. 'But I thought that was the name my parents – the Lattimores – gave me.'

'It was the only name she'd have for you. She said you were too beautiful to have just one name.'

'But my sister was called Anne. I always thought . . .'

'I'm so glad your parents kept your name. It pleased Emilia when she found out.'

She wiped a tear from her cheek. 'Why didn't she ever try to find me?'

'Oh, but she did. When we found out about the Lattimores, we kept an eye on you from afar. We knew when you started your job as a secretary and when you went away to university and when you got married and began work at Oxford University Press. And we couldn't believe it when we found out you were living right here in Parvington. It was as if you'd been drawn back home.'

'But she never came to see me.'

'No,' Mrs Beatty said with a sigh. 'She was anxious about making contact. She was so frail, you see, and she believed you were better off with your new family, your new life.'

'But that doesn't make any sense. I was just down the road.'

Mrs Beatty reached across the table and Anne Marie felt her hands moving instinctively towards hers to be held.

'You've got to understand how fragile she was. After losing you, she lost a part of herself too. She never left Morton Hall after that. Some days, she'd barely leave her room. She'd walk in the garden a little. She loved visiting the maze right until the last of her days. But she never went any further. In fact, she dismissed the gardener after Tobias died. She didn't like having too many people around and she thought it a waste to pay for that part of the garden to be kept tidy when nobody used it. So, for a while, things were left to get overgrown and, well, you saw the state of things. But she insisted that the maze was looked after because that was the one part of the garden that she truly loved and the one she felt connected her to your father. We hired a local company for a while. They seemed to send a different man every week, which we didn't like. We found Mr Colman more recently.' Mrs Beatty smiled. 'And then you came to us. Emilia told me of the time she saw you in the garden, walking down the path towards the churchyard.'

'She saw me, then?'

'Oh, yes,' Mrs Beatty said, squeezing her hands. 'She was so excited. She even thought about making contact with you, but her courage failed her. But it was after that day that she came up with the idea for restoring the garden. She wanted to find a way to bring you home without scaring you off.'

'It was a good idea,' Anne Marie confessed. 'To share this garden.'

'Then you're not angry at her not leaving the place to you?'

'How could I be?'

'I thought you'd feel that way. I knew Emilia's daughter – whoever she was – would have a kind heart.'

'Emilia's daughter,' Anne Marie repeated. 'That sounds so strange.'

'Not *too* strange, I hope.'

The two women looked at one another, their hands joined across the table.

'Why don't you take the rest of the day off?' Mrs Beatty suggested at last. 'Go outside – get some fresh air.'

Anne Marie nodded. 'That might not be a bad idea.'

As Cape rounded the corner of the garden, he saw Anne Marie walking out of the house and into the maze. He turned to see Mrs Beatty standing in the doorway.

'Is everything okay?' Cape asked.

'It will be,' Mrs Beatty said.

Cape frowned. 'What do you mean?'

'She's – well – she's had a bit of a shock.'

'What's happened?'

'Would you talk to her? I think it's best if she explains it all to you.'

Erin appeared behind Mrs Beatty in the doorway.

'Where's Annie?'

'She's in the maze,' Mrs Beatty said. 'No, leave her,' she added when Erin tried to go after her.

'I've got this,' Cape said.

Cape crossed the grass and entered the maze, making his way as quickly as possible to the centre. Sure enough, Anne Marie was sitting there, her face pale and her eyes shining with tears.

'Hey!' he said, sitting down beside her and picking up her hands. 'What's going on?'

She gave a strange laugh. 'I don't even know how to *begin* to tell you.'

'Mrs B said you'd had a shock.'

'A shock? Is that what she said?'

'Yep.'

'Queen of the understatement,' Anne Marie said.

'Has this got something to do with Grant?'

'Grant? No.'

'Then, what? Are you going to make me guess?' he said, giving her a little nudge. 'Because I'm not going to let you leave this maze until I find out.' He looked at her and could still see those tears in her eyes. 'Tell me,' he said, squeezing her hands gently.

She looked at him and he almost caught his breath at the rawness in her face.

'You know Emilia Morton?' she began.

He nodded. 'What about her?'

'She was my mother.'

Cape frowned. 'What?'

'Emilia Morton was my mother.'

'No way!'

'That's what Mrs Beatty told me.'

'And you believe her?'

'I don't think she's lying.'

'Oh, my god! What did she say?'

'She said that my parents bought me. Well, not officially, because the cheque was never cashed.'

'What cheque?'

'I found a cheque to Tobias Morton from my father. Tobias sold Emilia's baby, and that baby was me.'

Cape swore under his breath. 'Are you sure? I mean, are you *sure*?'

'I'm kind of putting the pieces together. You know I've always felt this distance between me and my mother. She was always comparing me to my sister.' Anne Marie paused. 'Only, she wasn't my sister, was she? Not if I was adopted. I wasn't related to her at all.'

'But I'm sure your mother still loved you. Your father too. I think it takes a special kind of love to adopt somebody,' Cape told her.

'All these years, I've felt different. She made me feel different. I was never good enough and now I know why. Because I wasn't really her daughter.'

Cape twisted his fingers through hers. He could feel her shaking.

'You know, it was Emilia who called me Anne Marie? I always thought . . .' The words died on her tongue.

'You always thought that you'd inherited your sister's name,' Cape finished for her. 'I'll tell you something else. If this is all true, then you're not a second daughter either. You're a first and *only*!'

She turned to face him, her lips parting ever so slightly.

'You're special,' he told her. 'An only child. The beloved child of a very special person.'

She shook her head. 'I can't take all this in.'

'I think you might need a while. I think *I* do and it isn't even happening to me!'

She managed a little smile at that.

'Oh, blimey,' Cape added. 'The house should have been passed to you, Anne Marie. You're a Morton.'

She shook her head. 'No. Emilia did the right thing. I wouldn't ever want to change her decision.'

'Are you sure? You know what's it's worth, don't you? I mean, the art collection alone—'

'I'd probably have done the same thing as she's done if I'd inherited it,' she said. 'I wouldn't want a place like this all to myself.'

'But you could have sold it or – well – done anything you wanted with it.'

'But I like what she's done, don't you? Being here with you and the others is the only thing keeping me together at the moment.'

'She's done an amazing thing, leaving the house and garden to the community,' Cape agreed. 'But are you sure you don't feel sore about that?'

'How could I? This was never mine.' A tear fell down her cheek.

'Hey, don't cry.'

'All this time, my real mother was here, alone, and I never knew it.'

Cape leaned in towards her and kissed her tear away. 'Perhaps a little part of you did.'

Anne Marie sniffed. 'How do you mean?'

'Maybe that's why you were drawn to the garden and why you came here time and time again.'

'Mrs Beatty said that too.'

'I think she's right.'

'You remember I said that I thought I saw Emilia at the window once?' She closed her eyes as if seeing Emilia again. 'If only I'd known. If only I'd reached out to her or her to me.'

'Did she know who you were then?'

'Yes. She'd been watching me from afar for years apparently.'

'Strange that she didn't make contact.'

'Mrs Beatty said she was fragile and she didn't want to disrupt my life. But I can't believe she wouldn't want to see me.'

'God, Anne Marie, this is the last thing I expected.'

'You remember the portrait we saw when we went into the house?' she said.

'The lady with the red hair?'

'That was her.'

'But I thought that was one of her ancestors.'

'She was wearing a Victorian dress. I don't know why.'

'And I said she had red hair just like yours.'

'Yes!'

'It *is* yours.'

Anne Marie nodded. 'She used to come into the maze. Mrs Beatty said it was the one part of the garden that she truly loved.'

'Hence my job.'

'Yes.'

'And there was that painting – the watercolour of her in the living room.'

'The one of her in the maze,' Anne Marie remembered.

Cape shifted on the bench. 'This is so weird,' he confessed. 'What are you going to do?'

Anne Marie wiped her eyes and then slowly stood up. 'I think I'd better talk to my mother.'

Cape stood up with her. 'What do you think she's going to say?'

Anne Marie took a deep breath. 'I have absolutely no idea.'

Chapter 24

Anne Marie recognised the car immediately as she pulled up outside her mother's house. It was Grant's. She sat there, mystified as to why he'd be there.

As if I don't have enough to deal with, she couldn't help thinking.

She got out of the car, walked up the path and knocked on the door. Her mother answered a moment later.

'Ah, Anne Marie! How funny you should turn up like this.'

'Mum, what's going on? Why's Grant here?'

Her mother looked perplexed by this question. 'He's your husband. Why shouldn't he be here talking to his mother-in-law?'

'Because we're getting divorced, Mum. I told you.'

'Oh, what nonsense,' her mother said, swatting a hand in her direction. 'You just need to sit down and talk things through.'

Anne Marie followed her into the living room in disbelief.

'Anne Marie!' Grant said, leaping out of the armchair he'd been sitting in.

'What are you doing here, Grant?'

'Grant's been explaining it all to me,' her mother said, 'and you've been letting yourself get worked up over nothing by the sounds of things, just as I thought you had been. But we've sorted it all out and you can go home with Grant now – back to your *real* home instead of that silly bed and breakfast.' Her mother gave a laugh that sounded brittle and forced to Anne Marie's ears.

'Mum,' she began, doing her best not to lose her temper, 'I'm not even going to talk about this right now. Grant, I'm sorry you've had a wasted journey. I think you should go because there's something I need to talk about with my mother.'

'He's not going anywhere,' her mother said.

'I'm not going anywhere,' Grant echoed, giving a wry grin.

'This is for your own good, Anne Marie. You can't turn your back on your family.'

The word *family* hit her like a spear in the chest.

'I really need to talk to you, Mum,' she said.

'There's nothing that can't be said in front of Grant,' her mother asserted.

'It's not his business.'

'I'm your husband, Anne Marie. Of course it's my business.'

Anne Marie couldn't believe what she was hearing, but the evidence was right there before her eyes.

'Very well,' she said, taking a deep breath. 'I spoke to Mrs Beatty today. The housekeeper at Morton Hall.'

Immediately, her mother started to shake her head. 'I won't have any talk of that place here. You know my feelings about it.'

'Well, that's just it, Mum – I *don't* know because you won't ever talk about it. Or, at least, I didn't use to know why you were unhappy with me going there, but I have a pretty good idea now.'

Her mother shook her head. 'You're obsessed with that place. Listen to her, Grant! It's not natural.'

'I agree,' Grant said. 'The sooner we get you back home and into your normal routine with the girls, the better.'

'Mum, will you *please* listen to me for a minute? This is important. Mrs Beatty told me—'

'I don't want to hear what nonsense she's told you,' her mother stated. 'She's got nothing to do with us.'

'She told me that I'm Emilia Morton's daughter.'

The silence that greeted this statement told Anne Marie all she needed to know: that it was true.

'Mum?'

Her mother refused to look at her. Instead, Janet turned to Grant. 'Grant – don't listen to her – she's talking nonsense.'

'She told me you and Dad adopted me,' Anne Marie went on. 'That Dad wrote the cheque I found to Tobias Morton. Remember the cheque I showed you?'

Her mother shook her head. 'I don't know what you're talking about. Grant, will you please take my daughter home?'

'We need to talk about this,' Anne Marie said. 'I need to hear your side. I want to understand. Did you adopt me? Could you not have any more children of your own after losing Anne? Was that the reason Dad went to the Mortons?'

She could tell from her mother's expression that she'd hit the mark.

'Mum? Please talk to me. I need to know.'

'Come on, Anne Marie,' Grant said. 'You're upsetting your mother.'

'*I'm* upsetting *her*?'

'Let's get you back.'

'Please take your hands off me, Grant. I'm not going anywhere with you and stop talking to me as if I were a child needing supervision.'

'You see?' her mother said. 'You see what she's like? She makes it so difficult for me to love her! She always has.'

'I know,' Grant said, nodding. 'I can see that.'

Anne Marie looked from one to the other and back again.

'I don't need this,' she said calmly. 'If you want to talk about this, Mum, you know where I am.'

'Where are you going?' Grant called, following her into the hallway.

But she didn't reply because neither of them were listening to her and she truly doubted that they ever really had.

Anne Marie drove through the Oxfordshire countryside for miles before parking in a lane that ended by the River Thames. She sat absolutely still, taking several deep fortifying breaths before leaving her car and walking towards the river. It was a beautiful evening. The wide stretch of water was a perfect blue and there were people out enjoying the late spring air. Anne Marie sat on a bench and watched two couples walking their spaniels, the dogs zigzagging along the bank ahead of them, tails wagging like mad metronomes.

Slowly, she began to process the day: the extraordinary revelation from Mrs Beatty, the knowledge that she was adopted, her mother's refusal to speak about any of it and Grant's misplaced belief that she was going to return home with him.

She gazed out across the water to the line of trees on the opposite bank. It was a scene worthy of a painting, and Anne Marie took a moment to simply soak it all in, to allow her breath to regulate itself, and to let go of the day, but still her mind felt like it was galloping.

She took out her phone and texted Kathleen to let her know where she was, and then she rang the number of the only person she felt she could truly talk to about all of this.

'Cape?' she said a moment later.

'Anne Marie? I've been worrying myself silly since you left. Where are you?'

'By the Thames.'

'What? Whereabouts?'

'Medmenham.'

'What are you doing there?'

'Contemplating drowning.'

'Anne Marie!'

'I'm joking!'

She heard him sigh. 'I take it things didn't go well with your mum?'

'You could say that. She refused to talk about it.'

'Oh, I'm sorry,' he said.

'And Grant was there.'

'Grant?'

'And he had the nerve to think I was going home with him. I can't believe he and my mum were talking as if I didn't have any opinions of my own. They thought everything was all right and I'd just been a bit silly.'

Cape cursed.

'Hey,' he said. 'You want to come over?'

'To yours?'

'Yeah, sure.'

'Well, I—'

'We could have something to eat. I was going to make chilli tonight.'

Anne Marie could almost feel her stomach rumble in response.

'Okay,' she said hesitantly.

'Good.'

He gave her his address and a list of directions which involved country junctions, potholes and blind bends, and Anne Marie walked back to her car, feeling a little bit calmer for having talked to him.

The cottage at Bixley Common was easy enough to find. Wonderfully isolated down a dead-end lane and completely surrounded by hills, it was an idyllic setting.

Anne Marie got out of the car, hearing the happy screech of swallows as they swooped through the late afternoon sky. Poppy, who was in the small front garden, waved as she saw her, and Cape soon appeared at the front door.

'You found us!' he called. 'Come on in and I'll get you a drink. What would you like? I've got some lime cordial if you fancy. It's pretty good with ice.'

'Sounds lovely.'

'Poppy – why don't you show Anne Marie the back garden while I fix the drinks?'

Poppy nodded and slipped her hand into Anne Marie's. The sweet gesture was almost enough to undo her and she did her best to blink back the tears as she allowed herself to be led through the house and out into the garden. As far as she could remember, Anne Marie had never held a child's hand before. She'd certainly never had any physical closeness to her step-daughters. It felt strange and wonderful – a gift, she thought.

'I love our garden,' Poppy announced. 'It's not as big as Morton Hall, but I love it all the same.'

Anne Marie could see why. What the garden lacked in size, it made up for in charm, with a tiny greenhouse in one corner, a couple of raised beds and borders full of spring colour.

'Here,' Poppy said. 'Sit beside me.'

Anne Marie sat down on a bench next to Poppy, who still had hold of her hand.

'I like to come here and think,' Poppy told her.

'Really? There's a bench at Morton Hall where I used to go to think.'

Poppy looked up at her. 'Did you go there when you were sad?'

'Yes. And when I was cross or stressed too. Or happy.'

'But you're sad today, aren't you? Daddy said.'

Anne Marie looked down at Poppy's sweet face, her large eyes staring up at her in wonder.

'Today's been a very odd day,' she confessed.

'How?'

Anne Marie frowned. How was she going to explain this? Simply and honestly, she decided.

'Well, I found out that I'm adopted and that my real mother had a brother who sold me to the parents who raised me.'

Poppy took a moment to digest this. 'That *is* odd!' she said, making Anne Marie laugh. 'I had an odd day too.'

'Did you?'

Poppy nodded. 'I went out in odd shoes. I have two pairs that are the same, only in different colours – pink and purple. They're my favourites. Mum let me buy them because I couldn't make up my mind and they were in the sale. And I went out in one pink and one purple today.'

'When did you notice?'

'Erm, I think I kind of knew when I was putting them on, but I didn't know where the others were so I just got on with it.'

Anne Marie smiled. 'And did anyone else notice?'

'My best friend said it looked good.'

'I bet it looked good too. I think we need lots of colour in our lives, don't we?'

'Like the flowers we're planting at Morton Hall.'

'Exactly!'

'Like dahlias, peonies and cornflowers,' Poppy said. 'They're Daddy's favourites. And poppies.'

'Of course.'

'He likes poppies.'

'I like Poppy too,' Anne Marie said, giving her a big smile which made her giggle.

'Are you happier now?' Poppy asked.

'Yes. I think so.'

'Good!'

Cape came out with a tray on which sat three glasses of lime cordial chinking musically with ice.

'You both look very comfortable,' he observed.

327

'We are!' Poppy said. 'And Anne Marie's much happier now.'

'I'm very glad to hear it,' he said. 'That'll be the Poppy effect.'

Poppy frowned. 'What's *that*?'

'It's what happens whenever you're around,' he said, bending to kiss her head before sitting on the bench next to them.

'Your bum's too big, Daddy!' Poppy said. 'You're taking up *all* the room.'

'Charming!' he said.

Anne Marie laughed. 'I think the Poppy effect is wearing off.'

'She always tells it like it is.'

'I do,' Poppy said.

Three in a row, they sat there on the bench sipping their lime cordials as the swallows screeched overhead. Poppy retold the story of her mismatched shoes to her dad and he confessed to her that he hadn't noticed, but that he had noticed that she'd only eaten half of the sandwiches he'd made for her packed lunch.

She pulled a face. 'They were soggy.'

'Soggy?'

'You put too much filling in them.'

'Oh,' he said. 'Sorry, Poppet.'

''S'alright.'

'I'm still learning the ropes,' he explained to Anne Marie.

'I'm sure you're doing a great job.'

'He is,' Poppy said and he ruffled her hair.

'Right, I'm going to finish dinner,' he said.

Half an hour later, they were all sitting at the kitchen table.

'This smells wonderful,' Anne Marie said as she dived into her bowl with a fork.

'We like to eat our chilli in a bowl,' Cape told her. 'I hope that's okay.'

'It's wonderful,' she said.

'Comforting,' Poppy said. 'I like bowls.'

Anne Marie and Cape exchanged smiles.

'But it feels funny eating at the table,' Poppy added.

Anne Marie looked up from her bowl. 'Don't you normally eat at the table?'

'Well, we did when Mum was here, but we've been eating on the sofa since she left, haven't we, Daddy?'

Cape almost choked on his chilli. 'You're making us sound like animals, Poppet.'

'Not animals, but Mum would hate it.'

'What do you think about eating on the sofa, Poppy?' Anne Marie asked.

She shrugged. 'I like it, I guess.'

'I do it all the time at Kath's.'

'You do?'

'It's fun.' She smiled at Poppy and Cape and he raised an eyebrow.

'You want to move to the sofa now?' he asked.

'I'd love to,' she said.

'Okay then.'

The three of them grabbed their bowls and went through to the living room, sitting down on the sofa together.

Poppy positioned herself in the middle of them and Anne Marie tried her best to hold her laughter in as she imagined sitting on the sofa with Irma and Rebecca. No, she just couldn't envisage that ever happening.

'And do you watch television while you're eating dinner on the sofa?' Anne Marie asked.

'Sometimes,' Poppy confessed, 'but Dad says we should talk about our day over dinner.'

'That's a nice idea,' Anne Marie said, again thinking about the impossibility of any sort of conversation around the dining table – or anywhere else – at Garrard House.

'Tell us about your day, Poppy.' Cape asked. 'She went to a friend's house.'

'In odd shoes,' she reminded them.

'Oh, I'm always going out in odd shoes,' Cape said and they all laughed.

'It was good,' Poppy said. 'She's got a doll's house and we played with that, but I got a bit bored. I told her it should have a garden because that's the most important part of any house, isn't it?'

'It's the bit I always like best,' Cape said.

'Me too,' Poppy said.

'Does your friend have a garden?'

'Yes, but it's only used for putting out the washing and the bins. They've not got any flowers or vegetable beds.'

Cape sucked his teeth in at that. 'I might have to stop you going over there,' he teased.

'Maybe she could come to Morton Hall sometime,' Poppy suggested.

Cape nodded. 'That's a very good idea.'

'She could get some ideas for her own garden.'

'Spoken like a true gardener,' Cape said.

'I'm not *like* a gardener,' Poppy said. 'I *am* one!'

And nobody could disagree with that.

After dinner, Poppy went up to her room and Anne Marie and Cape stepped out into the garden. The light was beginning to fade and the sun was setting behind a distant wood, leaving a trail of brilliant pink stripes in the sky.

'You've got a wonderful spot here,' she told him.

He nodded. 'I think so.' He gazed over the low hedge at the bottom of the garden towards the field beyond. 'I could never leave this place.' Anne Marie moved closer to him and slipped her hand in his. 'I often wonder if Renee misses it,' he added, 'but I doubt she does.'

'Have you heard from her?'

...ot dly. She emai... ppy though and they talk on the phone

... let twi... week. She'd

Ha found wor... ver there?'

... a job in a salon in downtown LA.' Cape huffed out a laugh.

... said she's ... recent clients' nails.

... me photo...

attach... me... s are for getting dirt under,' he said with some pride.

... did Pop... think?'

Oh, yeah.' He took a deep breath. 'And how are you?'

... really... a gardener, isn't she?'

... ppy says ... s are for... And how... that bowl of chilli on

'Feeling better for being here with you and that bowl of chilli on

... e sofa.'

'So, have you thought about what you're going to do about, well, everything?'

She swallowed hard. 'I'd like to talk to Mrs Beatty some more. And I told my mum to get in touch if she wants to discuss any of this, but I don't suppose she will. I think I'll just have to pretend I never found out about the adoption.'

'You really think she'll never talk about it?'

Anne Marie nodded. 'I think she's going to block it out for good.'

'And how do you feel about that?'

Anne Marie gazed out over the field. 'I'd love to speak to her about it, I really would, but we've never had the kind of relationship where we can discuss anything openly.'

'But she was talking to Grant, wasn't she?'

'Yes, she's good at giving her own opinion on things, but she's not so good at being accountable for her own actions.'

Cape reached an arm around her and rubbed her shoulder. 'You can always talk to me. You know that, don't you?'

She looked up at him, his eyes so loving and tender.

'I do,' she told him.

'You know, you should write about all this,' he said.

She frowned. 'You think so?'

Chapter 25

...on the garden at Morton Hall from dawn ...bs of the gardeners and making everything ...the raised beds were brimming with pro-...growing and surging towards the sun.

...hew and Elliot had planted and nur-...visting colourfully around their obe-...with delicious handfuls to take home each ...lug up the first potatoes for them all to share.

...made a picnic bench out of some old planks of wood he'd ...around the garden and they were all sitting at it having lunch one Saturday when Erin came running across the lawn from the house.

'What's the matter with you?' Kathleen asked.

Erin could barely contain her excitement.

'Mrs Beatty's offered me a job,' she told them. 'Full-time curator of the collection here.'

'Oh, Erin!' Dorothy said, getting up to hug her. 'I'm so pleased for you.'

'That's brilliant news,' Anne Marie enthused, knowing just how much the job would mean to her.

'I'll be continuing the cataloguing with Anne Marie when she's not needed in the garden,' Erin said, 'and liaising with experts to make

sure everything is kept in pristine condition and – I hope – curating exhibitions.'

'Exhibitions? Here at the hall?' Cape asked, obviously surprised.

Erin nodded. 'I think Mrs Beatty wants to test the waters with loaning pieces to museums first for short-term exhibitions, but she did say that Emilia's wish was to open the house to the public one day. The garden too.'

'Good,' Mac said. 'It's too lovely not to be seen and enjoyed by everyone.'

There was a pause while everybody took in this news.

'What's the matter, Kath?' Patrick asked and Anne Marie noticed that her friend's expression was sad.

'I'm not sure how I feel about sharing the garden,' she confessed. 'We've had it to ourselves for so long that I kind of selfishly want to keep it that way. Is that awful?'

'Yes!' Patrick said and everyone laughed.

'I know what you mean,' Anne Marie said. 'Before we started work here, I used to sneak into the walled garden and have it all to myself. I kind of miss that, but I have to say that it's a much nicer experience to share it.'

Cape beamed her a smile.

'I think it will be amazing to share this place with the rest of the village,' Erin said. 'We've had so much fun here but it would be mean to keep it all to ourselves. And I've been thinking – we could have all sorts of events like treasure hunts in the maze and concerts and theatre in the garden.'

Suddenly, everybody was talking at once, dreaming and planning for the future of Morton Hall.

'Can you believe we've been here for seven months?' Dorothy asked once things had calmed down. 'I'm so proud of what we've accomplished in that time.'

'Don't start getting complacent,' Cape warned. 'There's still an awful lot to do and then we've got to maintain it all.'

'Oh, I know,' Dorothy said, 'and I'm sure you'll keep us all in check.'

'I almost forgot,' Erin interrupted, 'Mrs Beatty's got something to show us.'

'What is it?' Patrick asked.

'I'm not sure. She was all mysterious about it, but it sounded important.'

The group tidied away their lunch things and followed Erin back towards the house. Mrs Beatty was there to greet them.

'I have something you might like to see,' she told them. 'I think it's time. But wash your hands first. I don't want greasy fingers on it.'

Everybody went to use the cloakroom in turn before Mrs Beatty led them through to the dining room. Anne Marie took a deep breath, remembering the news that had been told to her in that very room just a couple of months before. She felt she'd grown a great deal since then, accepting the past with wonder and, she hoped, grace. Her mother still hadn't spoken of it and Anne Marie believed that she never would, and she was trying to be okay with that. Cape was there to listen to her whenever she needed to talk about things and she'd also found a new closeness with Mrs Beatty, who had been surprisingly delighted to show Anne Marie the old family photo albums and to tell her stories about her ancestors. Little by little, she was coming to terms with being a Morton.

Now, as they all gathered around the dining room table, Anne Marie's gaze fell to a large book lying on it.

'What's that?' Patrick's son Elliot asked.

'It's a scrapbook,' Mrs Beatty explained. 'It belonged to Emilia.'

'Can we look through it?' Kathleen asked.

'Now that we've washed our hands?' Patrick added with a wry smile.

Mrs Beatty sent him a glare for his impudence, but then nodded.

'It's full of newspaper clippings,' Kathleen said a moment later as she turned the pages over.

The group gathered around.

'Hey, there's the story about Erin after she graduated,' Cape said.

'And the one about Kathleen's fire at the bed and breakfast.'

'And my husband's funeral,' Dorothy said, looking at the local report.

For a few moments, they stood in silence as they examined the newspaper clippings, turning over the pages and reading the pieces.

'What is this?' Patrick said at last. 'What was Miss Morton doing with all this?'

Mrs Beatty surveyed them before answering. 'She chose you,' she said. 'She chose each and every one of you.'

'*Chose* us?' Erin asked. 'How do you mean?'

'She said she wanted this place to make a difference and to bring people together,' Mrs Beatty continued. 'She knew that this garden had the power to heal and it was her wish to pass that on to others. She might not have known anybody in the village, but she took an interest all the same – only from a distance. She cared about you all. She felt your pain when your husband died, Dorothy, and she was so delighted to see you graduate, Erin.'

'Well, I can't thank her enough for choosing me. Being here has made a huge difference,' Dorothy admitted. 'I was in a really dark place for a time there, but coming here each week gave me a focus and a real purpose.'

'It's given me a job!' Erin said and Mrs Beatty nodded.

'But there's nothing about me,' Patrick stated. 'How did she find out about me?'

'Gossip,' Mrs Beatty said. 'We might be cut off here at the hall, but we're not completely immune to gossip.'

Everybody laughed at that, including Patrick.

'Well, I've never been closer to my boys,' he admitted, putting an arm around each of them and hugging them close.

'I suppose I was chosen for my brute strength,' Mac said with a grin.

Mrs Beatty looked at him. 'No,' she told him. 'She heard you on the local radio talking about gardening.'

'She heard that?'

'Yes.'

'That's the only radio interview I've ever done and that was under sufferance,' Mac said.

'Well, she remembered it. She said she loved your quiet passion.'

Mac's face heated up with colour at the attention. 'Well, I just try to do a good job,' he said, looking down at his boots.

'And we all know why she chose Anne Marie,' Kathleen said with a smile.

Mrs Beatty turned her attention to Anne Marie. There was a gentleness in her eyes when she spoke again.

'Emilia would be so pleased to know you were home.'

Anne Marie blinked back the tears that had arisen and managed a smile. Cape moved towards her and put his arm around her shoulder.

'Well, that's what I wanted to show you,' Mrs Beatty said. 'I thought you had a right to know.'

'Thank you,' Dorothy said. 'It was all such a mystery that day in the solicitors' office. When I was told about it, I thought you must surely have the wrong person.'

Mrs Beatty shook her head. 'I think Emilia got it absolutely right, don't you?'

The group exchanged smiles and Anne Marie couldn't help thinking how wonderful it was that they'd all been brought together in this way.

'Right, who's going to help me with the watering?' Patrick said, clapping his hands together at the prospect of getting back to his beloved plants in the walled garden. His question was met by a chorus of 'Me, Me, Me!' and everyone trooped through the hallway and back outside into the sunshine.

Anne Marie was the last to leave and she couldn't help looking back towards the house and smiling at Mrs Beatty, who was standing by the front door watching them all. It might be some time before Anne Marie thought of Morton Hall as a home, but there was one thing she was certain of – she knew she had found a family there.

ACKNOWLEDGMENTS

Huge thanks to Nicki Mattey for suggesting the fabulous name 'Capability' for my hero. I love it!

Thanks also to Mark Starte and Judith Thompson at Saffron Walden's Tourist Information Centre, and to John Bosworth – writer of *Bridge End Garden Creation and Restoration.*

Thank you to Andrew Sankey who gave a talk to the Nayland Horticultural Society and mentioned mazes, which gave me the light bulb moment for this novel.

And thanks to Saminia, Sophie, Bekah and the team at Lake Union for their enthusiasm and encouragement.

ABOUT THE AUTHOR

Photo © 2017 Roy Connelly

Victoria Connelly studied English Literature at Worcester University, got married in a medieval castle in the Yorkshire Dales and now lives in rural Suffolk with her artist husband, a young Springer Spaniel and a flock of ex-battery hens.

She is the author of two bestselling series, Austen Addicts and The Book Lovers, as well as many other novels and novellas. Her first published novel, *Flights of Angels*, was made into a film in 2008 by Ziegler Films in Germany. *The Runaway Actress* was shortlisted for the Romantic Novelists' Associations Romantic Comedy Novel award.

Ms Connelly loves books, films, walking, historic buildings and animals. If she isn't at her keyboard writing, she can usually be found in her garden either with a trowel in her hand or a hen on her lap.

Her website is www.victoriaconnelly.com and readers can follow her on Twitter @VictoriaDarcy and on Instagram @VictoriaConnellyAuthor.